JAYNEE MIKALOSA STARED INTO THE DUST-COVERED CRATE SHE'D JUST OPENED, ENGROSSED in the book of spells before her. She couldn't believe her find. Never had she expected to find an ancient, otherworldly spell-book in the unopened crate she'd purchased in this morning's auction. All that should have been inside were ancient Romancer Tomes.

Cautiously glancing around at the people perusing her bookshelves, she pulled the tome from the battered wooden box and set it under the counter. It wouldn't do to have that little treasure ending up in someone else's bag.

She and her coven had attempted nearly every spell known to them to bring lovers into their lives. Maybe this book from another world held the key. She waited for the last of her customers to leave, turned her sign to closed, and bolted the colorful double door.

Gazing through the *Illuma-glass* she peered up at the triad moons of *Carrillia*. Somewhere out there amongst the stars was her mate and one day she would find him. She glanced through the Book of Shadows and excitedly scanned the faded pages into the data-station behind her customer counter.

What is Earth and where would I find it? She mused. Soon she came to realize it is what the ancient off-worlders called the ground beneath their feet. She looked down at the brown *Shinosh* and wondered if she would have better luck if she named it Earth for her spells.

What could it hurt?

SEX ME

THE TRIAD SERIES

BY

TIANNA XANDER

BONNIE ROSE LEIGH

eXtasy books.com

explicitly exciting

Sex Me - The Triad Series books 1 - 6
Copyright © 2008
Tianna Xander and Bonnie Rose Leigh
ISBN: 978-1-55487-022-6
Cover art and design by Martine Jardin

Published by eXtasy Books
Look for us online at:
www.extasybooks.com

Library and Archives Canada Cataloguing in Publication

Xander, Tianna, 1963-
    Sex me : the triad series / Tianna Xander, Bonnie Rose Leigh.

Also available in electronic format.
ISBN 978-1-55487-022-6

    I. Leigh, Bonnie Rose, 1973- II. Title.

PS3624.A54S49 2008   813'.6   C2008-901504-5

To our mates...

SEX ME UP

J AYNEE MIKALOSA STARED INTO THE DUST-COVERED CRATE SHE'D JUST OPENED, engrossed in the book of spells before her. She couldn't believe her find. Never had she expected to find an ancient, otherworldly spell-book in the unopened crate she'd purchased in this morning's auction. All that should have been inside were ancient Romancer Tomes.

Cautiously glancing around at the people perusing her bookshelves, she pulled the tome from the battered wooden box and set it under the counter. It wouldn't do to have that little treasure ending up in someone else's bag.

She and her coven had attempted nearly every spell known to them to bring lovers into their lives. Maybe this book from another world held the key. She waited for the last of her customers to leave, turned her sign to closed, and bolted the colorful double door.

Gazing through the *Illuma-glass* she peered up at the triad moons of *Carrillia*. Somewhere out there amongst the stars was her mate and one day she would find him. She glanced through the Book of Shadows and excitedly scanned the faded pages into the data-station behind her customer counter.

What is Earth and where would I find it? She mused. Soon she came to realize it is what the ancient off-worlders called the ground beneath their feet. She looked down at the brown *Shinosh* and wondered if she would have better luck if she named it Earth for her spells.

What could it hurt?

Finishing her scans, she sent copies of the new book over the airwaves to her coven mates, so they too could begin their own rituals in their quest to find a husband.

For hours, Jaynee studied the book, looking for the perfect spell. Instead, she followed the instructions included on how to write her own. She'd never attempted that before. She usually played it safe, using tried and true spells that others had perfected. But this new book told her that sometimes spells worked best when designed by the witch who would use them. Turning off the lights, she carried the book to the stairs at the back of the shop and climbed up to her small apartment.

"Fire, earth, water and air, bring to me a man who cares." She shook her head and grimaced. "Yech. That won't work."

Jaynee pondered her words, yawned and decided to sleep on it. How could she write a passable spell when she was so tired? Carrying the book with her to her bed, she gave a dejected sigh, knowing she would have to wait another month to recite it anyway. And she was never good with rhymes. It would take forever to come up with a good one. The moons would cycle this night, forcing her to wait yet another turn before the three would be in the correct alignment again.

What was one more month? It was nothing if she could finally bring her mate to her. Nothing. Still, she worried, her thoughts troubled as she drifted off to sleep.

"EARTH AND WATER, fire and air, bring me together among a pair." Jaynee woke just before the moons reached their zenith, tested the words she dreamt and made a face. It was a horrible rhyme. One she wasn't sure she could recite with a straight face, even alone. Still, what could it hurt? If like the others it didn't work, she merely had to wait another month anyway. To her way of thinking, this way she would be a month ahead. Besides, there must be *some* reason she awoke just moments before the three moons merged in the sky.

She ran down the stairs and out into her backyard, grabbing a bottle of wine and her ritual chalice on the way out. Nervousness and anxiety ate at her. Lifting the open bottle to her mouth, she took a few healthy belts of the ceremonial wine before making her way to the center of her garden maze.

After pouring a more than generous amount in the cup and with no preparation, no lit tapers and as some would say no common sense, she raised her eyes and hands to the sky then recited her spell.

"Earth and water, fire and air, bring me together among a pair. Eyes of amber, eyes of green, bring to me what I have seen. Hair of walnut, hair of gold, embodied as in times of old." The wine started to take effect and her words began to slur.

"Pure of honor, heart and mind, bring me the love of all time. Kind and gentle, strong and wise, let's not forget, large in size."

Jaynee burped and giggled, laughing at her slurring words. Perhaps she shouldn't have drank so much. She shrugged. *Now where was I? Oh yeah.* "As surely as I drink of this cup, have my lover sex me up. Oh, Great Moon Goddess, I pray to thee, bring this love here to me. As I will it, so mote it be."

2

The cool breeze and a rumble of thunder in the distance made her rub her arms. There must be a storm brewing. She should get inside and await her fate. Whether it would still be loneliness, or regret, she didn't know. She weaved and bobbed, stumbling, as she slowly made her way to the back door. She paused and looked into the shop. She could have sworn she saw someone standing by the front door.

She shook her head. It was most likely a window shopper. Her first customer of the day tomorrow, no doubt. She glanced at the glowing timekeeper above the door and her eyes widened. It was way past her bedtime and she needed to get up early tomorrow. There was much preparation to do for next month's attempt at drawing a mate.

She stumbled back up the stairs, heading for her bed, and fell onto it exhausted. Still, sleep refused to come. Some sense of anticipation kept her eyes from closing. The rhythmic ticking of the timekeeper on her nightstand kept her awake and staring at the mirrored ceiling over her bed. The steady hum of hovercraft passing beneath her window bothered her to no end, when usually it lulled her to sleep with certain comfort.

Only when the nightlife below her window lulled and she muted the glow of the timekeeper with her blouse, did she slip into the peaceful world of the oblivious at last.

"Where am I and why did you summon me here?" a man snarled as he grabbed her arm and dragged her from beneath the warmth of her blankets.

Jaynee squealed out a protest as he switched on her light, dragged her semi-clad form from her bed, and stood glaring at her.

"What are you doing in my room?" she demanded. Only, once she stood shivering beneath his icy glare, did she really look at the tall man in front of her. Her heart stuttered in her chest as she realized he epitomized the talk, dark, and handsome, she'd often read about in the Romancer Tomes she sold in her store.

Towering over her the way he did, wearing a scowl even a Werewolf would be terrified of, there was no mistaking the man was furious. But that didn't stop her from staring at him.

His dark hair would have hung over his shoulders if it hadn't been tied back with a thin gold band. Amber eyes glittered at her with hate and derision. Wide, muscular shoulders that looked like they'd barely fit through her door, tapered down to a narrow waist, so defined, she could see the ripples of muscles beneath his shirt. Unconsciously, she licked her lips, and he sneered his revulsion.

"If this is some trick to get me to reconsider my declaration of war, you can be sure I will not be fooled."

"W—war?" *Oh, my gods! They've gone and done it! They will destroy the world!*

"You know as well as I do *Banart*—" he said the word as if it were a curse. "The *Savari* are not willing to stand about with their digits up their arses while you burn us out of our homes."

"Bone-arts?" she stuttered.

"Do not play the fool with me, female! You are in no position to act the part of the innocent either." He paced the room, agitatedly running his fingers through his hair. "I must get back to my ship. How will I launch an attack if I cannot reach my people?"

Jaynee grabbed the sheet from her bed when the sound of loud footsteps sounded on the stairs. Her eyes grew round with fright as she contemplated two complete strangers traipsing about her shop and home. She glanced over at her communicator sitting idle on her nightstand and inched closer. She must call the authorities before someone got hurt.

"Oh, no you don't," the stranger said, grabbing the communicator from her trembling hands. "One friend is enough. You are not calling for reinforcements." He threw the device against the wall and it shattered into a hundred pieces.

"F—friend?" Was the man delusional? He was the one with friends.

He grabbed her, turned her around, and placed her in front of him before the bedroom door crashed open.

WEARING NAUGHT BUT his street rags, Lucan Maedoc stormed up the stairs, prepared to gut the person that summoned him. He'd had the perfect cover, hiding in plain sight within feet of the *Carrillian Rebel* headquarters. The leader of the *Savari*, Dare Raden, was supposed to meet with them tonight and Lucan planned to gather whatever information he could, then report back to his superiors. If it looked like Raden really meant to fight against the *Banart*, then he'd arrange a private meeting. But until then, he needed more information about the mysterious ruler of *Savar*, a mostly forested planet few even knew existed.

Just as he intercepted a transmission announcing a delay in the meeting time, he found himself transported from his post to the center of a tiny shop filled with shelves of books and naught much else. His military training immediately kicked in. He needed to ascertain his position and locate any possible enemies, before plotting his next move.

A quick reconnaissance of the shop showed no one lay in wait downstairs. In fact, nothing about this place, or the town he'd spotted outside the glass, looked familiar to him. After he checked out the loft, he needed to find a way to contact his people.

How could he determine whether or not war with *Savari,* as well as the *Banart,* was necessary if he wasn't there to actually do any spying? Whoever had pulled him out before he completed his mission, better pray he was satisfied with whatever reason they chose to give him, or they'd regret toying with national security this way.

He scanned the shop once more before heading toward the stairway behind the counter. A raised voice at the top of the building drew his attention. He tilted his head in amazement. They weren't even trying to be quiet.

Shaking his head, he started up the stairs, a stunner wand grasped in one hand, a sharp blade in the other. If someone had brought him here to slaughter him, he'd not go down without one hell of a fight.

Feeling no need to keep his entrance quiet, he took one step back and rammed the door open with his shoulder. He quickly scanned the tiny room, only spotting two people—a man and a woman. And from the look of things they weren't on the friendliest of terms. Lovers spat, maybe? They stood together, one of the man's arms wrapped around her neck, the other holding her head. Was he going to break her neck?

"Don't come any closer, *Banart!*"

"What?" He looked from the man to the woman and she stared back at him, perhaps trying to ask for his help with a look. He may be there unwillingly but at least he wasn't threatening to kill her. Yet. And besides, this was the perfect opportunity to find out just what type of leader Dare Raden really was.

And, looking at the man, there was no doubt in his mind that's who held the trembling woman. He looked just like his brother at rebel headquarters. The rebels would have taken the man into custody to ensure his brother's cooperation if not for the fear of the reprisal such an action would cause. Suspicious, he narrowed his eyes. How had he managed to be exactly where he needed to be when even the *Carrillian Rebels* didn't know why the meeting was delayed?

His gaze once again settled on the terrified woman. If he hadn't worried that an ambush might lie in wait up here, he would have taken the time to really look at her. As it was now, knowing only the three of them were in the room, he couldn't help but stare at her unusual beauty.

Hair as black as sin hung in tousled waves, curling around her heaving breasts. Her smoky gray eyes were framed by the thickest sooty black lashes he'd ever seen. Purple markings of power were etched below her eyes and across her cheeks.

His attention was drawn to her lush lips when she wet them with her tongue. He could smell her nervousness, mixed with desire, and it only served to ratchet up the lust flowing through his body. True submissiveness was born, not trained and she had the scent of a true submissive.

His cock twitched, began to grow behind the closing of his pants when Raden's forearm brushed against her breasts, making her nipples hard. He could just imagine suckling on them as he drove his cock into her cunt. By the Lady Goddess, what was wrong with him?

THE NEW MAN, at least as tall as her assailant, was as fair as the man at her back was dark. His blonde hair stood up in short spikes on the top of his head. Green eyes, the color of *Caba* stones glittered menacingly over her shoulder at the man who threatened to do her harm.

His well-toned physique and costly weapons belied his worn clothing and she wondered if the man had recently fallen into dire straits or if he wasn't exactly what he portrayed. His expression looked too fierce, his stance overly aggressive, it made her question if he weren't more than his appearance made him seem.

Before she could think on that further, he tucked the knife behind his back and stepped closer to where she was being held.

"Let go of the female, Raden and explain where you've brought me, and why?"

"Brought you? It is you and this… this siren, who summoned me, *Banart*."

The light haired man shook his head, stepping even closer. Did he plan on attacking her too? Her mind spun. What was going on? Had she summoned these warriors to her last night when she cast the spell? That couldn't be right though. If this were her doing, only one man would have appeared, not two. Right? By the Lady Goddess, why were such trivial thoughts running through her mind when just the slightest squeeze by her attacker would cut off her air supply, and she'd see the three moons of *Calla* rise no more?

The golden man snorted in derision. "I am no *Banart*. I am Lucan Maedoc, a *Pantari*, from the planet of *Pantair*.

"And what do the *Pantari* want with the *Carrillian's*? I thought you were a peaceful planet."

"I was sent to spy on you, Raden. If it looked as though you were aligning yourself with the *Carrillian* government and the *Banart,* my orders were to terminate you."

"And if I'm not?"

"I'm to convince you to join the people of *Pantair* against the approaching *Banart* army."

Jaynee closed her eyes. Part of her was scared shitless. Another, bolder part of her was very aware of the two men in her bedroom. And did the one behind her call her a siren? Did that mean he thought she was attractive? She closed her eyes. *Focus, Jaynee. It's the middle of the night and there are two strange men in your home.* What could she do to get them out of her house?

She opened her eyes, her gaze darting around the room. "Um… there's a café down the street. Maybe you two could get to know each other there."

The man at her back let her go and pushed her away from him. She stumbled and landed on the bed. Rolling over, she looked up at the two men who now stood side by side, their trust for each other against a common enemy overruling their animosity for one another.

"You say you don't know how you got here?" the one called Dare asked the newcomer.

The other man shook his head and glanced her way, a thoughtful expression on his face. "No. I have no idea how I got here. One minute, I was standing outside the *Carrillian Rebel* headquarters and the next thing I knew I was downstairs standing amidst shelves full of books."

"It was the same for me," Dare said, his expression thoughtful. "One minute I was in my ship orbiting this planet, the next I was here, standing next to this woman's bed."

The blond tilted his head. "It is possible she brought us here. The power to call us is within her."

Turning toward the newcomer, the dark haired man frowned. "What do you mean?"

"The purple markings below her eyes denote her powers. If I'm not mistaken those particular tattoos mean she's one of the High Priestesses on this planet. That means she probably is not only spiritually powerful, but has psychic ability, and can communicate with people in high places—namely the Lady Goddess."

His gaze found her again. He didn't hide the fact that he was appraising her body. His amber-eyed gaze burned a trail over her flesh, pausing at her breasts until her chest burned with the effort to hold her breath. She didn't want him to think she thrust her breasts out for his inspection, though she'd wanted to do just that.

She gulped air into her lungs when he finally looked away to address the other man, Lucan. Jaynee glanced over at him, her heart stuttering at his masculine beauty. Even with his disguise, she knew him to be the epitome of masculine perfection. They both were. She swallowed around the lump in her throat when he turned his sparkling green eyes on her.

"She *is* a siren, isn't she?" he said, licking his lips. He looked down at himself then the corner of his mouth quirked up in a wry grin. "I don't look like much, though, do I?"

Dare grimaced and sniffed. "You don't smell like much either. Do they make you go days without a bath to go on one of these missions of yours?"

Lucan chuckled and rubbed the back of his neck. "No, it's a type of cologne they've developed. We merely squirt it on and we smell like a rancid beggar."

"Cologne is *not* a word I would have used." Dare said holding his hand over his mouth and nose as Lucan moved closer. "Find the woman's bathing chamber and wash that shit off. You stink."

They both glanced her way in question and she pointed to her door. "Down the hall, the second door on the left. There are towels in the cabinet under the sink and a new razor in the top drawer next to the tub." She didn't bother to tell him her soap smelled of flowers. Better he found that out after it was too late. The man *did* smell.

Dare sat down on the chair in front of her vanity when Lucan left. "What are we to do with you?"

Visions of various sexual positions flittered through her head and he smiled as he leaned back in the chair, stretched his long legs out in front of him, and crossed them at the ankles.

"I think it's only fair to tell you that as a *Savari*, I can read your mind." He grinned. "Such interesting thoughts you have." He leaned back and folded his hands behind his head. "I wonder if we should share your ideas with Lucan. We could kill two birds with one stone, so to speak. Get to know and trust each other and have a good time all at once."

Jaynee's face burned. Gods, why couldn't she control her thoughts? The more the man talked, the more her mind ran rampant with the idea.

What would it feel like to have two men want her, one at her front, the other at her back? She nearly groaned with embarrassment when he moved, drawing her attention to his long legs and the bulge at his crotch. Standing, he approached her slowly. His intent was clear as he sat on the edge of the bed.

"A *Savari* can read the minds of others when he or she is not angry or upset. In fact," he whispered, his head dipping to where her neck and shoulder met, "we can feel every emotion, every sensation of those we're linked with."

Jaynee tried to lean away, but warm air skittered across her skin as his tongue lightly stroked her pulse point. She felt the sharp edge of his teeth nip at her skin and she jumped. What was she doing letting him be so forward with her? She didn't even know him.

You want me.

"I want you," she repeated, closing her eyes. "Hey!" Her eyes flew open. "What kind of crap is that?" She pushed at his shoulders and he chuckled.

"You have a strong mind. I like that in a woman."

He bent his head to her neck again and she closed her eyes at the fluttering sensation in her stomach. This time she leaned into him as his mouth played over her flesh. She moaned when his hand moved up her thigh to her stomach before caressing her breast. Her nipple hardened beneath his experienced hand and she tilted her head to the side to give him better access to her neck. Soon, his hand moved up to cup her cheek. He turned her face to his and lowered his lips to hers.

She groaned when his tongue slid between her parted lips and delved into the warm recesses of her mouth. Liquid warmth pooled between her legs and she squeezed her thighs together in an effort to stem the raging need she felt building within her.

He palmed the back of her head, his hand fisting in her hair. Tilting her head to the side, he nibbled his way down her neck to the vee of her nightgown. Sharp teeth scraped the sensitive skin on the upper curve of her breast and she sucked in her breath.

"What are you doing?" She curled her fingers in his hair.

"Did it hurt?" he asked, laving the slight sting with his tongue.

She shook her head. "A little. I just wondered why your teeth are so sharp."

All else was forgotten as soon as his lips closed over the tip of her breast. She fisted her hands in his hair as he drew on the hard nub, and she groaned.

Cool air kissed her flesh as he released the buttons on the front of her nightgown.

What are you doing? Her inner-self screamed as his hand moved up her thigh. *You don't know this man—you can't have sex with him.*

He is your destiny, a strange female voice rang through her head. *He and the other are your mates, brought to you through time and space. Together you will form a triad. A three bound circle of power that will add to the power of three. We must have many such as you to bring down the Banarts. Embrace them, embrace your new life, and help the universe to survive the Banart siege.*

With the last button on her gown released from its buttonhole, Dare moved his hand further up her thigh. His fingers sank into the warm moist heat of her sex and she groaned. Expert fingers circled her clit and she spread her legs, giving him more room to caress her slick flesh.

She bent her knees, further opening herself up to him. There was little else she could do. If the voice in her head was to be believed, this was for the good of all. The Banarts were an evil race, conquering everyone in their path and obliterating all who refused to comply with their doctrine.

What was one night of pure blissful sex to prove or disprove her theory? If she were merely hearing things, if this man was doing naught else but planting ideas in her head, she would still have this one night to call her own. She would still have this one night where not one, but two gorgeous men would love her. She let him ease her back onto the bed and he moved to lie beside her.

The floorboard in the hall creaked and she knew just when her other guest entered her room. If the sharp intake of his breath and heavy breathing was any indication, he was just as aroused she was. She smiled, raised her head, and held out her hand.

He dropped his towel with nothing less than a growl and approached the bed slowly. She watched him, loving the way he moved, so gracefully, like a cat. Every movement was slow, precise, as if extra movement was a waste. He lowered himself to his knees and crawled up the foot of the bed to settle between her thighs.

"Is this the way of your culture, *Carrillian?* If so, I must commend your people on their hospitality," he said just before he lowered his head to her sex.

Jaynee screamed as the rough pad of his tongue stroked her flesh. He lapped at her, suckling her. The pleasure pain continued. He'd bring her to the edge then pull back. For what seemed hours, but were mere minutes, he tormented her by taking her to her peak then bringing her back down. Once again, he stopped, and lifted his head away from her sex. "I'll have the name of the woman I'm with."

Jaynee gasped, shocked she'd let this go on without even exchanging her name. What kind of woman was she? How could she give herself to two complete strangers this way? What was wrong with her?

He nipped her thigh. "Your name. Now."

She licked her lips, arched her back. "Jay…" Dare's teeth bit down on one nipple then laved it with his tongue, sending shards of sensation straight to her empty pussy. Again she tried to answer Lucan. "Jaynee. My name is Jaynee."

Finally, his lips circled around her clit, giving her the touch she wanted, desperately needed. Her thighs quivered. Her pulse pounded. Her hips lifted into the air in a desperate search for relief. One sharp pull on her clit, one hard draw on her breast and she came into his mouth, her cum pouring from her sex. Wave upon wave of pleasure washed through her as he continued to suckle her clit while Dare suckled and laved her breasts, alternately fondling and pinching each one in turn.

How could something feel so right and still be so wrong? She'd wished for a mate and gotten two instead. Would she be allowed to keep them, or would this only be for the night?

"Shh…" Dare whispered into her ear as he laved the outer shell. "Don't worry about such things." He chuckled softly. "It pleases me to know you brought me here with a spell. On my world, such an occurrence means the two are mated by divinity." His arms wrapped around her, holding her closer so he could whisper into her ear. She shivered when warm, moist air wafted over the nape of her neck. "Shall we complete the bonding?"

She squeezed her eyes shut. This could be naught but a dream. She had two men to love her, to please her, to send her screaming over the edge of heaven's precipice. Would she survive it? Did she really care if she would not? And if it was a dream, could she bear to wake once it was over?

Strong hands lifted her astride Dare as he lay back upon her bed. Somehow, his clothing had melted away, as if they had never been there. Never been a part of him. She straddled his lean form, her hands splaying over the rigid muscles of his chest and abdomen. His amber eyes sparkled with heat, the hunger raging inside should have burned her rather than make her feel safe, cherished.

Reaching down, he positioned himself at the entrance of her needy pussy, and flexed his hips upward, as she lowered herself over his massive sex. The feeling of being stretched so full was exquisite, beyond anything she'd ever imagined, and yet she knew something wasn't right. It wasn't enough. Even as huge as he was, he didn't fill her as she should be filled.

"Enter her from behind, Luc. She's as wet as she'll ever be and she wants this." He gazed deep into her eyes, his gaze searching. "Don't you?"

She nodded, unable to stop herself. She knew this is what she wanted, needed. Only then could she find the completeness she'd always lacked, the wholeness of spirit that she'd always missed during sex.

"Yes. God, yes. I want it. Give it to me. Give it all to me," she panted as she rode the massive cock of the man beneath her. "Fuck me in my ass, Luc."

She groaned when Dare's hands rose to her breasts and pulled on her sensitive nipples. Still she didn't know what had come over her. It was almost as though the appearance of these two men had turned her into a nymphomaniac. What would she say to them when it was over?

It will never be over, natoya. You will never be free of me. This is our mating night. You have agreed. What Luc wants is up to him, Dare whispered into her mind as she felt the ripples of another orgasm begin.

Using his fingers, Lucan traced the folds of her dripping pussy, gathering her cream and dragging it to her nether hole. Had he known in advance what was in store this night, he would have come prepared. When he knew her back entrance was sufficiently lubricated he began to stretch her ass. When she could take three fingers comfortably and began to fuck herself on them, he knew she was ready for his cock.

"Do you want to know what I feel, Jaynee? I know if I enter you now, I will never find my way out. Our people have gone too long with a shortage of women." He looked toward Dare. "If she will have me, she will belong to the both of us, thus creating a binding alliance between all our people."

With Dare's nod of acceptance, Lucan focused his attention back on his mate. Removing his fingers, he placed his cock against the opening of her ass. "Do you accept me as your mate as well?"

"Yes. Yes, oh god, yes!" she cried as he began to slide into her.

He moved slowly, his cock inching its way inside her virgin hole. He moved forward, inch by inch, until he was fully seated in her ass. Then he stilled, waiting for her to become accustomed to his cock. After a minute, she

"I can't—" She gasped when Luc suckled the other into the warmth of his mouth.

The restraints fell to the mattress obviously forgotten and she relaxed. Two warm mouths pulled erotically on her breasts. Her insides melted, turned to mush, as they both worshipped her body. Two large, male hands splayed over her stomach and caressed her thighs. Her whole body quivered as they suckled and laved at her breasts.

At last she was able to trust them, to relax into their loving. She reached up and thrust her fingers through their hair, each hand savoring the silky softness of a different length, different texture. They reached up and, trailing their fingers along her sensitized flesh, tangled their fingers with hers. It felt right, this loving, this closeness. If someone had told her a day ago she would submit to a loving such as this, she would have thought them mad. Nothing in her life had ever felt so right, so good.

It wasn't until the restraints closed around her wrists that she realized what they were up to.

She pulled against them, to no avail. They were anchored at each corner of the bed. She lay on her back, both arms spread wide.

"Don't do this," she said as they each grabbed an ankle. A shaft of both fear and desire shot through her and she again tugged at her bonds.

WHILE HE SECURED Jaynee's leg to the post with the silken tie, Lucan couldn't help but run his hand down the satin smoothness of her thigh, until his fingers lightly gripped her ankle. Only after he made sure she couldn't slip her leg free, did he once again allow his hands to roam over her legs, her thighs. Out of the corner of his eye, he watched Dare secure her other leg then he, too, began to stroke her quivering body.

The panther within him purred out his pleasure, thankful to have this chance to master his mate. Her musky scent wafted from her swollen channel and the beast inside him wanted to scream out his joy at finally having a mate. He couldn't wait to plant his cubs in her, wait to see her heavy with his children, feeding them at her breast.

Though he wasn't happy about sharing a mate with the *Savari* leader, he wasn't opposed to it either. Among the *Pantari,* triad matches were common, thus the overwhelming urge to destroy the other male didn't ride him as it would if he were of her species, a *Carrillian* by birth.

After meeting Dare's gaze, and seeing his subtle nod, Lucan reluctantly lifted his hand from her seductive curves. Walking to the head of the bed, he looked down at his mate, raised his eyebrows in amusement when he saw the erotic edge of both desire and fear glimmer in her eyes. He could feel her defiance, her belief that they would not truly withhold climax from her. Never before had he felt another's emotions rather than scenting them. It must be a result of the triad bond forming between them.

Knowing that he needed to show her that in the bedroom he and Dare were not to be disobeyed, he stared into her eyes, letting the panther inside him rise to the surface. He could feel his eyes change shape, changing to those of the panther, his other form. His ears tingled, as he held off a full change, only allowing her to glimpse he wasn't humanoid—not entirely anyway.

His hands and arms itched as fur began to spread upon his skin. His canine teeth elongated, became fangs. A low feral growl vibrated from his chest. When her startled gasp and indrawn breath satisfied the beast within him, he halted his shift. Lucan let her see what he was capable of, but not enough to terrify her. "In the bedroom, you answer to us. Your pleasure is ours to give, not yours to take." He stopped speaking, to allow her time to let the words sink in.

Dare cleared his throat, ran his hands up her body, as he slowly made his way toward the head of the bed. Jaynee's head whipped toward her other mate, her eyes growing wider at his approach. His voice was rough when he spoke, harsh to even Lucan's ears. "When we tell you to do something in the bedroom, you are not to hesitate, not to question our demands."

Jaynee paled, her lips trembled. Her whole body began to quake. Lucan realized instantly they were throwing too much at her too quickly. He needed to set her fears at ease. He had to remember that she didn't know them yet, had no real reason to trust them. "If at any time we do something that hurts or frightens you, you need only tell us, and we'll either stop immediately or at least put you at ease. Do you understand what we're telling you?"

Out of the corner of his eye, he watched as Dare clenched his fists, obviously reluctant to even give her this much freedom. The *Savari* were mostly an unknown in the galaxy, their mating practices and social customs a complete mystery. He'd need to talk to Dare and make sure they were on the same page as to how to treat their mate.

He wouldn't—couldn't—allow his triad partner to scare her away with his dominance, though he could not allow Jaynee to deny submission in the bedroom either. The three of them needed to find what would work best for them as a Triad, combining the best of all their traditions if they wanted to be a functional and loving familial unit.

He watched myriad emotions flash across Jaynee's expressive face. Her gaze skittered from him to Dare and back again. Finally, she gave a jerky nod, though he could still see the fear and trepidation in her eyes. The only thing they could do at this point is show her that no harm would ever befall her by their hands.

With determination to do just that, he fisted his hands at his side and firmed his voice. When he knew he was in control, he could see Jaynee's nerves begin to fray. He climbed onto her bed, straddling her head. Looking down into his mate's eyes, he once again spoke, his voice raspy even to his own ears. "Now, you will suck my cock and swallow every drop of my seed when I cum. Dare is going to eat that luscious pussy of yours and *you* are *not* to cum."

Her eyes flashed fire, and her body tensed. "Do you understand me, mate?"

She bit down on her bottom lip and after turning her head toward Dare and back, she raised her eyes to his and swallowed. Once more, she passed her tongue over her lips as she stalled for an answer, and his cocked twitched, growing larger and thicker. Her eyes widened, though he hadn't thought it possible—they were already so large.

"Lucan is waiting for your answer, female. Best not to make him wait too long." Her head whipped toward Dare and after only a slight hesitation, she nodded. "I understand," she whispered, her voice shaky and uncertain.

His eyes never left hers as he spoke to Dare. "Dare, climb up here and make a meal out of Jaynee's cunt. And make sure you take your time to savor it, we wouldn't want her to feel as though we don't worship her, do we?"

Dare's answering growl was all the answer he needed. "Now, mate. Suck my cock. I want to feel your luscious lips wrap around my shaft, feel the strong pull as you take me down your throat and swallow my seed."

Once more, she licked her lips. After a long moment, she lifted her head, her gaze never leaving his as she swiped the head of his weeping cock with the tip of her tongue. His entire body shuddered. The touch of her tongue lapping up his pre-cum, swirling around the head of his cock, was almost more than he could bear.

A rumbling growl vibrated in his chest. "Take it in your mouth, Jaynee. Now."

Without any hesitation this time, she wrapped her lips around his shaft. Grabbing the headboard, he leaned toward her, thrusting into her mouth to make it easier on her. He kept his movements measured and slow, even though all he really wanted to do was pound into her mouth, fuck it with an urgency he'd never before felt.

Jaynee began to squirm beneath him. Her moans vibrated against his cock, and he snapped, losing all control. He shafted into her mouth, her moans and the slurping noises of Dare going down on their mate, drove him toward his release much sooner than he wanted. His balls drew up, tingling spread up his spine and through his extremities. His thighs quivered. The pressure built and built, and at last his release boiled out of his body, flooding her mouth with ropes of thick cum. "Swallow it all, Jaynee." He could feel her shake, choking on the jets of semen pouring down her throat. Long minutes passed, longer than he ever thought possible, even though his kind were known to take a quarter of the dial at times to release all their seed during a mating.

When every drop of cum left his body, he reluctantly pulled his still hard cock from her mouth. Her lips were puffy, raw looking, and he knew he'd been too rough on her, but she hadn't protested, hadn't signaled him to stop. Even though he regretted his rough treatment, he couldn't help but feel proud of her submission, her willingness to see to his needs. Now it was time to show their compassion and see to hers.

After giving her a tender smile, he turned toward his other triad partner. "I think she's waited long enough and she's being so obedient. She needs a reward." Dropping his gaze to Dare's cock, he twisted his lips in an understanding smile. "Looks like you can use some ease as well." He raised his gaze to Dare's, watched his meaning sink in. Knowing the pair could use some alone time together and hoping for the same soon, Lucan lifted himself away from his mate.

"I'm going to take a shower and scrounge up some food, before we try to contact your ship. Why don't you both take care of your mutual…" he paused looking for the right word. He shrugged. "…problem, while I do so."

Without waiting for an answer, Lucan quickly left the room. He just hoped that Dare didn't take too long returning the favor, giving him some one-on-one time with their mate as well.

USING HIS TELEPATHIC abilities, Dare focused on his newfound bond with Lucan so he could establish communication with the departing man. *Thank you for giving us this time.*

He could feel Lucan's begrudging amusement. *Just don't forget to reciprocate when time isn't so short.*

Understood, Lucan. This means more to me than you can imagine.

I understand. It's how I feel as well. We will have to work this out, set aside some time where we can have her to ourselves. Now stop talking to me and make our mate cum.

Shaking his head at Lucan's attitude, Dare's gaze focused on the plump lips of Jaynee's creamy pussy. He swallowed the saliva pooling in his mouth and did his best to keep his fangs sheathed within his gums. *As you command.*

Turning his attention back to his mate, Dare raised his gaze. He felt Jaynee's desperate need through their bond, could feel her raging desire as her entire body quivered. He needed to make love to her soon. She couldn't lay spread out as she was for much longer, before her pleasure would turn to pain. But he could ease her just a little.

Reaching back, he untied the scarves around her ankles, allowing her some freedom. He couldn't wait to feel her legs wrap around his waist as he fucked her hard and deep. "Is that better, my mate?"

She nodded, straining against the bonds still holding her outstretched arms. He could tell she wanted to speak, to ask why he didn't release her hands as well. "You can speak freely, Jaynee. I'm sure you have many questions."

She licked her lips, heaved a sigh, then nodded. "I do. Why won't you untie me? Why tie me up at all? It's not like I'm going anywhere."

Lining up his turgid cock with her slit, Dare pretended to think about it. Slowly, he slid his shaft just inside her pussy. A gush of cream coated his dick and it was all he could do not to ram into her. But, no. He needed to maintain control, draw this out, and make it good for her.

Shaking his head at his lack of control, Dare once again met her questioning gaze. "Why? It's to draw out your pleasure, Jaynee. If all you can do is lie there, accept our touch, the sensation will be that much more extreme, your need more urgent. And when you finally are allowed to cum, the explosion will be greater and more pleasurable than you can imagine."

When she gave him a doubt-filled look, Dare had no choice but to prove her wrong, and he was about to do just that. Without any further foreplay, Dare drove into her cunt, hitting deep inside her with a single thrust. Her strangled gasp rang through the room, firing Dare's lust higher than it had ever burned before.

JAYNEE COULDN'T BELIEVE her luck. She now had two gorgeous, dominant men to love. It had been her fondest desire to have a dominant man. She'd never dared to dream for two. She struggled against her bonds, wanting—needing—to feel the silk of his hair. Her fingers itched to score his back with her nails as he drove into her. Still she waited, knowing he would free her when he deemed it appropriate. They hadn't hurt her thus far, so she remained content to follow Dare's lead.

Grateful for the reprieve, she wrapped her legs around Dare's waist and pulled him to her, reveling in the wondrous heights his thick cock took her to. She arched her back, silently begging to feel his mouth on her flesh. Her breasts tingled with anticipation as his eyes lit up at her unspoken request. Already hard nipples turned to diamond-hard peaks, jutting up toward his lowering mouth. She groaned and quivered beneath him as he nuzzled her heated skin.

"So responsive," he breathed against her flesh. Taking her left nipple in his mouth, he suckled hungrily, laving then gently nibbling the turgid peak. She fisted her hands, pulled at her bonds and whimpered.

She needed to cum, needed a climax more than he could know. Still, he held something of himself from her. He moved slowly, almost reverently against her as she writhed beneath him. His hands slowly roved over her flesh, teasing.

"Please!" She begged. How could he be so cruel? Why did he withhold her climax this way? He said he would make her cum. When would he allow her the release she so desperately needed?

"Tell me what you want," he said, panting as he surged forward. "Tell me, Jaynee."

Her face blazed. Why did he want her to tell him? She showed him with every movement, every arch of her back, every intense moan as he moved above her and still he tortured her mercilessly.

"I need." She licked her lips and squeezed her eyes shut with mortification that she'd reached this level of need. "Ram it into me, Dare. Fuck me so hard, so deep that you'll never find your way out."

"As you wish, *natoya*."

He surged forward a few more times, then withdrew from her. She nearly screamed with frustration. Why was he doing this to her? Her body vibrated with the need to climax and he still toyed with her, still brought her to the very edge, and left her to sob with frustration.

She sighed with relief when he released her wrists from the bonds. She brought her hands down, rubbed her wrists for a moment, then sent her hand to her quivering cunt, seeking relief. If he wouldn't give it to her, she would see to her own climax.

"Do not, *natoya*," Dare said, gently removing her hand from between her legs, and stood. "I will care for you. I will see to your needs." He stared deep into her eyes, his gaze compassionate. "I promise you. You will cum as you never have before."

She let him pull her from the bed, and into his arms. He drew her against him, pressing his hard body against her softer one. Dare bent, pressed his lips to hers and begged entrance to her mouth. She opened for him, reveling in the heady taste of him as the wet velvet of his tongue dueled with hers.

At last, able to give into the need to feel the silky softness, she speared her fingers through his inky hair and pulled his head to hers. She wanted nothing more than to meld with him, crawl inside him where he would keep her safe and content forever.

Gently, he pulled his lips from hers, his hands reaching up to disentangle her fingers from his hair. He kissed her knuckles and stared deep into her eyes.

"Your thoughts humble me, *natoya*. I also wish to keep you with me. I cannot tell you how many years I have searched for you. If you only knew how many of my people suffer with no mate. How many more go to war, becoming mercenaries to fuel their death wish, because they tire of living their life alone. You are a precious gift."

"What does that mean, Dare?" she asked, when she found her voice. "*Natoya*? Is that your language?" She ran her hands over his smooth chest, unable to keep herself from touching him.

He nodded, smiled, and rested his hand against her cheek. "It means many things—my heart—my love—precious gift—beloved. You are all those things to me." He dropped his gaze to her lips. "You are everything to me."

He kissed her again, his mouth trailing over her sensitized flesh to her ear and the crook of her neck. Her skin prickled with anticipation as she waited for him to sink his teeth into her once more. She needed it as surely as she needed to breathe. She needed to see to his every want, his every need.

Easily, he lifted her in his arms. "Wrap your legs around my waist."

Wrapping her arms around his neck, she complied. She was more than ready for him to take her over the edge. She screamed with frustration when he teased her first, circling her clit with his fingers, thrusting them into her empty channel. When would he let her cum? When would he allow them both a release? Surely, by now, he needed it just as much as she.

She bit her lip when the thick head of his shaft pushed against the opening of her channel. His hands on her hips guided her down. He slid into her with ease as her cream coated his shaft.

"By the Lady Goddess, you're wet, Jaynee," he breathed against her neck.

The scrape of his teeth against her flesh drove her closer to her climax. Frantic for her release, she fought his measured thrusts, needing him harder, deeper.

"Please, Dare. I need this. I need to—" the words caught in her throat when he reached between them and squeezed her clit. She screamed his name as she came, her channel clasping his cock as he continued to ram into her seeking his own release.

Turning, he laid her across the top of her dressing table. Her toiletries crashed to the floor and his frenzied thrusts drove the dressing table across the floor. Taking her legs in his hands, he drew them apart and pushed them to her chest, opening her up to his pounding cock.

Another climax crawled through her blood. A scream bubbled from her throat as he groaned above her and sank his teeth into her breast, once again sharing his elation through their newly formed bond.

He came into her. Thick jets of warm semen bathed the inside of her grasping channel. He pulled his head back, the glow in his eyes receded and he leaned down to lick the wound on her breast.

His flaccid penis slipped from her cunt, leaving her feeling empty and bereft. How would she ever function without one of them inside her? She needed him again, *now*. What had this mating done to her? Somehow, it changed her into a grasping woman. A nymphomaniac. A slut.

Dare smiled, still breathing heavily above her. He leaned down, lapped at her nipple, and grinned. "That is a common reaction to the semen of a *Savari*. That is why we rarely interact with other races. We have been named monster and sex gods, by the same people. We do not wish to war with others. We only wish our race to survive."

He ran his fingers through his hair. "We would not be here now if it weren't for the Banarts. We are forced to seek alliances with others to ensure the continuation of our race."

Dare straightened and lifted her from the dressing table. He looked down at the mess on the floor and grimaced. "I'm sorry about your broken things. I shall replace them at the first opportunity."

He carried her into the bathroom and set her on the rug. "I'll need to contact my ship after we shower. My people are going to be worried about my disappearance. I don't want them to do anything drastic."

Thirty minutes later, they strolled into the kitchen fresh from the shower. Luc looked up, glanced at their wet hair, and grinned. At least he didn't look jealous. His relief was so great Dare almost laughed out loud.

He watched his triad mate stare appreciatively at their female. He didn't blame him. He himself could barely stop staring at her when she'd first sauntered from her closet wearing an off the shoulder clinging dress. It was blue, the color of *minia* flowers, draped over her body, hugging her feminine curves.

He needed to discuss this arrangement with Lucan. There was no getting around it.

Their mating triad, while not traditional for the *Savari,* would ensure an unbreakable bond between his people and that of Jaynee and Luc's worlds. It must. The three worlds needed each other, whether they wished to believe that or not.

"Have you contacted your people?" he asked, taking the seat next to Luc while Jaynee poured him a cup of *Jabba* juice. He didn't need sustenance the way she and Luc did, but it wouldn't hurt him and, in fact, may strengthen their bond. Giving her a smile and a wink that made her blush, he took a sip of the dark juice.

"Mmm… This is good, Luc." He gave the other man a grudging salute. "You make a good cup of juice."

"It wasn't my doing," Luc grinned and shrugged. "I merely switched the pot on when I came in here." He nodded to Jaynee. "Our mate seems to be a wonderful cook."

They both glanced at her and raised their cups. "Thank you, Jaynee," they said in unison.

She blushed. Dare reached down and rubbed his crotch, already needing to bury his cock in her tight sheath again.

He glanced in Luc's direction. He noticed the pained expression on the other man's face and was relieved to see that he wasn't the only one affected by her beauty.

Luc shifted in his seat. "I contacted my people to let them know I'm fine." He tossed the communicator at Dare. "I would suggest that you do the same. Your people are threatening war against both my people and the *Carillians*." He gave them a rueful smile. "I don't think war between our people is in any of our best interests. Better to save our enmity for the *Banarts*."

Dare inhaled sharply. "You are correct in that it would not be in our people's best interest. Together we have a chance to defeat the *Banarts*. Divided, we shall surely fall."

Luc stood and began to pace. "On the other hand, should our people band together, we could spell the end of the marauding *Banarts*."

Dare nodded, strode to the corner of the room, and spoke to his people in low tones. Looking up, he pinned Jaynee with his stare.

"Where are we?" he pushed aside her gauzy curtain to peer outside. There were no obvious landmarks near. Only gray, nondescript two-story buildings with small signs surrounded her small shop.

Jaynee cleared her throat. "We are two minutes south of the timekeeper in the *Carrillian City* Centre Square. Shop number Oh-two-four-two."

Dare relayed the address to his people, closed the communicator and set it on the counter. He turned toward his newly acquired mates. "They're sending a transport. They want us to meet them in the square." He turned to Jaynee and raised his brow. "They will be there within the hour awaiting us. Is there anything you wish to pack?"

"Pack?" Jaynee swallowed and licked her lips. Her gaze darted nervously between them. "I don't plan to go anywhere. This is my home." She held her arms wide, as if to encompass the entire shop and dwelling. "You can't expect me to just pick up and leave."

Dare sat down at the table and sighed. He should have known it was too good to be true. He should have known this was all too easy. What if he didn't have a mate and allies after all? What if they refused him, refused his needs? If they did, he'd never have another family, children of his own. He had to try and make her understand, make them both understand.

"You don't realize what your decision means. You must return to *Savar* with me. If we do not complete the mating ritual on *Savar* within the next four days, you will doom us all."

Jaynee gasped. How could she not? "What do you mean, doom us all?" Somehow she knew—knew with absolute certainty—that whatever he was about to tell them would change her life, would force her to do as he wanted.

She watched as he straightened in his chair, looked from her to Lucan and back. "If we don't perform the mating ritual on the night of *Savar's* full moons, then our mating, our true binding will never be complete. Not only will we never link as we are meant to, completely, soul to soul to soul, but having any children of this union will be an impossibility."

Pain shafted through her at the knowledge that children might not be part of their union. Always, in the back of her mind, she'd hoped for children, a home. She rose, took a step toward Dare, feeling his pain as though it were her own. Behind her, she heard Lucan's chair scrape back as he too made to rise. Apparently, neither she nor Lucan could handle seeing the crushing blow her words had wrought on this strong man.

Reaching out to him, Jaynee ran her hand down his face, using her touch to soothe the pain away. "Talk to me, Dare. Tell me what's going on." She turned her head, saw the worry in Lucan's eyes and with his slight nod of encouragement, she dropped to her knees in front of Dare. She laid her hands upon his clenched fists, trying to soothe away his tension, his pain. "Tell us," she pleaded, needing to understand, to make things right.

Dare raised his head, looking at her through haunted eyes. So much pain and weariness shadowed his face. "There are some things about the *Savar* that you need to understand, some things that might shock you." He looked over her shoulder. His concentration now centered on Lucan, who, had at some point, moved to kneel behind her. Luc placed his hands on her shoulders, a solid presence to lean on if she needed it. She didn't know how she knew that's why he was there, but she did. She'd have to think more on that at a more appropriate time. "Shock you both, actually."

Behind her, she could feel Lucan stiffen. Waves of tension and anger seemed to emanate from him. Was Dare talking to Lucan? Was he keeping something from her? At the thought that either man would purposely withhold information from her, something inside her snapped. She'd be damned if they'd treat her like she wasn't an equal outside of the bedroom, and best they learn that now.

"Will one of you please tell me what is going on? I don't like you talking behind my back. In fact, all you're doing is pissing me off, and an angry witch is not a good thing."

They must have sensed her outrage because as one they moved to wrap their arms around her, cocooning her in their warmth, making her feel loved and cherished. How could she stay mad at them when they worked together to thwart her anger? How could any woman remain upset when two gorgeous men focused all their attention on her, showing her with gentle touches and heated glances how they felt about her?

"I'm sorry, *natoya*. I never meant to leave you out," Dare whispered. She could feel the scrape of his teeth against her neck, knew he was trying to distract her from her anger. She huffed out a breath. His damned plan was working because she could barely think, never mind stay angry with him.

"I too apologize, mate," Lucan mumbled, his voice a raspy caress as he nuzzled her ear. Shivers raced up and down her spine. Her womb clenched. Her clit throbbed in need. Soon, she'd be a blubbering blob of desperate need, and then she wouldn't get any answers.

"I know what you're both doing, and this isn't going to get you out of telling me exactly what's going on." Both men stiffened, but neither moved away from her, rather, they both seemed to move even closer to her, if that were even possible. Already she could feel every muscle and ridge of their firm bodies pressed against her.

Seconds passed, and still they didn't answer, didn't tell her what she needed to know. Worry and fear invaded her mind. Her stomach seized, cramping, as horrid images of what might happen flashed through her mind. A light sheen of sweat coated her skin and her entire body began to quiver. She couldn't take much more of this unnerving silence.

Dare lightly nipped the pulse point at her neck, then sighed. When he finally raised his head and looked at her, she could see the worry in his eyes. By the Lady Goddess, what did he have to tell her that worried him so?

Against her throat, Lucan growled before lifting his head. After placing a tender kiss at her temple, he rested his chin atop her head. "Just tell her, Dare. She doesn't need you dragging this out. All you're doing is scaring her. Better she knows just what's she getting into, than find out later on."

Dare nodded, then lowered his hands. Scooting his chair back, he stood, turned away from her. Pain pierced her heart. Why would he turn away from her? Tears welled in her eyes, her hands fisted at her sides. Lucan stood, pulled her into his arms, and braced her against his chest. She watched the flex of Dare's back as he steadily moved away from her, from them. "Why do you turn your back on me? What could be so horrible that you can't look me in the eye when you tell me?"

A wave of rage washed over her and she knew it came from Dare, knew he didn't like the fact she'd called him on his cowardice. Good. Let him be mad, maybe then she'd get some straight answers.

I suggest you don't try my temper, natoya. I won't be as lenient in your punishment as I was earlier.

Go to hell, Dare.

Outraged, hurt, and disillusioned, Jaynee shrugged out of Lucan's arms and ran out of the kitchen. They'd expect her to hide in her room, to lock herself away in familiar surroundings. They didn't know her at all.

She couldn't bear to be in the same room—the same building—as the two men who claimed to want to share their lives with her. If they couldn't share the truth, couldn't be honest with her, then there was nothing more for her to hope for. Their relationship was over before it ever really began. With tears blinding her, and the aching loss and despair driving her on, she raced away from her store, from her home, and from the missing part of her heart, her soul.

She ran as far and as fast as she could, blindly running to a place where she knew she would be alone. A place where she knew she could find solace. She reached the square in record time. Usually she walked to the square, she didn't run, until now. She sat on the bench and contemplated what Dare said.

Could she just pick up and leave? She didn't know either of those men. Not really. What about her home, her shop? And what would happen if things didn't work out between them? She would have nowhere to go, nothing to do.

She wiped her damp hands on her legs. Such a decision couldn't be made in a day. It was unfair for him to think she could do so. Something this huge, took months to decide. Yet, according to Dare, she no longer had months. She had days to make such a momentous decision. Days spent aboard a stranger's ship, living by his people's rules and laws. What if she made the worst decision of her life?

Jaynee rested her head in her hands and finally gave in to the urge to cry. A life without Dare, Lucan and children, or facing the unknown with two men she barely knew. What kind of choice was that?

She felt two people sit down next to her on the bench. Knew without looking who had joined her. Besides, she knew Dare and Luc's scents already. It was ingrained in her mind, like the scents her mother and father always wore. She refused to look up. Refused to acknowledge they sat next to her on the bench. Her whole body quivered with need for these two men. She literally shook with the desire to couple with them both again. When had she lost control over her own body?

"I can't go with you, Dare," she said. At last she had come to a decision on this. There, she'd told him. Now he knew she couldn't go with him to his planet. She would stay here alone, or perhaps she could convince Luc to stay with her.

Dare sighed and shook his head. "I wish you had not just said that."

He stood and moved to the side and she felt bereft. How could his absence be so heartrending? What would it be like after he left her here?

"Take her to the transport and hurry up about it. We don't need her people causing a scene over her abduction."

"What?" She raised her tear-filled eyes and saw three men approach from the trees surrounding her. They must have been hiding there, waiting for a signal from Dare. She whipped her head toward Dare, watched the satisfaction fill his eyes. Rage filled her. Rage and fear. She stood and made to run away again. "I'm not going anywhere with you!"

One of the men reached out with a glowing rod and touched it to her middle. Every one of her muscles went slack. She felt nothing, could do nothing. She fell, could only lie in a heap, her eyes open, as Luc bent over her, a grim expression on his face.

"I hope you can find it in your heart to forgive me for this one day," he said as he threw her over his shoulder and carried her to the waiting shuttle.

She raged and screamed in her mind. She begged people for help as they walked by. None of them heard her. She couldn't say a thing. When Luc shifted her in his arms, it must have looked as though she were there willingly. Her eyes were open, yet she couldn't say a thing. If only the people could have heard her mental screams, maybe someone would have helped her.

When they reached the transport, Luc bent and set her gently on a plush seat. She'd never seen such a luxurious shuttle before. Dare sat down beside her, touched her with a small needle and feeling began to return to her extremities.

"I hope you know I'll never forgive either of you for this. Kidnapping is a crime in every system. You must know that. My people will not stand still for this, you know."

The corner of Dare's mouth lifted. "I contacted your people the moment you ran from us, *natoya*. They believe you to be a willing participant in our coming nuptials on *Savar*. Even your esteemed leaders plan to attend your wedding. Will you have them killed on *Savar* for your own selfishness? Or will you come to terms with the fact that you are the mate of the *Savari* leader and a *Pantari* spy?"

Jaynee licked her lips. There was nothing to do for now. For now, she would sit here and listen to what Dare had to say. Then, when his guard was down, she would find a way to escape.

Dare lifted his hand and cupped her chin. "You will not escape me, Jaynee. The only way to escape me now, is death. I will always know where you are. I will always be able to find you. No matter how far or how fast you run, you will never be able to hide from me."

Tears pooled in her eyes as the engines whirred and the transport left the ground, taking them to the *Savari* vessel orbiting her planet, taking her away from everything she ever knew and loved. She cast her gaze to her lap. Her heart breaking, she twisted her fingers together, and sobbed.

"Oh, my Lady Goddess, how could you abandon me so?"

LUCAN WATCHED FROM beneath lowered lashes as Jaynee sobbed her heart out. The panther inside him stretched, screamed out its rage. Its mate should not hurt. Should not cry. Unable to stop himself, he took the seat on the other side of her, effectively boxing her in between them.

He knew she'd try to escape. He'd do the same in her situation and because of that, he and Dare needed to come up with a plan to subdue her. They needed her. He couldn't allow her to escape them. She had to know, to understand, that she belonged to them, as they belonged to her. And he knew just how to do it.

Unable to sit near her without touching her smooth skin, Lucan reached over and wrapped his hand around hers. Using the pad of his thumb, he gently rubbed circles against her clenched fist, doing his best to offer what little comfort he could. She tensed beneath his hand, tried to move away but seated between them as she was, she couldn't escape his touch. He vowed before this night ended and a new dawn approached, she would welcome their touch, would beg for it. For that, he'd need Dare to work a miracle before they reached his ship.

Tell me you have a pleasure chamber aboard your ship, Dare.

Dare lifted his eyebrows. His eyes glittered and a wry smile spread across his face. Lucan caught a glimpse of fang and knew his triad partner understood exactly what he planned for their mate.

There are several aboard my ship, actually.

Can you make one unavailable to the rest of the crew?

I can do better than that. My personal quarters have such a room, though our people call it a training room rather than pleasure chamber. All Savari *men are taught the proper way to train their mate to submit, to relinquish all their fears and concerns to us during intimate times.*

Lucan nodded his understanding. The *Pantari* weren't so very different when it came to the need to sexually dominate their mates. In all other areas of their life, the *Pantari* embraced their women's strengths, their independence. But in love play their need to take charge was an inherent instinct, a drive so strong it was impossible to ignore for long.

Good, then have your people prepare the room. Jaynee will not leave it until she submits to us and to her own desires. She likes to be dominated during mating, needs it as much as we need to dominate. It is only the suddenness of the changes we've wrought upon her, the need for her to give up all she knew and loved, which keeps her from surrendering her heart to us. It is that which we must overcome.

You speak wisely, Luc. Perhaps there is a way in which we could give her back that which she believes lost to her. I shall think on that as well.

Good. It is settled then. Luc looked down upon his mate. Her eyes were closed. Dried tear tracks marred the delicate beauty of her ivory skin and her cheeks were flushed. His breath caught in his chest as he gazed upon her. To him, she was the most beautiful woman he'd ever seen. Nothing could—or would—ever change that for him.

THE MOMENT THE shuttle landed upon the deck of the *Savari* ship, Jaynee opened her eyes. If she were to escape this would be her best chance for success. Before she could even rise from her chair, she felt the current enter her again. She looked down, saw the glowing wand and raised stunned eyes to the wielder. Lucan, looking almost feral, turned toward one of the warriors from the square and handed him back the weapon.

"Thank you. I hope this is the last time I'll need your assistance." His gaze, filled with determination, dropped to hers and if she could have moved, she would have moved as far away from him as she could. The predator was unleashed and she was his prey of choice.

Focused on Lucan, unable to move, unable to speak, there was no way for her to avoid Dare when he once again leaned over and gave her an injection. Warmth flooded her body. Her pussy clenched. Her clit twitched. Cream slid down the inside of her thighs. Her eyes widened in disbelief. What the hell had he given her?

"It is a mild aphrodisiac, *natoya*. It will heighten every sensation, every movement you make, until you beg us for relief, and even then, until we feel your spirit willingly merging with ours, we will not join with you."

Her mind raged and screamed. Fear and anger, desperation and heartbreak warred within her. What would she do? How would she ever get away from them? They would torture her. Rape her. How could they do such a thing if they loved her as they claimed?

"We only do what we must. It is you who won't allow us into your heart. You hold yourself back from us. Do you think we would make you give up all that you know and not do the same?"

Lucan bent down, met her angry glare with his own. A growl rumbled from his chest, his lips lifted in a snarl. "If you truly loved us, believed in our ability to provide you with all that you need, you'd not be in this situation. Before the night is out, you'll know in your soul that we belong with each other, despite whatever circumstances brought us together.

Dare lifted her into his arms, before she slumped to the floor. Her arms and legs had grown leaden, useless. Would they continue to keep her like this if she refused to submit? How long would they try to force her into submission? How long must she endure their cruelty?

She didn't know if she could ever trust them now. What little trust that formed at her home, was destroyed, shattered into a million shards, like broken glass upon a sidewalk.

Have faith in your men. Have faith that they have your best interests at heart.

Who are you?

You know. There is nothing to fear. Your mates love you. Let them prove it to you.

Unable to think of anything to say, she closed her eyes, avoiding the stares of Dare's crew as they carried her from the shuttle and to whatever fate awaited her.

It took but minutes for them to reach their destination. She could feel their excitement, their desire. Their hunger burned. The desire raged inside them, a ravenous beast desperately waiting for permission to break free. And she'd be the meal they would feast upon.

Before she knew it, they stopped, then placed her on something plush and soothing. Still, she refused to open her eyes, to acknowledge them. She wouldn't give them the satisfaction. The rustle of clothes, the metallic sounds of metal meeting metal, and the heavy breathing of her mates made her curious, but still she refused to allow her curiosity free reign. That would only lead to more heartbreak.

Her eyes snapped open when she felt a needle slide under her skin. Another wave of heat washed over her but this time the sexual need didn't increase. Instead her fingers and toes began to tingle. Confused, she looked from one male to the other.

"We don't want to just use your body against you, mate." Lucan's raspy voice brushed against her, sending shards of tingling sensation straight to her dripping pussy.

"No, we want you to enjoy this night, *natoya*. We want you to know that we'll never leave you wanting. We will provide all that you need, as you will do for us."

Before she could get full feeling in her extremities, Dare picked her up, cradling her against his chest as Lucan made his way toward a door she'd not noticed until it silently swung open in front of him. She gasped. Her mind raced. Every wall, every surface was dedicated to carnal pursuits. When her gaze landed on the hanging restraint system, she knew exactly what they had planned for her. Oh, Lady Goddess. How would she ever survive?

SHE SHUDDERED, DESPERATE to escape her bonds so she could make herself cum. Hours had passed since they brought her into this room, strapped her into this netting where they had access to all parts of her body as she hung suspended in midair.

She needed release, needed it with ravenous greed. "Please?" she begged, forgetting their decree she not speak without permission. Luc's sharp slap on her ass caused her gasp. Heat flared in her sopping cunt. Fire tingled up her spine.

"You were told not to speak, mate," he growled. His gentle caress rubbed away the sting. She gasped when Lucan's fingers stroked her pussy. Gently, he parted her lips, his fingers circling her clit, before he lowered his head and sucked her pulsing nub. He inserted one finger, then another, stretching her. The strong pull accompanied by the deep stroking of his fingers inside her channel threatened to send her over the edge.

Her thighs quivered, her hands trembled. By the Lady Goddess, she couldn't take much more. They needed to stop this torture. They needed to fuck her, to let her cum.

She'd do anything, say anything, just to get relief. How could they let this go on for so long? She wanted to sob, she wanted to scream, but most of all she wanted to be fucked. Now.

UNWILLING TO JUST watch any longer, Dare approached his mate. Watching Lucan devour her pussy, listening as she begged him mentally to ease her ravenous need, had driven every sane thought out of his head.

His cock bobbed in front of her face, heavy with need. Her eyes flicked up to his, desperate need warred with anxious anticipation. She moistened her lips with her tongue and a drop of pre-cum greeted her in response.

"I won't tell you again, *natoya*. Take my cock in your mouth and suck it dry. I want you to take every drop of my seed when it spills. I want you to lap it up, as a *Pantari* feline would sweet cream."

Finally, after what seemed hours instead of just the few seconds that passed, she dragged her tongue over the head of his cock. More pre-cum spilled into her mouth.

His hips began to jackhammer against her mouth, and as she squirmed beneath the simultaneous assault Lucan was making to her cunt, moaning around his shaft, his aggression, his need to dominate her, increased. He knew he was being too rough, but he couldn't help himself. His *Savari* instincts demanded she take him as he was—all male aggression and driving need.

Her breathing grew ragged, and still he didn't slow down, didn't ease off the pressure or tempo. His strokes were deep, hard, forceful, and she took it, took all of him. Dare sensed no protest in her mind, in her heart, though the fact that Lucan was doing his best to drive her out of her mind, probably helped matters.

The pressure around his shaft increased, and his balls drew taut against his body. Tingles raced up his spine and his hands began to shake, and still he forced his cock even deeper, wedging it down her throat. Dare groaned as he felt his cum rip out of his balls and down the length of his cock.

Savage pleasure raced through him as his body found release. "Swallow it, Jaynee. I want to see you consume every last bit of my seed. And when you're finished, you'll do the same for Lucan."

Dare clasped her head, wrapping her hair around his fingers just as hot jets of semen spilled down her throat. Ropes of cum shot out of his cock, and still he didn't let up his grip. Dare could see the tension running through his mate's body. It wouldn't take much to send her careening over the edge of release. Now was the time to get her to agree to their terms.

Dare dropped his gaze, meeting Lucan's hungry stare from beneath her weeping cunt. At his slight nod, Dare looked into his mate's passion glazed eyes. "If you agree to go through with the Binding Ritual, we'll let you come, *natoya*. We'll love you all night, and through the rest of the trip to *Savar*. All your needs, your desires will be seen to. I'll fuck your ass, as Lucan fills your empty channel and only when you can't take any more, will we let you rest."

Lucan's rumbling purr interrupted the tense silence as they waited for her to make her decision. *It may not be fair to pressure her, to force her to go through this on such a short acquaintance.*

Yes, they'd only known each other a very short time, and had no courting to speak of, but he knew, as Lucan knew, they were a part of each other, and nothing would change that. He couldn't let her fears keep them from having a happy future, and he'd spend the next thousand years showing her how much he adored her, needed her in his life, so she never regretted mating with them.

When he thought she'd refuse out of sheer stubbornness, she heaved a shuddering breath then nodded her acquiescence. Joy winged its way through his heart. Beneath her, Lucan's throaty purr announced his own happiness with her agreement.

"Then let us now see to your needs, *natoya*. We can't have word reach the outside that we're not men who will honor their vows. And this promise, we are more than happy to fulfill."

And love her they did. For three days and nights until they reached *Savar*, Dare and Lucan did their best to see that her every waking desire was seen to, from making sure her favorite foods were available to quenching her body's demands to mate.

It was up to Jaynee whether or not she fulfilled her promise to them, and they could only hope they'd earned her trust, her belief in them. With much trepidation the men left her, giving her time alone for the first time since they'd abducted her. All their hopes for the future rested in her hands.

.

GIANT TREES LOOMED over her head. They were so tall, it made her dizzy when she craned her neck to see the tops. The large leaves were a vibrant shade of purple. As big as her hand, they resembled those pressed between the pages of the spell-book she'd found. Oak, though the color was something she'd never before seen. The author of the book wrote in her own hand that the tree was called oak. This must be a hybrid of those Earthen trees.

It seemed strange to find this world so much like her own, yet still so foreign. She bit her lip, still trying to overcome her silent rage at being brought here against her will. Still she promised to cooperate and she would not have her males punish her again for her disobedience.

Her face burned at the thought of her punishment. She hated it and enjoyed it at the same time. There must be something wrong with her. Normal women didn't like to be spanked and restrained during sex, did they? She shuddered, remembering Luc's sharp slaps followed by his gentle caress, rubbing away the sting.

She spun in a circle, looking around. The wide band of trees surrounded her, the vivid colors of their purple and blue leaves, breathtaking beneath the moons beams. A thick carpet of purple and blue leaves covered the grove inside the stone circle. An altar, marbled with veins of pink, stood between the two largest upright stones. *Casta* blooms of pink and white decorated the circle. Their star-shaped buds glittered with dew and their stems—braided together in a delicate rope—were draped over most of the shorter standing stones. Tears filled her eyes at the collective beauty. It seemed even though his people were strange and hard at times, their souls were pure.

Dare and Luc still stood outside the circle of stones. Their glimmering black robes made them appear sinister somehow. Maybe it was the hoods pulled up over their heads, or the way they kept their heads down and their hands tucked into their sleeves.

It still irked her that Luc knew what the hell was to happen during this ceremony and she was kept in the dark. She still hadn't forgiven them for stealing her away from her world, her life, but she *had* grown to trust them during the three day trip to this world.

A wedding ceremony with witnesses she could understand. But this…this not knowing their secrets was really beginning to grate on her nerves.

Jaynee, whatever should happen in this circle is an affirmation of your love and your trust in your mates. If you refuse them, if you show you do not trust them by not following their requests, you will forfeit your right to bond with them. You will also doom the three of you to a childless existence. You can only bear the children of these two men. To any other you are sterile. Remember this when you think to refuse them something in the next few hours.

Jaynee chewed her thumbnail and wondered if the voice she heard was that of the Lady Goddess? Who else could it be? She looked over at her two mates and knew she trusted them. She vowed to herself, that come what may, she would do everything they asked of her, as long as she remained in this circle.

Soon, cloaked figures moved from the cover of the trees, silently approaching them. They surrounded her and her mates. Dozens of people gathered around them, clasping hands as they formed a circle. Only the whisper of wind through the trees broke the unnatural silence.

Two men broke off from the rest, entering the circle. One wore a robe of red, the other green. They entered the circle and stood before her.

They looked her up and down, their faces blank. She fought the urge to draw her own covering closer about her as they looked right through the transparent material to the naked flesh underneath. Their eyes probed her. It was almost as if they thought her unworthy to take her men to mate. Perhaps they did.

"Who petitions the council of *Savar* to bond with this woman?" the man wearing red asked.

"We do, illustrious priest, druid of the *Non*," Dare answered for them both as he and Luc finally entered the circle and took their places beside her.

The man in green lowered his hood. Jaynee's head snapped up in surprise. He wasn't a man at all, but a woman. "Who petitions the council of *Savar* to bond with these men?" She stared at Jaynee, waiting for an answer and the circle of witnesses hushed at her hesitance.

Jaynee stepped forward, willing strength to her body and her voice. "I do," she said, her voice carrying over the circle with a forcefulness she didn't realize she possessed. The man and woman took each other's hands and reached out to take theirs.

The five of them formed a loose circle around the altar and they all began to chant. Everyone in the grove began chanting in a foreign tongue. Dare prepared her for this. He told her the language was ancient, a rite to draw the power from the moon to bless their union, uniting the three of them together.

A small moonbeam filtered down from the sky, it touched Dare, the light growing, expanding around him. The robed man and woman left the circle, still chanting as the bright glow surrounded Dare, encompassing Jaynee and Luc and the marbled stone altar.

Her robe shimmered, grew brighter, the soft blue of the gauzy transparent garment lit up as the moon kissed her skin through the transparent fabric. Her nipples tightened, puckering into hard peaks as they stood within the moon's ethereal glow.

Soon, they all began to sway in a strange rhythm following the chant of the others outside the circle. Jaynee began to feel strange, light headed. The tips of her breasts began to tingle. Her clit pulsed between her legs. Still she stood holding the hand of each mate surrounded by their warmth. Feeling their desire envelop her as she waited for them to take her home and love her.

Dare moved behind her, his hands moved to her shoulders, his mouth trailing damp kisses along the curve of her neck. Luc stepped forward and cupped her breasts as the folds of her robe parted and it fell to the ground.

Cool air kissed her skin and she shivered with both the cold and desire. A touch of embarrassment rode her, knowing dozens of others looked on. She attempted to shrug it off, and allowed Dare to turn her in his arms.

His lips covered hers and she opened for him. She needed this. She needed for him to help her forget they had an audience. Part of her raged that he could do this to her, lead her here and force her to have sex in front of dozens of people. Yet she couldn't stay angry with him. She was too caught up in the moment. What was it about that silvery shaft of light that made her feel so feminine, so loved?

Luc's hand caressed her from behind and she groaned. What would these people do, stand there and watch them fuck her? Did she really want to be put on display like this?

Trust them, Jaynee. They only have your best interests at heart. Trust them to know what is best.

Whose voice was that in her head? The goddess? She hoped so. If not, she could be entrusting herself to these men on the word of some creature of the netherworld.

She gasped when Dare's fingers stroked her pussy. Gently, he parted her lips, his fingers circling her clit. Her legs gave out. Luc caught her and lifted her to the altar. Laying her down, he gently spread her arms, securing them to the base.

Her eyes widened, certainly filled with the fear she felt. Still, she gazed into Dare's eyes and trusted him. Trusted him and Luc not to hurt her. In fact, she fully expected them to take her pleasure to new heights.

Dare secured her legs to the other end of the altar and they moved around her, turning her on with their heated looks. She wriggled on the cold stone, wanting, needing their caresses. She needed to feel their thick cocks pounding into her as she screamed their names in ecstasy.

Before she could beg them to touch her, she heard the rustle of their robes, the soft sigh as material landed on the grass at their feet.

Lucan's strong hands stroked her inner thighs as Dare made his way toward the head of the altar. Luc stopped, looked down into her eyes. She could see the hunger, the driving need flare in his eyes. Out of the corner of her eyes she saw the robed woman enter the sacred circle and hand something to Dare, before stepping back to rejoin the others.

Questions flared in her mind but were silenced when he lifted his hand, showing her the silken material. "For the ritual you will be blindfolded. Give yourself over to us."

She shuddered when he put the blindfold over her eyes. Every touch, every breath of air stirred her sensitized flesh. Her every nerve ending sang with the need to have her mates take her here, now, despite the fact that people watched. Hell, maybe it was because she knew they watched.

Her nipples hardened to a point of pain and she gasped when one of her men grasped one between his fingers and twisted. The pleasure-pain made her groan and she bit her lip. A warm mouth covered the tip of her breast and she groaned aloud. They didn't tell her not to make noise. It was one rule they never tried to implement. They probably knew it would be unfair to expect her to remain silent during such an onslaught.

Fingers delved into the moist flesh between her legs. She squirmed on the altar, raising her hips when the fingers left her. She screamed her rage, her frustration that they would do this to her. That they would bring her to such a level of desire without giving her the means to climax and relieve the burning need that rode her.

Warm breath caressed her thighs and she gasped. Her own breath came in short pants as she anticipated the pleasure that awaited her when those soft, warm lips closed around her erect clit. She wriggled, raised her hips again, reaching for the mouth she knew was just out of reach.

She felt one of her men straddle her chest, felt a hard cock press against her mouth at the same time as a warm tongue stroked the length of her wet slit.

"Suck my cock, mate." Luc's voice grated over her sensitive flesh. His voice was low, harsh, as if he couldn't control the need to come into her mouth right this instant.

Jaynee opened her mouth without hesitation. He moved, placing his cock against her lips. Sticking her tongue out, she laved the weeping head, tonguing the ridge, tasting the pre-cum that dribbled from the small hole.

Dare ate at her pussy, his mouth working between her legs like a starving man. She groaned as he suckled her clit, raising her hips to intensify the sensation.

Luc groaned. "Suck it!" He grasped her hair, held her to him in an unbreakable grip. She did her best to take his full length down her throat as he drove his cock into her mouth. She caressed him with her tongue, wishing she could reach up to fondle his sac.

Her climax grew closer as Dare worked at her cunt and she groaned. Luc's hand grasped her head. Bolts of pure energy shot up her legs, to her groin, to her nipples and she attempted a scream of release.

"God, baby, I'm going to cum. I want you to swallow it. Swallow my cum, mate." He leaned closer to whisper, "You're doing everything as you should and I'm proud of you. We both are. Trust us just a bit longer, Jaynee."

He stiffened above her as thick jets of semen shot down her throat. She gulped the thick, bitter fluid and tried not to gag. She didn't want to disappoint him. She didn't want to disappoint either of them.

Luc climbed off her and loosened the bonds on her wrists while Dare released her ankles. She reached up to remove the blindfold and gentle hands stopped her.

"Not yet, *natoya*," Dare said. His lips pressed against her, kissing her softly, showing her without out words the depths of his feelings. "You must leave the blindfold on a while longer yet. When it is time for it to come off, one of us shall remove it."

They helped her stand and led her to another spot she assumed was within the circle. Raising her hands above her head, they secured them with the restraints that still bound her wrists. She hung there in this mystic circle like some virgin sacrifice of old. Jaynee resisted the urge to giggle. She was certainly no virgin.

Soon her men began to touch her, lave her nipples, nibble at her skin. She groaned deep in her throat when they both suckled the tips of her breasts into their mouths at the same time.

Razor sharp teeth grazed her left breast and she knew it was Dare. Luc moved around behind her. He wrapped his arms around her, his mouth working at her neck. She whimpered, canted her head to the side.

"Do you submit to us, mate?" Dare asked, his voice rough. "Do you lay your trust at our feet and submit to us in every way?"

She nodded, then gasped as Luc's hand sank deep into her pussy from behind. His fingers delved deep, then pulled her slick juices to the tight bud of her ass and inserted his fingers, readying her for his invasion.

"Say it!" Dare demanded. He fisted his hands in her hair and pulled her head back. She reveled in the pleasure-pain and rocked back, swinging on the ties that held her upright.

"Yes! Yes, I submit to you and Luc in every way."

Dare growled and lifted her into his arms. Placing his cock at the entrance to her channel, he drove into her and she screamed.

"You are mine, you are Luc's, you belong to us. Say it!" Dare demanded.

"I belong to you." She sobbed.

"And?"

"I belong to Luc!"

With those words Dare slowed his pace and Luc entered her ass. His long, thick cock slid easily into her prepared hole and he moved within her, steadily bringing her closer and closer to another orgasm. Shards of ecstasy rushed through her blood scorching her heart, her soul and she knew she was one with these two men.

Jaynee tightened her legs around Dare's waist, pulled him deeper as Luc drove into her ass. She screamed out her release as she felt them both swell within her, growing larger as they neared their own climax.

She came again, as Dare sank his teeth in her breast, as Luc plunged his own into her neck, and they both drank the nectar of life she knew would make them truly one.

Dare lifted his head, swiped his tongue over her breast, and ripped his wrist open with his fangs. "Drink and we shall be one."

Her trust in him never wavering, she dipped her head and drank from the wound at his wrist. Luc reached forward, leaning in to give his wrist to Dare.

Still they both surged within her, seeking their own release.

Dare sank his teeth in Luc's wrist and drank deep. When he was through, he raised Luc's wrist to Jaynee. Nodding, she took Luc's essence into her mouth, swallowing the liquid that would combine their lives, their love and their species.

Jaynee came again, screaming her climax to the heavens as her mates spilled their seed into the depths of her body.

"*Jaynee of Carrillia*, we accept you into our lives, into our blood, as we become one." Dare and Luc said simultaneously. "Reach for that which is ours within you. Feel our bond, our blood flowing in your veins and embrace us. It is time. Embrace your other side, your animal side." They lowered her to the ground and held her until she stopped swaying.

As they moved toward the line of trees, she felt another presence living inside her, growing in strength and insistence. She needed to run, to explore the world around her, but not as a *Carrillian* or a *Savari* but as a *Pantari*. Once they were safely hidden from sight, Lucan stopped.

"It's time, my mates. Visualize your animal spirit in your mind. See the great black cat as it prepares to hunt, to chase down its prey."

Jaynee watched in awe as her mates began their change. Their eyes glowed brilliant amber. Their pupils lengthened. Their teeth grew, muzzles shaped. Hair sprouted on their arms and legs, before their backs bowed and they were forced to drop to all fours.

Only after her mates stared at her from their feline bodies did she close her eyes and do as Lucan instructed. Power and heat blasted through her body as the great cat emerged from its slumber. Jaynee expected the shift to hurt, but the sense of freedom and joy that flooded her body swept any thought of pain away. When next she opened her eyes, the world had changed. She had changed.

Her mates surrounded her, buffeting her with their bodies, licked her muzzle then darted away. Unable to help herself, she gave chase.

Now you are one, Jaynee. You are of the Pantari as is Dare. You are of The Savar as is Luc. The two men now have the power of three, as do you. You three are the beginning of an army. An army of powerful triads that will one day defeat the Banart plague. One triad shall form every moon cycle on Carrillia. You must contact the next female in the line of three.

Carrillia, Two weeks later...

"HELLO?" LAYNEE ANSWERED the buzz of her communication terminal. Sound crackled and the *vid-screen* was full of static before it cleared to show her a familiar yet beloved face, the face of her twin, older by but a few ticks of a timepiece. "Jaynee! Where have you been? The store has been closed for two weeks and I've not seen you."

Jaynee nodded. "Yes, Laynee. Tell mother and father that I'm fine." She smiled softly. "I have to tell you something."

"What?" Laynee asked moving to sit at her table in the seat nearest the terminal. "That your spell-book doesn't work?" She shrugged. "I've already figured that out for myself."

Jaynee shook her head. "No. It does work. But it will only work for one specific witch per moon cycle."

"One a month? What good is that?" Laynee grimaced and took a sip of the steaming *Jabba* juice at her elbow.

"It is very good if you are the chosen witch."

Laynee made a face. "Yeah, and you would know...how?"

"I was the first. I woke from a dream and the words spilled from my mind. It was a spell which brought me not one, but two virile males with which to mate."

"Two?" Laynee sputtered, her face heating with a blush. It was one of her greatest fantasies.

"You too?" Jaynee asked with a knowing smile as her mates stepped beside her to wrap her in loving arms. She glanced at them and smiled before looking back at her sister. "It was a dream come true for me, Laynee. Don't fear it, embrace it." She suddenly became somber. "Now for the reason I've called." She leveled her gaze at her sister. "You are the next."

SEX ME DOWN

LAYNEE MIKALOSA SAT AT HER COMMUNICATIONS TERMINAL, STUNNED. "WHAT DO YOU mean, I'm the next?"

"This is your month, Laynee. When the moons reach their zenith, if you chant the correct spell, you shall draw your mates to you."

Laynee swallowed past the lump suddenly lodged in her throat. Her hands trembled, so she wrapped them around the mug of *Jabba* Juice in front of her. It wouldn't do to have her big sister return home if she thought Laynee needed her here. Jaynee had two new mates to take care of now. She didn't want her sister feeling like she needed to step in to make things right.

Not that she ever asked Jaynee to fix her mistakes, but she'd never stopped her sister from coming in and making things better either. She'd much rather surround herself with ancient tomes and lose herself in the worlds and adventures of others than venture out on her own. Laynee bit her bottom lip, then sighed.

Perhaps, it was time to stretch her wings a bit. What harm could there be in casting this spell to find her mate—or mates—if she believed Jaynee's story? And seeing the two gorgeous men who stood behind her sister, she didn't doubt the possibility that a mate or two awaited her somewhere in the far reaches of space and time. The question she needed to ask herself though was whether she had the courage to cast the spell or would she sit back and let the opportunity pass her by.

Her tummy flipped in nervous apprehension, but the growing dampness in her panties was proof enough she didn't find the idea totally repugnant either.

With her resolve strengthened, Laynee straightened her spine, dropped her hands from around her cup, leaned back, and crossed her arms beneath her breasts.

"Tell me what I need to know, Jaynee." She leveled her gaze at her sister and the two men behind her. "And don't leave anything out, please."

Laynee watched as her sister fidgeted in her seat. The blond man reached out and placed his hand on Jaynee's shoulder, while the darker one lightly stroked her hair. She could see her sister relax beneath their touch and that alone was enough evidence for her to know that Jaynee had finally found the happiness that had so long eluded her.

Lost in thought, she was startled when Jaynee started to speak. It wasn't until she heard the word *Banart* that a chill of premonition rippled down her back and she realized she needed to pay attention to exactly what her sister was saying.

"What did you say?"

"You will not just be calling your mates to you, Laynee, but you three shall be the next triad necessary to the coming war. Many of us are needed to defeat the *Banarts.*"

Unwilling for her sister and her mates to see her fear, she lowered her head to her chest and closed her eyes in thought. By the Goddess, the *Banarts* were feared in every known galaxy across the universe. How could she, a glorified librarian and bookseller, help defeat them? She was a nobody. She had no courage. No strength. Nothing inside her that could be used in such a battle. No matter what her sister believed, she was obviously mistaken if she thought that the Lady Goddess had told Jaynee her shy sister was the next to be called to this duty.

Feeling defeated, Laynee clenched her fists and sighed before raising her head and meeting Jaynee's gaze through the communication's terminal.

"I know that look, Laynee. Have faith in the Lady Goddess. Have faith in me. I would never steer you wrong."

"And if you're not wrong... What should I do?"

"I received the words to the spell in a dream the night of the three moon's alignment. Spend the next few weeks coming up with a spell of your own using the pages of the book I sent you before my own mating, but if you dream have faith in what it tells you. Believe in the Lady Goddess, but above all, believe in yourself, Laynee."

"I'll try, Jaynee. That's all I can promise you."

"That's all I can ask. I must go, sissy. There is a meeting we must attend and time grows short. I've sent you the frequency of our quarters so you can always reach us in an emergency. Take care."

"Take care, Jaynee and many blessings on your mating."

"Thank you and may the Lady Goddess bless you. Give my love to mother and father."

As the *vid-screen* went dark, Laynee slouched in her seat. In frustrated silence, she ran her hands through her hair, grimacing as they got caught in the knots that seemed to perpetually form, even moments after brushing her wild black mane.

Laynee pushed her chair back and stood, needing to walk off some of her anxiety. Even though her apartment was tiny, a little pacing room was better than none.

If only Jaynee knew how hard it was to live up to her. She'd never been outgoing and adventurous. She'd never been spontaneous or the life of the party. If she believed, took that leap of faith, she didn't know where she'd land. Could she do that? Could she really rely on blind faith that everything would work out as it should? She just didn't know.

WITH HIS HEAD lowered to his chest, Fane used his hair to shield his eyes as he watched his captor pace in front of him. After weeks of torture, his Banart guard had been unable to force Fane to answer any of his questions and from the looks of things, his patience—if one could call enduring the systematic and endless beatings that went on for days, patience—had reached its limits.

Fane could feel the creature's anger, could sense the hate hanging in the air ready to pounce on him at any time. He ignored the pain in his outstretched shoulders where he'd been manacled to the wall. He ignored the broken ribs that made breathing difficult. The cuts along his torso where his tormentor tried bleeding the answers out of him were but a nuisance at this point. He could even ignore the burn marks on his balls from the pain rod he'd been repeatedly zapped with. He could ignore it all, knowing full well that soon his captor would let his anger take over his common sense. When that happened, he'd finally get a chance to see his enemy's weakness. Once he knew that, all bets were off. That's when he would finally let the beast that lived inside him take control.

He hung limply from the manacles on the wall. He'd tried breaking the bonds, but he wasn't strong enough in this form. His captors had weakened him too much. If only he'd been more vigilant. If only he hadn't been so intent on searching worlds to find suitable mates for his people. Their blood had grown thin. They could no longer breed among their own kind. With too few separate families they needed new blood. He refused to marry his cousin. The idea of that sickened him.

He tried to sleep, knowing he would need his strength the moment the opportunity to escape presented itself. He'd slept standing up before though it wouldn't do to let them know that. It would be no hardship to do so again. Fane relaxed into his bonds when he heard footsteps beyond the door. He intended to escape and if he managed that feat, he would be the first non-conformist to ever speak of the *Banart*.

His people never involved themselves in wars before now, but this enemy knew no words such as neutrality. They came. They conquered. They killed. Entire worlds were destroyed beneath the *Banart's* cruelty. And until now, no one knew what the *Banarts* looked like. He glanced up at the man who entered his small cell and smiled mirthlessly. He refused to die. He would never go to his end knowing the man who killed him had taken on the shape of the one person he respected most. His father.

Apparently the *Banarts* could shift at will. They became the people they conquered—most likely to make it easier to infiltrate their ranks. He must escape. He must get to his people before his enemy found out their location. He hadn't broken yet, but he feared he might, given enough of their torture. He wasn't a weak *Tigerian*—none of them were—but he grew weaker every day under his host's careful ministrations.

"Tell me where you are from," the man reached out with the pain rod and threatened to shove it against his balls again.

Fane stood firm, his expression didn't change from contempt to fear the way his captor had hoped. He didn't know what type of creatures the *Banarts* truly were, but one thing was certain. They had the ability to shift their form at will and someone had to warn his people. He would prove his worth to the council. They may not want to listen to him on the subject of mating but, by the Goddess, they *would* listen to him about this.

He stared back at the cruel creature, the defiance showing in his eyes. "I will not betray my people and you will not force me to."

The man kicked him, using the pain rod against the back of his thighs.

"Thank you. My feet were sore anyway," he said, provoking the man.

The *Banart's* anger was close to the surface. Fane could see it. The exact duplicate of his father paced in front of him, nearly shaking with the effort to control his ire, and Fane almost smiled.

He was close, so close to angering the creature before him. He wanted to laugh, to shout with triumph, but he stood silent, willing his captor to finally show him his ire—to show him one weakness he could exploit.

It came most unexpectedly. One moment the man paced before him, the next he'd hunched over, shuddering, stuck between forms. One form was his father's tall well-built frame, the other was that of a diminutive creature with gray skin and small black eyes. The creature stood before him. It continued to spasm as the pain rod fell from its grip.

Fane wanted to growl, to roar with triumph. Instead, he concentrated on the change. He pushed it faster than he ever had before. He had to escape. His muscles thickened, bones popped and cracked. His arms became the heavily muscled forepaws of the large tiger he knew he could become. His legs, too large for the manacles that were tight on the man, burst the shackles to pieces and he landed on the floor on all four paws.

He looked at the smaller creature as it faded in and out and wondered if that was what a *Banart* truly looked like. He may never know. He stepped over the pain rod, hitting it with his paw. It slammed against the wall and broke. Then he turned to his captor and lifted his lip in a silent snarl. Killing him would be easy. Almost too easy. He felt like he should let the creature out of his hell and give him a weapon. But he wasn't stupid. He didn't know what kind of tricks the thing had up its sleeve.

LAYNEE STEPPED OVER the outer circle. She glanced around, making sure everything was in place. She'd had two weeks to prepare for this ritual. But for her, two weeks weren't nearly enough. She would screw something up—even if the spell had been given to her in a dream from the Lady Goddess. She hurried inside and took her ritual shower, visualizing the negativity swirling down the drain. She would have preferred to bathe, but that would have taken too long and she needed to complete this spell as the moons reached their zenith—or so Jaynee said. Wrapping herself in her black ritual robe, she hurried back outside to her hastily prepared circle.

It had taken days to find the trees specified in the spell-book. The trees were the same, just called by a different name. She tried not to think of a world so similar to her own, yet so foreign that it would be on another planet thousands of light years away.

The small bits of willow and apple winked up at her in the moonlight, their leaves shining, glossy in the bright moon light. Four candles graced her altar. There was pink for true love, red for true passion, green for fertility and purple to help boost her magical powers. She may be her sister's twin, but she'd never had the power Jaynee had in her little finger.

Stepping within the sphere, she closed her eyes, said a small prayer and raised her hands to the heavens. The power of the three moons poured into her as she stood waiting for the right time to begin her spell. She only hoped it wasn't foolish to use a spell from her dreams, especially since she didn't know what half of it meant. Yet it worked for her sister.

Bending, she lit the candles while she chanted her spell. She said the words softly as she touched the flame to each of them, leaving the purple for last.

"Eyes of amber, eyes of blue, bring to me love that is true. Hair of black, hair of white, bring my loves within my sight. The time has come, the moons have risen, release my love from his prison. The time has come, the moons rise above, bring my mates to their love." She chanted the words over and over, visualizing them in her heart and in her mind.

When she finished chanting the spell nine times, she turned to the east and closed her circle. It was up to the universe now. Either she got what she asked for or she didn't. Only time would tell. She left the candles to burn out and went back inside. It wasn't until she'd started climbing the stairs that she heard the soft rumble of a big cat's chuff.

Scanning her darkened basement apartment, she tried to pinpoint where the sound came from, but only an eerie silence permeated the room. Even the steady tick of the timekeeper on her entry wall seemed to go silent.

Her palms were slick with sweat. Her heartbeat galloped in her chest. Her knees threatened to buckle. "Is anyone there?"

Nothing. Just more of that eerie silence. Seconds passed before she finally convinced herself that no one had snuck into her apartment. A whoosh of air escaped her lungs. She hadn't even realized she'd held her breath in fear until the flood of fresh air filled her lungs.

Finding her way unerringly toward her darkened bedroom, she couldn't help but shake her head. "You're imagining things, girl."

"I wouldn't say that, exactly."

Unable to control her reaction, Laynee squeaked, spun in a circle and darted back toward her front door. Unfortunately, she only made it a few feet before someone—or something—took her down, and none too gently either.

Warm breath caressed her neck, and a rumbling growl skittered along her nerves. By the Lady Goddess, what kind of animal had attacked her? And who was the man that had managed to break into her apartment?

She squeezed her eyes shut and counted to ten. When she opened her eyes, she would see there was no one here. She had merely fallen and the voice was naught but her imagination. She refused to think her spell had actually worked and so quickly. She couldn't think of sharing herself with one male, let alone two. Dear Goddess, what had she done?

Breathing shallowly because of the heavy weight on her chest, she cracked one eye open slowly. Hoping against hope that there was no animal sitting atop her and no strange man in her home, she peered up and almost fainted. She froze, her eyes wide, as she stared up into the ice blue eyes of a great, white tiger.

Panic welled up in her throat and choked her. She couldn't even scream. Not that anyone would hear her. Her gaze darted around her. Of course she kept nothing on the floor that she could use as a weapon. She fought the urge to reach up and stroke the glossy-looking pelt. He looked so soft her fingers itched to touch him.

Her fingers curved inward, her nails pressing into her palms. She couldn't touch this animal. She had no idea where it belonged or to whom. It could have a disease for all she knew.

I do not have a disease, human.

She blinked. Did the big cat just talk to her?

"He is not just a big cat, lady. He is *Tigerian*," said a man as he stepped from the shadows. His mouth quirked in a grin and his dark hair fell over his eyes as he assessed her.

"Dare? Dare Raden?" She looked at the newcomer confused. How could he be her mate? He belonged to her sister. He didn't think she'd actually betray her sister, did he? No force would ever compel her to do such a thing to her sister. Her love for Jaynee wouldn't allow such treachery.

The man took another step toward her. "You know my brother?"

"Y—your brother?" She tried to turn to get a better look at him but the cat chuffed at her again, drawing her attention.

"Dare is my brother. My identical twin, actually."

Tell him to leave. Now.

Even with the ferocious white tiger crouched over her and a stranger not two feet away, her body began to warm as the first stirrings of desire tickled beneath her skin. What was wrong with her? How could she lie here practically at their feet and not do her best to seek help?

The crouching tiger chuffed again. His warm breath teased the nape of her neck, sending shards of sensation down her spine and causing her skin to prickle with awareness. Her nipples grew rigid, scraping across the wood floor. She could do naught to resist moaning out her pleasure. By the Lady Goddess, what was wrong with her?

Tell him to leave.

The tiger's rumbling voice sent shivers of awareness racing down her spine. She didn't know whether to moan with need or scream with fright. When had she lost all control over her body, her sense? This was wrong, so wrong. Two strangers—one a man with a familiar face, the other a rare white tiger, a *Tigerian*—were in her home and yet she'd done naught to make them leave.

With her hands flat against the floor, she pushed herself to her elbows, needing to escape, needing to reach safety. Again the tiger chuffed. His muzzle pressed against the nape of her neck as though he were scenting her. His big paw pressed down upon her spine, pinning her in place. The rough texture of his tongue rasped her skin as he licked her. Lady Goddess, don't let him eat me. Please?

When I eat you, mate, it won't be to fill my stomach but to taste the sweet cream found between your thighs.

Laynee squeaked. How could she not? She did not know these men, this tiger crouched above her. They were strangers to her. Even if her spell worked and she called them to her, she didn't know them. The fact that her nether parts quivered, and her heart raced with both fear and an uncertainty of what was to come, must be ignored. That was the right thing to do, the safe thing to do.

No, the safe thing to do, mate, is get rid of the other male before I kill him in your home.

She couldn't think, couldn't breathe. This was too much. Deep down, she never believed the spell would work, that it would bring her one mate, never mind two. How was she ever going to cope? She didn't have the strength or the courage to mate with them. The only thing she could do with any efficiency was work her sister's tome shoppe and even then her sister always made sure to keep an eye on her.

Why had the Lady Goddess chosen her? It must be a mistake. That was the only explanation that made sense. Her shoulders sagged. She shook her head in defeat. "You're wrong. I'm not your mate. I'm nobody. I'm just a plain sparrow amidst a sea of pure doves." She knew she was neither brave, nor beautiful. She didn't have the courage to mate with these males.

The sound of an indrawn breath, accompanied by the tiger's withdrawal, was all the proof she needed that the men agreed with her. Defeated, she lowered her head, squeezing her eyes closed as she tried to stifle the tears she could feel welling in her eyes.

Laynee flinched when a ferocious growl echoed eerily throughout her home. What now?

"What did you say, *Tigerian,* to make our mate say such a thing? What did you do to her?"

Raising her head, she watched them circle each other. The white tiger would lunge toward Dare's brother and he'd retreat. What should she do?

Should she get between them, or try to get away?

Tell him to leave now if he wants to live.

By the Lady Goddess, why was she hearing the tiger's voice in her mind? She'd only ever shared such a connection with one other, her twin sister. If she could hear him, could he hear her? She wouldn't know until she tried. Swallowing past her fear, she focused her thoughts toward the tiger. *Can you hear me?*

Of course I can hear you, mate.

Knowing that at any minute the two could come to blows, Laynee began to scoot back, away from the still circling pair. Once she was far enough away that neither could reach her easily, only then did she turn her gaze toward Dare's brother. She needed to get him out of here, both of them out of here. She was not what they wanted—what they needed for a mate. "He wants you to leave."

As fierce as the tiger looked, as big as he was and knowing what kind of damage he could do, she didn't expect the man's reaction. Rather than move a safe distance away, he laughed, closing the distance between him and the beast.

"Never. You are my mate and I won't be made to walk away from you. Not by him." His gaze flickered quickly to her before he once again focused on the enraged tiger. "And not by you either, *natoya.*"

Laynee gasped. How had he known what she'd been thinking? "You must leave, both of you. This is all a big misunderstanding. You don't even know why or how you got here."

The man snorted, dodged out of the way of the tiger's swiping paw. "Of course I know why I'm here. My own brother mated your twin. How could I not know why I found myself in your home?"

The tiger reared back, standing on his two back legs, swiping the air where Dare's brother had stood. Instead of facing the tiger as he had before, he now stood behind the ferocious beast, his legs apart, braced for battle. How had he moved so quickly? What powers did this man have?

The tiger once again chuffed his displeasure. It almost sounded like a snort. *What is he talking about?*

I... I...

Spit it out, mate? What does he speak of? Why is he here?

"I'm here because she is my mate and she called me to her."

As though he'd only been waiting for the male to speak, in a move so blindingly fast she hadn't even seen it, the tiger turned and swiped his clawed paw across the man's chest and stomach. Four long furrows stretched across the width of his torso. Blood began to seep from the open wounds. Rivulets of his life's essence ran down his torso, disappearing beneath his pants—the only clothes he wore. Even his feet were bare.

Unable to help herself, Laynee gasped as the blood began to flow more freely. At that rate he would bleed out and yet he didn't slow, didn't stumble. By the Lady Goddess what should she do? How could she stop them?

"Nice job, *Tigerian*." She watched with wide eyes as he dipped his finger into his own blood and brought it to his mouth. Without dropping his gaze from the tiger, he licked the blood off his finger. She shook, unable to believe what she witnessed. But it wasn't revulsion that caused her to shudder, but a desperate desire to be the one to be taking his essence into her body. By all that was holy, why was she reacting this way?

"Let's see how much you like being clawed." Before she could even comprehend what the male was about, she watched as his hand shifted from that of a human male to that of an animal. Fingers changed to claws and before she could warn the cat of the man's intentions, he'd already swiped at the tiger, raking its belly.

The tiger roared in outrage. She could see the furrows through the tigers white fur, see the stark red of its blood mar the purity of its white coat. The two males had to be in pain and instead of running to them, stopping them from their battle, she could only watch.

How much more proof did they need that she was a coward, that she wasn't worthy of them, either of them? Lost in her own misery, she didn't realize that they were once again battling, not until she watched the tiger knock the male into her end table, shattering the precious *Illuma-glass* that covered it. Both tumbled to the floor amidst the shattered glass. Neither stayed on the ground, each doing their best to pin the other as they rolled across her floor, knocking her furniture down, breaking the more delicate pieces in their desperate attempt to kill each other.

When she was sure that neither would notice her disappearance, she darted toward her bedroom door. As soon as she reached the relative safety of her bedchamber, she slammed the door closed, jamming the locking-bolt home. She rested her head against the only barrier separating her from her mates, and let out the breath she didn't realize she'd been holding.

Even with the door muffling most of the noise, she could hear the fight. Shattering glass and breaking wood echoed through her small cottage. Unable to control her quivering body, she turned, pressing her back against her door.

Her gaze darted around the room looking for anything she might have to defend herself if she needed it. Before she could step away from the door, the cottage grew silent. She turned her ear to the door, doing her best to hear what was happening on the other side of her barrier. What were they up to now? Or had one finally killed the other?

"You have to listen to me. I know what is happening." Sayre faced down the huge cat, his breath coming in gasps as he gulped much needed air into his lungs.

The tiger lunged at him, swiping his big paw over a low glass-topped table, clearing it of its contents with a single swipe. *As do I, Savari. I realize now that it is your people who call themselves the Banarts. Did you think yourselves too clever to not be found out?* The tiger snarled his voice gravelly and his breath came in short pants. *Yours are the only people in the galaxy who can shift shape on a whim. Tell me, is this your real form, or only one you took on to capture the woman?*

"You don't understand. I am not *Banart*. They are our common enemy. I only know what is happening because the same thing just happened to my twin. We are mated to this woman. Both of us. Not just you, not just me, both of us." Sayre stretched, releasing the tension building up in his already healing muscles. New skin tightened over his chest as the deep gouges left by the cat repaired themselves and he absently rubbed at the restored flesh. Healing—no matter the form he was in—never failed to itch.

The large cat paced in front of him, agitated. *I would not share my precious mate with one of my own kind, let alone share her with Banart scum such as you.*

Sayre kept the furniture between them. He couldn't afford to hurt the tiger, regardless of the other man's feelings. He knew exactly what was at stake even if the other male did not.

"Then you doom all of our people to death, *Tigerian*," Sayre said, the fight leaving him. They obviously weren't going to settle this in battle. They needed to find a way to get along. "If we can't find a way to share this woman between us, the battle against the *Banart* will be over before it has truly begun." He ran his hands through his hair. "This is not only about us. It is not about our wants and needs. It is about the needs of our people. All of our people."

The tiger sat back on his haunches and pierced him with his blue-eyed gaze, not relaxing his scrutiny one bit. *Continue.*

The big cat yawned giving the appearance of one who was bored, one who may make a mistake, but Sayre wasn't fooled. He knew the tiger sat waiting to pounce if he sensed a lie in his words. One thing he knew about the creature standing before him was that a *Tigerian* could sense fear and falsehoods before one of his species could even realize the lie was out. Complete truth was his only ally in this.

"I do not like the idea that I must share her any more than you do but we are both the woman's mates. We have only four days to get to *Savar* for this to be a true union between us or none of us will ever bear offspring of our own."

The tiger coughed. *I have heard of the rare triad bonding of the Savari but why only four days?*

"Because the three moons of *Carrillia's* zenith precedes that of Savar by only four days. We must mate in the *Hallowed Glenn* before the next full moon's rise or all of us will be rendered sterile. It is the way of our people. The magic of the Lady Goddess makes us so. It ties us and our mates to the same laws of nature. As our triad mate, it binds you with the same laws."

Why should this affect me in any way?" The tiger stood and began to pace again. "Why should I believe any of this?

Sayre took a deep breath and let it out on a sigh. They were doomed to a barren existence if he couldn't get this cat to believe him. He could kill the tiger in a heartbeat, but that wouldn't help him. Now that all three of them were brought together, if they didn't all three mate under the moons of Savar in four day's time they would never be truly bonded.

"Because you know the power of your people better than I do. What do your instincts tell you?"

My base instincts tell me to take my mate and run, he growled then sat down again. The air shimmered around him as he changed forms to that of a man.

Sayre almost breathed a sigh of relief when the *Tigerian* changed to his human form. He'd never seen one of their kind as a man before. They tended to keep their cat form when in situations where they felt their lives were at risk. The *Tigerian* showed a semblance of trust changing to his weaker self in front of a virtual stranger.

Long white hair fell over his shoulders, the black tips brushing his chest and upper arms. Sayre supposed he was a good-looking male in his right. At least he wouldn't be stuck raising the ugly cubs of a *Hienial* triad mate. Given the nature of those beasts, however, he saw them in an alliance with the unfeeling *Banarts* before anyone else.

56

"Shall we go find our mate and apologize for destroying her home? I'm sure our male posturing and aggressive behavior has not ingratiated us to her in the least." Sayre offered his hand to the *Tigerian*. "I am Sayre, brother to Dare Raden of the *Savari*."

Taking his proffered hand in a warrior's grip, the tiger bowed his head over their clasped arms. "Fane, Fane Gavaire, head of the house of Gavaire of *Tigeria*."

Sayre blinked. "Not *the* Fane of Gavaire."

"The one and the same." He smiled wryly. "It seems being faced with the scent of a true mate brings out the worst in even the purest of royal families of *Tigeria*. If only it hadn't been so long since my people have had the privilege of finding their one true mate." He thrust his fingers through his hair and walked through the broken glass to sit on a chair at the bar. "Go get the female. I fear what I may do if she chooses to struggle. The beast in me may rise once more."

Sayre inhaled deeply, scenting the animal just below the surface of the other man. "You change quickly. I've never seen one of your kind during transformation before, is it normal to change from one form to another so fast?"

Fane shrugged. "It is my ability. I have always been this way. Even when I was nothing more than a young cub, I was able to shift fast." His gaze met Sayre's telling him without words that he spoke of *Tigerian* secrets. "Even as a cub, *Savari*. Our people normally cannot change as cubs, not until well past puberty can they do so."

Sayre bowed. "Then I find myself in rare company indeed. Not only are you *Tigerian* royalty but one of the rare *Shinsai*. What else can you do?"

Fane shook his head. "Better to leave the rest until we know each other a bit better. I feel I've told you too much already. Go get the woman. She listens to us even now and yet, it's doing nothing to dispel her fears. Only the touch and scents of her mates will do that."

Sayre turned toward the door his mate had disappeared through just moments before, knowing the *Tigerian* was correct. He flexed his fingers as he remembered hearing the solid sound of her jamming the lock into place. It wouldn't do to face his mate with his hands balled into nervous fists. It could give her the wrong impression.

He wiped his damp palms on his pants and raised his hand to knock on the door. Swallowing past the thick lump lodged in his throat, he wondered when his confidence with women had deserted him. Perhaps it was because he knew she was finally *The One*. All of his previous encounters had only led him to this moment, to this woman, to his mate.

"We know you are still there. We have stopped our fighting and we wish only to speak with you. Will you come out and meet your mates?"

He cocked his head to the side. Was that a whimper? Could they really have frightened her so thoroughly that she may never come to them on her own? He closed his eyes and wished they could have been brought together under better circumstances. Still he knew it had taken great courage for the *Tigerian* to believe him and give up his stronger form. He could do no less in facing their mate.

It didn't take a healer to see the wounds inflicted by obvious torture on the other man's flesh. He may heal fast, but he didn't heal as fast as a *Savari* and no one knew the signs of torture as well as his people. He shuddered with the memory of his last encounter with the *Hienial* people. They took great pleasure in causing their prisoners extreme pain before leaving them to die.

He'd been lucky that Dare had suggested that as second in the line of succession, he should have a tracking device inserted. Beneath his hair, the device was undetectable by scans due to the nature of *Savari* electrical impulses in the brain. Without that device, he would have died on the planet his captors left him on, surrounded by nothing but rock and dirt.

Sayre pushed the memories of torture aside, needing a clear mind to deal with the fears of Jaynee's twin sister. The corner of his mouth quirked up in a half smile. Twins. They were certain to have at least one set between them now. How fortuitous that his mate should be the twin of his brother's mate. He knew at least a little about her.

He knew her name was Laynee and she was very, very reserved. She lived the life of an introvert, almost completely shut away from the real world. Jaynee talked about her, worried about her constantly. Jaynee feared the woman would lose herself in her books without her sister here to prod her into experiencing life.

Resting his head against the cool wood, he reached up and rubbed the back of his neck. They would be lucky if they could convince the woman to appear from behind this door, let alone emerge from the protection of her wall of diffidence.

Fane and he may have shown great courage to overcome their differences, even to have overcome their individual capture and torture by their enemies. Still, he knew it would take even greater courage for their female to face them both alone.

"Please come out, Laynee. We aren't fighting anymore and we wish to speak with you."

"How do you know my name?" Muffled by the door, the trembling voice sought out his heart and squeezed.

"Your sister is my twin brother's mate. You look exactly as she, as I am identical to Dare. It's something we have in common, you and I."

"Oh." She spoke so softly he barely heard it through the thick wood. "You only want to talk?"

Sayre and Fane both inhaled sharply at the sound of her voice so filled with hesitance and fear. When they first appeared, she'd practically materialized from the dark before them. She'd been a brave woman, ready to face intruders in her home, to face her future with her mates. Their fighting caused her to take refuge inside her protective shell. She closed herself off to them. She stood hiding behind the wall of her room.

"Yes, Laynee. For now we shall only talk."

He refused to lie to her. They would need to claim her this night. He especially. Once he mated with her the first time, it would be simple to acquire her consent or her forgiveness. If he could only manage to make love with her just once, it would begin her addiction to his seed, her dependence upon him as her mate.

THE SNICK OF the lock echoed through the small apartment, seeming loud in the silence of the night. The wooden door stood closed for several moments as they waited for her to gather her courage to come out and greet her mates. The sound of a mumbled prayer reached Fane's ears as she openly debated whether or not she should trust the two strange men she found in her home.

His heart in his throat, Fane watched as the doorknob turned. His palms began to sweat as he imagined a million reasons she could have for not exiting that room. He sighed with relief as the door cracked open in small increments. She moved slowly, almost as if she expected to slam it in their faces if they attempted to accost her.

Sayre backed away from the door, giving her the necessary space to step from the other room.

Fane panted, his lungs laboring to draw in great gulps of air. The atmosphere in her small home was thick with tension as she inched herself within view. Muscles he didn't know he'd held clenched, relaxed. He released the breath he'd been holding and sucked in another lungful of her unique scent. Her gaze darted toward him, obviously startled.

A huge bed sat against the wall in the room behind her. Bathed in silvery moonlight, it tempted him. It taunted him with her nearness. He wanted nothing more than to drag her to that bed and make her his. She may not know it, but she was already his. The Lady Goddess had deemed it so. Already her scent permeated his body. His very cells were fraught with the delicate aroma of her fear and arousal. He wanted nothing more than to sink his cock into her up to his balls. He wanted her beneath him so much, he ached with it.

A soft light shone through her bedroom windows. It left her in silhouette, bathing her in the pale radiance of *Carrillia's* three moons. He swallowed thickly, already loving the woman whose sleek body tempted him even before he'd seen her face. He knew she was beautiful. There was no doubt. The moonlight bathed her, leaving her standing within a glowing halo of light. This woman was more to him than a mere mate. She was a gift from the Lady Goddess herself. A woman—a mate—he would cherish till the end of his days. What had he done to deserve such a precious gift? Squeezing his eyes closed, he gave thanks for the woman whose life had just been irrevocably tied to his.

A terrible need slammed through his body as a soft breeze carried more of her enticing scent to him. The tiger in him rose, snarling to be set free. It demanded he claim his mate. His teeth elongated, his nails cut into the palms of his hands. It was all he could do to tame the beast down, hold it leashed deep within him.

Opening his eyes, he looked at her, drinking in the sight of the woman who would bear his cubs. She was nearly close enough to touch. He fought the urge to sniff the air like the untamed animal he was. His clenched fingers itched to feel the ebony silk of her hair. They longed to touch her milky skin. Still, he managed to keep his hands to himself and the beast leashed. This night must be for her. She must accept him—accept them both. He knew that Sayre told the truth because unbeknownst to the *Savari* people, he'd traveled to their world undetected and witnessed their customs. There would be no children for any of them if they did not complete the ritual. As one of the rare *Savari* triads, they *must* confirm their mating under the moons of *Savar*.

Fane's body burned just as surely as if he'd been struck by lightning. Fire raced through his blood at just the sight of her. The arch of her back, the gentle curve of her breasts with their hard peaks nearly undid him. It was all he could do to keep himself from pouncing on her and laying claim despite her fears.

She stepped further from the protection of her room and into the soft light from the window behind him. Thick, glossy black hair fell over her shoulders in long waves curling around her full breasts. Gray eyes, framed by the thickest ebony lashes he'd ever seen, rounded with fright as she looked between them. The purple markings of a *Carrillian* High Priestess graced her cheeks. The intricate tattoos showing the world her high rank among the witches. She licked her full pink lips nervously. His cock sprang to life as he imagined those luscious lips closing around his shaft as he thrust himself inside her perfect mouth.

Sayre sucked in his breath and Fane almost growled. The bred-in aggression of his kind was hard to overcome. He would rein it in soon. He must. But for now it was hard to swallow the fact that he would have to share his mate after all. He didn't want to share his woman with another. That had been one of his reasons for searching off-world for a female.

Still, glancing back at his beautiful mate, his chest expanded with pride. She was even more beautiful than he ever could have hoped. He couldn't blame the other man for his reaction. She was the loveliest creature Fane had ever seen. His cock twitched out a reminder that he'd not been with a woman in several cycles and he grinned wryly. If he could not control his body's reaction to his mate, how could he condemn the actions of Sayre?

Still, the thought of sharing her rankled. His people had begun to war amongst themselves over the lack of available mates. Fane wasn't the only one of his kind who didn't want to share his mate with another. Many of the males of his species shared their females with their close friends or brothers, yet some wanted a mate of their own. He and his twin cousins left *Tigeria* together on this quest for a mate. They too searched the worlds for a woman of their own. Since they always shared everything between them, he could only hope they would be as lucky in finding a willing woman with the courage to love them both. Men were killing each other in the streets over fickle women who could not decide between them. *That* was what sent him off-world in search of his one true mate. Only a true bond-mate would keep to him and him alone. He had found her. And still he had to share. He tightened his fists, blood welling in his palms as his frustration called to his inner beast.

He braced himself as he waited for her to approach, hiding his clenched hands behind his back. He'd agreed to this. If not vocally, at the very least he had approved this triad bond by changing to his human form in front of two off-worlders.

He watched as Laynee took one hesitant step after another away from the safety of her bedroom and he smiled encouragingly. Not only was she beautiful, but she was courageous. A fitting mate for him. The alpha female of his house must be a woman of courage and strong character. She was frightened. He could smell it. And still she moved to join them. He found that he could do no other than admire the demonstration of her courage through her fear as she entered the room and gave them both a wobbly smile.

WHAT NOW? LAYNEE asked herself as she glanced between the two men. Sayre looked just like his brother. She blinked slowly. Tall, dark and handsome, he was the epitome of masculine beauty. Though something about him was different from Dare. Was it the same type of difference she saw between herself and her sister? Or was it just that her mate was the more handsome of the two men? *Age before beauty.* The thought came unbidden as she realized she stood gaping at the younger of the two Raden brothers. Perhaps it was the inner strength she could sense beneath his mental shield to his soul beneath. What she saw awed her. Here was a man worthy of love. But was she worthy of his love?

She couldn't help the shiver of desire that shot up her spine, or the answering moisture she felt in her nether parts, soaking her panties.

A half smile on Sayre's face gave him an almost dangerous, rakish look and she wondered what thoughts danced behind his strange amber eyes to give him such an enigmatic expression.

"I don't wish to alarm you, Laynee, but ..." He grinned. "... I can read your mind." He gave her a shallow bow. "Thank you."

"Oh!" Blood rushed to her face, searing her cheeks in a blush. She dropped her gaze to the floor. *Lady, how could I be so stupid, so...so wanton?* She attempted to clear her mind of its rampant thoughts to play hostess to her guests. What more could she do? She certainly must get to know them before she agreed to mate with them.

A rumbling growl distracted her and she turned to the other man. She nearly gasped when he stepped into the light. Goddess, he was tall. White-blonde hair fell over his tanned, well-muscled shoulders. The pitch-black ends nearly brushed his flat brown nipples. Startling blue eyes stared back at her unblinking, like the cat he was. High, wide cheekbones gave his straight nose prominence in his too handsome face. She would have been hard pressed to choose between the two men if the need ever arose.

She let her gaze rove recklessly over his perfect form as she admired his muscular arms and chest. A light dusting of hair tapered down over his stomach to his—Laynee jerked her gaze back up, her face burning hot with another blush. By all that is holy, she should have realized he would have no clothes! The last thing she'd expected was to see the man's erect penis winking at her as if she were a *Carrillia-faire* prize.

Desire coiled through her at the sight of his large uncovered shaft. Moisture pooled in her middle, making her womb clench. The inner contraction sent her woman's cream out to wet the silk of her panties. She must clear her mind of that sight! Laynee closed her eyes and swallowed. Gathering what little of her wits remained about her, she tried to start a conversation.

"Would you," she said licking her lips, trying to forget the experience of seeing her first naked male. "Would you care to have a seat?" she asked, her gaze shifting to Sayre. It was easier to talk to him--he was clothed.

"I don't mind if I do." He strode over to the couch, picked up the lap-blanket she used to cover herself on cold nights and tossed it to the *Tigerian*. What had he said his name was again?

"Fane," the man said as he accepted the blanket from Sayre and wrapped it around his waist. "My name is Fane. I am glad to finally meet you, mate."

She covered her face with her hands. "Don't tell me you can read my mind too!" Her cheeks burned, rivaling the liquid fires of *Mount Galinor*. She was no stranger to telepathy though she'd gotten out of practice since Jaynee left *Carrillia*. It was too difficult to communicate over long distances.

He graced her with a crooked smile that nearly drove the breath from her lungs. The flash of those even white teeth was nearly her undoing. How could any man be so devastatingly handsome? Both of them were. Sayre was much more handsome than his brother. Fane, with his light blue eyes and sinful body was obviously Sayre's equal in all things. Each one of her mates by himself was more man than she'd ever dared hope to have. And there were *two* of them.

She strode over to the sofa and collapsed onto the center cushion, her eyes closed tight. Lady Goddess, how did she ever get into these messes? She was a good girl, always an avid student and a voracious reader. How had she come to this end?

Sitting up straight, her eyes opened wide when the cushions on either side of her dipped with the weight of an occupant. Looking from one to the other, she couldn't manage to say a thing. With Sayre on her right and Fane on her left, she could do nothing but gape at the two men as they sat close, boxing her in between them. Her entire body quivered. What was happening to her? Was this feeling in the pit of her stomach the desire she'd read so much about in her romancer tomes?

Sayre rested his arm on the back of the sofa at her neck and Fane half turned to face her, keeping her within his sight.

"Um ..." she licked her lips, not quite knowing what to say. "I—I don't think this is a very good idea." Of course it wasn't. She couldn't think when they were this close to her. She needed space to keep her head clear. Her inner alarm shrieked with their closeness. Her insides melted with the knowledge that these two wonderful male specimens were her mates and sooner or later they would want to claim her for their own. Her heart slammed in her chest at the idea that they would both want to claim her this night and she nearly whimpered with trepidation.

Would they understand that she feared the union? Would they be patient with her because she'd never known the touch of a man?

She stared down into her lap, twisting her fingers as she worried about the things to come, nearly forgetting the two men could read her every thought. A gentle finger slid down her right cheek and she turned to Sayre.

"I—I don't think I can do this." Her whole body began to tremble and she started to stand.

"Do what, *natoya?*" Sayre asked, moving to bring her back against the sofa, his hands gentle. "We are only talking. No one has insisted you do something you are not ready to do."

She looked up at him, needing to make him understand. "But I know you will. Eventually you will want me to—to ..." She waved her hands. "You know what I mean. Don't make me say it." Her cheeks heated with her mortification. Must they always make her voice everything? They knew what she meant. They had to. Did they really need to hear that she feared the physical intimacy they would both expect from her this night? It was one thing to read about it, to crave it in her dreams. It was something completely different to live it. She wasn't sure she could.

"It is your destiny," Fane said, resting his hand lightly on her thigh.

"Will you two stay out of my head?" She wrenched away and stood, trying to escape them. All she wanted to do was to run back to her room where she could lock herself in, where she would once again be safe.

And alone, Laynee. Do you really want to remain alone, with only your dreams to warm you?

The strange voice in her head gave her pause. *Who are you?*

You know who I am. Your sister told you I would come to you. The universe needs your unique talents to defeat the Banarts. Without you and your mates, all is for naught. I must have you all.

Laynee nearly cried out with her frustration. *I don't think I can. I don't know how to love. Not like that. I'm not who you want, who you need.* She paced across the room, her hands wrapped around her middle, trying to sort out the myriad feelings zinging through her.

Never fear, you know how to love these two men just the way they each need to be loved. You are the only one capable of it. Only you have the power to see deep into these men's souls. Only you can see their true worth. This is your one chance at love, Laynee. At life. Do not pass this up for fear or your need for safety. Remember, the truly courageous are those who are frightened of the unknown, yet do not allow that fear to stop them from doing what they most want to do. You know you want those two men. Your mind may lie to you but your body and your heart never learned how to lie. Listen to them.

Laynee stopped pacing and sighed. She wasn't sure, but she suspected the voice was that of the Lady Goddess. Who would know more about what she was capable of than the Great Mother herself? She knew Laynee's every strength, every weakness and still the Lady insisted that this was the one thing she was meant to do.

She turned back to the men sitting on her sofa and suppressed a smile. She knew one thing. She really needed to get Fane some clothes. He couldn't seem to keep himself covered. She blushed and looked away when she remembered they could read her mind. Fane covered himself and they both held out their hands, inviting her to join them. Should she join them, or should she run for the relative safety of her bedroom? She looked from them to her bedroom door and gauged the distance. She was sure she could make it.

Turning back to the two drop dead gorgeous men sitting in her living room, she sighed and turned her back on her room. She wanted this. She wanted *them* and the only way to have them was to agree to the claiming. Swallowing around the lump in her throat she gathered her courage around her like a blanket, lifted her chin and approached her mates.

SAYRE SWALLOWED THICKLY. *Do you see that, Fane? She wears her courage like a badge. It shimmers around her, keeping her warm in its embrace.*

Fane's eyes widened. *Is that what that is? I see the magic surrounding her.*

I'm not sure she's aware she does that. It makes her even more beautiful than before and I didn't think that was possible.

Neither did I, Sayre agreed. He watched silently, waiting for her to approach on her own. It must be her choice to join with them. He would not be a party to taking any female—especially his mate—against her will. He knew Fane would not either. It was just as well. Being so much alike would make them good triad mates.

Laynee took their outstretched hands and they attempted to pull her down beside them. She shook her head and pulled, urging them to stand. She released them when they did so.

Staring down at her feet, she twisted her fingers in her robe. The glow surrounding her grew stronger, brighter as she stood before them, her head bowed. Raising her head, she stared over their shoulders, obviously unable to meet their gaze. Taking a deep breath, she stubbornly thrust out her chin and took turns looking between them.

"I know that I must accept you—accept both of you. I know who you are." Her gaze faltered and she took a deep breath. Closing her eyes, she drew more energy into the sphere surrounding her. "I know *what* you are—what you need of me. But I'm afraid."

She turned to pace away from them, her hands still twisting the fabric of her robe, a nervous reaction Sayre was sure she was unaware of.

"I need you to understand. I've lived my life in the shadow of my sister. I've never been recognized for doing anything in my own right. I finally have the chance to show myself…" she paused, her gaze darting around the room as if searching for what to say next. "To show others who I really am. Not as Jaynee's little sister. But as me, as Laynee." She bit her lip, fat tears streaking down her face.

She held her hand up when he would have stopped her. "Now you're asking me to give it all up. Plus, I'm not as strong as my sister. Ask anyone. They will tell you. I've never even been with one man before, never mind two. I don't—" Her breath came out on a sob. "I don't know what to do. I don't have the first idea how to please you both."

She bowed her head again, held her hands clenched together in front of her as she danced from foot to foot. An action that proved her fears, but even her standing up to them enough to talk this way, was an act of true courage.

What do you think, Fane? Sayre asked, needing to have a private moment with the other male so he would know exactly where he stood before he proceeded. *I do not need our mate to give up herself to be with me. I have been at the hands of the Hienial people. They try to kill what they don't understand. They attempted to force me to admit my weakness to them. I have no desire to do the same to my mate. What say you?*

I agree. My time with the Banart left a bad taste in my mouth for such pursuits. I only wish to love our mate and give her the pleasure she deserves, while receiving the same from her. Fane growled low in his throat. *What I want to know is who made our mate think so little of herself. I refuse to believe it was her sister. Is she merely shy and doesn't know how to assert herself?*

Sayre stepped forward, slowly moving closer to her as Fane slipped around behind her. She needed to begin to trust them. This was a good first step. "Just you being yourself pleases us. Forget about what you think we need or want from you. Instead, let us pleasure you." He reached out, picked up a lock of her hair and brought it to his face. "Even your scent pleases me."

Fane stepped up behind her, his chest pressed against her back. He lowered his head, his breath brushing her neck. Tendrils of hair stirred as he spoke and Sayre saw gooseflesh rise on her skin. "Be at ease, *la nisa*. We shall only take this as far as you are willing to go. Your needs must come first in all things."

She licked her lips and Sayre felt an answering surge in his cock. His balls tightened against him and he moved closer, trying to hide his reaction lest he frighten her.

"But—but it is not fair to you." She half turned and looked between them both. "It isn't fair to either of you for me to take while giving nothing in return." She bowed her head again and whispered. "I'm such a coward."

Sayre and Fane both shook their heads.

"No, Laynee," Fane responded. "You are the most courageous woman I have ever met." He cupped her cheek and lightly pressed his lips against hers. "Giving you pleasure will please us. In this way, you will give back. If all we wanted from you was pure sex, we could get that anywhere. But you are our mate. We want more from you than mere sex." He trailed his fingers down her arm, pressed his chest against her back. "Will you let us pleasure you?"

Sayre stepped forward, pressed against his mate. He could feel her pebbled nipples through her robe as they pressed against his torso and it was all he could do not to drop his head and suckle them through the fabric. "Please, Laynee, let us pleasure you."

LAYNEE TENSED, NOT out of fear, as she would have expected but more out of nervousness. Could she really do this, really give herself sexually and emotionally to two strangers?

Deep in her soul, she knew that she didn't really have a choice. Her heart and her soul had called them, and if her sweaty palms, accelerated heartbeat and quivering tummy were any indication, her body wanted them to mate with her. The only question that remained was whether she had the courage to listen to her heart for a change rather than the nagging voice in her mind that always made her feel that she would never be good enough.

She could feel the heat from Fane behind her and Sayre in front and feel their strength. She stood there, soaking in their warmth, gathering her courage around her like a winter's cloak. It was time, time to take the first step to her future, the future she'd share with these two strong and courageous men. She only hoped they didn't regret their decision to mate with her.

Time passed. Seconds, minutes, she didn't know. All she knew for sure was the longer she stood between their bodies the more her heart raced and her breasts ached. Her nipples tingled, began to sting as they grew harder. Pressed against Sayre the way she was, there was no doubt in her mind he wasn't aware of her body's reaction to them. Her clit twitched and her pussy ached for she knew not what. Soon, her panties would be drenched with her woman's cream.

Fine tremors spread over her body, firing along her nerve endings. She had no choice. Her soul burned, her body demanded. Her heart pleaded for them. "Make me yours."

Sayre smiled a half smile. His eyes seemed to blaze. Slowly, he raised his hands, then reached for the fastening on her robe. Rather than just rip it open, stripping off her clothes, he stopped. Waited. Was he asking permission? If she didn't encourage them to take her now, she would probably never have the courage to do so again. "Go ahead. I want to be with you." She turned her head toward Fane, once again gathering her courage before speaking. "I want to be with both of you and I can't do that if I hide behind my robes."

She watched as Sayre's hands trembled as he loosened the clasp at her throat. Was he nervous? She snorted causing his gaze to jump to hers. "Of course, I'm nervous. You're my mate, Laynee. I—we—don't want to do anything that might frighten you."

When her robe was naught but a pile of silken fabric on her floor, Fane wrapped his arms around her, nestled his cock against the crease of her bottom, slid one hand down her flat belly. His palm was rough. She could feel calluses along his fingers and palm and knew that he had a warrior's hands.

His hands lingered on the waistband of her panties. Her stomach tightened. Fane must have realized her nervousness had grown because he stopped his downward movements, pressed a kiss to her shoulder, her neck. Slowly, as though he were afraid she might protest, his fingers slipped beneath the thin fabric, through netherlips bathed with her woman's cream, and found her clit. He pressed against it once, twice, then flicked it with his fingernail. She cried out, bucking into his hand as pleasure speared through her, sending shards of intense sensation through her entire body. By the Lady Goddess, never had she felt such sensations.

Her thighs quivered, and even though the pleasure was intense, she knew something was missing. "You like that, don't you, *la nisä*?" he whispered. She could feel his warm breath brush against her ear and another wave of heat rippled through her body. "You're so wet, Laynee. So hot. Are you ready for Sayre to see you, mate? Are you ready for us to pleasure you, to claim you as our triad mate?" Fane's mouth settled at the spot where her neck met her shoulder. The gentle rasp of his tongue, the sharp edge of his teeth had yet more cream running down her inner thighs. His kisses changed from gentle exploration to sucking bites and all she could do was let herself feel. Sayre's gaze dropped to her waistband. She watched his eyes glaze in passion. She couldn't help but drop her own gaze, watch Fane's fingers beneath her panties working her clit harder, pressing against her in ever increasing movements.

Laynee couldn't look away. His touches grew unrelenting, making her whimper. She couldn't breathe, couldn't think. Her heart felt like it would beat right out of her chest. Her hands dropped to her panties, clutching at his. She didn't know whether to ask him to stop or beg him for more. She hovered on the edge of a desperate need she didn't understand, didn't know what to do about. "Are you ready to take these off?" Fane whispered. Once again the smoky edge to his voice made her quiver beneath his touch.

Her voice shook as she answered, "Yes."

"That's our girl," Fane said. He pressed two fingers into her empty channel, stroked her once, twice, then withdrew. She couldn't help but feel the loss of his touch. What was wrong with her? Why was she acting this way with them? Had her hormones finally caught up with her age, or was it these two men, her mates, that made her feel so wanton?

Taking a deep breath, she decided to take charge, let her men know that this was her decision. Without stopping to think about it, her hands moved to her hips, slipped beneath her waistband of her panties and shoved her panties down. She heard Sayre's gasp, watched his trembling hand reach down. His fingers trailed over the smooth skin of her woman's mound, touched Fane's hand before sliding past to slip through her slick and swollen folds.

Sayre crowded closer, so that no space seemed to separate them. It forced her attention back to his face. She dropped her gaze, winced inwardly at her cowardice before once again raising her head. She wet her lips, nervous. Would he be disgusted at what she'd done to her mound? Did he and Fane find it distasteful?

Sayre's eyes narrowed. "How can you think anything about you would disgust us? You are all that either of us could ever imagine for a mate." He pulled her naked body tightly against his clothed one. Fane's hand remained trapped between her thighs. One finger entered her, two, stroking her. Sayre's eyes flashed. His mouth descended and covered hers. She softened—unable not to with their combined attention. Her body rested against Sayre, unconsciously submitting to both of their needs. His touch gentled and when he lifted his mouth from hers, Laynee not only saw, but felt the heat, hunger and a vulnerability she hadn't witnessed before in any male.

Fane stepped back, reached for her hand. "Take us to your bed, *la nisa*. Show us your inner sanctum."

Laynee nodded, unable to do anything but acquiesce to their desires. Slowly, they made their way to her room, each holding one of her hands. Did they think she would run from them? Something burned inside her. Something both frightening and unstoppable. She couldn't run now if she wanted to, not until she knew what the burning fire in her blood meant. Not until the ache in her loins was quenched.

She led them into her room, embarrassed by the severity of her inner haven. There were no candles to light, no silken curtains upon her windows. Only utilitarian blinds covered the *illuma-glass* that allowed the soft light of the triad moons of *Carrillia* to bathe her room in a silvery glow. The only saving grace in her stark bedroom was the mauve cover on her bed, the silken material glistened in the soft light of the moons and she sent up a soft prayer of thanks that Jaynee insisted she purchase it.

As they approached her four-poster bed, they dropped her hands. "Get on the bed, *natoya*. Let us love you." She paused only long enough to take a deep breath before crawling onto her bed. Even though her nerves were shrieking at her to move, to do something, she didn't. She just watched as her mates stopped and stood at the end of her bed. Her eyes widened as they undressed—Fane dropped the lap-blanket, Sayre shucked the silk-linen trousers that hung loose on his waist. Her heart raced and her lungs struggled to get enough air.

When they crawled onto her feather mattress, they lay on their sides, each bracketing her. She didn't know whether to lie flat on her back and spread her legs or reach out and touch them. Why hadn't she asked them what they needed, what they wanted her to do? She bit her bottom lip.

Indecision and anxiety worked their way through her hazy mind. Her gaze shifted from one masculine face to the other, looking for a hint as to what they expected. She could tell nothing from their fierce expressions. By the Lady Goddess, she was so unsure and nervous. She needed strength and courage to get through this, and she wanted more than to just get through this, she wanted to enjoy this night. Enjoy the night with her mates, her claiming night. She swallowed back her fear. "Tell me what you want me to do," she finally whispered.

A sexy smile stretched across Fane's face. Her heart lurched, sped up if that were even possible. He moved forward, draping his upper body over her, his chest half covering hers. She could feel his cock hard and wet against her side. He pressed a tentative kiss to her lips, pulled back only to return to nip her bottom lip.

Her gaze flew to Sayre, needing to know he wasn't upset at being left out. His soul reeled with pain and she wouldn't be the cause of any more hurt. He moved closer, seeming to understand her fear, positioning himself in the same way Fane had, hovering over her prone form. She could feel his thick cock press against her thigh and warmth spread through her as she thought about where they would want to put their large cocks.

His hand moved to her woman's mound, his fingers petted her netherlips before they slid slowly inside. His fingers tapped her erect clit. She gasped. Her nerve endings seemed to become charged with an energy she'd never experienced before this evening. Sayre's smile grew naughty, his eyes glistened with heat, then he dropped his hand.

She whimpered, feeling the loss as though a part of her heart, her soul had been taken away. "Sshh... I'm not leaving you, *natoya*. Never will I leave you." Sayre leaned back, and a movement on her other side drew her attention.

Laynee turned her head and looked into Fane's sapphire eyes. Slowly his head lowered. His lips were soft, gentle as he kissed her. Not normally an empath, it surprised her to feel his need to shower her with tenderness, with care. His touch turned whisper soft and loving.

Emptiness filled her when the kiss ended. She needed something, needed to feel him—them—inside her. Tears ran down her cheeks unchecked and she had no idea when they had begun or why she was even crying. Fane caressed her cheek with his rough tongue, lapping up her tears and soothing her with his gentle caress. "Ssshh, *la nisa.* Quiet, little warrior. All will be well. We will give you what you need."

FANE'S MOUTH MOVED from her cheek to her neck, trailing kisses down her body. The quivering slopes of her breasts drew his gaze and he became desperate to take her nipple in his mouth and suckle. His heart clenched as he imagined his cubs sucking on her breasts. He couldn't wait until they reached Savar, combined their life forces, and impregnated their mate. To see her body swell with his cubs couldn't come soon enough for him.

Fane's cock surged against her thigh seeming to understand his need to fill her with his seed. It grew wetter, spilling pre-cum. Unable to wait any longer, he latched onto a dark nipple and started suckling, aware that Sayre had latched on to its twin.

Laynee began to squirm, her moans echoing through her bedchamber. Her fingers speared through their hair, holding them both to her as she thrashed underneath them, pressing upward against their thighs where they had her pinned. She may not understand what she was doing, but both he and Sayre knew it for what it was, an unconscious plea for them to fill her. His hand moved to pet her cunt only to find Sayre's already there, lazily stroking her.

Fane took a deep breath and suckled her with new fervor—anything to keep himself from thinking about his desperate need to sink his cock into her empty pussy. This night was about her needs, not theirs. With a desperate groan he left her nipple, knowing if he stayed where he was he'd be unable to stop himself from claiming her before she was ready. He trailed his lips downward. He nudged Sayre's hand aside then latched onto Laynee's turgid clit.

She squirmed beneath his tender assault almost dislodging him. Beside him, Sayre moved up her body, holding her down as he kissed her. As she succumbed to Sayre's passion, Fane attacked her pussy with a desperation he'd never before felt. He laved and suckled her clit before he finally burrowed into her dripping channel with his tongue, desperate that she reach fulfillment with them. He wanted her introduction to lovemaking to leave a lasting memory.

Minutes passed, then she screamed, sobbing out her release. Fane pulled back. He wanted to continue loving her throughout the night, to keep pleasuring her with his mouth even if it meant he could do naught but cum on the sheets.

He gasped, his shoulders quivered as he braced himself between her shaking thighs. Her pussy glistened with her cream and his saliva. Finally, he lifted his mouth away from her woman's mound. He needed to share with Sayre, though everything inside him rebelled at the idea. He shook his head. No. He wouldn't start out their family unit with jealousy and strife. With one last whisper soft kiss on her sopping mound, Fane moved away, gesturing to Sayre to take his turn.

SAYRE MOVED DOWN her lithe form, loving every smooth inch laid out before him. He never believed himself lucky enough to draw a real mate to him. He always knew his brother would find his mate. As ruler, he must. Everyone on their world was honor bound to report if they found a female whose manner and DNA seemed compatible. Yet, he'd never dreamed he would find his one true mate. He never expected to find the one woman whose soul would match his, whom he could love and commune with on a truly spiritual level.

He trailed his lips over her breast to caress her smooth, flat stomach. Lingering over her middle, he laved her navel with his tongue, reveling in her soft moans and her quivering flesh. Her body squirmed beneath him as his breath stirred the glistening hairs between her legs.

"Please," she begged. Her hands fisted in the sheets, her head thrashing on the silken sheets as he ran his tongue over her wet slit.

He drew the sensitive nub into his mouth and suckled. Gently pushing a finger into her virgin channel, he worked it in and out of her. Her tight pussy clasped his finger as he pushed it into her. First one, then another. One by one, he continued to push his fingers into her tight sheath readying her for their possession. Sayre scissored his fingers and her back arched off the bed and she screamed another release. She lay on the bed panting when he raised his head. Fane sucked and fondled her breasts. Her fingers buried in his hair, she clutched him to her.

How do you wish to proceed, Fane? he asked, working his way back up her torso.

I don't think I can wait, Sayre. My tiger demands to claim its mate. I fear I'll change and it will inadvertently kill her while attacking you, if you attempt to mount her first.

Sayre exhaled forcibly, clenching and unclenching his fists. It was a no win situation. Each of them wanted to be her first. He rubbed the back of his neck knowing that, like it or not, he must assume the less dominate part in their relationship. Fane was the head of his house, the alpha male of his clan. He could not be expected to take the submissive male role in this. There was no other choice, that role must fall to Sayre.

Having always been second to Dare's alpha on his own world, it was a familiar position. One he didn't want to continue, but he was certain that Fane would not force him into the submissive role all of the time. The other man knew his background. He must, given the nature of his genetic gifts.

I bow to the needs of your inner beast, Fane. I won't fight you for the honor, as we both know I would win such a battle. We both must complete the ritual. There is no choice in this matter.

Fane smiled wryly. *You think you would be the victor in such a battle, blood drinker. But we shall not argue the point. Besides, I give you leave to be the first to fuck her tight ass after she becomes used to the two of us screwing her luscious cunt.*

Sayre fought the smile tugging at the corners of his mouth. At least he would not be second in all things. Somehow he had known his triad mate wouldn't be so cruel as to keep him in the submissive role permanently.

Sayre moved to kiss her, allowing her to taste her body's sweet cream upon his lips. His tongue rasped against the wet velvet of hers as she pulled him to her by his hair. He thrust his tongue into her mouth, loving the feel of her hard nipples rasping against his chest.

Fane moved to position himself between her legs, rising over her to rest the thick head of his cock against the entrance to her slick channel.

LAYNEE WHIMPERED AS Fane rose over her. When would they end this torment? Something was missing within her. Her body craved something real, something tangible. What happened next? Would they never show her? A part of her knew they must. It was surely something they wanted as well.

She gasped when she felt Fane rest his shaft against her netherlips. He pushed forward, entering her slowly until he reached her virgin's barrier. He raised his head and looked into her eyes.

"You are my mate, Laynee. From this night forth you shall be known as the mate to the alpha male of the house of Gavaire. You belong to me." His eyes changed, reflected the low light like the predator he was. "Say it. Tell me you belong with me. From this night forth, you belong to me. You shall rule by my side as my equal, mate."

As his equal? A part of her both rejoiced over and feared his statement. She would be his equal—their equal. Licking her lips, she cast a glance to Sayre, not wanting to leave him out. She would *not* be a party to hurting him, even by accident. Turning back to Fane, she stared deep into his eyes, silently asking him to include Sayre in this.

Fane closed his eyes then amended his statement. "You belong to us, Laynee. Say it. Say you belong to Sayre and me."

She took a deep breath and gathered her courage. "I—I belong to you." She shot a glance toward Sayre. "I belong to you and Sayre." She screamed both with pain and arousal when he drove the rest of the way into her, his sac resting against her rear. The pain was intense but still bearable. He held himself deep within her unmoving to allow her body to grow accustomed to his invasion.

Sayre's mouth left her flesh. He blew across her breasts, her nipples tightening as the air caressed the damp peaks. She noticed the transparent barrier behind him and frowned. Reaching up to touch it, she realized it surrounded her, was a part of her and she stared at it, awed.

Laynee stared at her new mates, looking from one to the other as she noticed the barrier surrounded them all in its protective light. Fane moved then and she forgot about everything but the sensation of his hard cock moving in and out of her. His flesh slid back and forth, the friction rubbing against an inner part of her that nearly drove her mad.

Sayre's hands were gentle, moving over her sensitive flesh, touching her in places she never knew could bring her such pleasure. She arched off the bed, the sensations they introduced her to almost too much for her to bear. Still Fane thrust his hard shaft within her, and Sayre kissed and fondled her breasts. Her throat worked convulsively as Fane lowered his head to suckle her right breast while Sayre suckled the left.

She screamed another release as the two men continued to suckle her, the pleasure so intense she was sure she would die from it. Fane reached down and lifted her legs, seating himself further inside her. His cock rammed deep and she screamed again. She thrust her fingers through their hair, digging her nails into their scalps.

"Please," she begged again, still unsure what it was she wanted, what she needed. "It isn't enough. I—I don't know what—"she sobbed. "It just isn't enough."

She looked at Sayre. "I need...more."

"What do you want, *natoya?*" Sayre kissed her lightly.

Fane stilled over her, waiting for her to voice her needs. That was the problem. She didn't know what she needed. The only thing she knew for certain was that what they were doing wasn't enough. Something was missing from their lovemaking.

"I—I don't know." She looked at Fane. "I only know that what you are doing isn't enough," she sobbed, feeling so inadequate. "I'm sorry, it just isn't enough."

Fane pulled from her and she whimpered. He didn't want her now that he knew she was some sort of weirdo. A deviant. Tears tracked down her face and she turned her head, trying to hide her mortification.

"Go to her bathing chamber and find some lubricant, Sayre. I think I know what she needs." He raised a brow. "If I'm correct, you won't be left out tonight after all." He glanced back at Laynee. "I must heal you before we continue, *la nisa.*" He moved down over her, lowering his head to her sex once more. "Those of my house have healing agents in their saliva. I know what you want. You will not find pleasure in what is to come if I do not heal the tearing of your barrier first."

Laynee groaned as he laved the stinging flesh between her legs. The sound came from deep within her. Her chest heaved as his tongue snaked inside her, laving the tender flesh. He pulled back a bit, kissing her netherlips, suckling her clit until she was mindless once again. A thick finger pushed past the tight opening of her ass. Surprisingly, it didn't hurt. At first it was merely a bit uncomfortable. After a moment, it felt good, too good.

Fane's mouth still worked at healing her as he pushed another finger into her ass, then still another. Soon, she wriggled on his thick fingers, begging for more, needing to feel more. This was what she'd been missing, what she'd needed as he rammed himself inside her.

Sayre returned from her bathroom with a bottle of the oil she used to make her skin smooth. It was the kind specifically for use on one's nether parts. Her face burned at the thought that he knew she'd dreamt of this. Needed this.

"It—it's for..." her gaze darted around the room.

"I know what it is for, *natoya.*" Sayre grinned, setting the bottle on the table next to the bed. He brushed the hair from her face and kissed her softly. "There is no need to be embarrassed, mate. It is good you are so well prepared."

"It's the best oil for making sure my skin is smooth. It has no odor and I have no allergic reaction to it." It had never given her a rash like so many other oils. She'd bought it on the suggestion of one of her coven mates. Since it was designed for use in such sensitive areas, it was less likely to cause an adverse reaction.

Her embarrassment was so great she hadn't noticed that Fane had stopped his ministrations. Looking at her two mates, her heart slammed against her ribs. Desire tore through her and she felt an answering moisture gather between her legs. She never dreamt she would be so lucky to attract the attention of one such male, let alone two.

With a boldness she didn't know she possessed, she sat up and reached out. Taking Fane's still hard cock in her hand, she feathered her fingers over the velvety flesh. She examined it, loving the way it looked, the way she knew it could make her feel. She gasped when Sayre leaned over and took the tip of her breast in his mouth.

Overwhelming sensation flowed through her as they both continued the assault on her senses. Soon, she forgot her curiosity as they continued to move over her, their gentle hands skimming her flesh, once again bringing her to the very edge of sanity.

Fane moved to lie on his back. Taking her hand, he brought her over him. Straddling him, she reached down and positioned herself over his massive organ, sliding herself over it like a slick glove. She groaned at the new level of penetration. Circling her pelvis, she moved over him. With his hands gripping her hips, Fane guided her movements.

Reaching up, he pulled her head down to his, kissing her deeply. His tongue thrust into her mouth, parrying with hers and he held her, one hand in her hair, the other on the cheek of her ass, spreading her for Sayre's invasion.

Cool oil ran down her thighs when Sayre squirted the oil on the opening of her ass. A spear of doubt—of fear—shot through her and she almost cried out for them to stop. Instead, she pressed her lips together, refusing to disappoint either of them, or herself. She wanted this, almost as much as they did. She needed it. Deep in her soul she knew that this was meant to be.

The white light surrounded them more closely, the light brighter, the veil between them and the bedroom thicker. It was almost as if a force field surrounded her and her lovers. Feeling the head of Sayre's cock at her small opening, she once again gathered her courage and pushed back against him, helping him seat the thick flesh deep inside her ass.

After he sank the length deep into her flesh, neither of them moved for a moment. Sayre, behind her, rested his head between her shoulder blades and Fane contented himself with fondling her breasts.

It was Sayre who moved first. Slowly, he pulled out, then thrust back into her, moving even deeper than he did before. They set up a rhythm, each thrusting and counter thrusting. It soon had her screaming with ecstasy. Flames licked at her skin. Singing currents of electricity flowed through her. Her blood flowed through her veins like liquid fire as another climax gradually built within her.

Her mind fragmented, splintered into a million pieces as another orgasm overtook her and she screamed when Sayre sank his teeth in the back of her neck. She'd never believed any of the stories she'd read about the blood drinkers. Now she knew them to be true.

The pulse of her mates' combined orgasms drove her over the edge once more and she collapsed onto Fane, exhausted.

Sayre licked the crook of her neck where he'd bitten her and kissed her back. He eased his still semi-hard shaft from her ass, stood and padded from the room. He returned a while later, rolled her from atop Fane and placed a warm cloth between her legs. He gently washed the remains of their lovemaking from her and kissed her forehead.

"Sleep mate. You are fatigued." He placed two fingers over her mouth when she would have spoken. "There will be enough time for your questions tomorrow after you've rested." He placed more soft kisses on her eyelids. "I'm so proud of you, Laynee. We both are. You are indeed courageous to put your trust in us so soon."

Laynee relaxed into their arms, allowing herself to drift to sleep wrapped in the warmth of her mates' embrace.

FANE LEFT THE room carrying another of her bags. She refused to leave her things behind. If they expected her to live with them they would take her things and like it. She smiled shyly at Sayre as he entered the room for another box.

Making a detour to where she stood, he took her into his arms and kissed her deeply. "I thank you for your trust in this."

"It's enough that you told me what to expect, Sayre." She smiled and lowered her eyes. "I realize you broke some sort of rule for your people by telling me what to expect. I appreciate your trust in me as well." She licked her lips needing to ask him about what she saw last night.

"What was that energy field that surrounded us as we made love? I didn't notice it until you returned from . . ." She let her voice trail off as heat bloomed in her cheeks. "Until you returned with the oil."

He reached up and cupped her cheek, a soft smile on his face. "It wasn't me who made that, *natoya*. It was you."

"Me? I don't know how to do that. Why would you say it was me?"

"Fane and I both noticed it. We wondered if you knew you could do it. You seemed oblivious to it." Taking her hand, he pulled her to the couch, sat and pulled her down onto his lap. "We first noticed it when you made your decision. We think it's a protective aura you draw around yourself when you are frightened. The glowing sphere is present whenever you make the decision to do something that frightens you. I believe it is a manifestation of your powers and courage."

She turned to look him in the eyes. "But I have no powers and I usually have no courage. I don't know what came over me, giving me the nerve to accept you both into my life the way I did last night." She bowed her head, ashamed that he must know of her weakness.

Gentle fingers under her chin lifted her head and she peered into his beautiful amber eyes.

"Never tell me you have no courage, *natoya*. You have heard what Fane calls you?"

"Yes." She nodded. She knew *la* meant little. She could only guess what *nisa* meant. Chicken and baby came to mind.

"It means little warrior. Even Fane has seen your courage. Do not tell us you are not courageous. You are the most courageous woman I have ever met."

Her mouth dropped open at his words. "It really means little warrior?"

"Why would I lie? What could I possibly gain from it?" He nodded toward the door. "He comes now. Ask him what it means."

Fane stopped just inside the door. He searched the room briefly and smiled when he saw them resting on the sofa. "Mind if I join you?"

They both shook their heads. Sayre nudged her and she licked her lips, suddenly afraid. What if Sayre didn't really expect her to ask him, what if it did mean little chicken after all?

She squared her shoulders and prepared herself for the worst.

"Fane, I'd like to ask you a question about your language."

"Yes, *la nisa*," he replied, taking her hand and bringing it to his mouth. Goddess, she didn't know if she could think with him kissing the palm of her hand like that. It was very disconcerting. Very arousing. Her pussy clenched and her clit pulsed out a rhythm with his mouth.

"That thing you just called me. What does it mean?"

He raised his head and stared deep into her eyes. "Let there be no mistake, Laynee. I call you that because I both love and respect you. It is a name I felt suited you last night when you fought back your fears and accepted both Sayre and me into your life." He leaned over and pressed a soft kiss to her lips. "It means, little warrior. I call you that because you face your fears. You do not hide from them as others do. You are our little warrior."

Tears burned her eyes as she looked between them. "I don't deserve you. I don't deserve either of you."

"No," they said in unison. "It is we who do not deserve you."

Three Days Later, Savar

As LAYNEE FOLLOWED her mates to *The Hallowed Glenn* she couldn't help but feel awed and humbled. Trees unlike any she'd ever seen before surrounded her. Their leaves shimmered in breathtaking hues of blue and purple, fascinating her. Moonbeams shone down on the tops of the trees giving the leaves an eerie mystical glow. She wanted to reach out and grasp the delicate fronds, but knew even if the moons hadn't reached their zenith leaving little time before the ceremony must begin, she wouldn't risk destroying such beauty by touching them just so she could ensure they were real.

She followed behind her mates, her eyes fastened on their asses. Even beneath their black leather pants and capes, she had no trouble remembering just how firm their muscular backsides felt beneath her hands. She'd spoken with her sister on their trip to *Savar*, and even though Jaynee was mated to the *Savari* leader, she didn't withhold answers from her as the *Savari* Council of Elders insisted. She knew that her mates were supposed to be wearing naught but ritual robes for the ceremony, but in deference to Fane and his position in *Tigerian Society*, they instead wore warrior trews and cloaks.

Her wandering thoughts halted as they stepped through the wall of trees into a clearing. Her breath caught in her lungs as she spied the stones standing in a circle in the middle of the clearing. She could feel power—

ancient power—encircle her, buffeting her like a warm wind. She straightened her spine, drawing on her own strength, visualizing the aura her mates had pointed out after their first mating. She wouldn't back down. She wouldn't give in to fear. No longer was she the wimpy girl afraid of her own shadow. Now, she knew her own strength, her own power, and was secure in both her abilities and the love of her mates. Nothing would deter her from joining with her men, not even the ancient spirits of *Savar.*

Her gaze drifted around the glen, trying to take in everything at once. A thick carpet of purple and blue leaves covered the grove inside the stone circle. An altar, marbled with veins of deep pink, stood between the two largest upright stones. *Casta* blooms of pink and white decorated the circle. Their star shaped buds shimmered. Their stems were braided together in a delicate rope and draped over most of the shorter standing stones, though how they could still be alive she didn't know. Then there were the plants that she couldn't identify.

Towering flora of purple and pink butted up against the tallest of the stones, though they held no leaves of any kind. Instead it looked as though they were naught but colored stalks. Ferns of vibrant purple were growing in the shadow of the mystical *Stones of Savar.* She followed Sayre and Fane until they stopped, standing just outside the circle of stones. Their glimmering black and burgundy capes combined with their black leather trews made them appear more sinister than ever before. Though she knew in her heart they'd never hurt her, perhaps it was this place that made her shiver in fear, in dread.

Nervous now about what would happen, even though all had been explained to her, Laynee couldn't seem to stand still. After all, she would be making love to her mates, pleasuring them in front of witnesses. That thought should have scared her, infuriated her, knowing their lovemaking would be put on display, but instead her pussy grew wet with the thought. Her thighs trembled. Her clit grew turgid, twitching in need. What happened to the woman she used to be just four days ago? Where had the wanton woman that now dwelled within her heart come from?

Laynee, you know that what happens in this circle is an affirmation of your love and your trust in your mates. You are only now seeing yourself as I have always seen you. You had the strength, courage, and passion in your soul just waiting until the right time to burst forth. The love of your mates and the love you feel for them was all that was needed to show you what you've always been. You have much still to learn, more growing yet to do, but with Fane and

Sayre by your side, you will become so much more than you can ever imagine.

As Sayre explained to you, if you refuse them, if you show you do not trust them by not following their requests, you will forfeit your right to bond with them. You will also doom the three of you to a childless existence. You can only bear the children of these two men. To any other you are sterile.

Sayre honored you, honored the strength he has always seen, by telling you of this ceremony though custom dictates the woman enter The Hallowed Glenn ignorant of what will occur. Don't worry about what others will see, will think. Just enjoy this time. This is your mating night, Laynee. Blessed Be.

Laynee closed her eyes and sighed. She knew the Lady Goddess was right. She could not worry about the others. This night was about her and her mates and the unbreakable bond they'd forge together. Once she managed to push all negative thoughts and worries aside, she opened her eyes and looked over at her two mates. Her heartbeat pounded out a rapid beat and she knew she could trust them with all that she was and would ever be. She vowed she wouldn't let them—or herself—down. She would do everything they asked of her, anything to prove her love to them.

Soon, cloaked figures moved from the cover of the trees, silently approaching them. Dozens of people calmly walked toward them, their faces and genders hidden by the heavy robes they wore. How long had they hidden behind the foliage, watching them? And why did the thought of them watching unseen disturb her more than the fact they'd watch her make love to her men?

Soon, she and her mates were surrounded, encircled by the robed witnesses. As one, they reached out, clasping their hands, one to the next to the next until a circle formed around them. No one spoke, no one so much as moved once they formed their circle. In fact, only the whisper of wind through the trees and her own harsh breathing broke the unnatural silence.

Two robed figures approached from the tree line. Ducking beneath the clasped hands, they entered the stone circle, stopping only a few feet before them. One wore a robe of red, the other green.

Though she couldn't see their faces, she could feel their penetrating stares, felt them searching inside her soul into the very heart of her. Even though she wore a yellow sarong that adequately covered her, she felt naked and exposed beneath their searching gaze.

"Who petitions the council of *Savar* to bond with this woman?" the man wearing red asked.

"We do, illustrious priest, druid of the *Non*," Sayre answered for them both as he and Fane each reached out and grabbed her hands, pulling her to stand beside them rather than slightly behind them as custom dictated.

The green robed figure lowered his hood. Only a slight gasp announced Laynee's surprise when she discovered the council member was female. Apparently, Sayre hadn't told her everything about tonight, though in his defense, he probably didn't think the sex of the officiators important enough to mention. "Who petitions the council of *Savar* to bond with these men?" She stared at Laynee, waiting for an answer and the circle of witnesses stilled. Even the winds quieted in anticipation.

Laynee stepped forward, willing strength to her body and her voice, building the aura-shield she'd learned to depend on in the short time since Sayre and Fane pointed out this particular skill she'd had and never known about. Knowing now wasn't the appropriate time to wonder how she could have been so ignorant of her own abilities. Laynee shoved it to the back of her mind to think on later.

Knowing she could show no doubt, no fear, she raised her voice, determined that all within hearing distance would find the truth in her vows. "I do." The man and woman took each other's hands and reached out to take theirs.

She knew what came next, knew the appropriate words to say. The five of them formed a loose circle around the altar and they all began to chant the Savar Binding Spell. Everyone in the grove began chanting, giving their strength to ensure none could beak the bonds being forged between the new Triad. Sayre prepared her well for this, for what would come next. He told her the language was ancient, a rite to draw the power from the moon to bless their union, uniting the three of them together. Though she didn't know what all the words meant, she knew enough to know they were asking for the Lady Goddess' blessing.

A small moonbeam filtered down from the sky, it touched Sayre, the light growing, expanding around him. The robed man and woman left the circle, still chanting as the bright glow surrounded Sayre, encompassing Laynee and Fane and the marbled stone altar. What happened next surprised her, and from Sayre's shocked gasp and those of the witnesses, it had not been expected.

Her own aura began to expand. The shimmering blue of her aura merged with the brilliant yellow of Sayre's, forming a green bubble around her and her mates. A solid wall formed around them, blocking out all sound from the outside. What in the world?

You have power within you. Together the three of you will be able to do many things never before realized. While you're encased in this shield, the three of you can not be heard by others, and only those with magick in their blood can even see this shield. To all others, you are invisible. Now you know the truth depth of your strengths, your powers. You and your mates are necessary if the Banart plague is to be defeated before your worlds fall.

She could feel her mates tense beside her, knew without asking they too could hear the words of the Lady Goddess. Before she could speak, she could feel the Goddess withdrawal, could feel the protective shield around them thin until it was no more.

Once the green aura-shield disappeared, her gown appeared to shimmer beneath *Savar's* Triad Moons. The fabric grew brighter. The soft yellow of the gauzy silken material seemed nearly transparent beneath the moons mystical glow. Her nipples tightened, puckering into hard peaks, begging for the touch of her mates, the feel of their tongues caressing her needy flesh. Her pussy grew wet with need. Lust and love boiled through her body, sending it aflame. Though she'd been warned the mating heat would hit her suddenly, she had not been prepared for the intensity of her need.

As the witnesses continued to chant, she found herself swaying, her thoughts disconnected. Laynee began to feel strange, light headed, almost as though she was outside her body looking down. Rather than allowing her fears to overrule her, a strange sense of calm and expectation washed over her. The tips of her breasts began to tingle. Her clit pulsed and twitched between her legs. Her woman's cream coated her thighs and instead of embarrassment, pride filled her. This cream was for her mates, proof of her desire for them. Still she stood holding the hand of each mate surrounded by their warmth. Feeling their desire envelop her as she waited for them to take her home and love her.

As though he knew she was on the edge of climaxing, just holding their hands, Sayre moved behind her. His hands moved to her shoulders, caressing her glowing skin. His mouth trailed damp kisses along her forehead to her temple, drifted down her cheek, until he reached the curve of her neck. Fane stepped forward and cupped her breasts, tweaking her nipples between strong fingers. She gasped, unable to stand quietly a moment longer.

With gentle urgency, he reached up, pulled down the thin scrap of material keeping the gauzy confection on her trembling body. The sinful dress fell to the ground in a pool of silken fabric, though she could care less. All she wanted was to become one with her mates, no other concerns mattered right now. No other thoughts or worries would intrude.

Before she could even think about the others that watched, Sayre turned her in his arms so that she faced him. His lips covered hers in desperate urgency and she was powerless to withhold her affection, opening to him. She curled her tongue around his, dueled with him. She needed this, needed to become one with him. Fane's hand caressed her from behind and she groaned. She needed to feel him pressed against her, feel him sinking his cock into her ass as Sayre fucked her needy pussy. Her skin burned. Her heart raced. Her empty pussy ached.

She gasped when Sayre's fingers stroked her pussy. Gently, he parted her lips, his fingers circling her clit. His touch was light, dreamy, but never enough to send her over the edge but enough to make her beg for relief if she were allowed to speak. Once, twice, he tweaked her clit. Her legs gave out. Fane caught her from behind and lifted her to the altar. Laying her down, he gently spread her arms, securing them to the base while Sayre secured her legs.

She watched through hooded eyes as the men stripped. The cloaks dropped to the grass, their leather trews soon followed. Her eyes widened. She licked her lips, desperate to taste their cocks, cocks that even now stood rigid, filled with their seed.

She wriggled on the cold stone, wanting, needing their caresses. She needed to feel their thick cocks pounding into her as she screamed with completion, but she knew that first she needed to swallow their seed. They'd need to spill their seed in every orifice to prove their dominance and her trust before this evening ended.

Fane's strong hands stroked her inner thighs as Sayre made his way toward the head of the altar. Fane stopped, gazed deeply into her eyes then gave her a slow, heart-melting smile. She shivered beneath his gaze as driving need flared in his eyes. Out of the corner of her eyes, she watched him step over to the robed woman and take something from her hands. He quickly returned after muttering his thanks.

He lifted his hand, showing her the silken material. A moment of panic washed over her before she quickly quelled it, knowing that she must be blindfolded for the next part of the mating ritual.

Sayre's voice echoed through the glen, bouncing off the mystical stones. "For the ritual you will be blindfolded. You must give yourself over to us, mind, body, and soul."

She swallowed nervously, then nodded her agreement. Within seconds she was shrouded in darkness, unable to see what happened around her. All she could do was wait for the next part of the ceremony.

Just thinking about pleasuring her men, taking their thick cocks in her mouth and swallowing their seed, made her nipples harder. Rough fingers grasped a pebbled nipple between his fingers and twisted. The pleasure-pain made her groan. She bit her lip, desperate and hungry. Needy. A warm mouth covered the tip of her breast. Another mouth latched onto her other breast. She wanted to reach out, run her fingers through her mates' hair, hold them to her, but all she could do was accept their attention.

Fire zipped down her spine. Her woman's cream seeped from her pussy, preparing her cunt for her mates. They didn't tell her not to make noise. It was one rule they never tried to implement. They probably knew it would be unfair to expect her to remain silent during such an onslaught.

Fingers delved into the moist flesh between her legs. She squirmed on the altar, raising her hips, grinding against them as she sought her release. Only a few more strokes and she would finally have sweet release. On the edge of climax, the fingers left her. Warm breath caressed her thighs and she gasped. Her flesh tingled as hot air bathed her erect clit. A warm wet tongue delved between her folds, suckled on her clit.

She felt one of her men straddle her chest, felt a hard cock press against her lips. She knew what was required, looked forward to pleasuring her men.

"Suck my cock, *la nisa.*" Fane's voice grated was low, rough with need and desire. It made her feel powerful, strong.

Laynee opened her mouth, wanting, no needing, to feel Fane's cock between her lips. Even blinded, she'd know Fane's cock, the texture of it, the length and width. She could picture it in her mind exactly. She knew his very scent. She laved the weeping slit, swirled her tongue around the head, tasting his pre-cum. When his groans became desperate pleas, she took his length between her lips, worked his cock until he reached the back of her throat.

Sayre ate at her pussy, his mouth working between her legs like a starving man sitting before a banquet in his honor. The slurping noises echoed through the glen but she felt no embarrassment, just love. Love for her mates. She groaned as he suckled her clit, raising her hips the best she could tied down as she was.

Fane grasped her hair, held her to him as he thrust into her mouth. She did her best to take his full length down her throat, swallowing both his cock and her pooling saliva as he drove into her mouth. She caressed him with her tongue, wishing she could reach up to fondle his sac. She wanted to show him just how much he meant to her, touch him, caress him, love him.

Her climax grew closer and the world around them was naught but a hazy memory. Nothing existed in this grove beyond her mates. Her thighs quivered. Her back arched, desperate in her need to get closer to Sayre as he continued to lap at her cunt.

"I'm going to cum now, *la nisa*." She knew she needed to swallow his cum, take his essence into her and she did so willingly. Jets of his creamy semen shot down her throat. She gulped the thick fluid, knowing they were one step closer to becoming bound triad mates. He thrust deeply into her mouth groaning out his release before pulling his spent cock from between her lips.

Fane climbed off her and loosened the bonds on her wrists while Sayre released her ankles. She'd give anything to remove her blindfold so she could look into her mates' eyes, but she knew the time had not yet come. Battling back her disappointment, she waited for the next phase of the ritual.

Once her mates had released the binding and helped her stand, they led her a few steps away. Raising her hands above her head, they secured them with the restraints that still bound her wrists. Even knowing that she would be trussed, when she hadn't seen any sort of restraint devise when they entered the circle, she'd assumed the ritual had changed. What was she connected to?

Her thoughts drifted away as her mates began to touch her, worship her with their hands and mouths. They nibbled on her skin, stroked her pussy and laved her nipples with their tongues. It almost seemed their hands and mouths were everywhere at once.

She groaned deep in her throat when they both suckled the tips of her breasts into their mouths at the same time. She gasped as they both bit down, sending shards of pleasure pain straight from her abused peaks to her throbbing clit.

Razor sharp teeth grazed her right breast, scraping her with pointed fangs and she knew it was Sayre. Fane moved around behind her, stroked her ass with the tip of one finger. Her entire being quivered in need, dripped with desire. His teeth scraped along her neck and goose bumps flared across her skin. She whimpered, tilted her head to the side to give him better access.

"Do you submit to us, *la nisa?*" Fane asked.

From in front of her, she heard Sayre suck in a breath, then his rough voice washed over her, asking her the next ritual question. "Do you lay your trust at our feet and submit to us in every way?"

She felt no hesitation, no fear. She wanted to shout her joy, her love, but instead in as strong and honest a voice as possible, answered him. "Yes, I submit to you and Fane in every way."

Sayre growled and lifted her into his arms. Placing his cock at the entrance to her channel, he drove into her and she screamed.

"You are mine, *natoya*. You are Fane's. You shall forever belong to us."

Knowing her submission wouldn't be complete until she agreed with his pronouncement, she swallowed before answering his silent demand. "I belong to you. I belong to Fane. From this day forward I belong to you both."

Behind her, Fane stretched her back hole with her own cream, preparing her for his invasion. When she was ready, he slowly entered her ass. His long, thick cock slid easily into her prepared hole. She trembled, caught on the razor's edge of pleasure and pain as he moved within her. Closer and closer, she came to reaching her climax. Her mates stroked into her in tandem. In. Out. In. Out. Finally her pussy clenched. Her clit spasmed as fire and heat rushed through her body. She came again, as Sayre sank his teeth in her breast. Fane plunged his own into her neck. They continued to shaft into her as they took her blood, desperate to find their own release.

Sayre lifted his head, swiped his tongue over her breast, and ripped his wrist open with his fangs. "Drink and we shall be one."

Knowing neither of her mates would ever cause her harm, she dipped her head and drank from the wound at his wrist when he pressed it to her mouth. Fane reached forward, leaning in to give his wrist to Sayre.

Still they both surged within her, even as Sayre sank his teeth into Fane's wrist and drank deep. When he was through, he raised Fane's wrist to Laynee. Without hesitation, she took Fane's essence into her mouth, swallowing the liquid that would combine their lives, their love and their species.

Her mates surged into her body one last time. Their cocks expanded, thickened inside her already tight channel. As her mates spilled their seed into the depths of her body, Laynee came again, screaming her climax to the Lady Goddess.

"Laynee of *Carrillia*, we accept you into our lives, into our blood as one," Sayre and Fane said simultaneously. "Reach for that which is ours within you. Feel our bond, our blood flowing in your veins and embrace us. It is time. Embrace your other side, your animal side." After unclasping her wrists, they lowered her to the ground and massaged her shoulders until the tension and trembling eased.

When they were sure her strength had returned, they led her toward the line of trees. As they left the circle she felt another presence living inside her, growing in strength and insistence. She had an insane desire to run, to hunt, to explore the world around her. Not as a *Carrillian* Priestess, but as a *Tigerian*. Suddenly, overwhelmed with the foreign need, she ran and her mates followed. Only after they'd left everyone behind, did they stop.

Fane turned toward her, concern in his gaze. "Are you ready to run as a Tigerian, *la nisa*?

Unwilling to wait even one more moment to experience shape shifting for the first time, she nodded. "More than ready, Fane."

"Good. Sayre already knows how to shift, so watch us. Visualize your animal spirit in your mind. See the great white tiger as it prepares to hunt, to chase down its prey."

Laynee watched in awe as her mates began their change. Their eyes glowed. Sayre's a brilliant amber and Fane's a pure deep blue of a bottomless ocean. Their pupils lengthened. Their teeth grew, muzzles shaped. Hair sprouted on their arms and legs, before their backs bowed and they were forced to drop to all fours.

The change happened in only moments and she couldn't wait to try it herself. She closed her eyes and did exactly as Fane instructed. Power and heat rushed through her body as her inner tiger stretched, emerging from its slumber. Not knowing exactly what to expect, Laynee was surprised that other than exhilaration, only the need for freedom flooded her. She opened her eyes, looked around. She had changed. Tonight her entire world changed and she couldn't help but wonder just what else was in store for her and her mates.

Unable to help herself, she ran, knowing her mates would soon catch up to her. For tonight, only pleasure and happiness existed. She'd worry about the *Banarts* tomorrow.

Now you are one, Laynee. You are of the Tigerian as is Sayre. You are of The Savar as is Fane. The two men now have the power of three as do you. You three will play an essential part in our army. An army of powerful triads that will one day defeat the Banart plague. Remember Laynee, as your sister did you, you must contact the next female in the line of three.

Dax Gavaire sat at the communications terminal researching the letters and *vid-conferences* he'd intercepted over the last couple of weeks as they zinged their way across the surface of the planet. This late at night it was easy to read all of the communiqués sent back and forth. There weren't so many when most of the planet slept.

"Hmm… This is interesting." He took a close look at one sent from a Laynee Mikalosa to Rachana Salura, a coven mate apparently readying to go off world on an historical artifact expedition. His lip curled. Historians were naught but boring bookworms with nothing better to do with their time than live in the past. Better to face the future then die stagnating in the past.

"I know you're frightened, Ana, but you mustn't be. I'm forwarding another copy of the text to you." Laynee Mikalosa said. He watched the transmission with interest as she pushed a button on her console. "I know you, and I know you destroyed it as soon as you received it. You must conduct the spell, bring your mate to you. It works."

"I don't want a mate." Rachana said, her bottom lip pushing out in a full pout. "I refuse to do this."

"You cannot refuse, Ana. The world, the entire galaxy relies on you, on us, to rid the universe of the *Banart* scum. What is a little thing like sharing your life with others when it can destroy those who are so evil?"

"I will think about it, Laynee. I cannot promise you more."

Laynee sighed. "That's better than a firm refusal, I guess. Please think hard on this before you destroy the spell book."

Ana sighed. "I will. Have a nice trip with your new mates. I hope everything turns out just the way you want it to."

The screen went dark and Dax sat staring at the attachment he'd downloaded. A book of spells designed to bring mates? His face broke into a smile as he stood and went in search of his brother. Perhaps what worked for the women of *Carrillia* would work for them as well.

"It certainly won't hurt to try."

SEX ME ALL AROUND

the smoking grass and buildings of the town three miles away and prayed the *Hienial* people would finally leave her planet and her people alone. If only she could escape this place. If only she could manage to find someone who would come to *G'Recio* and help, they could defeat the monsters who loved to laugh as they tortured her people.

Minna closed her eyes and tried to forget the unimaginable pain, the horrors of being a woman in the hands of such monsters. She'd finally managed to escape, but she knew it was only a matter of time before they broadened their search and found her. Then the beatings, the probes, and the humiliation, would start all over as she waited for them to decide which three would mount her again.

She curled her fingers, balling her hands into fists. She couldn't allow that to happen. She looked down to the *fazac* on her belt and smiled grimly. No, they would not capture her again. Not alive, anyway. She'd been lucky the last time. She hadn't conceived. She didn't know if she could end the life of an innocent child. But, how could she knowingly help such a deviant race continue their existence?

Her eyes widened as her whole body began to tingle and she reached for the weapon on her belt.

Too late! Her scream of frustration was silent as she temporarily lost the use of her mouth. They'd already trapped her in their transportation device. It somehow dissolved you into millions of tiny pieces before stacking you back together in another location–just as good as you were before, only not as free.

When she reached her destination, a hard body knocked her to the floor. Immediately, she wrestled her attacker for possession of her weapon. They wouldn't let her kill herself. They enjoyed the torture too much. Besides, they needed women to continue their race.

When her assailant had her pinned, another man stepped up and took her weapon. "You won't need this."

"Better to kill you with," she bit out between clenched teeth.

"My, my, Dax. What a bloodthirsty little hellion you've wished upon us."

The man atop her raised his head with a snort. "Me? You're the one who wanted a female warrior, Rage. And I quote, "I want a woman not afraid to defend her cubs, her world and her mates." Don't tell me *I've* wished this upon us."

Minna stopped struggling long enough to hear their conversation and realized they were much too handsome and clean to be members of the

Hienial race. She sniffed delicately and almost sagged with relief when she didn't smell the hideous odor of one of the marauding *Hienials.*

The one called Rage stepped closer, giving her a better look at his laughing blue eyes, eyes the same color of the deep waters of Lake *Brakia.* The one lying atop her pressed her bones into the soil. He glanced down at her sharply indrawn breath and it was then she got a good look at his face. Her eyes widened. Brothers, they were brothers. Twins, by the looks of it. Both had the same white-blonde hair with black tips, ice blue eyes and full lips that made her think of things other than doing battle.

The man above her moved—pressing the hard evidence of his obvious arousal between her spread legs—and her face heated. Blood pounded in her ears and her heart slammed erratically in her chest when she realized of what they spoke.

"You drew me here with a spell," she said with a frown. "I thought only women could use the spells to bring their mates to them." She squeezed her eyes shut when she realized what she'd blurted out. Damn, why could nothing go right for her?

Perhaps it has already gone right for you. We wished for a well-educated, well-endowed warrior woman, and here you are, Dax said, slipping into her mind and letting her know he could read her thoughts. "How do you know of the spells?" he asked aloud, with a frown.

Her face blazed with mortification. Was she to have no privacy with these two? How—how ungentlemanly it was of him to make such a comment! It wasn't her fault her breasts were too large and her hips a bit too wide. It was what her grandfather had always called an hourglass figure. Whatever *that* was.

"I intercepted a couple of communications." She blinked slowly, hoping their masculine beauty was merely an illusion. "They don't work though, I tried."

"We are more alike than you know, woman."

She shoved at the wall of his chest when he grinned down at her. If they wanted to kill her for taking such liberties, so be it. They would merely be putting her out of her misery. Her only regret would be that she was unable to help her people.

RAGE BARELY STOPPED himself from gaping at the woman tucked beneath his brother. As he hoped, the wish-spell had brought them one woman, not two. Her long golden hair would stand out amongst his kind. She was unique. Full lips that begged for his kisses pouted at him and her violet eyes would look stunning when she finally changed to her inner cat. Her large breasts nearly spilled from her robe as she struggled beneath his brother. He found himself licking his lips in anticipation of closing his mouth around her erect nipples. The woman was perfect in every way. But, would she welcome the advances of two men? There was really only one way to find out.

After waiting years for their own mate, neither he nor Dax were of a temperament to give her the time or the opportunity to reject them. They'd planned for her seduction and he didn't see any reason to delay the mating, especially after seeing how fierce their mate could be. Besides, he thought, looking down at his brutal erection, his cock was in full agreement.

Rage watched his mate tense beneath Dax's body, could see her fighting to gain control. He could hear her chaotic thoughts whirl as she tried to figure out how to get the upper hand. Their mate wouldn't willingly submit to them—at least not yet. Yes, seduction was definitely the best route to take in subduing their spirited mate. He couldn't keep calling her mate, either. The first thing they needed to find out was her name and where she'd called home before they'd cast the spell. Then, they could seduce her.

Though it pained him not to loosen the ties on his trews thus releasing the pressure on his throbbing cock, Rage didn't dare show her the affect she had over him. Later, when they knew she was theirs he would shower her with attention, show her through his actions that his body would only burn for her.

Dax grunted, capturing Rage's attention. From the grimace on his twin's face, she must have elbowed him in a very delicate place. Enough was enough. "Cease and desist, woman. We mean you no harm."

"I have naught but your word of that." Though her words were firm even as she struggled beneath his brother's weight, he could feel her fear as though it were a living thing. Her fear crawled through her, demanding she find a way to escape them. This wouldn't do. They wanted her submission, yes, but through her trust, not because she feared they'd do her harm otherwise.

"Let her go, Dax."

"What?" Her eyes went wide, clearly not believing she'd heard him right.

What? Are you out of your mind? She'll try to escape the first chance she gets.

I don't think so. She needs to learn to trust us. She knows we are bigger and stronger than she is. That alone will keep her from fully trusting us.

95

Unless, or until, she feels she has the advantage, anyway. "Hand her the weapon back, too."

Are you sure about this, Rage? She might turn the weapon on us and try to run.

It's the chance we have to take. She'll not come to us willingly otherwise. For our mating to be acknowledged, she must be a willing participant in the binding ceremony.

"You will continue to believe we mean you harm if you remain unarmed. We know we would never hurt you, but until you realize that, you'll feel compelled to question everything we say. If having your weapon makes you comfortable, then have it you shall."

"I could just shoot you," she said, sitting up to assess her injuries. She had hit the ground hard when the other jumped on her. Doing a mental inventory, she realized she had a few aches, but nothing serious.

"You could, but then you'll never know if we spoke true about being your mates. Will you?"

She bit her lip, obviously deep in thought. "You're right. I wouldn't know." She looked around. "Where are we? Where have you brought me? I would at least like to know where I am before I make such a momentous decision as accepting you two for my mates."

Dax smiled, using the grin he'd practiced on females many times. He and his brother had used the same smile to get what they wanted from women for years. This time he used it with the knowledge that the woman he wanted would be the last.

"You are on our home world, *Tigeria.* Welcome to our home, mate."

MINNA ALMOST SLUMPED with relief. She'd heard about the *Tigerians.* Knew their honor was renowned throughout the galaxy. If they made a promise, they kept it. Still, she made a grab for the *Fazac* as soon as he held it within reach. She may have heard of their ways but it didn't mean she trusted them. She held it up, pointing it at first one, then the other. She felt ridiculous, knowing they could have killed her any number of times when she'd first arrived. Plus, they could have done anything to her while she lay helpless beneath the one. Yet they hadn't and it was that alone, which made her begin to trust them.

She looked from one brother to the other, both so handsome, so alike and knew that she must succumb to them. She must find the courage to mate with them and find a way to convince them to help her sisters or her entire world was lost to the cruel invaders who would do no more than use them for receptacles for their horrible smelling ejaculate and bearers of their hideous children.

No matter how she weighed her options, these two gorgeous men were infinitely better than dealing with the several *Hienial* people who would insist on mounting her. The *Hienials* were huge, ugly, smelled of death, sweat and had rotten teeth. What sane woman would want to mate with them? For some reason, they always birthed males. Never did a girl child come from a union with one of their kind and never did a child take on *any* characteristics of the mother's race. Too bad they did not simply cease to exist.

Again, she looked from one twin to the other, counted her blessings and nodded. "I—I don't have much choice. I cannot go home. The hideous *Hienial* have overrun my planet. I know you must be better than what awaits me there. I only hope you will not do me harm."

"What a lovely compliment, mate," Rage said, quirking the corner of his mouth in a wry grin.

"Stop teasing her, Rage," Dax said to his brother. "We will never harm you, love. We have waited too many years for you. We want you to know that you can trust us with your life."

She alternated her gaze between them. Surprisingly, she did trust them with her life. She just wasn't sure if she could trust them with the lives of all the women of her world—and her heart.

MINNA BIT HER lip, wary about what was in store for her. She had no idea where they were leading her, and even though she thought they spoke true when they said she was their intended mate, she still had her doubts. But, were they the doubts of a frightened woman or those of a warrior wary of a potential enemy? She just didn't know. They still hadn't done anything to prove to her that they were the *Tigerians* they claimed to be. They could have easily lied to her.

She watched the flex of the one called Dax's ass as he led the way. They'd started out in some sort of standing stone circle in the middle of a meadow before heading toward the tree line of the darkened forest. Before long, they'd left a well-worn path through the trees and began following an overgrown trail deeper into the woods. By the Lady Goddess, where were they taking her?

She wanted to look at everything at once. The trees stood taller than the largest building on *G'Recio*. Their red veined leaves were larger than her head. Her gaze was locked onto the treetops when the sounds of running water caught her attention. "Where are we going?"

Rage cleared his throat behind her, but he didn't say anything else. She could practically feel his gaze burning holes through her clothes. Unwilling to walk blindly into any situation, no matter if they were her supposed mates or not, she wasn't stepping one foot farther until they answered a few questions. They were asking an awful lot of her, and now they were reluctant to tell her where they were taking her.

By the Lady Goddess, they'd soon find out that she wasn't anyone's pushover. And they'd find out right now. Without any warning, she stopped in her tracks, turned on her mates, and pulled her *Fazac*.

She edged around until she could see both Dax and Rage. Now wasn't the time to let down her guard, even if she never intended to actually shoot them. They, however, didn't need to know that. "You can stop right there, Rage. I want to know where you're taking me."

Minna had to hand it to them. Neither male so much as flinched. Their breathing never altered. Their gazes never wavered. As far as she could tell, they weren't worried in the slightest that she might do them harm. She wasn't sure if it was courage that left them facing her with no worry or stupidity.

Perhaps it is trust. She ignored the voice in her head and voiced her demand once more.

"Well? Tell me where you are taking me."

"We are taking you to the hot springs, where a natural pool formed eons ago. Among our people, it is common for mates to bathe together there, to purify not only our bodies, but our hearts and souls as well. It's a sacred spot shown only to the males upon reaching maturity. Females only learn the location upon their mating night. We shall reveal another such place after the official ceremony." This time, Dax spoke. His rough voice swept over her, caressing her flesh. Goose bumps spread across her skin. She wanted to beg him to keep speaking. To stroke the rough pad of his tongue over her heated skin. Instead, she straightened her spine, and quirked one brow in disbelief.

"Let me get this straight. You're taking me to a *sacred pool* where we'll bathe together, and then mate? Here? Now? With the both of you?" She didn't know why she was so surprised. She knew they both wanted to mate with her, were taking her somewhere to do that very thing. But until right this minute, it hadn't seemed real somehow.

She swallowed the saliva pooling in her mouth. By the Lady Goddess, could she actually go through with this? Could she mate with two men, strangers, based on a gut feeling they spoke true when they said she was destined to be the third in their triad?

She watched as both the males nodded. "Yes, Minna. That is precisely what we mean. It's exactly what will happen. Or will you go back on your word?" Rage growled.

She grimaced. How did this get all turned around? All she wanted— needed—were answers. "No," she said, shaking her head. "I have no intention of going back on my word. But I'm not just a woman. I'm a warrior, and if there is one thing I've learned, it's never to walk into any situation blind."

Rage seemed to relax at that. She could see the tension ease from his frame. Was he worried she'd refuse to mate with them if they told her all the details of what would happen, about where they were taking her and its significance to them?

Unable and unwilling to worry him further—and unsure why she had such strong feelings about two virtual strangers—she tossed her weapon to Rage. Let him make what he would of her actions.

Dax closed the distance between them, encircled her with his arms, pulling her back to his front. Minna leaned back into him. She could feel the solid pressure of his erection pressed against her back and her heart thundered inside her chest in reaction. Her nipples tightened into hard, aching points. Every time she inhaled, the rough fabric of her woolen robe brushed against their sensitive tips. Her pussy felt empty. It desperately needed to be filled. Cream slid down her thighs, proof of her body's desire to mate.

By the Lady Goddess, never had she felt such overwhelming sensations. Every nerve in her body felt electrified. How would she feel when no clothing separated her from them, when the only thing rubbing against her painfully taut nipples would be their fingers and tongues? She shuddered and her womb clenched just thinking about it.

Dax slowly began to lift her robe and all she could do was stand there, frozen in his embrace. When it reached mid thigh, he eased his hands underneath. His palms were rough against her skin. They rasped sensually over her and another wave of goose bumps rippled across her flesh.

Minutes passed, or mayhap only seconds before he slipped his fingers inside her nether parts. She widened her stance, making it easier for him to slide his fingers through her slick folds. She cried out in reaction, quivered when his fingers pressed against her erect clit before thrusting them into her sopping wet channel.

Her vision glazed over with need and still her gaze remained locked on

Rage's. She watched his pupils dilate while his brother fingered her mound. His chest vibrated when he let out a primal growl. It was too much. Too much sensation. Too much passion. Too much need. By all she found holy, what was happening to her?

Dax's lips brushed against her neck. She wanted him to suck on the sensitive flesh, to bite down and mark her as his mate. She was raw. Desperate. Craving domination. She didn't even understand where these needs, these desires, came from when never before had she wanted to give up control to another. Not like this.

As if sensing where she needed to be touched, Dax's other hand lifted to the fastening at her throat. Only a single cloak pin kept the garment closed, and he quickly opened it, leaving her bare body exposed to both the brothers' heated looks. With infinite slowness, Dax moved to cup her breast, then teased her turgid nipple with quick flicks and light pinches of his finger and thumb.

Pleasure pain zipped from her breast to her pussy. Her empty channel clenched and a wave of white-hot need rushed over her. She closed her eyes, dropped her head back against Dax's chest. Rage gasped and still she couldn't manage to raise her head and meet his heated stare with one of her own.

His hand retreated, forcing her to snap her eyes open. Before she could ask why he stopped, he stepped back and groaned. Rage growled and she could see the tip of fangs peek out the corner of his mouth. Somehow, she didn't think he let others see him when he was this close to losing control. That thought alone empowered her, gave her a sense of satisfaction.

Rage's eyes had darkened. His nostrils flared. His fists were clenched, pressed against his sides. Another drop of cream slid down her thighs in response. Minna's gaze moved to where the large outline of his cock pressed against the front of his trews.

He must have sensed the invitation in her gaze for he stepped forward, and stopped directly in front her. Unable to resist the need she could see burning in Rage's eyes, she leaned forward, still held firmly within Dax's embrace and covered his lips with hers.

Her tongue teased his bottom lip, seeking entrance. Her hands trailed down his ribcage, his sides, until settling atop his clenched fists. He growled again, low and deep, a rumbling purr of need and desire. Minna moaned when Dax continued his almost painful assault on her breast as Rage continued to kiss her.

Both brothers grew more aggressive. Dax's fingers tightened against her already rigid nipple. Rage's kiss grew brutal, his tongue mating, warring with hers in a heated battle for dominance. She whimpered, needing to submit to him and still she didn't understand why she felt this way.

One of her hands moved from Rage's clenched fists to the front of his trews. She needed to feel his cock. Her touch made him even more aggressive as he stepped closer, trapping her hand between their bodies.

Behind her, Dax stilled. "Let us continue this at the *Sacred Pool*. Let us become truly one there, not amidst the dirt and grass of the forest."

Rage nodded. Dax stepped back, releasing her from his touch. Before she could blink, Rage bent, put his shoulder to her tummy, and lifted her over his shoulder like a barbarian from ancient times. She gasped, surprised. Though the move was sudden, she wasn't afraid, merely intrigued. Even the jostle of his quickening steps or the rough hand that kneaded her buttock didn't cause her an upset. She must have lost all common sense the moment they disrobed her.

Within minutes, they left the forest behind. They crossed first one, then another meadow covered in wild flowers. The pleasant scent relaxed her somehow. Listening, she noticed the sound of trickling water grew louder. They were obviously closing in on their destination. She bit her lip to block the bubble of nervous laughter. She was barely able to believe that she would soon be willingly submitting to the sexual needs of these two men.

Though she couldn't see much with her face pressed against Rage's back, all her other senses were alive, teeming with information.

A plethora of birds called to one another across the vast meadow. The fragrance of the blossoming *nightblooms* she could see hidden within the deep grass filled her nose with their sweet scent. Even the feel of Rage's back beneath her hands as muscles rippled and flexed with his every step seemed more vivid.

Lost in experiencing the rush of information her senses were gathering, she almost missed the fact they'd stopped moving. Only when her head bounced off his back when he came to a stop let her know they reached the *Tigerian's Sacred Pool*.

Without warning, she found herself back on her feet, her robe open. What was the point of wearing it when it didn't do anything to cover her? Self-conscious, she reached out to pull the gaping sides of her robed closed, only to have her efforts halted by Dax's hands.

He laughed when she tried to swat his hands away. The husky sound rushed through her. From the corner of her eye, she watched Rage strip off his trews. When his clothes were naught but a pile of fabric on the grass at his feet he stepped forward, stopping in front of her, a hand's span from his brother.

Her eyes widened, darted between Rage's naked cock and Dax's clothed one. Apparently that was the only encouragement Dax needed, because he too stripped, shucking his pants and underwear, while never dropping his gaze from hers. Before long, he too stood in front of her, naked and aroused. Both their cocks stood full and ready. She swallowed in trepidation. What had she gotten herself into?

Her hand shook as she reached out to touch them. Both the men stepped back, out of reach.

"Strip, Minna. I want nothing caressing your flesh but the wind, the water and our tongues." Rage practically growled his demand and she couldn't help but respond, her nipples pebbling against the material into rigid points.

Minna gasped. Bit her bottom lip in indecision. She watched Dax's eyes flare, and made her choice, shrugging the ceremonial robe off her shoulders and letting it drop to the ground.

She stepped forward and watched Rage's eyes as she ran a finger down the length of his shaft before gently cupping his heavy balls. When his big body shuddered, she released his sac and moved to Dax's erect cock. A small bead of pre-cum spilled forth and it took everything she had to resist leaning forward to take him into her mouth.

Needing a distraction from doing just that, Minna returned to Rage's shaft, stroking him with a firm grip, somehow knowing that was what he'd prefer.

"You're playing with fire," Dax warned. "You keep that up and you'll get more than you're ready for."

She jerked her head up at his implied threat. Even though she knew they'd never harm her—not if they believed her to be their mate as they'd repeatedly told her—a different type of fear ran through her, causing another quiver deep inside her.

Whatever she might have said was wiped from her mind when Rage and Dax each grabbed one of her hands and began walking backwards, pulling her with them. Only then did she really take in her surroundings.

Behind the men stood a small wall of rocks, obviously formed by nature and not machines. The grey stone was faded with age, worn in places that only the flow of water over time could achieve. Moss and ferns were interspersed with an abundance of flora she'd never seen before. Flowers topped with blooms of such amazing colors they seemed to weep their vivid hues of pinks and blues, oranges and purples.

Steam rose from the rippling water of the natural pool just as a wave of cool air wafted across her exposed skin. She shivered, but not because of the sudden breeze. How could she possibly be cold when two of the hottest males she'd ever seen stood before her wearing naught but their smiles?

As though reading her mind—and maybe they could—they led her into the steaming waters and guided her toward a flat area on the natural rock barrier surrounding the pool. Water swirled around her thighs, sending pulses of heat through her aroused body.

Her nipples drew even impossibly tighter and she had to quiet the moan she could feel bubbling up inside her. She closed her eyes, doing her best to gain control over her raging libido.

Large hands wrapped around her waist, lifted her, forcing her to open her eyes. Before she could focus, Rage leaned forward, pressed his lips to hers. She gasped and Rage took that opportunity to sweep his tongue inside. The kiss went on and on. When he finally lifted his mouth from hers, it left her in a sensual haze she could barely see through. "There's a small ledge beneath the water just in front of you. Kneel on it facing me, Minna. Love me with your mouth, mate."

She nodded, barely aware when he placed her on the ledge he'd spoken of. She quickly moved into position, her mouth facing his erect cock, her ass facing Dax.

Rage's eyes flared as she leaned forward, eager now to take his cock between her lips. From the corner of her eyes, she watched Dax slowly stroke his own erection before moving behind her.

Closing her eyes, she lowered her head, her tongue sweeping across the weeping head of his cock. It pulsed and jumped against her lips and she smiled, feeling the power she held over him. His hands fisted in her hair, holding her to him. Yet she wasn't afraid or repulsed by his show of dominance. Slowly, she lowered her mouth to the head of his cock, taking as much of his length as she could.

Minna moaned and spread her legs, being careful not to lose her balance on the underwater ledge nor ruin the rhythm she needed to maintain to give Rage the pleasure he wanted, needed.

Something was missing. Someone. Without Dax, the mating wouldn't be complete. As if he knew just what she required, he slid his palms across her ass, gripped her hips then drove his cock deep into her needy channel. No hesitation. No foreplay.

For a moment, they all stilled. Heat and passion radiated off the three of them, swirled around them on the air just as the water swirled around their legs. The bubbling water lashed at her clit and she shivered in reaction. That simple movement caused both her males to surge into her, setting up a driving rhythm between her thighs and lips. All she could do was take it. Her tongue lashed at the head of Rage's cock on her every downward stroke. She moaned as Dax drove himself into her even deeper. She could feel him at the mouth of her womb, striking it relentlessly with every thrust. The pleasure pain was exquisite.

She lost herself in the sensations, let herself sink into the moment, experiencing something she'd never even conceived of before this evening.

RAGE CLOSED HIS eyes and moaned in pleasure as she continued to work his cock. His thighs quivered. His heart raced. His fingers tightened in her hair. His back arched. His testicles pulled taut, filled with his seed. He forced his eyes open, needing to share this moment with his twin. He looked first at Minna whose luscious lips were wrapped around his cock, and then at his brother whose face held naught but pure ecstasy.

He watched Dax's cock tunnel into their mate and knew nothing could be better than this, nothing more profound than loving his mate at the same time as his brother. As though sensing his increased desire, Minna's mouth became more aggressive, taking his length down her throat in her attempt to milk him of his seed. He lost control, shouting out his release long before he wanted to.

His senses were muffled, his thoughts sluggish. Only Dax's cries and Minna's moans as they reached their own orgasms brought him back from the brink of collapse. Rage's legs grew weak, his body too tired to even hold himself up any longer. Before he could sink beneath the churning water, he scooped Minna up determined to have her before his legs completely gave out. "Wrap your legs around my waist, mate."

Unbelievably, he felt his cock surge anew with desire, and strength returned to his body. It was as though she rejuvenated him. He had to have her. Again. This time he needed to slide his cock into her tight pussy, feel her spasm around him as she reached her own climax.

Once her legs wrapped around his waist he moved to the ledge and sat down, lifting her just slightly so he could slide his now hard shaft into her wet slit. Only once he was in as deep inside her as he could go, did he meet his brother's heated gaze.

SATISFACTION WHIPPED THROUGH Dax at the sight of Minna taking Rage into her body. Needing to be a part of their joining, he straddled Rage's legs and slid the head of his cock along the crease of her ass. He wanted to fuck her there, take her from behind as his brother took her pussy.

"Take us both at the same time, Minna," he whispered, "love us both at the same time."

She didn't answer in words but instead with her actions, lowering her chest until she was plastered against Rage, leaving her ass open to him. Dax's cock pulsed with the thought of what he was about to do. He reached down, waited for Rage to pull out of her sopping pussy, slipped his fingers into her channel and gathered their combined juices so he could prepare her back hole for his penetration.

Slowly, so not to cause her too much discomfort, he stretched her ass with his fingers, starting with one finger, adding another and another until she could handle three with relative ease. When he was confident the girth of his shaft wouldn't harm her, he slowly entered her.

Once fully seated, with only a thin membrane of tissue separating him from his brother, Minna began to thrash between them. He met his brother's gaze over her shoulder, and as one, they began to thrust.

As Dax thrust into her ass, Rage eased out of her pussy, until they established a rhythm of give and take. Harder and harder, they drove into her. Minna's cries and pleas egged them on farther, pushed them harder. Dax was desperate for relief, desperate to feel her clench upon his cock as she reached her climax.

All too soon, he felt the telltale ripple in her cunt and he was lost, unable to stop his seed from exploding even if he wanted to. Wanting to give his brother some one-on-one time with Minna, Dax eased his shaft from his mate's ass, and stepped away, sliding deeper into the pool and away from them.

"I'll be back in a few minutes, Minna. Enjoy this time with my brother for when it's over, you'll be mine for a time. "

From the shadow end of the *Sacred Pool*, Dax watched as Rage completely wrapped Minna within the safety of his arms. "I don't have the strength to push you away, mate," he muttered. She rose up on her elbows and looked down on his brother's face. Rage loosened his grip from around her waist, cupping her breasts instead. Beneath the churning waters, Dax's cock once again surged, need whipped through him, but he was content to watch—for now.

Rage's fingers tightened on her nipples and she arched her back in response. When he captured her rigid peak in his mouth, she cried out. Sweat began to bead up on Dax's brow as he watched his brother and mate in the throes of their passion. He watched as Rage hammered into her, taking her as though he hadn't just emptied his seed into her moments before.

Dax knew this night was special to the three of them, the first night of their mating. His brother needed Minna as much as he did, and because of that, he was content to watch their fevered joining. Whispered pleas and fevered moans echoed across the cove and finally came the sharp cry of their mutual release.

Satisfaction moved through Dax, satisfaction and contentment. This was what he'd always wanted for himself and his brother. She was all they'd ever need to warm their bed and warm their hearts.

With hooded eyes, he watched Minna succumb to sleep wrapped in his brother's arms. She hadn't even managed to get out of the swirling waters of the *Sacred Pool* before giving in to her exhaustion. Dax's soul overflowed with love—the love for his brother—and now love for their shared mate.

He loved knowing Minna was theirs to take, either separately or together. Even more, he loved knowing that even while wary of them and the situation she was in, deep down she felt safe enough to fall asleep in Rage's arms. With a desperate desire to take Minna to her new home, he left the relaxing waters of the *Sacred Pool.*

Rage, let us take our mate home now, so that we may awaken with her in our arms, in our bed.

MINNA WOKE TO silence. The cold sheets twisted around her told her she was alone at last. Thank the Lady Goddess for that at least. She stretched, wincing when muscles she never knew she had before, protested her every movement.

"It wasn't a dream." She was disappointed. She'd gone from one type of enslavement to another. It didn't matter that she'd tried to call the men to her first. On her world, with her weapons, they would have been under her control. Instead, the two males had made her scream and beg for release as they continued to assault her senses.

Her face burned with mortification at the things she had willingly done with them. The very same things she'd deemed deviant and disgusting with the cruel *Hienial* people. But then, the two brothers never forced her to do

who seemed to want to help her people. She arched her back further, grasping his hair and holding his head to her as he suckled her breast. Her legs spread almost of their own accord. His fingers continued to stroke her heated flesh as he moved between them and his clothes melted from his body.

She could feel his long thick cock pressed against her thigh. The moist head dribbled precum on her leg and she longed to take him into her mouth. Wanted—no—needed to have the hard male flesh driving between her lips as she raked her fingernails over his sensitive sac. She licked her lips and he groaned, taking her mouth with his. His tongue thrust into the warm depths, tangling with hers.

Warmth spread within her, crawled through her as his fingers brought her to the edge of her climax and she screamed.

"Please," she begged, her head thrashing on the mattress. "I need—" *more. I need so much more.* Still she couldn't bring herself to ask for what she needed. Too many encounters, too many bouts of torture had taught her that begging would get her nothing but more laughter and pain.

Dax moved between her legs, gently pressed his shaft into her and groaned.

"You're so tight, Minna. So hot. I don't know how long I can remain gentle, *mo fria.*"

She didn't want his gentleness. She wanted his caresses, his pleasure his…love. Minna gasped when he surged into her. His thick cock rubbing those places she'd only heard about before, yet never experienced before meeting the two brothers. Perhaps, this was naught more than a dream and she was still on her world hiding from its invaders. If that were so, she could only wish to die in her sleep, still in this dream—still with the cry of her climax on her lips.

DAX WATCHED HER as he slid into her. Her eyelids lowered. Still she looked at him with a hooded gaze. She threw her head back, her eyes glazing over, as he fully seated himself within her. Clenching his teeth, he managed to slide into her slowly several times before the mating lust took over and he began to ram into her with everything he had. He fought it. He wanted to be gentle—show her that not every male was the type of animal that had attacked her on her home world.

Her hands fluttered around his shoulders for a moment before one finally cupped his cheek and the other fisted in his hair, pulling his head to her breast. He feasted on the succulent flesh, needing the succor of her embrace as much as he needed to cum with his prick seated firmly inside her. He sucked her nipple into his mouth, laving the hardened peak with the flat of his tongue.

He set a hard rhythm, his cock pounding into her flesh as her hips rose to meet him. "Wrap your legs around my waist." The words came out rough, his voice gravelly as though he were about to change. He felt the familiar tickling sensation as his tiger tried to take over. Gathering his control, he pushed it back, filtering the need through his eyes and extremities. His cock grew impossibly larger as her wet velvet flesh grasped at him, sucking his shaft back inside her as he pulled nearly all the way out before plunging back in.

She wrapped her legs around his waist and he immediately grabbed her thighs, shoving them to her chest. Angling himself to thrust inside her deeper, he growled out his pleasure, his cat demanding he bring his mate more pleasure, more joy. His sac lifted, tightening against his body. The head of his cock flared out slightly as he neared his orgasm. Minna gurgled with surprised delight as the head of his shaft widened, rubbing areas in her velvety channel that had never been touched before. He shared her surprise, her elation and felt the utter triumph of knowing she had never cum so forcefully before in her life.

Her scream echoed throughout the room as he gathered control over his inner beast. His shaft returned to its normal dimensions as he emptied his seed deep into her womb. He lay panting over her, his weight on his elbows. He watched her throat work as she tried to speak. Ripples of aftershocks tore through them both and for a few moments, he knew neither of them could do much more than tremble and pant.

Minutes passed, or perhaps only a few seconds. In his stunned mind, he'd lost all sense of time. He hadn't expected that, hadn't expected their mating to have such a monumental significance. He quirked his lips in a small smile, careful to keep his cheek buried in Minna's hair. A small shudder worked through his body. Rage was going to be as stunned as he was when he told him what happened.

"Are you okay, Dax?"

How could he put into words how blessed he felt at this moment? He cleared his throat. "Yes, mate. I'm fine. I must be crushing you."

"No, it feels good, safe. I haven't felt safe in a long time."

"You'll always be safe with us." He sighed, hating the necessity of leaving her body. "We'll protect you even from ourselves."

He gently eased out of her clasping warmth and rolled to his side, dragging her into the shelter of his body. Curving himself around her, he brushed his hand over her belly where he hoped one day she would carry their cub.

He continued to smooth his hand over her tummy, petting her, showing her the devotion he felt but couldn't seem to put into words. He wanted to lie with her longer, just bask in the moment, but they had a ceremony to attend and already they were running late. "Though I want naught more than to lie with you the rest of this dawning, we must prepare for the joining ceremony, Minna."

He felt her tense within his arms, then relax, melding into him. "I'm nervous, Dax."

"There is naught to fear, my mate. The joining ceremony is a blessing in front of family. The bonding itself doesn't come until later, in the *Crystal Caverns of Goashi*, and is an intimate celebration."

"So, tonight, only you and Rage will be there?"

He could feel her quivering in his arms, his answer obviously very important to her. "Yes, Minna. Only the three of us. Only the Lady Goddess herself can intrude upon us tonight and it's been many, many years since she's blessed a union among our people in such a way."

He felt her sigh then relax back into his arms. No matter how much he enjoyed lying in their bed with her, it would have to wait. There was much to do still before the ceremony this evening. After placing a chaste kiss atop her head, he massaged her tummy once more before easing himself away. "It's time, Minna. The matrons will be meet us at the transport to prepare you for the joining."

RAGE WATCHED AS the transport approached the docking center. He couldn't wait to see his cousin Fane and his new Triad mates. They'd been away on *Savar* since their *Savari* mating and returned to *Tigeria* to have their mating recognized by their people. As the leader of the Gavaire *Tigerians*, there could be no doubt to the legitimacy of Fane's mating. Without a recognized *Tigerian* mating ceremony, when the time came for him to step down, his heir would be unable to take over leadership of the pride.

The shuttle door opened with a hiss. Fane was the first to leave the transport. As soon as his feet touched *Tigerian* soil, the Council Elders rushed to greet him. He ignored them all and turned to help his mate out of the shuttle, though it could be no more than a footspan drop between the transport and the ground.

Rage's breath caught in his throat when the woman first emerged from the vehicle. She was beautiful. Certainly no more beautiful than his own mate, but she had an air about her. One that said she was born to be the mate of a king. She held her head high, surveying the people gathered around. A man stepped up behind her and placed his hands on her shoulders. She tilted her head back and smiled. The man must be the other mate he'd heard about. He cast a look toward Minna and Dax.

Minna stood between them nervously clasping their hands. She'd been afraid to come, sure that she didn't belong at such an important state event. It took every bit of his and Dax's powers of persuasion to convince her, as their mate, she belonged here with them.

He watched as Fane tucked his mate beneath his arm and turned to face them. "This is Laynee," he turned to the man who stepped up on the other side of his woman and smiled. "And this is Sayre. You will welcome them to *Tigeria* in the warrior way. They are my triad mates and I claim them as my own." He turned to look out over the gathered crowd, his expression filled with aggression. "If anyone wishes to refute my claim on my mates, speak now or forever remain silent." His face told anyone who bothered to look, that he would fight for his mates. No one moved. No one made a single sound of protest. Who would want to attack their king?

Rage put his hands together. He looked over at Dax, raised his brow and continued his show of support. Soon, Dax and others followed suit, showing their ruler that they approved of his mates. Many would do anything to stop the fighting amongst themselves—anything to keep from mating with blood kin. Applause echoed through the compound as they celebrated the mating of their king. With luck there would soon be a royal heir. He looked between them, not missing the secret smiles and furtive touches, and grinned. Perhaps there would be many heirs.

A group of robed women pushed their way through the crowd and Rage knew it was time to bring Minna forward. Fane's gaze searched the throng, expecting to see them. He had insisted they join in the same ceremony. Time was precious and there was no reason to risk one's mate. Once tied to them by blood, the women would never be without protection. Blood ties made it possible to scent them anywhere and feel them even off world.

They stepped forward. Minna moved reluctantly. His hand at the small of her back, he gently pushed her forward until she was but a hand span from his cousin who looked down at her and smiled.

"I do not bite, my lady."

Her face tinged red with his words and she ducked her head. Rage nearly laughed with his joy. Soon he would be mated and there was no greater honor than an invitation to share the king's own ceremony.

Fane turned to his mate. "Laynee, this is the lady Minna. She is to share your mating day. I knew you would be a bit nervous and frightened but," he turned back to Minna, "She is even more so. Would you welcome her into your circle of friends?"

Laynee stepped forward and held out her hand. She glanced over her shoulder toward the approaching matrons. "Come with me, Minna. I just know we're going to be the best of friends. I'm from Calla. Where are you from, if you don't mind my asking?"

MINNA GAPED AT the young woman before her. She'd never seen a more beautiful woman in her life! Glossy black hair fell to her waist in long waves. Her large, gray eyes gazed at her with the promise of friendship and solidarity. She felt the goodwill radiating from Laynee. The woman was the ideal mate for royalty. Her aura glowed, nearly sang with her power, and her beauty could not be matched. The other woman's slender body, with its curves in all the right places, put Minna to shame. Even the purple markings, high on her cheekbones, couldn't detract from her loveliness. Warmth flooded her at the woman's soft touch and she smiled. This woman was compassion personified.

A discordant wave of energy passed through her as the matrons surrounded them. She glanced back at the males. All four of them watched as the matrons began to drag them away. Soon they would be alone with them. Soon she would be at their mercy.

"No!" she screamed, pulling her arm from the tight grasp of one of the women.

Rage and Dax rushed to her side. "What is it, *mo fria?*" Dax asked as he glanced around them searching for an intruder. "Why do you not wish to accompany the matrons so they may prepare you for your mating night?"

"I—I don't know." Still, she couldn't force herself to accompany them.

A noise sounded overhead and Fane sighed. "So much for my surprise," he said as another transport landed nearby.

"Laynee!" a female voice squealed and a woman ran to pull Laynee from the clutches of the matron at her side.

Minna gaped at the exact replicas of Laynee and Sayre. Two sets of twins mated to each other. She turned to look at her own mates. Three sets of twins, three people in a triad, and the three moons of the planets involved in such a phenomena. Was it coincidence or destiny?

It means you are fated to be a part of this, Minna. Do not question the will of the Great Mother.

She felt the blood drain from her face even as another wave of malevolence washed over her. She stumbled and Rage caught her, pulling her up against his hard frame.

"Something—" She shook her head. "No. Someone means to do us harm. I can feel it." She placed her hand over her stomach. "Someone doesn't feel right."

"What do you mean, my love?" Rage asked, as both he and Dax moved to hold her between them.

She wanted to sink inside them, just seep through their flesh and bone to hide within them where she would be safe. Steeling her resolve, she moved away, forcing herself to find the disharmonious chord in the music of their gathered energy. She moved slowly through the crowd of people and still, she couldn't find the cause.

Moving back to her mates, she took their hands. "I feel stronger when I am with you." She glanced over at the other two triads, watched as the men circled the women. "Perhaps if we band together, we can find the evil that attempts to form a bond with one or all of us."

After several anxious seconds, everyone nodded and formed a small circle. The nine people took each other's hands. The two sisters began to hum low, before beginning a ritual chant.

"With the power of one, this is begun. With the power of three, so shall it be. Three times three, let us see, let us see."

Soon, a bright circle of light surrounded them and Minna could only gape at the others who gathered round. Everyone's face was aglow with the show of such powerful magic. Except one. The matron who had gripped Laynee's arm with so much enthusiasm moved slowly through the crowd, backward.

Minna pointed to the woman. "There she is. It's her. She's different." She covered her stomach with her hand. "She appears to be *Tigerian* but she is not. She is something else."

The woman attempted to run, but the others captured her and dragged her to Fane and he glanced at Minna. "Are you certain she is not *Tigerian?*"

She nodded. "This woman is not what she appears to be." She furrowed her brow. "To tell the truth, I'm not even sure it's a woman." Fane growled, his canines extended. Beside her, she felt Rage and Dax stiffen.

"What are you if not one of our people, woman?" Fane demanded. Minna could see his aura quiver, darkening as his rage mounted.

The woman's lips turned up at the corners, yet it wasn't a smile. It seemed cold, somehow. Even cruel. "I am *Banart*, you *Tigerian* scum. You will comply with the doctrine or you shall perish like countless others."

RAGE TENSED, READY to take down the enemy among them—ready to protect Minna with his life if the need arose. Only the feel of Dax's hand on his shoulder kept him from attacking the treacherous *Banart*.

Thank you, brother.

You're welcome. Might I suggest we move to somewhere more secluded, somewhere we can interrogate the prisoner. I would wager you are not the only one who would like to rip into the enemy, and until we receive answers to our questions, we can't allow that to happen. There was a brief pause before Dax continued. *No matter how much I might enjoy watching a Banart suffer at the hands of our people as we have suffered at the hands of theirs.*

Rage nodded, turned his attention back to Fane, though carefully shielding his mate with his body. No way would he allow their enemy to get his hands on his mate. The cursed *Banart* would have to go through him first.

Us, Rage. They'd have to go through both of us before they'll lay a filthy hand on her.

You are right, he agreed with a curt nod.

"Fane, if I might suggest moving our prisoner to another location so that we may interrogate her."

Through their strengthening bond, Rage felt Minna's unease. Turning to her, he gazed into her eyes. Saw the very real fear there. "What is it, my love?"

"You don't know she is the only one. If I might suggest, send someone you trust explicitly to guard her, until the nine of us can check everyone here. There may be more *Banart* among you and while we're questioning her, another enemy could still be out here, doing whatever he—or she—came to do."

Rage's appreciation of his mate's intelligence and warrior spirit continued to grow. "Very wise advice, *mo fria*."

Turning toward the crowd of onlookers, he looked for his second in command of the *Tigerian* Security Forces, and outside his own family, his closest friend. It didn't take long for him to spot Kelson Galbar or for their gazes to lock. The *Galbar* Beta chose to join the *Gavaire Pride* when the *Banarts* had obliterated his entire village while he was away on a mate hunt and though it pained him that his friend had lost all his loved ones, he could only be thankful he now served at his side.

Kel must have sensed Rage's need because he quickly stepped away from the crowd he was attempting to hold back and made his way toward their small group. He stopped, gave a respectful bow then straightened his spine, his eyes never wavering from the *Banart* scum Fane and Sayre had within their grasp. "What can I do for you, Sirs?"

"I need you and three others to watch this imposter. Take her to the holding cells until we can interrogate her. Under no circumstances should anyone approach her. Detain anyone who approaches and hold them for questioning later. If it tries to escape or does anything you find might jeopardize the safety of our people, terminate it immediately. Understood?"

"Of course, Sir." Rage watched as Kel quickly called for assistance using the tiny transmitter interwoven in the cuffs of his uniform. It was a useful device in these times of war. Unless you knew the device was there, you'd never know to look for it. "They will be but a moment."

Rage nodded then turned his focus back toward their prisoner. The *Banart* stood defiantly, sneering at them in hatred. Even held firm, and surrounded, the creature showed no fear. That is what made this entire state of affairs dangerous.

Something was not right about this situation. Behind him, Dax straightened, stepped closer to Rage's side, completely blocking their mate from the *Banart's* view.

What is it you sense, Rage?

I'm not sure. This is not right. We've captured it and it is unafraid. It plans something.

"Do you think you can question me? That you can control me? I am a *Banart* and you are naught but animals." It spit on the ground at its feet. "You are beneath me. I am all. There are too many of us for you to conquer. Bow now before our power and might and we might let you live to serve our needs."

Rage watched as Fane's lip curled up, exposing his canines. Sayre, too, stepped closer to the prisoner. Fury and menace wafted off the pair in waves, and still the *Banart* did not flinch beneath their hate-filled gaze. His eyes glinted with deadly cold. A shiver worked down his spine and the hairs at the back of his neck stood on end. That alone sent warning waves through him.

He knew, just knew, something horrendous was about to happen.

"Fane, Sayre, all of you step away. Kel, have security lock on to the *Banart's* energy pattern and enclose it in an impenetrable shield." At almost the same moment the energy shield shimmered around the prisoner, she reached inside her left sleeve. He had no time to shout out a further warning as a second later, an explosion rocked the ground, sending everyone sprawling.

"Quick, don't let anyone out of your sight. Not until we have ensured no other enemies hide amongst us," Fane bellowed. Seconds later, *Tigerian* Security Forces surrounded everyone who'd attended the arrival ceremony, herding them together until the three Triads confirmed no other *Banarts* were hiding among them.

Knowing that his security forces were doing their job, Rage reached for Minna's hand, pulling her into his arms. Dax quickly stepped behind her, pressing her closer to Rage, wrapping them in their touch, their scent. Her entire frame quivered within their embrace. "Ssshh, *mo fria*. All will be well."

"It's all right, Minna. No one was harmed but the one who infiltrated us," Dax whispered against her temple.

"What if we'd gone with her? Every one of the matrons as well as your Alpha's mate would be dead right now."

"And you, mate. You too would have perished. But you used your gift, and such a tragedy was averted."

"Listen to your mates, little warrior." After kissing Laynee, Fane stepped forward. "If you'd not stopped my mate from going with the Matrons, we would have lost her, and all the other mated women of our pride. You have done a great service to the *Tigerian* people and we are indebted to you."

Minna lifted her head from where she'd had it buried against Rage's chest. Both he and Dax were aware that though she'd stopped any visible trembling, inside she still quaked with fear. She bit her bottom lip, worrying it, and Rage inwardly groaned. Now was not the time to let his hormones get the better of him. "My job is not done yet."

Behind her, Dax straightened, placed his hands atop her shoulders and squeezed gently in reassurance. "Our job, my love. Together, the nine of us, will make sure that no other *Banarts* hide among our people"

MINNA'S EYES GREW round as their craft flew over the wide plains. Farmers tended their crops. Animals that resembled the *p'lebies* she used to ride grazed lazily in the open fields. The pungent scent of freshly turned soil wafted up to the transport and she inhaled deeply. She'd never smelled anything like it in her life.

The entire countryside looked strange compared to *G'Recio*. The blue-green grass was so different from the golden fields of her home. Yet, the disparity was comforting. She knew she was no longer on her world. She knew there was no way she merely dreamed this up. She would never be at the mercy of the *Hienial* males ever again and that thought comforted her more than any other ever could.

"Look, Minna," Dax said, pointing to their left. A giant blue water lake stretched to the horizon. "That is the great lake, *Soribu*. The blue water tells us that the lake is healthy and the weather is just right for planting. Green water means there is little time before a storm arrives and brown . . ." He trailed off, a frown creasing his brow. "Murky brown means the world is dying and vast changes must be made or the world will perish. The lake has only been brown once in recorded history. Our people made changes to help our world heal. After ten years, the lake returned to its state of perpetual blue and green cycles."

"And we hope to keep it that way," Rage added as he turned from talking to the pilot. "Our scientists monitor the waters daily. We do not want another worrisome decade such as that one, ever again."

The craft moved lower, flying through the dense underbrush as they neared their destination. The jungle-like atmosphere surprised her. She hadn't expected such thick foliage after seeing the open plains with crops and grazing animals.

"Where are we?" she asked, leaning forward to look through the thick *illuma-glass*. She watched as they continued to drop closer to the ground. Rage wrapped his arm around her waist and smiled down at her. Swallowing, she couldn't help but think about how lucky she was to have these two men for her own. Her stomach quivered and gooseflesh rose on her skin. Dax moved around her other side and they boxed her in between them. She liked nothing more than keeping her men close. She sighed, loving the feel of their warm bodies pressed close to hers. With them, she was safe and would never need fear anything ever again.

"We approach the area near the crystal caves." He nodded toward the man at the controls. "Triston will drop us near our area, while the other transport will drop Fane and his mates near the royal arena. We shall have twelve hours of complete privacy before he returns for us."

"Oh." Her face blazed anew at what she knew awaited her here. It didn't seem to matter that she'd been with her mates many times. The things they did to her still seemed so new and fresh. She was unsure if she would ever grow used to it. Perhaps it was better if she didn't.

The transport slowed to a stop, resting on the ground. The vehicle hummed as the pilot held it in place while they disembarked. A large black bag and a good-sized basket were the only things they carried with them.

"Where did those come from?" she asked, as Dax threw the bag over his shoulder.

"It's full of things we will need this night." He waggled his brows and tossed a glance toward Rage. "He has our dinner. I hope it's packed full. We'll need all our strength," he cast a brilliant smile her way.

Minna almost swooned and reminded herself how lucky she was to have two such caring and virile mates. She only wished she could convince them to go to her world and save her sisters from the monsters that continually attacked them.

"After our ceremonial mating night is over we shall take a journey to rid your world of the *Hienial* plague. An army is being gathered as we speak."

Minna nearly slumped with relief at the knowledge. She still didn't like the thought that they could read her mind, but she supposed, it could come in handy in the future. Finally, her people would get the help they needed. She only hoped it wouldn't be too late.

They led her through the dense underbrush to a large outcropping of rock. She frowned, wondering how they expected to go any further—then she looked up.

"I'm not climbing up there." She shook her head and backed away. Looking from one mate to the other, she bit her lip. They had to understand, she couldn't do what they wished. "I—I'm not climbing up there," she pointed to the dark hole in the side of the cliff above them, before backing away. "I can't go into a cave." Tears pooled in her eyes and her vision blurred. "I—I just can't."

Her whole body trembled as she moved away from them. She stumbled over a large stone and would have fallen, had Dax not rushed to catch her. He pulled her close, palming the back of her head. Visions, memories of the dark, dank dungeon the *Hienials* kept her in, invaded her thoughts. She placed a hand between them, protectively covering her heaving stomach—just the though of being trapped in the close confines of a dark cave made her ill.

A mental picture of the cruel men, with their horrible grins, coming to violate her, nearly brought her to her knees. *How can a man—of any race— be so uncaring, so cruel, that he can use a woman then discard her like a broken toy when he's through?*

"Shh …, Minna. No one will force you to do something you do not wish," Dax said, pressing his lips to her ear. He trailed tiny kisses along her jawbone and neck. "We do not want this night to frighten you. We shall all stay here in the forest if that is your wish."

She looked between them, knowing—trusting—that they would respect her wishes. She sighed in relief when he sat on a large rock nearby and pulled her down onto his lap. They held her like that for almost two hours. When the sun set and the darkness settled in, her anxiety returned tenfold.

"I'm such a baby," she said through her chattering teeth.

"Sshhh…*mo fria.* You are no infant. You have reason to fear. We understand your concern. I only wish we could give you the light you need without entering the caves." Dax squeezed her hand.

"Why—why can't you?" She sniffed. "A lantern would work just as well out here as it would in the cave."

"Look up, my brave mate, and tell me what you see," Rage added, settling close to stroke the back of her head.

She tilted her head back, glanced up at the cave and her mouth fell open. Light spilled from the entrance. Like a beacon in the darkness, it drew her like a moth to a flame.

"How…?" She couldn't voice the rest of her sentence. She turned to Dax before glancing over at Rage. "How is the cave filled with light?"

"We cannot explain it as well as one of our scientists could." Rage smiled, looking a bit sheepish. "We can only tell you of our own theories." He continued at Dax's nod. "During the daylight hours, the crystals absorb the light and energy from the suns. They will continue to glow, only fading near sunrise when the cycle begins anew."

Minna glanced around her, wary of the creatures lurking in the dark. She never once thought that Dax and Rage wouldn't protect her from them. Yet she still didn't like the thought that they were there. She didn't like the idea of the close confines of a cave, either but she couldn't bear the darkness. Too many things hid in the darkness…

She ran a trembling hand through her hair and licked her lips. "Well then, the cave it is, I guess." She stood and stepped closer to the sheer rock face, reached out and placed her hand against the cool stone. "How do we get up there? I think it's only fair to warn you that I do not climb well."

Rage and Dax merely smiled at her as they each took one of her hands. "You will not need to climb, *mo fria*, we shall carry you." She looked up toward the cave and snorted. "Yeah, right. I'm too heavy to carry. You'll slip and we'll all fall to our deaths." Her eyes widened as Rage began to remove his clothes. "What are you doing? You can't climb this thing naked!"

She shrieked, jumping into Dax's arms as Rage transformed from a man to a huge white tiger.

"It is Rage, Minna," Dax said, pushing her closer to the big cat. "You know he would never harm you."

She looked into the tiger's eyes and somehow saw Rage within the cerulean depths. Reaching out, she placed a hand on his head and curled her fingers through the soft fur behind his ears. He purred loud and made a slight coughing noise that made her jump.

"Climb onto his back, Minna. He will carry you to the cave." Dax shed his clothes beside her, stuffed them and Rage's into the bag and hung the strap around his neck. "Do not be frightened of us, Minna. We are the same men who gave you such pleasure last night. Allow us to do so again."

She swallowed a scream as her other mate transformed into a tiger as well. Looking between them, she climbed onto Rage's back, wrapped her arms around his neck and let him carry her to the cave. It was strange, this new life of hers, and she wondered if she would ever get used to it.

Tighten your hold on me, mate. I do not wish you to fall.

She squeezed him tighter, digging her heels into his side, the way she'd always done with the *p'lebies* she rode on her uncle's farm when she visited him in the summer.

Rage's muscles bunched and flexed just before he leapt into the air. Large claws appeared from his giant paws and dug into the rock ledge. He pulled with his front legs while his back legs scrambled for purchase. Another long leap brought them to the ledge in front of the cave and she slipped from his back, speechless. It didn't take long for Dax to join them. Unencumbered by her extra weight, he made the leaps easily and soon stood beside them, staring into the wondrous cave, with the handle of the basket in his mouth.

Minna stood looking between them for a long moment. Her heart slammed in her chest as they changed back to their human form. They stood naked before her, their hearts visible in their eyes. Those eyes pleaded with her for acceptance, not to call them monster, and suddenly she knew. They may have strange, unbelievable powers but, deep down, she knew they would never harm her. And she loved them.

When faced with entering the cave, she ached to run screaming into the darkness but she lacked the courage, even for that. One foot in front of the other, one step after another, she let them lead her into the cave.

Lined with the colorful stones that seemed to wink at her, the glowing caves looked magical. Awed, she continued down the narrow passage until it widened to a vast cavern. The interior of the cavern looked larger than her entire village on *G'Recio*. She lifted her head, ensuring no flying creatures were hovering above her and gasped in awe. The cavern seemed to reach into the heavens themselves.

In the center of the huge, glowing room, surrounded by a ring of standing stones, lay a large pool of steaming water. Clouds of moisture hovered over the small lake. A soft breeze coming from another passage blew the tufts of steam into small whirls over the bubbling water. Colorful crystals beneath the churning surface gave the pool an ethereal glow.

"It's beautiful." She gazed around her, thinking nothing could be further from the dank dungeon where the *Hienials* held her prisoner. She threw her arms around Rage. "It's so magical. How did your people ever discover it?" she asked, releasing Rage to hug Dax to her. She didn't want him to feel left out. She never wanted to hurt them, either of them.

"It has been our ceremonial mating area for eons. I don't think anyone knows when it was first discovered."

Rage pressed against her back, his hard cock pressing into her rear. "This has been the private area for newly mated pairs and triads since the beginning of recorded history. I'm glad you approve of it, mate. It is a beautiful place."

Minna leaned back, pressing her ass against his jutting hardness. Dax, at her front, separated the robe covering her. It slid off her shoulders, to land in a puddle of silk on the cavern floor. Warm air caressed her hardened nipples and she moaned. Rage kissed her throat, gently suckling and biting the sensitive flesh where her shoulder met her neck.

Water splashed as Dax backed down into the water, drawing her with him. She went willingly, this was their night and she would do whatever it took to see that they received their pleasure.

Rage, at her back, continued to massage her neck and shoulders. She attempted to turn, to tell him that she wished this night to be theirs. He grasped her by the shoulders and kept her turned away.

"This night is for you, *mo fria*. Tonight, we shall gift you with all the pleasure you can stand." Rage moved closer behind her, crowding her into Dax's front.

They sandwiched her between them, pressing their bodies ever closer and she groaned with longing and frustration. Would they never give her the chance to show them she could pleasure them? Didn't she please them?

We know what you wish to do, Minna, and we cannot wait to feel your hands on our flesh. But, you come first. Dax's voice rang in her head.

You shall always come first, Rage said, his lips caressing her shoulders. Pushing her hair aside, he trailed kisses to her ear, his tongue laving the outer shell. *We will allow you your way soon enough, but first, we want to feel your flesh around us, milking us of every last drop of cum. After Dax is through fucking your pussy and I am done with your sweet, tight ass then you shall have your way with us.*

Rage's arms snaked around her and she groaned when his hands covered her breasts. Gentle fingers plucked at her nipples and she felt Dax kneel in the water before her.

Strong hands lifted her, placing her legs over Dax's wide shoulders, opening her up for him. Her entire body quivered with anticipation as his warm breath caressed her thighs. Too long. It had been too long since her mates had touched her, been with her. She nearly smiled at the thought. If one would have told her even a week ago that she would crave the touch of a man, she would have thought them mad.

Dax's tongue snaked out and tasted her flesh and she mewled with pleasure. Arching up, she pressed her legs into his shoulders, seeking the warm silk of his mouth.

"Yesss," she hissed when his tongue slid through her slit. Her legs tightened around his shoulders as he parted her swollen lips and suckled her clit. He alternated between lapping up her cream and suckling her swollen nub.

Rage, still at her back, supported her upper body, his hands busy at her breasts. A rush of sensation moved between her breasts to her pussy. Invisible threads of pure pleasure rode through her body, invading her very soul until she couldn't think. She could only feel. Rage thrust his tongue into her ear and she screamed out her pleasure as Dax continued to suckle her clit and feast at her pussy. Never in her life had she ever dreamed that such pleasure was possible.

When Dax finished lapping up the cream from her orgasm, he gently pulled her legs from his shoulders. She sagged, her body held upright by Rage's embrace. She had no doubt that if he'd have let her go, she would have slumped into the water and happily drowned.

"What was it you were saying about pleasuring us?" Dax asked with a chuckle. He glanced over at Rage and grinned. "I think our mate is going to be too exhausted to do as she wants." Turning back, he looked into her eyes. "Because we are far from through with you, mate."

"Oh, my!" she said when Dax stood and she got a good look at his hard cock.

He grinned at her while he stroked the length of his shaft. "Shifting always makes us bigger. This will be a night to remember, Minna. For Rage and I both are going to fuck you tonight and our cocks are bigger than you are used to. I want to feel your pussy wrapped around me, milking my cum from my balls." He shivered slightly. "Even now, I can feel them tingling with the urge to cum deep inside you." His hips shifted forward, pressing his cock closer as Rage steered her into the deeper water.

"Feel the water, Minna? It's silky, smooth. It is the best lubricant our people have for a mating night such as this," Rage whispered in her ear. "A natural oil in the water will soothe your ass as I press into it. Can you feel how hard I am for you?"

She hadn't until just that moment. His question made her hyperaware of the impossibly large erection pressed against her back. She squeezed her eyes shut, her anxiety causing her heart to slam erratically in her chest. How would the two of them ever fit inside her at the same time? It wasn't possible, was it?

She gasped when Dax bent forward and took her nipple in his mouth. His hand worked at her other breast as Rage moved his hand down between her legs, his finger circling her clit.

"Please," she gasped.

"Please, what?" Rage whispered in her ear. "Tell us what you want, Minna."

"Please, you two. Fuck me. Please!" Her face blazed as the words left her lips. She couldn't believe she needed their hard cocks inside her so much that she ached with it—that she literally begged for it. She'd come a long way from the abused woman she was only a few short days ago. She had her handsome mates to thank for that.

"Look at me, Minna," Rage whispered while he laved her ear. She turned to look and he said, "No, look at me while I touch you."

She looked down at him while his hand worked between her legs. She spread her legs wider, giving him better access as she thrust her hips out to get a better look at his hand between her legs.

"That is me pleasuring you. Do you like what you see?"

crossed beneath her breasts. She did not have time for this. She needed to get to the surface before her former co-workers. Otherwise, she'd never be recognized as an Archeologist in her own right. But, what could she do? If she didn't inform Laynee of what she discovered, didn't tell her or her coven sister what had befallen this planet, how could she live with herself? She had to tell someone.

She'd worked too hard, her innate goodness and naiveté always used against her by her peers. They stole her research, her findings, time and again, always passing them off as their own. Not this time. Even if she were of a mind to do as her sister witch requested, and performed the spell, she had no time for a mate right now. If she did have the inclination to follow her vows to harm none she would put her mates second, after her work, where they must stay.

Running her hand through her hair, Ana knew in her soul she couldn't just not sit idly by just because she didn't want to be browbeaten about the spell. Though she'd lose her chance at reaching the ruins, there was no justification for not making a transmission that could save thousands of lives.

Ana couldn't help but recall the last conversation she'd had with her priestess just over a moon ago, before she'd set off on her mission alone. As she looked down at the planet below, all she could see was the past.

"I know you're frightened, Ana, but you mustn't be. I'm forwarding another copy of the text to you," Laynee Mikalosa said, as she pushed a button on her console. "I know you, and I know you destroyed it as soon as you received it. You must conduct the spell, and bring your mate to you. It works."

"I don't want a mate." Rachana said, her bottom lip pushing out in a full pout as she crossed her arms beneath her breasts. "I refuse to do this."

"You cannot refuse, Ana. The world, the entire galaxy is relying on you, on us, to rid the universe of the *Banart* evil. What is a little thing like sharing your life with others when it can destroy those who are so evil?"

"I will think about it, Laynee. I cannot promise you more."

Laynee sighed. "That's better than a firm refusal, I guess. Please think hard on this before you destroy the spell book."

Ana sighed. "I will. Have a nice trip with your new mates. I hope everything turns out just the way you want it to."

After disconnecting the transmission, Ana looked around her. Her gaze wandered around the small shuttle she'd use to escape *Carrillia* in her effort to get to the *Great Desert of Briama* on *G'Recio's* Southern Hemisphere. There she hoped to find the ruins of the Mother Goddess' sacred temple of Wisdom.

Legends spoke of a time where one could sit with the Mother Goddess herself, absorb her wisdom and her teachings. She wanted—no needed—to discover if such a place existed. It was the sole reason she had become an archeologist and she would let no man stand between her and what she wanted most. Not ever again.

The near-collision warning system began to blare, tugging Rachana back to the here and now. Knowing that more than likely her dream would never come to pass, she pulled out of orbit and headed for deep space. She needed to be far enough away to have a chance of escape if the *Hienial* people learned of her communication.

Six hours later, Rachana made the call that would forever change her life.

"This is Rachana Salura, calling Fane Gavaire of the planet *Tigeria* and Dare Raden of the planet *Savar*. The people of *G'Recio* are under attack. I repeat. The *Banart* and the *Hienial* have attacked the planet of *G'Recio*. Immediate assistance is required."

With that done, Ana leaned back in her seat and stared out into the vastness of space. She'd given up her dream, and now her heart felt as bleak and empty as the cold space that surrounded her small ship.

SEX ME IN

Rachana Salura watched from the safety of her cloaked ship as she waited for help to arrive. How long would those animals stay? She hoped they stayed long enough for a rescue party to arrive and wipe them from the face of this planet—from the entire galaxy. A week had passed since she'd made the call, begging for assistance. Sometimes she wondered if help would ever arrive.

She did another surface scan. The men were attacking the defenseless women again. They were disgusting and repugnant. Their very existence caused entire worlds to shudder. Thankfully, she'd never been captured and used by the *Hienials*, but she'd known too many who had. The *Banarts* were cruel, worthless enemies. Many times they had infiltrated planets, killing and maiming as they went. Still, they weren't as bad as this. At least they put their victims out of their misery when they finished with them. These monsters forced their victims to live.

The *Hienials* were no better than animals. They used the poor, unwilling women of the planets they conquered as human incubators for their bastard children. She shuddered at the thought. They were beasts, plain and simple.

She jumped when her reminder alarm went off. Settling back down in her seat, she made a face at the note on the screen in front of her. Tonight was the night. It was time to fulfill her coven vow to allow harm to none—it was time to at least attempt to draw a mate into her life. How one ambitious archaeologist having a mate could make a difference in the war against tyranny, she would never understand. Besides, it wasn't acquiring a mate that she wanted to avoid. One mate she could deal with. It was the warning from her coven sisters that she may have a second mate waiting for her that rankled. One man she could control. Two men would control her. It was unacceptable.

First things first though, she must break orbit before someone detected her. She would be an easy target on this research vessel alone. Ana tapped her chin, wondering if she should break orbit and call for help again. She bit her lip. But was anyone even close? She'd called for help several times and no one answered her pleas.

She brought her craft around and hid behind one of the moons. The last thing she wanted was for someone to sneak up on her while she was distracted and performing her ritual.

"This is Rachana Salura, the Captain of the *Carrillian* research ship *Adventurer* requesting assistance—I repeat, I require assistance. The *Hienials* have invaded *G'Recio.* They are attacking the *G'Recians.* It is an unprotected populace, mainly women and the elderly with no weapons or warriors to protect them. Please," she begged. "We need assistance!"

Ana glanced around the inside of her small shuttle and knew that if no one answered her call, they would all perish. She'd stayed in orbit around this planet too long to travel to another occupied system and her resources were running low. Soon, she would have no food or water. More importantly, in three days she would run out of oxygen.

At that time she would either have to land on the surface, making herself vulnerable to attack or she would perish here in this small craft. She chuckled mirthlessly. The *Adventurer* was no more a research vessel than her small niece's *walk-around* buggy. The craft was nothing more than a small shuttle she'd appropriated during an attempt to escape the academic thievery of her peers. She'd escaped them all right.

"Well, nothing to be done about it now," she said to herself as she scanned through the pages of the spell book. Having decided not to use any of the spells and making up her mind to try the visualization techniques provided in the large, digital book of shadows, she skipped to the directions and read them one more time before she started her mental ritual.

A small smile curved her lips. She would fulfill her vow to attempt to help the galaxy by performing the rite, but no one ever said she had to mean it. Perhaps if there wasn't immense power behind it, she would only draw one male to her. One male she could handle—perhaps even dominate. If she couldn't dominate she would, at least, demand equality.

Equality was a laughable concept among most males she'd ever had the pleasure of meeting. They demanded fidelity while not giving any of their own. They demanded her submission when she needed some semblance of control to reach her pleasure. They demanded her love while remaining aloof. She would never succumb to the advances of a *Carrillian* male ever again.

Closing her eyes, Ana pictured her ideal male. When the faces of two men filled her mind, she stopped, cursing. She refused to have two males. Determined to choose between them, she closed her eyes fully intending to banish one from her thoughts. Yet she couldn't. How could she choose between two such gorgeous men? Instead, she concentrated on thinking of their characters. Her male must be brave, yet kind. He must be handsome, yet not narcissistic. A good sense of humor was also good. He must allow her to stand by his side, instead of shoving her behind him. And, most importantly, he must love her above all others.

Ana pictured her two males and included her stipulations for her mate's character. No two males would meet her criteria. If—by some small miracle of fate—they did, she must accept them both. She would never have the heart to choose between two such ideal specimens. Several moments passed as she visualized her perfect men. Strong, handsome men—at least one of which who would love her, cherish her, forever.

Suddenly, her proximity alarms began to shriek. "Warning, warning, collision imminent!" the computer generated voice blared over the speakers.

Rachana rushed back to the pilot's seat, frantically pressing buttons. Bringing up the viewscreen, she cloaked the ship just before two large warships blinked into view. Their sudden arrival could only mean one thing— her much anticipated help had arrived.

She frowned down at her scanner console. Why were they arming their weapons against each other? Her fingers flew over the console as she searched radio frequencies, hoping to hear something, anything, from these people before they blew each other to hell. She needed them. The *G'recians* need them.

"Stand down, unknown vessel. We demand the return of our leader!"

"We do not deal with kidnappers and terrorists. We demand the return of our captain!"

The two disembodied voices demanded the same thing.

"Men!" she spat, disgusted. She dismissed the coincidence though the hairs on the back of her neck stood on end. "Why must they always insist on getting their way without giving in return? They each would go to war before admitting that the other has taken another prisoner." She almost scoffed at the two ships, willing to destroy each other rather than admit their transgressions. "They would rather go to war than release the two men. Utter stupidity." She shook her head. "But what did I expect? They *are* males."

Again, the hairs on the back of her neck prickled and a shiver of unease shimmied down her spine.

"You don't seem to have much regard for males, woman. Perhaps you haven't met one to your liking? Yet."

Turning, she shrieked and jumped from her seat. "How—how did you get here?" she asked the strange man standing before her. Yet she knew. This man had visited her dreams. She watched him warily as he stepped closer. The same orange-gold hair with black tips graced his head. The same muscular body stood before her. The muscles of his large arms flexed as he moved. She loved the way they bunched and released as he moved to sit at the console she had just vacated. His green gaze bored into her, pinning her feet to the deck. Her mouth had gone dry with the effort to speak as her mouth opened and closed several times in an effort to communicate. She closed her eyes and opened them slowly, berating herself for her apparent loss of wits.

"I must tell my ship where I am before they fire on an innocent vessel," he said, his fingers flying over the flat panel. "*Tigerian* vessel *Bengalli*, stand down. This is Kel Galbar, Commander of the *Tigerian* security forces. I repeat—stand down. I am not being held on the unidentified ship." He looked around the cramped bridge of her stolen craft. "I appear to be aboard a small shuttle." He turned to look at her. "Where the hell am I and how did I get here?"

Ana licked her lips. Her heart stuttered in her chest as she stared at her dream man. He was broad of shoulder and handsome as a *Truan* actor. Who could ever resist a man like him? What woman in her right mind would want to? His strange golden hair, with its black tips, hung around his shoulders in silky waves. It appeared soft. She fisted her hands. Her fingers itched to feather through it to see if it was truly as soft as it looked. His broad shoulders tapered down to a hard stomach she could see even through the thick material of his *shert.* Thick muscles rippled beneath the rough fabric. A movement in his lower regions set her to blush as she realized her scrutiny gave the poor man a hard cock he couldn't hide, though he tried as he turned sideways to talk into the radio once more.

"Advise the unidentified ship that we believe their leader is aboard this vessel as well. I will investigate the matter and contact you as soon as possible." He turned and pierced Ana with a fierce gaze. "Where am I?" He stood. "Answer me." His lips tipped up at the corners. "Or would you prefer I convince you to answer?" A perfect golden brow arched in question. "I can be quite persuasive."

Ana swallowed thickly. *What to do, what to do…* Her gaze darted around the small room and she gauged the distance to the door. Maybe she could make it off the bridge and lock herself in her small sleeping quarters. He could just radio his ship and have them transport him off her shuttle. Taking a deep breath, she lunged for the door. She took several steps more than she figured she'd be able to when she turned back to see if the man followed her, just before she ran into a wall.

A very hard wall of delectable male flesh. "Oh, my!" Her heart stuttered at the sight of the man before her. He had to be over two meters tall. His short black hair curled around his collar and his broad chest tapered down to a narrow waist and hips. He was the epitome of tall, dark and handsome with dark eyes that reminded her of the cocoa bean that her uncle brought back from a distant planet.

Her breath came in short pants as she tried to bring her breathing under control. Her hand fluttered to her chest and she stood staring between the two men who now occupied her small craft, making it smaller by the minute.

"Who are you, woman, and why am I here?" the new man asked, his thinned lips told her he would demand true answers.

Her face blazed as she stood gawking between them. She knew she must explain her actions, but she also knew he would most likely not believe her. Besides, why would one so handsome care to mate with one such as her? She was certainly nothing special and, well, this man was nothing short of a god! They both were.

"I—I"

The first man, the red head, stepped forward. "I think I can explain."

"And who are you? Her accomplice in this?" His stance became more aggressive. "Know this *Tigerian,* I am the leader of my people. They will not stand for my abduction."

The *Tigerian* stepped forward. "I have nothing to do with your presence, *my lord,*" he said, scathingly. "I merely appeared here myself. Yet I know, from my own leader, that women such as she can call forth the men meant to be their bound mates." He smiled, the gesture never reaching his eyes. "Believe me, if you wish to forego your rights as her triad mate, I would be more than happy to remain with her as a pair."

The man turned to stare at Ana and she squirmed under his scrutiny. "I am Wray Navedis, alpha of my people. They will not stand silent over my disappearance long. We have come in answer to a distress call, knowing full well that it could be a trap, yet unwilling to gamble the innocent lives of rare females."

"Women are few among your people as well?" the one called Kel asked. "It seems that women are scarce everywhere in the universe with the exception of two planets." He flicked a glance to the view screen as if he could see the planet on the other side of the moon. "This planet and *Carrillia.*"

Wray shook his head. "No, there is another. We were on our way there for a mate hunt. We have been told it is a planet rich with life where the women outnumber the men three to one."

Kel shook his head. "The lucky bastards. I hope you will share the whereabouts of this world with my people. We need women as well."

"That remains to be seen." He moved over to the console and slid his hand along the smooth surface. "Wray Navedis to the *Lupin* starship *Nomad.* Cease your aggression." He turned to face Ana once again, pinning her with a stare. "How and why did you bring us here, woman?"

WRAY STARED AT the miracle before him, clenching and unclenching his hands at his sides. The female was beauty personified. If he had the privilege of choosing a woman for his mate, he would choose her. But his people did not have that luxury. Fate chose their women for them. His people had learned hard lessons throughout the millennia that fate was not a force to trifle with.

He closed his eyes and breathed in her delicate scent—the scent of her soap, her perfume and the musky scent of her arousal. His body hardened with her close proximity. Would she accept him as was required? He must find his mate and bear heirs or his would be a short occupation of the throne, like his alpha before him. The last thing their people needed was another campaign. They needed a leader and they needed him now. Still, no female had ever garnered such a reaction from him. Snapping his eyes open, he fought the urge to lean close and immerse himself in her tantalizing scent. Perhaps he could pull it in through his pores. She stirred a response in him that was unfamiliar. He hoped she was his mate, his salvation. Could he be that lucky?

Wray couldn't help but stare at the woman standing so regally before him. She was a goddess, plain and simple. Her dark hair hung about her shoulders in long waves. The color reminded him of the mahogany chest his father brought back from that distant planet so rich with females. Her amber eyes nearly glowed with the intensity of her resolve.

She stubbornly raised her chin and, despite her obvious fear, looked him square in the eyes. "I have made a vow, sir. To fulfill it, I was required to recite a spell. One that would bring my—" She cut herself off and nervously licked her lips.

His cock jerked in response, what he wouldn't give to feel those full lips wrapped around his shaft. He wanted nothing more than to bury his fingers deep in her hair as he thrust his cock deep into her perfect mouth. He felt her fear and excitement, the rush of adrenaline and sexual energy rolled off her, bombarding him with a depth of feeling he never knew was possible.

"I—I'm a witch. I made vow with my coven mates to do everything in my power to keep harm from all who have no evil in their hearts."

She swallowed and licked her lips again. Goddess, he didn't know whether he could control himself if she didn't stop doing that. His whole body ached with the need to bury his thick length inside her over and over until she screamed her climax to the heavens. He blinked slowly, trying to keep himself from jumping on the poor woman. Every hair on his body stood on end, reaching for the amazing creature before him. His skin tingled, and even though he knew it was impossible, his skin prickled anew each time she exhaled. It was as if he could feel her breath caressing his skin, increasing his incredible desire to have the woman beneath him on the deck, both of them as naked as the day they were born.

"And?" He prompted, needing to keep her talking before he pounced on her and made her his. "That doesn't explain how I merely blinked and found myself in your sleeping chamber." Her face blazed at that and he almost felt sorry for her. Almost.

"We must bring our mates into our lives to fulfill our vow."

This keeps getting better and better. Very interesting that she called forth her mate and he had been the one to arrive. It was quite propitious. "Your mates," he asked, giving her a level look. "Plural. As in you want more than one?"

Frowning, she stomped her foot like a petulant child. "Of course I don't want more than one." She closed her eyes and appeared to count to herself before she continued. "According to the High Priestess, we must all call our mates into our lives using a spell we take from this spell book." She pulled out a communications device, opened the saved spell book and thrust it at him. "We are to call our mates to us using one of those spells or make one of our own. The three then form a powerful triad that is necessary to fight the evil *Banarts* before they enslave the entire galaxy."

"Necessary how?" he asked, merely to keep her talking. He loved the sound of her voice. It was so sexy. Low and sultry, it sent tendrils of desire shooting through his blood, making it burn with the need to have her, to possess her. His cock jerked with the anticipation of sinking into her moist heat. "How could three people possibly make any difference?"

"How am I supposed to know?" she asked with an elegant shrug. "I merely followed the instructions sent to me by my priestess and here you are." She cast a glance back to the *Tigerian*. "Here you both are." She flung herself down into the nearest seat, pushing the console out of her way. Turning, she stared dejectedly through the *illuma-glass* into the cold darkness of space. "If I'd have known this was expected of me before the vows, I never would have spoken them. Any of them."

Wray felt a strange wrenching in his chest. Putting his hand over his heart, he knelt beside her. "Why would you have refrained, little one?" he asked, surprised that he felt the need to know—surprised that he even gave a damn. "Why do you resist taking a mate?" He gave her a crooked grin, glanced at the other man then added, "Or two for that matter. I'm not such a bad sort and I hear the *Tigerians* are honorable men of their word."

"Because I—I…"

Her face reddened and he knew it was something to do with the mating itself. He suppressed a grin and placed a gentle hand over hers. "Because you what, little one?"

"Rachana, call me Rachana or Ana. Little one makes me seem like some small child." She swiped at a tear, not realizing how much like a child she looked with the tears streaming down her face, coupled with her small stature.

Wray reached up and thumbed a tear from her cheek. "Rachana is a beautiful name." Resting back on his heels, he pressed her further. "Why do you fear the mating, Ana?"

"Because," she said, twisting the material of her jumper with trembling fingers. "I need…" She shook her head. "I can't. I can't tell you. It's too personal."

"Ana," he said, placing his fingers beneath her chin to tip her head back. "By your own admission, we are your mates. If you cannot share something so personal with us, who can you share it with?"

KEL STEPPED FORWARD, unwilling to remain silent any longer. As they both had said, they were all mates. He would have his say in this as well. "I find I must agree with him, Ana. It would seem that we are all in this together. If you cannot share your secret with us, then you must bear it alone."

He found himself staring at her. He couldn't help it. She sat with her large amber eyes glowing up at him. Delicate hands she held in her lap, fumbled with the material of her jumpsuit. The tiger in him snarled, needed to rip her clothes from her trim body and make her his in every sense of the deed. He wanted this woman with an intensity he didn't know was possible. His body itched with the need to change. His bones ached from holding it at bay. Yet he held it back, using every power, every force he held within him. Frightening her was the last thing he wanted to do.

He glanced over at the stranger, wondering how the man had heard of the *Tigerians* but they had heard nothing of Wray Navedis and his people. "How do you know of us, sir?" he asked, needing to know how many other races knew of his people when they tried so hard to keep themselves secret. Apparently, there were no secrets in the galaxy, except perhaps, that of Wray Navedis and his people. "Where do you come from, Navedis? Why have I not heard of you before?"

"I have just taken on the mantle of leadership for my people. Perhaps the name Oreside Lupin would mean a bit more."

Kel stepped back. It felt like someone had just punched him in the gut. "Yes," he said, after swallowing thickly. "That name does ring a bell. I take it that he has expired?"

Wray gave a short nod. "Yes. He was murdered in his sleep. Since he had no mate, the bitch he tried to breed with had him murdered when he couldn't get her with child."

"Some women are strange creatures when it comes to wanting a cub in their arms," Kel said with a nod.

"It wasn't the lack of cubs that made her do so. It was greed, plain and simple. She wanted to mate with the alpha and a leader with no heirs is always challenged. She merely chose her champion poorly. Our people will not follow an alpha with no honor. They arrested him and campaigned for a new alpha." He smiled, baring lethal-looking canines. "Care to guess who won?"

Kel snorted. "I don't need to guess. Anyone willing to look can see that you're an alpha."

"Then most of my people were blind. None of them could see that," Wray said with a shrug. "Until I made them."

"That can be so with any government. The people refuse to see what is right before their eyes. Refuse to see that sometimes, things must come to pass no matter how much they abhor the idea," Kel agreed. Still he knew being beta to this man would be preferable than having no mate at all. He'd already resigned himself to remaining an unmated male. As the last of his line, with females growing so scarce, he'd never expected to bond with anyone. He didn't want to take a precious female from a male of a strong house. He didn't feel he had the right.

Turning back to the woman he wondered what secret she held that kept her silent on her own ship. Loath to press her to answer when she clearly wasn't comfortable with them, he continued to steer the conversation away from the matter.

"We should help those in need before the *Hienials* kill them all."

Ana moved to her console, her fingers flying over the glassy smooth surface, "They will not kill them outright, though most of them may wish they were dead. The *Hienials* use them to breed. They have no females of their own and the women never bear a female child."

"What is it with the lack of females?" Wray asked, shaking his head. "You would think it would be an isolated problem. Not one so widespread throughout the galaxy."

"It must be something that happened several generations ago. We started noticing a decline in female births five generations ago. It's only been recently that the decline has become sharp enough to alarm anyone." Kel watched the woman to see how she would react to his next declaration. "Our scientists believe it could have been a virus, one that has spread among those of us who have the power to shift."

Wray snorted. "A disease specifically designed to eradicate shifters? Not likely."

"Why not?" Kel continued quickly before Wray could interrupt him. "It appears as though the only races affected are those of us who have the ability to shift. It would make sense that there is something in our genetic make-up that could give us a disease or virus that would affect only us." He glanced at Ana. "Perhaps the humans are immune."

Wray looked at him with a new understanding dawning on his face. "You're right. It does make sense. It also makes sense that the *Hienials* are attacking these women. They have been unable to breed for generations. If they can get children on these women, they have a whole new way to perpetuate a species that never should have been." He glanced through the *illuma-glass,* a thoughtful expression on his face. "I've heard of an ancient civilization who attempted to rid the galaxy of a parasitical race who thrived on attacking and killing those whom they deemed weaker, regardless of their ability to fight." He turned and strode back to a console and sat, his fingers flying over the keyboard. "The ancient race attempted genocide on a brutal dog-like species with an engineered virus. I'd never agreed with the practice before. But now…" He glanced up at them. "I think the *Hienials* are the people they attempted to eradicate—and they have infected us all. Our only hope is to mate with the human women who seem to be immune to it."

Kel felt his eyes widen. "Then we must do our best to kill them all. I have heard of the ancient plan myself. It's taught to us during our primary school years. According to the ancient texts, they are a vile, disgusting people who not only torture their enemies, but eat them alive when they are through." He turned to see Ana pale at his declaration and wished he'd kept that last to himself. Striding over to her, he stood close enough to catch her, lest she should faint. "We must notify our ships immediately. Those animals must be stopped as soon as possible."

ANA STARED AT the two beautiful men before her then gave a curt nod. They were right. They needed to save the people on the planet they orbited. Her secrets could wait for another time. Standing she looked from one to the other. "Whose ship will I be on?" She turned her attention back to the console, brought up her life-support screen and indicated it with a negligent sweep of her hand. "You two have nearly depleted what little oxygen there was left on my craft. I need to dock." She looked between them. "Which one of you will invite me to your vessel?"

"I will."

"Come to my ship."

They both spoke at once.

Wray held up his hand. "She will come to my ship. As leader of my people I can guarantee her safety." He looked over at Kel. "Can you say the same?"

Kel nodded. "I can. It would not mean so much as your declaration. But, know this Navedis. If she goes with you, so do I."

The other man nodded. "A fair proposal, *Tigerian*."

She gave her console attention again as the proximity alarms began to blare again. "Three more ships have arrived. According to the sensors, one *Tigerian* and one *Savari* vessel and another ship that looks just like yours, Wray Navedis."

"All the more reason for her to go to my ship," Wray said with a growl.

Kel nodded. "I have no argument, wolf."

SEATED AROUND THE conference table in Strategic Command aboard the *Lupin* Starship, *Nomad*, were all four of the newly formed Triads. They were introduced to her as soon as she entered the conference room and she'd found each of them interesting in their own right.

Everyone—men and women alike—sat in stony silence as Rachana reported *G'Recio's* current situation. Only Minna's unflinching courage gave Ana the courage to speak of the atrocities she witnessed on the planet below.

"Minna, is there anything you can add? Anything you can think of that might help us defeat them? Perhaps, you know of a weakness we can exploit?" Ana hated having to put the woman through this after what she'd already suffered, but for now, she was the best source of intel they had.

Minna, the only female of the third Triad, grimaced then straightened her spine. Though her eyes were open, Ana knew the only thing Minna could see was the past. Her mates must have sensed the same thing because Rage reached for her hand and gave it a quick squeeze, while Dax spoke to her in a soothing tone. "We're here baby, remember that. You'll never be alone again, my love. That's a vow Rage and I will never break."

She placed a slow tender kiss first on Rage's lips then Dax's before she began her tale. "Looking back, we have only ourselves to blame." When everyone at the table started to rise to refute her statement, she shook her head. "No, it's the truth. You need to hear it—all of it."

After everyone settled back into his or her chairs, she continued. "About eighteen moon cycles ago, we received an urgent message from the *Carrillian* government, requesting—no, begging—to send in military reinforcements. The message claimed the *Banart* army invaded their home world while their own military forces were off planet fighting their own battles with the *Banart* in the far reaches of the galaxy.

Ana could visualize the *G'recians* scrambling to get to *Carrillia* in time, desperate to protect those that couldn't protect themselves. The *G'recians* were known throughout the known universe as a protectorate race. They didn't start wars, but they would not sit idly by while another world suffered under the cruel hands of marauding armies either. The *Banart* used the perfect ploy to force the *G'recian* warriors to leave their own world virtually undefended.

"The Warriors left within two days. Once they left our air space, they should have reached *Carrillia* three days later. We never heard another word from them. Within days of their departure, the *Banart* and *Hienials* descended on *G'Recio*. We've been under their control ever since.

"They take the woman and young girls into breeding camps where they rape them until they're with child. Those that don't breed within six lunar cycles disappear. I can only imagine what happens to them when they leave the planet.

"They killed all of the men and elderly outright as soon as they arrived and the young males became slave labor. When they grow big enough to fight back, they are terminated in the public square."

Ana's heart went out to Minna and her people. The *G'recians* were such a devoted and faithful people who loved everyone, despite the differences between the galaxy's various species. Only the *Banarts* and the *Hienials* are their enemies, and only because the *G'recians* had watched what those creatures had done to the people they'd attacked.

In a sudden move, Dare Raden, the *Savari* leader, shoved his chair back from the table and began to pace from one end of the cabin to the other. His quick movements, though fluid, were definitely agitated, not that Ana could blame the powerful blood-drinker.

Dax and Rage, *Tigerian* twins, looked like they wanted to kill someone with their bare hands. Fane, the *Tigerian* Leader and his Triad mate Sayre, both wore pained expressions, something between despair and rage. Lucan, a *Pantari* and Dare's Triad mate, Wray and Kel also appeared lost in murderous thoughts of their own if the clenched jaws, furrowed brows and white-knuckled fists were any indication. She wasn't about to dip into their emotions to confirm her suspicions, though. There were enough rampant emotions to deal with. She needn't ask for trouble.

Jaynee and Laynee, identical High Priestess twins, had tears of compassion running down their cheeks. No one in the room was unaffected by the tale Minna wove.

Minna herself looked as though a small island breeze could blow her away, but she held firm, strong no matter the pain that obviously battered her. Ana's heart clenched as the woman's pain and torment seeped into her, flooding her with anguish.

She needed to help Minna, help her deal with all the poor woman had been through, all the memories that continually ripped at her soul. There was only one way to do that effectively, though. She'd have to draw the pain of the memories out of Minna and into herself in an empathic healing.

No one knew of her gift but her mother and she had long since passed away. If she did this, she would expose her greatest secret to virtual strangers, but she couldn't allow Minna to suffer anymore than she already had. Enough was enough. Her conscience would not allow her to sit idly by when she could do something to help. Her heart was too close to breaking to allow the woman her continued suffering.

With a soft sigh, Ana stood and made her way around the table to where Minna sat straight in her chair, her back stiff. The other woman looked up at her as she approached. Ana tried to give her a reassuring smile, but she wasn't sure how successful she'd been when she felt a wave of panic roll through Minna's mind.

Dropping to her knees beside the surprised woman, Rachana reached for Minna's hand. "Let me help you, Minna. Let me ease your pain."

Minna's eyes widened. The pulse beating at her throat sped up. Minna licked her lips nervously. "Wh—what do you mean?"

Ana swallowed passed the lump that seemed to lodge in her throat. It was now or never. "I can draw the pain away from you… If you allow it, that is."

Behind Minna, Dax and Rage each placed their hands on their mate's shoulders, in support or in defense, Rachana didn't know. "Whatever you think of me, I would never use my gift to hurt your mate. Or anyone else for that matter," she whispered to the two men ready and able to defend the shaken woman.

Behind her, she felt her own mates approach, both the powerful *Tigerian,* Kel and the ruthless leader of the *Lupin,* Wray. This was too much. She could feel the testosterone build as the angry and defensive vibes poured off all four men. She couldn't take all these feelings bombarding her or the unvoiced threat building between them on top of the desperate pain Minna's memories invoked. It was too much. It was why she'd chosen the lonely profession of archeology. She loved the solitary work. The haven of ancient cultures and the puzzles of the past were her family and her friends. People felt too much, happiness and misery, pain and joy, need and desire. Rachana sighed. She was better off alone, away from all this, but she knew she wouldn't go anywhere, couldn't.

As though they may have sensed her need, or maybe it was all in her mind, the turmoil from her mates that had pounded at her mind, lessened, becoming more of a gentle breeze that brushed against her rather than a roiling wave battering her barriers.

Soon, Kel and Wray too had their hands upon her, caressing her arms, her hair, in a show of what, she wondered. Sympathy? Support? Understanding? She didn't really know. Only the feel of their hands, the brush of their clothing against her back centered her in the storm of feelings lashing her mind. She knew right then, she'd never be able to hold herself back from giving completely to them, body, heart and soul. They were her mates. Who was she to question the will of the Lady Goddess?

Drawing a deep breath, Ana closed her eyes in preparation. Only when her own heartbeat returned to its normal steady rhythm did she open her mind for the empathic healing. The healing itself was easy. Opening herself to the pain of others, to their personal horrors and fears, and allowing them to flood her consciousness was much more difficult.

It didn't take long for her subconscious to find Minna's pain. It was a writhing mass of turmoil and despair, byproducts of her haunting memories. Rachana couldn't do anything about Minna's past, about what happened to her, but by taking some of her pain into herself, perhaps she could give her the final push she needed to become whole in spirit, as she was meant to be.

After drawing one last deep breath, Ana let her power unfurl. With Minna's hands clasped in hers, she drew the pain from the other woman, absorbed it through her mind, her heart and her soul, letting it flood her in ever-increasing waves.

Pain gripped her. Her body trembled. Her stomach cramped and she gagged, almost vomiting up her last meal. A layer of sweat coated her skin. When she thought she could bear no more pain, no more torment, she found she *could* take more. She allowed her own soul, her own feelings of self-worth to flood through her hands into Minna, gifting her with happiness and joy.

The more pain and torment Rachana drew from Minna, the more she showered her with feelings of contentment, pleasure, fulfillment and confidence. Ana refused to allow herself to dwell on her own pain, concentrating only on the healing she could feel in Minna, the changes she could already sense in Minna's mind.

Minutes passed or maybe hours. Rachana had no way of knowing how much time passed as she continued to heal the woman seated before her. All her thoughts, her energy, went to giving the gift of happiness to Minna. Only once she was certain that the shadows of torment had left Minna's soul, did Rachana begin to break the connection between them.

The more she lessened the strength of the bond between them, the more she felt the pain of Minna's memories ravaging her own body. She needed to get away, to purge the fear, the horror from her own body before it began to take a toll on her own well-being.

Shuddering, Ana eased away from Minna and opened her eyes. She could see the tension around Minna's eyes had lessened; her body no longer remained rigid and tense. No matter how much the healing hurt, she couldn't regret that she'd lightened the other woman's burdens. No one should know such suffering as Minna and all the other victims of *Banart* and *Hienial* cruelty had. No one.

Knowing she'd done all she could, Rachana moved to stand. Her legs quaked, her entire body swayed with fatigue. Only the strong arms of her mates made it possible to keep standing.

Beside her, Wray tightened his hold on her arms, searched her gaze with his. "Come, Ana. You must rest."

Before she could move away, she felt Kel stiffen behind her. A surge of awareness blasted between them. She jerked her gaze up, searched the room for whatever threat Kel had felt, trying to sense the danger that she knew they both were aware of.

Turning her head, her wary gaze met Kel's. "What is it, Kel? What do you feel?"

He looked deep into her eyes, seemed to search her very soul before he answered. "I'm not sure. Something is about to happen. I feel it. My Tiger feels it."

She nodded, accepting his feelings as truth. Some may have written his thoughts off as nonsense, but Ana knew that the Lady Goddess had bestowed heightened senses upon many, allowing them to know when danger approached.

Glancing around the room, she noticed that Kel was not the only one who obviously sensed the impending danger. "Come, my mate," Wray urged. "I must warn my crew. If you both feel that danger approaches, then we must prepare." Nodding, Ana allowed her mates to pull her toward the seat she'd vacated before the healing. Seconds after she'd settled against the soft fur covering of the chair, warning alarms sounded throughout the room.

"Dammit! Those are proximity alarms." Wray grimaced, stroked his hand through her long tresses. "I will be back. Stay here with Kel and the others until I can determine just what is going on."

Before she could object, Wray turned on his heel and raced out of the room.

RUNNING A HAND through his hair, Wray quickly made his way toward the command deck. No matter how much he wanted to remain by his mate's side, this was his ship. As alpha, it was his duty to prepare for whatever danger might be out there. He must meet this situation head on. He would face any newcomers, whether they were friend or foe.

As soon as he reached the command center, another proximity alarm began to clamor. "What do you see, Officer Boneget?" Wray asked his second in command. Though Kaylen Boneget was his closest friend and ally, on board ship, he couldn't let his personal ties influence the command protocols established for all those serving aboard the *Lupin* fleet.

"I detect five *Banart* Attack Vessels and four *Hienial* transport ships approaching our location, Alpha. What are our orders?" Officer Boneget announced.

Damn, he thought. *How can we defeat nine ships?* Wray had to think fast. He needed to protect his ship and all the people on it, but he couldn't just leave the people below susceptible to their vile attackers either. "Are there any ally ships nearby other than the ones already here?'

"Let me run some long range scans, Alpha." Seconds passed that felt like hours, and with each second they waited, the enemies ships grew closer.

"It looks like a *Lioni* Warship and an Attack Vessel of the Great Bear Clan are within communication range, Sir."

"Hail them, Boneget. And pray to the Goddess that they are both close enough and willing to offer assistance."

"Yes, Alpha."

"I need to inform our visitors of our enemies' arrival. Contact me in the Strategic Command Center."

"Yes, Alpha."

Without further delay, Wray headed back toward his Triad mates and the other three Triads. Hopefully, the coming battle would be in their favor. If not, they would go down fighting. When he finally reached the others, he could feel the tension thickening the air.

"What have you learned?" Dare, the *Savari* leader asked.

Ana must have sensed his fear, his worry because she quickly made her way to his side. "Is all well, Wray?"

He shook his head. "I'm afraid the situation has gone from mildly dangerous to downright hostile. Nine enemy vessels are approaching—five *Banart* warships and four armed *Hienial* Slave Transports."

All the men stiffened where they stood. "Well," Fane grunted, "let us contact our ships and prepare for battle."

Wray nodded. "I've had my crew contact two of our Allies that are within communication range—the *Lioni* and the Great Bear Clan. Hopefully, they too will be able to assist us in this upcoming battle."

Ana reached out to him, placed her hand upon his chest. Kel stepped forward as well, clasped his forearm in a warrior's acknowledgement, a silent vow to stand by his side. "What can the rest of us do?"

"Pray to the Lady Goddess. Until we know more, that is all we can do."

As the others left the Strategic command center to contact their ships, Wray followed his own advice and offered up a silent prayer to the Lady that today's battle would end with their victory.

ABOARD THE COMMAND deck of the *Lioni* Attack Vessel, *Revenge*, Drace Vanier paced, his movements agitated, his mind a jumble of chaotic impressions. Why was he out here, hiding behind a planet that had no strategic worth? What had driven him to ignore his councilors and make his way out here, so far from his own home world? Why did he feel—no—know that this is where he needed to be at this time?

Drace sighed, stopped in front of the viewscreen. "Commander Vanier," his communications officer announced. "We have received an urgent communiqué from the *Lupin* ship, *Nomad.* They request our help in fending off an impending attack."

Well, I guess that answers that. Now I know why I'm here. "Tell Navedis we will be there as soon as possible. What are they facing?"

"According to their missive, nine enemy vessels are approaching and will be upon them in less than a quarter of a dial."

Drace clasped his hands behind his back, let out a deep breath, then turned toward his crew, eying each of the men he'd hand chosen to join him on this trip. "Prepare battle stations. Proceed with caution, with our ship fully cloaked, but inform Navedis where we are at all times."

"Done, Sir."

With a nod of his head, Drace quickly moved toward the weapons console and took a seat. He may be the commander, but he loved a good battle.

OUT OF THE CORNER of his eye, Kel watched Ana pace. Wray's cabin had seemed large when they'd first entered it, but with her agitation growing, the chamber seemed to be shrinking with every minute that passed. Back and forth, from one side of the room to the other, she walked, her arms wrapped around her waist. What was upsetting her so? The danger they were about to face or something else?

"Please tell me what is bothering you so, my mate?" he asked, unable to keep silent any longer. Something was upsetting her and he'd do whatever he could to set her mind at ease.

Ana bit her bottom lip then raised her worried gaze to his before turning her head away. "I feel—I—someone out there, someone is in terrible trouble. Their fear is choking me. I don't know how much more I can take, Kel." Rubbing her arms, Ana went back to pacing. The minutes slowly passed and the shadows beneath Ana's eyes continued to darken.

"Are you okay, Rachana?"

Ana shook her head, made her way over to the bed and slumped down. Her head rested against her chest. She looked defeated.

"What is it, my mate?"

She raised her head, holding his gaze directly for the first time since they'd entered the chamber. So much hurt and fear had pooled in her eyes. He couldn't stay away from her. Settling next to her on the bed, he pulled her into his arms and pressed her head against his chest. With as much tenderness as he possessed, he ran his hand over her hair, petting her, soothing her to the best of his ability.

"Tell me, Ana. What do you need from me? What do you feel?"

"Someone on the surface is in dire need. I feel her terror, never have I felt such raw fear and determination. Somehow, I must save her, Kel. I must. I feel it all the way to my soul that if we are ever to defeat the *Banart*, then we must rescue this woman."

He didn't like her gift. It hurt her. Too much pain made it past her natural barriers and into her heart and mind. One day it would be unbearable and she would have a breakdown. Kel fisted his hands at his side and simmered with impotent rage at his unseen enemy.

Walking to a nearby console, he contacted Wray. "Ana is beside herself with pain and worry over an unseen woman on the surface of this planet. She's convinced the woman is of great need to us in our battle against our enemies."

"How?" Wray asked, obviously attempting to divide his attention between his two loyalties, his mate and his people.

"She's not sure. She knows only that the woman is instrumental in the battle with the *Banart* and their eventual destruction." Kel paced in front of the viewscreen, his gaze constantly returning to Ana. She lay curled in a tight ball, her body wracked with tension as she attempted to draw the negative energy from the unknown woman. "Give me a few men, Wray. Let me take her down to the surface and get this woman."

Wray shook his head. "Absolutely not. I'll not have you endanger our mate's life so carelessly."

"Look Wray," Kel said, grasping either side of the vid screen. "We endanger her either way. Her tie to this woman is so strong, I fear for Ana if the other dies."

Wray's eyes suddenly changed to that of his wolf. Kel had just told him of a threat to his mate. If he'd thought him all business before, the man he saw now was like a robot.

"Kaylen!" He turned to face the people behind them.

An exceptionally tall man broke apart from the others to move to Wray. He gave a short bow. "Yes, Alpha?"

"Don't 'yes Alpha' me now. Get your ass over here and take command. Something threatens my mate and I intend to eradicate it." Wray led the other man over to a console in the corner. "I'm going to take a contingent of men down to the surface and remove the threat from my mate. You will stay here as my emissary and carry out my orders. Defeat the *Banarts* at all costs."

"You should not be the one to go, sir." The other man said. "Allow me to—"

"She is my mate! It is my right. Do as I say." Wray looked around the bridge. "Take care of my people and if I don't return," he grabbed Kaylen by the arms. "Do not let it be said that I shirked my duty to name a beta. Kaylen is named my successor."

Kel watched Wray through the video link and admired the man even more for knowing how to lead like the king he so obviously was. Still he wasn't sure it was necessary for them both to accompany Ana. Given the choice though, he knew he would never allow her to go down there without him. How could he expect Wray to do any less? Switching off the video link, he turned to comfort his mate while he waited for Wray to join them. She still lay curled in a ball on the bed, tears running down her face.

Fisting his hands at his sides, he strode to the bed to stare down at her. He must try to control his feelings. The rage he felt swirling inside him would only further upset his sensitive mate. He concentrated on her scent and her goodness as he lowered himself to the bed to take her in his arms. Here they would await Wray and the small army he knew would accompany them to the surface. Neither of them would take any chances with her well-being.

WRAY BARKED HIS orders and left the bridge in a killing rage. What could affect his mate so strongly? He stopped short when he entered their room. Ana and

Kel lay on the bed. She was curled in a trembling ball with Kel wrapped tightly around her. It was almost as though he attempted to block the psychic onslaught with the protection of his body. If only it were that easy. He stood and stared at his two mates, amazed at the depth of feeling he already felt for both of them.

He hated to wake them but the men accompanying them were ready to go and he couldn't bear to see her suffer any longer. If the look on her face was any indication, the pain and fear even assaulted her in her sleep. He drew his hands over his face and sighed. It was time. Sitting on the edge of the bed, he pushed the hair back from Ana's face and pressed his lips to her forehead.

Her eyes fluttered open and she looked around the room, her expression confused. "What?" She looked behind her to Kel, still wrapped around her. "Where am I?"

"We're in my room, love." He cupped her cheeks, his thumbs feathering across the dark circles under her eyes. "I know you don't feel well but—"

She pulled from Kel's embrace and sat up, keeping her arms wrapped around her middle. Kel woke and rolled off the other side. Like any good warrior, he was instantly awake and warily looking around the room for an enemy.

"Is it time?"

Wray nodded at Kel's question. "The landing party awaits us in the disembarking chamber. A shuttle awaits us there as Ana will be needed to point the way to the woman in need."

Ana relaxed her hold around her waist. A look of relief crossed her face before she nibbled on her bottom lip in worry. His cock jumped at the sight and he had to force his libido in check. There would be time to mate with her later, after he rescued the woman from the surface and defeated the enemy quickly approaching their location. "Thank you, Wray. I know this isn't the best time, but I feel…"

"What do you feel, sweetness?"

She shrugged her shoulders. "She's important and we—no—I have to be there if she is to be found."

Wray nodded. "Then so be it. I have put together a landing party. We shall do all in our power to find this woman, and lead her to safety."

FROM THE COMMAND Deck of his ship, Drace watched the small shuttlecraft leave the *Nomad* and head toward the surface of the planet below. *Now what is up with that?* Knowing that his ship would be safe with his brother Vane at the helm should battle erupt, Drace made an instinctive decision. Whatever the crew of the shuttle was up to, he needed to be a part of it.

Turning toward the communication terminal, Drace connected to his brother's cabin, audio only, unwilling to spy on his brother and whatever playmate he'd taken to bed this eve. "Vane you have the helm. If it looks like our allies are in need, step in. Keep the ship cloaked but move as close to the action as you can. I'm heading down to the surface."

Before his brother could argue with him, Drace cut the transmission and headed to his shuttle bay. He had someplace he needed to be and wasting time arguing with his brother about his safety wouldn't change his mind, only slow him down. And somehow, he thought—no, knew—that time was something he didn't have.

As the shuttle scanned the surface looking for life signs, Ana looked into herself, trying to hone in on the woman she came down here to search for. "South. We need to head south."

The shuttle pilot shook his head. "I'm not detecting anything in the southern hemisphere."

"It doesn't matter. That's where she is." She turned her head, searched out both Wray and Kel. "I know that's where she is."

Wray nodded then turned back to the pilot. "Head south. If that's where my mate said we need to go, then that's where we go."

The pilot nodded hesitantly, but did indeed turn south. Relief washed through her, an almost giddy sense of happiness that her mates appeared to trust her instincts over their own technology. She wanted to thank her mates, show them how much their support meant to her, and she knew just how to do it. Even though she'd known since their meeting on her ship that they were her mates she'd done nothing to show that she'd accepted it, and in fact had taken their kindness, their caring and their warmth and hadn't reciprocated. Well, that would stop now.

Knowing they were her mates, she knew she'd have a telepathic bond with them, but she'd chosen not to use it, to ignore that mental bond, just as she'd tried to pretend they weren't her mates. Well, no more. It was time to show them that she accepted them as they had shown her that they accepted her. Her relationship with these two wonderful men was a gift she would not squander.

Thank you both for standing by me, for trusting me when I've given you no reason to do so.

Kel quirked his lips and gave her a slight nod in acknowledgement. Wray's eyes widened then seemed to flood with joy.

Think nothing of it, my love. Wray's husky voice whispering in her mind sent goose bumps pebbling across her arms.

I will always stand by you, mate. Kel's voice, equally sexy, sent a pulse of warmth through her woman's core. She squeezed her thighs in reaction. This wouldn't do. She must concentrate on the woman who needed her, not on her body's reaction to her mates.

As though just the thought of the unknown woman strengthened their connection, Ana felt the woman's nearness through their bond. Lower. I need you to get lower. They were just above a jungle, or at least that's what it appeared to be through their viewscreen. She knew to the depths of her soul, what they were seeing was only what they were meant to, not what was actually there.

"Stop. You must land here."

The pilot shook his head. "There is nowhere within a day's walk to land."

She fisted her hands by her sides. "Please, trust in me. What you see is what you are meant to. Have faith in the Goddess, for she is the one who has bestowed my talents upon me. We are where we need to be."

The pilot looked to Wray for an answer. "I trust in my mate. If she says this is where we need to be then I believe her."

"Yes, Alpha." Even though the pilot shook his head in disbelief and began to mutter to himself, he slowly lowered the ship. Closer and closer to the forest canopy they moved and Ana didn't flinch. She knew in this she wasn't wrong. The forest was just an illusion.

Both Wray and Kel moved up beside her. Even though they said they trusted her, deep down she hadn't believed them. But, when she searched their feelings, only trust and a sense of purpose flooded her. Happiness flooded her heart. Yes, her mates truly did believe in her.

Of course, we do, they both said simultaneously.

"Goddess she was right," the pilot exclaimed as they continued toward the ground. As soon as they bypassed where the treetops should be, the illusion disappeared.

Ana gasped. "It's real. The Lost Temple of the Lady Goddess really does exist." Tears flooded her eyes and her mates each wrapped an arm around her waist in support. In front of her, a tall pyramid of white marble stood.

G'Recio's trio of suns bathed it in glorious white. She could see standing stones in the distance, and between them and the temple, a glen with the greenest grass she'd ever seen. Her heart stuttered then sped up. Her hands shook and her tummy cramped.

"All my life, I dreamed of the day I'd find it. Ever since I was naught but a child, I've felt it was my duty to find this place. I dedicated my entire life, my career, everything I am to fulfill the vow I'd made myself. It is said in myth, that only the purest of souls can set foot in the temple itself. Evil may surround it, but if a pure soul shelters inside, no one with ill intent shall be able to step a foot through the door. No wonder she chose to seek refuge here," she whispered, awe and satisfaction filling her.

Each of her mates stroked her hair, and then over her head Wray addressed them all. "Beware. The woman inside is frightened, scared. She has taken refuge in the temple for a reason. I imagine the enemy above is also down here. My mate and the woman within these walls must be protected above all else."

"Yes, Alpha. No one shall be allowed to harm them. You have our vow."

Wray nodded then clasped Kel's shoulder as he pulled Ana beneath the shelter of his arm. "It is time."

Kel fisted his hands at his sides. "Yes," he agreed. "It is time."

Behind the marble walls of the temple, Kiri Leran clasped the hand of the small boy she considered her own. Born of a *Hienial* father and a *G'recian* woman, it had been Kiri who'd cut the premature child from his dying mother. Too small at birth to be separated from her, she'd raised the child as her own. But, when the time came for them to take Ryo from her, to infect him with their evil, she'd attacked the guards with a weapon she'd fashioned from the undercarriage of her metal bed, stolen a transport ship, and after crashing three days walk from here, finally managed to get them to safety.

She had hoped they'd be able to remain hidden longer, that the *Hienials* would have given up looking for her. It was a false hope. They guarded their captives with zeal. She should have known they'd never let her or Ryo go. Well, they'd make their last stand here. She'd fight to her last breath to ensure that Ryo remained free of the *Hienial* plague, do whatever she had to in order to ensure he wasn't exposed to their evil.

The thundering at the temple doors grew louder as more *Hienials* attempted to break through the barrier to the temple proper. Beside her, Ryo quaked in fear. She lifted the toddler in her arms, cuddled him against her chest. "Fear not, little one. We are in the Lady Goddess' Temple. No one who has evil in their soul can enter here."

His little voice shook with fear. "But I am evil. I am *Hienial*, just like them."

Her heart clenched. "Oh, my son. You are not evil. You are all that is good or the Goddess would not have let you shelter here. You have a pure soul, unmarred by their ugliness."

As she found a seat against one of the marble pillars, she pulled Ryo onto her lap and began to gently rock him back and forth. As always when she sat here, her gaze strayed toward the altar where seventeen amulets lay upon a silken pillow. As she so often wondered since arriving here, she couldn't help but ask herself why the odd number. What was significant about there only being seventeen amulets? On the other hand, was the number important at all?

It is important, my child. When the others come and defeat those awaiting you outside, let them in and tell them my words. Four Triads have formed and two more are due. Before you sit seventeen amulets, to enhance the energy your triads have sown. One will come from a far distant place, wearing an amulet of her own. When eighteen wear an amulet of power, the time to fight has reached its final hour.

When no more words were spoken, she asked the question uppermost in her mind. *Who are you?*

You know who I am. Tell all who enter the temple tonight to be at the standing stones tomorrow just as the new day dawns. All four Triads must be present at that time, as well. Take care of your cub, young lioness.

As quickly as she appeared in her mind, the Lady Goddess was gone and all that was left were the shouts outside the temple and the soft snores of her son laying nestled against her breast.

An hour passed or maybe more as she rocked her son, listening to the sounds of battle just outside the temple doors. As the day slowly turned to night, she continued to wait for those that would enter, thinking upon the Goddess' words. *Why would she speak to me?*

KEL GRIMACED AS another *Hienial* mercenary shot at him. Ducking behind the standing stone he'd chosen to shield Ana behind, he waited for the shooting to stop. As soon as the laser fire hit the marble protecting him, he whirled around it into the open and fired, hitting the *Hienial* square in the chest. *One more down, a dozen or so more to go.*

He ducked behind the stone again, glanced at his mate. "Are you okay?" he asked, though why he bothered when he could see what the evil surrounding them was doing to her. Lying near his feet, she had plastered herself around the stone, her body curved inward as she shuddered. As an empath, she was drawn to others emotions, and the evil living inside the *Hienials* seemed to be slowly poisoning her. They needed to defeat them soon, before Rachana succumbed to their hatred.

Wray, we need to end this now. Ana can't take too much more.

A pause, then Wray's voice grew strong in his mind. *It seems the Lioni Pride Leader, Drace Vanier, has arrived with a landing party of his own. I don't know why he's here, but I'm not going to question it right now. With two teams attacking the Hienials, it won't take long to destroy them.*

You had better hope so. If we lose her, no one will be safe from my wrath.
Understood.

Within minutes the tide had turned. Several of their crew sported injuries and they'd suffered two deaths, but all the attacking *Hienials* had died. They would honor their fallen, but first they had to retrieve the woman who even now was sheltered inside the temple. Only then, would they celebrate the lives of those who given their life to protect another.

Bending down, Kel lifted Ana and carried her toward the Temple gates to meet up with Wray and the others. Ana barely responded as he carried her toward the others. Deep shadows marred her cheeks. Her skin has a sickly gray cast to it. Once they were assured the other woman was brought to safety, he planned to pamper his mate.

So, you agree, Wray. Once we're back on your ship, and our enemy is defeated we devote our evening to our mate.

Definitely. I have felt her pain, her exhaustion through our bond. Once the enemy above is defeated, we'll bathe her, and put her to bed. She needs a healing sleep.

I agree. Kel stepped up next to Wray and nodded toward the *Lioni* male. "Thank you for your timely assistance." He shifted Ana in his arms. "I don't know how much more she could have taken."

Drace nodded then his gaze darted once again toward the temple doors. His brows pinched down in thought. "What is it that you search for here?"

"A woman sought shelter here. We came to rescue her. Our mate tells us she is important if we are to defeat the *Banart* and the *Hienials.*"

He raised his brows in surprise then tilted his head in acknowledgement.

"Then let us go in and see that she is brought to safety."

Both Kel and Wray nodded. Drace pulled open the temple doors. The three men, and the two squads of soldiers that had followed them into battle, stepped through the entryway. Before they'd taken two steps into the temple, a woman approached them. In her arms, she held a small child of no more than three winters, who looked at them with adult eyes, eyes that had already seen too much.

Drace gasped. Both Kel and Wray whipped their heads around, looking for danger. Instead, the *Lioni* male growled low in his throat, as he spoke words that shocked them all. "She is mine to protect, as is her cub."

The tiny red haired woman quirked her eyebrows before turning her gaze toward Ana. "Will she be all right?" she asked, her voice soft and soothing.

"She will be after she rests. We are here to take you to safety. You and your son."

She nodded then turned her attention toward Wray. "I have a message for all of you from the Lady Goddess, even the *Lioni* male among you."

Kel watched as Drace leaned against the nearest marble column and slowly nodded.

"What is your message?" Wray asked.

The woman sighed then began to speak. "Four Triads have formed and two more are due. Before you sit seventeen amulets, to enhance the energy your triads have sown. One will come from a far distance place, wearing an amulet of her own. When eighteen wear an amulet of power, the time to fight has reached the final hour."

At that, Drace straightened. "Was there anything else she said, little one?"

"Only that anyone who entered the temple tonight needed to return tomorrow at dawn, as well as her four Triads. You are to meet at the standing stones."

Wray nodded and Kel watched as he headed towards the altar where the amulets rested. Lifting the pillow they lay upon, he carefully carried them toward the temple doors, speaking over his shoulder as he went. "Then let us get back to the *Nomad.* I've already received word that the *Banarts* and *Hienials* above were destroyed in battle. It seems not only had the Great Bear Clan and the *Lioni* arrived in time, the *Savari* elders sent four cloaked ships of their own to protect their leader and his brother. With eleven to nine odds, and the superior weaponry of the *Tigerians* and the *Savari*, not to mention the invisibility of the *Lioni* during the fighting, the battle was over shortly after it began."

ANA WOKE TOASTY warm and comfortably sandwiched between her two future mates. Even with her eyes closed as they were, she could tell that her head rested against Kel and Wray had his chest pressed against her back. The heat and warmth filling her had more to do with the press of their bodies against hers rather than the coverlet currently wrapped tightly around her. She could get used to waking this way. Ana sighed then began to worry her bottom lip with her teeth.

How did she get into to bed with them anyway and were they still aboard ship? The last thing she remembered was the near exhaustion she'd suffered while trying to locate the woman and child hiding on the surface. She had hazy memories of returning to the ship and someone—or, two someone's—bathing her. Or, was that a dream?

She could feel the heat rising in her cheeks just thinking that her mates might have bathed her, seen her completely open and exposed. And, if it wasn't a dream, what must they think of her? Goose bumps pebbled across her skin just thinking about it.

Well, no matter how much she'd like to lie abed with her mates, she needed to get up and search for the woman they'd rescued from the surface, Kiri and her son, Ryo. There would be much healing she'd need to do today, if she wanted to make sure their trauma was but a distant memory rather than a constant source of torment and misery.

Sighing, Ana tried to wiggle out from beneath the heavy weight of Kel and Wray's arms. As close as they were holding her, getting up without waking them might be near impossible. Within seconds, she realized that getting up without their knowledge was just not going to happen.

Behind her, Wray's arms tightened. He pressed his lips against the nape of her neck, nuzzled his way beneath her hair. His warm breath wafted across her cheek, sending another ripple of goose bumps to rise along her flesh. "Good morning, my mate."

Wray's voice was husky with sleep, and oh so sexy. By the Lady Goddess, how would she ever resist him—them—when the time came to mate? She snorted. Why would she want to?

In front of her, Kel shifted closer, pressing his front more tightly against her chest. She could feel every muscle in his torso, hear his heartbeat grow louder and faster. "I, too, wish you a good morning, Rachana. Did you sleep well?" he asked.

She knew they were both awaiting an answer but her body began to grow even warmer. Knowing her mates lie so close, their bodies pressed against her, skin to skin, made her stomach roil in nervous anticipation. Would they expect to mate with her now? Was she ready, if they did?

She licked her lips, let out the breath she hadn't realized she's been holding. "I'm well." She opened her eyes, took a quick peek up at Kel. She felt another wave of heat flow beneath her skin when she looked into his hungry eyes.

Turning her head, she met the equally heated gaze of Wray. She swallowed. Her arms, her legs began to tremble. Oh Goddess, it looked like they were indeed ready to make her theirs in every sense of the word.

"Thank you for taking care of me last night, when I was too weak to take care of myself. I used more energy than I'm used to, it seems."

Kel pressed his lips against her forehead, before trailing them down her cheek. Finally, they settled against her mouth, sipping at her in exquisite gentleness. Snuggled behind her, she could feel the firm press of Wray's shaft nudging her back, sending shards of heated awareness winging through her blood. Her breath hitched. Her heart stuttered.

How could she do it? How could she let these two virtual strangers mate with her so soon? Always she shied away from intimacy because of the emotions, the feelings that the males bombarded her with. The few times she had allowed herself to get close to a male, their disregard for naught but their own wants and desires blasted into her mind, making any desire she may have felt wither and die. She'd never been able to allow someone this close before.

She'd never made love to one man, never mind two at one time. How could she even think of continuing with this? Could she really submit to these men? She didn't know them. If she submitted, afterwards they would be forever her mates, able to dictate her life, her choices? They were two against one. What if she learned she was naught to them but a vessel for their seed? What would she do then?

She felt intense pain emanating from them at her mental accusation. She closed her eyes with shame as their grief tore through her. They attempted to save her from their intense suffering as they hurried to block their feelings, but not before their pain fisted her heart and wounded her soul.

She bowed her head. Tears trailed down her cheeks, dripped onto the coverlet as she processed their pain, let it flow through her body and out her pores.

"Please forgive me," she begged, shifting her gaze to her feet. "I wanted to believe you would never hurt me, never force me to do something against my will." Her voice quavered and she buried her face in her hands. "I just didn't know for sure until I … until your denial bombarded me." She sobbed into her hands, knowing she would never, could never deserve them. Leaning forward, she buried her face in the crook of Kel's neck, scenting his male musk beneath the aroma of the soaps they'd bathed her with earlier.

They both caressed her hair, whispered sweet nothings into her ear as tears of frustration fell from her eyes. "Do not worry, mate," Wray whispered against her hair. "You are all that we want, all that we will ever need. If you need more time, we will give it to you. Your emotional needs are more important than the desires of our flesh."

"I do want you." She looked up; searching first Kel's eyes then Wray's. "Even though I've never been more than passably interested in a man before, I want you both." She shrugged. "Maybe I'm just scared."

Ana gathered her courage, reaching toward Kel with trembling hands. Whether they shook with nerves or desire, she didn't know. Her mouth grew dry at the sight of the honed muscles of his chest and abdomen. She dared not look lower. Just the thought of seeing his hard male member drove her knees to quake. How would she ever overcome her fears and allow them to do what she knew they wanted?

She steeled herself, bolstering her nerve. She knew that sooner or later she would have to see him … there. Touch him there. She would have to touch them both. Her stomach did a little flop and, gathering her courage, she lowered her gaze. Her eyes widened at her first glimpse of his hardened member. She'd been careful not to look at her mates too closely in the bath. Instead, she kept her eyes closed not wanting to incite their passion. Now she gaped, her eyes wide, amazed at the length and width of him. Pre-cum seeped from the meaty head, and she wanted to lick it away. What would it taste like?

She swallowed past the lump once again lodged in her throat. Was Wray just as large? She fought the urge to turn and look. Her body began to tremble and they wrapped their arms around her, soothing her with long soothing strokes of their hands upon her back, her arms.

Behind her, Wray tucked an errant lock of glossy ebony hair behind her ear. Both of her mates had a strange fascination with her long mane, not that she would ever think to complain. She found that she loved the feel of their hands caressing her.

Kel eased his body away from hers, giving her space to make her decision. "Have you changed your mind, love? We can wait. Your health, comfort and well-being will always come before our desires. You merely need to say the word."

She looked from one to the other and wondered exactly what they thought. She could feel their emotions, even their wants and fears but what they truly thought was a mystery to her. Could she go through with it or would she deny them. If she did, she would also be denying herself. Would they keep their word? Did they really wish to please her as they claimed?

Yes.

She believed they did. Besides, she couldn't deny them the one thing each of them longed for most of all. A mate. A woman to love and call their own.

She closed her eyes and nodded her acceptance. Behind her, Wray's shaft once again prodded her backside, pulsing with need. Dare she turn around? Did she even want to know the size of her other mate's erection?

Curiosity killed the *sauri,* or so they said. Still, she couldn't keep herself from turning to see the size of his erection. Her eyes widened to the point of pain. How would they ever all make love at once? She could never take them both at the same time. She just couldn't, at least not tonight. Not her first time. They would certainly tear her in two!

Kel pulled her tight against his body, his hands splaying over her back and buttocks. "Do not fear us, little one." He chuckled at her expression. "Forgive me. I forgot that you do not like that appellation." Tucking his fingers beneath her chin, he pressed a fleeting kiss to her lips. "I didn't wish to upset you."

"Move from her presence you great hairy beast. Our princess deserves better than your bumbling attempts at romance." Wray said with a laugh. "She needs a male who will treat her as she deserves. She certainly doesn't need some large bumbling oaf who would frighten her with his ugliness at every turn." His grin and laughing eyes took the sting from his reprimand and Ana laughed as she finally managed to relax just a bit.

"Seriously though," Wray added. "You needn't fear us this night. If you wish to wait another night or another year for that matter, we shall oblige. As we said, your comfort and your needs will always come above our own."

Ana's heart filled with pleasure at their declaration. She could feel the honesty behind their words. They truly would wait for her. And, just like that, she decided she didn't want to wait any longer. She was ready to take them as her mates. Now.

Licking her lips, Ana allowed her gaze to meet first Kel's, then Wray's. "I would like to make love to you—both of you, but…"

"But what," Wray whispered, his voice now husky with desire.

"I've never been with a man. Can we take it slow? I—I mean, one at a time? I'm not sure I could take you both inside my body. Not yet, anyway."

"Anything you want, my mate," Kel promised. "Anything."

Behind her, Wray eased away, leaving the bed to her and Kel. Ana lifted wary eyes to him, watching as he dressed. She worried that he'd be upset that she wasn't ready to take them both at the same time. He must have sensed her thoughts, because he gave her a wry smile and took another step back. "You need time to get to know us, time to learn each of us. I will check in with my second in command and return to you. Enjoy your time with Kel."

"Are you—are you sure? I don't want to make you feel second best, because you're not." She raced to add, reaching her hand out to him, needing him to take it, to reassure her that she was doing the right thing and hadn't hurt his feelings.

Wray took her hand, gave it a slight squeeze before placing a kiss on her open palm. "Don't worry, Ana. Enjoy your time with Kel. I'll be back shortly to make you mine. I want you to have as much pleasure today as you can take. We'll join as a triad during the final ceremony. Each of us are going to want to have one-on-one time with you, so Kel is just the lucky one to get you first."

Bending down, Wray tenderly kissed her trembling lips. After nodding at Kel, he walked to the door, giving her once last glance over his shoulder before silently leaving the cabin and his triad mates behind.

"Are you ready, my mate?" Kel asked as he slowly settled himself between her thighs, opening her legs wider until he'd spread them as far apart as they could go. Her thighs trembled, and her stomach muscles tightened. Her fingers clutched the bedding beneath her, anxiety of the unknown making her more nervous than she expected she'd be.

Kel lowered his head and moaned against her woman's mound. Ana arched her back, whether in desire to scoot away or lift herself closer to his mouth, she didn't know. Silently, she waited for his first touch. It wasn't long in coming.

He softly blew a puff of warm air against her quivering mound before nuzzling his face against her creamy center. Gently, so as not to startle her, Kel ran his tongue up between her pretty, pink folds and stopped at her clit. He pressed the tip of his tongue against the nub and held it there.

She squirmed beneath him, trying to evade his seeking mouth. This was her first time with a man, the first time being devoured by a man's mouth. Only when she reached her woman's pleasure would he take her completely.

He swirled his tongue around and around, in and out of her tight sheath, lapping up her woman's cream, inhaling her scent deep into his lungs. He'd never get enough of her. Over and over, he ate at her, until she was writhing beneath him. She panted and moaned as his tongue danced around her pussy, propelling her higher and higher.

Kel separated her folds with his finger and circled her hole, spreading her moisture on his finger. Then he pressed into her tight core, catching her hips as they shot off the bed. She arched so high his finger nearly slipped out of her.

After he settled her body again, he went to work, alternately licking her in long and short strokes. He penetrated her sheath with first one then two fingers, stretching her so she'd be able to take him with the least amount of pain possible. She never once let go of the bedding beneath her.

"By the Lady Goddess, Kel, please! I need… I need more!" She screamed into her pillow, her body writhing in agonizing need.

Kel lifted his mouth from her, watching her passion with his hungry gaze. He was starving for her, desperate to feel her pussy sheathe his cock.

"By the Goddess, don't stop, don't…" Her head shot back and forth on the pillow as she pleaded with him to end her misery.

He laid into her once more with his mouth, sucking her clit between his lips and biting gently. She screamed, her entire body shaking with her release. Her orgasm ripped through her body, squeezing his fingers still embedded deep within her woman's channel.

He climbed higher on the bed and knelt between her thighs, keeping one finger on her clit to keep the sensations rolling. Her eyes were squeezed shut and sweat beaded on her forehead. She never opened her eyes as he reached for another pillow and slid it beneath her still arching hips.

Still caressing her clit with the tip of his finger, he brought the meaty head of his shaft to her wet channel. Pushing gently against it, he watched it slowly sink inside her clasping sheath.

Kel pulled out, his cock bobbing up and down, slick with Ana's dew, and weeping with his own juices.

"Don't stop…you…can't," she cried.

"I promise, my love. I won't stop." He pressed forward again, lodging his cock's head more firmly inside her this time. He stayed that way, unmoving as he waited for some sign she was ready for more.

Ana bit down on her lip and shifted against his cock that now stretched her tight pussy. He pulled back a tiny bit, watching the relief cross her face before thrusting deeper still.

Her hips jerked, impaling herself on his cock, and she screamed with the pain as he breached her virgin's barrier. Kel again waited for her body to accept his, for her pain to turn to pleasure.

When she began to move beneath him, he lifted her knees into the crooks of his elbows, placed his palms on the bed beside her shoulders and slowly sank deeper into Ana's welcoming body.

Slowly he withdrew until only the head of his cock remained lodged inside her. Only when she began to squirm, arching up against him, did he drive himself into her softness. Over and over, he thrust, the pace picking up with his ever-increasing need to cum.

Ana screamed, her orgasm hitting her hard. Kel groaned and buried his cock as far as it would go, her climax triggering his own. His seed shot deep into her womb, bathing her with his life's essence.

Their sweaty bodies stuck together as they lay, their chests heaving, in a mass of quivering flesh on the bed. His shaft was still deep inside her. He would be content staying forevermore inside her clasping channel, but he knew that Wray waited patiently to take her as mate, as well. He couldn't award Wray's selflessness by ignoring the other man's needs.

Even though he'd rather stay embedded deep inside her, Kel slowly withdrew from his mate's body, careful not to hurt her. He felt deprived of her body's heat almost immediately, but he knew he couldn't be selfish with his desire for her. Knowing that Wray waited elsewhere, he slowly ran his hand through her tangled mane, and then rolled to his side and off the bed. "Rest, Ana. Wray will be here shortly to love you as well. Just rest."

Anna nodded then closed her eyes, wearing a smile of sated contentment. Kel grinned at his accomplishment and with happiness flooding his heart, went in search of Wray, the third member of their Triad.

WRAY HAD TRIED his best not to think about what was happening between Kel and their mate. That way laid madness. He wanted to make love to her so badly he hadn't been able to concentrate on anything his Beta had said. If Kel didn't show up soon, he'd probably find himself standing outside his cabin, waiting in the corridor until they called for him. *By the Goddess, I hope she'll be ready for me soon.*

Wray sighed, ran his fingers through his hair as he stared out of the viewport and down on the planet below. The sound of approaching footsteps shook him out of his reverie, and he looked over his shoulder. Kel, wearing an intensely sated expression stood just a few feet away from him.

"Is Rachana all right?" he asked, needing to know that her first lovemaking experience had been pleasant for her, even if it hadn't been him loving her.

Kel quickly closed the distance between them and pulled him into a warrior's embrace. "She is resting now. I must thank you for gifting me with her innocence. It is a memory I shall always cherish."

"So long as the pleasure outweighed the pain, then it was worth it. I'd do anything—give her anything—to make her happy."

Kel nodded. "So would I. So, go to her. She's waiting for you. I shall find the others and make arrangements for our travel to *Tigeria*."

Wray watched as Kel quickly walked away. After dragging in a deep breath, he left the command deck and headed toward his cabin, toward his mate.

Once he entered their cabin, and undressed, Wray slowly approached the bed, his gaze hungrily feasting on his lovely mate. Her eyes fluttered open and his heart hitched when her lips turned up into a smile. She held out her hand to him. Sheer joy and love flooded his soul. Finally, he was where he was supposed to be. In her, he would finally be complete.

While Ana struggled to sit up beneath the coverlet, he eased himself onto the bed beside her, bent down and took her mouth with all the love and tenderness he possessed.

Still kissing her, Wray lowered the blanket she'd been clutching against her breasts, leaving her completely exposed to his gaze. She ducked her head in shyness. Unwilling to let her hide from him, he lifted her chin. "You are beautiful, my love. There is no need to hide from me."

He slowly raised his hands, caressed her face, her shoulders, and then trailed his fingers down her chest until his palms covered her full breasts. He took both of her nipples in his fingers and began pulling and softly pinching them, showing her that even small pain can lead to the ultimate pleasure.

She pulled her mouth away and arched her back, thrusting her breasts more fully into his hands. He sucked in a deep breath then followed the line of her neck with his mouth, nipping and licking his way down to her chest. Once there, he stopped, lifted his gaze toward hers.

"Please Wray, I need you. I ache. Make it go away."

He nodded, swirling his tongue around her breasts, being careful to avoid the pebbled peaks. Ana fisted her hands in his hair and tried to force him to her nipples.

Wray didn't hesitate. He latched on to one of Ana's turgid nipples and suckled it, before lashing it with his tongue and teeth. Ana cried out her pleasure and shoved more of her breast into his mouth. He went back and forth, from one breast to the other until they were both swollen and red.

Only then did Wray nudge her gently to her back. He knelt on the floor beside the bed and pulled her gently by the hips to the edge. Once there, he placed her knees over his shoulders. He bent forward and inhaled deeply of her intoxicating scent before swiping his tongue from her dripping channel to her swollen clit. Ana gave a keening cry when Wray began to suckle it gently.

Within seconds, she came, flooding his mouth with her woman's cream. She cried out his name and he thought his heart would stop, so much love filled him.

Before she could catch her breath, Wray began to ravage her with tongue and teeth. He licked and sucked at her pussy, lapping up all of the juice that was gushing from her.

Wray slid a finger into her swollen channel and slowly began working it in and out. Then he had two fingers in her, widening her, stretching her for his cock. Impatient to make love to his mate, he lifted her, placing her on her hands and knees before him. He stepped behind her and pushed against her upper back so that her head and shoulders rested upon the bed. As soon as he had her positioned how he wanted her, he thrust home.

Ana cried out. Wray stopped, holding himself completely still, deep inside her.

"Are you okay? Did I hurt you?" He didn't know what he'd do if he hurt her. She was everything to him.

Ana thrust her hips back against him, forcing him deeper. Wray groaned. "Please, Wray. It's not enough. Never enough. I need more."

That was all it took to set Wray off again. He pulled back until only the swollen head of his cock remained inside her and then slammed deep again. Again and again, he thrust hard in her tight pussy, reveling in the tight, hot depths of her, the way her muscles clenched his shaft.

Reaching around her hips with his right hand, he found her clit and began pinching it between his fingers. Ana came with a guttural moan, squeezing his shaft in her clasping channel. That was all it took to send Wray over as well.

Together, they collapsed upon the bedding, panting, their bodies covered in a sheen of sweat. Their scents mingled, the heavy musk of his seed and her woman's cream combining into a perfect blend.

"Sleep now, Ana," Wray whispered. "Tomorrow we will be mated on the surface outside the Lady Goddess' Temple with the others before heading to

Tigeria."

The Next Day... Outside the Lady Goddess' Temple~ Planet of G'Recio

THEY ENTERED THE circle. Large standing stones surrounded them. Ana watched the other couples as they gazed at each other lovingly with smiles on their comely faces. Glancing up at the huge stone pillars, she felt small, dwarfed by the enormous stones. How long had they stood here in this magical glen, she wondered.

Her fingers—her entire body—itched as the mystical power poured from the ancient ring. It enshrouded them in the warmth of its teeming energy. Worried, she feared she would never live up to the expectations of her mates. Would they ever show pride in her abilities, or would she forever be an embarrassment to them? Ana shook off her trepidation and placed her hands in those of her mates, allowing them to lead her further into the grass-covered ring.

No sooner had the four triads reached the center, than the wind gathered strength around the outer ring. Eddies of leaves danced around the edge, small whirlwinds of swirling sand drove the onlookers away from the powerful glen. A vortex of swirling stars and darkness appeared in front of them before the wind suddenly died. The vortex disappeared and in its place was a woman with beauty and strength beyond measure.

Drawing herself to her impressive height, the woman stepped forward, a smile on her glorious face. She looked between the four triads and nodded.

"All is as it should be." She gazed through the standing stones and lifted her hand. She motioned for Jaynee, Dare and Luc to join them. "My first triads of power," she said raising her arms to encompass them all. "You have listened and heeded my will well—though some of you wished not to." She turned her gaze to Ana and lifted her brow.

Ana's face blazed with mortification. She wanted nothing more than to crawl beneath one of the large stones and hide.

The woman smiled kindly. "Still, I would reward such obedience, not punish it." She threw her head back and allowed the wind to whip her hair about her. "All ye gathered here, bear witness—these men and women are joined together by my hand." She approached each triad and placed their hands together, each three forming a pyramid. "They are now, and forever will be, under my protection. Together they are everyone's salvation." She turned as if to leave and stopped. "There will be more. Let us all rejoice in the knowledge of the inevitable defeat of the cruel *Banart* army."

The woman raised her voice louder, so those gathered round the circle could hear and celebrate. "Take each other's hands," she instructed each triad in turn. "Feel the power flowing through you." She moved to clasp Sayre and Fane's hands together. She paused before Luc before giving him a beauteous smile. "You look much better thus." She feathered her fingers through his dark hair. "I—" She turned to glance back at the others before returning her wondrous silver-eyed gaze back to Luc. "Like the others—wish there was no need for the subterfuge—for your need to become something you are not. I—as does your beautiful mate—prefer your ebony color to that of the blonde you must so often conceal yourself with."

The Goddess, for Ana realized it could be no other, returned her attention to the others once more. She checked to see that their hands were clasped, each triad a pyramid raising a cone of power of their own. A fissure of light shot from one group to the other, linking first three, then all four triads together by one thin band, one thin ribbon of pure silvery white light. Their eyes widened as they all gazed at the thin band of power, charged by their clasped hands and unified front.

"So you see the power granted you by the Universe—the power that awaits those who would be strong enough to join our cause. You finally see the means by which you shall defeat the enemy. "I wish—" She stopped, silvery tears glimmering in her eyes. "I wish I could do more, but even *I* am bound by nature's laws. I am forbidden to use my powers against those who would harm you." She smiled mischievously. "Yet I am not forbidden to bring those together who would have the power to rival even that of a god." She looked at them all in turn, her gaze boring into their very souls. "Use this power wisely, lest we all perish."

The strange echoing voice ceased and a bright light momentarily filled the circle, spilling out into the surrounding fields and forest. Blinded, Ana put her hands to her face to block the intense light. When the light disappeared, so had their powerful visitor.

Ana's hands—no—her entire body tingled with the residual power as the males turned to their mates and spoke as one.

"I claim you both as my triad mate. Forever are we bound. You are forever in my keeping."

The women threw their heads back, drew down the power of the universe, and gazed at their men, their eyes nearly glowing as they spoke their own binding vows.

"I accept your claim as I stake a claim of my own. I claim you males as my true triad mates. Your hearts are forever bound, forever in my keeping."

The bolt of energy returned, joining each triad together, snaking to the next, until the light bound all four triads. The bolt of pure, blue-white energy shot from the bound triads, seeking out those who would harm them. Several screams rent the air as explosions sounded near and far.

"*Banarts,*" someone exclaimed. "There were *Banarts* among us!"

Ana ran toward the muffled cries. Wray grabbed her and swung her behind him. "You are no warrior, my sweet. Do not rush headlong into danger. That is my job."

Communiqués came from all over the planet. "Several *Banarts* have been found dead. They have all been burned alive by the same energy bolt that killed those near the circle." Drace said, holding his large hand to his ear, his free arm looped around Kiri's shoulder, in an effort to keep her safe as she clutched at the tiny hand of her son beside her.

The four triads traded looks with the grim realization that together they possessed a mighty weapon.

"We could free every one of the *Banart* controlled planets," Laynee whispered, as she held her trembling fingers over her lips.

"Perhaps," Sayre agreed, stepping up to encircle her in the protection of his arms. "But once we are gone, we leave them to face our enemy's wrath."

"Maybe the more of us there are, the farther reaching our powers will be," Jaynee added. "Just as the cone of power grows as our coven grows, perhaps this new power—this weapon—shall also grow as more triads are formed."

"We can only hope. The enemy is widespread and far-reaching. Any planet we free would only be enslaved once more as we moved on to free others. We must find a way to rid the universe of them." Wray pulled her closer and Ana fought to keep herself from closing her eyes. Every breath he took, every word he spoke drove her nearer to a desire she couldn't name, couldn't fathom.

You await the real claiming, Ana. Kel whispered into her mind. *Your body yearns for mine. It yearns for Wray's. Together the three of us will quench your desire—your undeniable thirst for our bodies.*

She shivered in response, waiting, needing them to do the things they promised to do. How could it be that only a few short days ago she feared this mating, this meeting of the flesh? Now she craved it with everything within her. Her body trembled at the thought of their inevitable possession and she hungered for it. She couldn't wait to be alone with them—couldn't wait to feel them pressing their hard hot bodies against her as she cried out her pleasure between them. Where before she feared it, she now feared she would never have it—have them.

Wray pressed his groin against her buttocks. "You shall have us as you desire, Ana," he breathed in her ear. "Soon we shall be alone in my quarters aboard the *Nomad* and we will give you what your body craves."

Two hours later… Lupin Starship Nomad

KEL BREATHED HER scent deep. He needed her as badly as she obviously needed him. Needed them. Her body gave her desire away. Her nipples pebbled, tenting the thin scrap of material that covered her breasts. The sheer material wrapped around her hips, hung to her ankles in strips, barely covering her shapely legs.

He closed his eyes in an attempt to bring his raging hormones under control. What would he do if he suddenly shifted to his tiger and scared her? He would never forgive himself. Fisting his hands at his sides, he contented himself to just stand beside her and breathe in her intoxicating scent.

Wray moved to embrace her, burying his face in the crook of her neck. What Kel wouldn't do to have the control over his body that he needed to do just that.

Gently, Ana pulled away from Wray. Smiling, obviously to not cause him pain or distress, she licked her full lips and turned to Kel, her gaze searching his. "You cannot make me believe you would hurt me, even in your other form." She reached out her free hand, keeping one clasped within Wray's firm grip.

Her free hand grasped the waistband of his slacks and she tugged him to her. "I do not fear you," she said cupping his cheek. "Please do not pull away. You cannot isolate yourself from us like this. I—I," she paused, licking her lips. "I love you. I need you." She glanced back at Wray. "I need you both."

Kel couldn't believe his ears. He never expected her to accept him—all of him. She even accepted that part of him that wasn't human. He could see it on her face, in her beautiful amber eyes. He couldn't keep himself from her any longer. Moving forward, he crushed her to him, reveling in her soft acceptance.

Wray moved behind her, wrapping his arms around her to fondle her breasts, as she leaned forward to press her mouth against Kel's.

Kel groaned when she parted her lips and moaned into his mouth. His heart raced, pounding against his ribs as her silky hands pushed up his *shert.* Petal smooth thumbs brushed over his flat nipples and his knees turned to mush. He backed toward the bed, pulling her with him, lest he fall at the floor at her feet in supplication.

"But that is what I want, Kel," she breathed against his mouth. Pressing her lips to his cheek, she moved boldly to his ear. "I need you to worship me on occasion, just as Wray also needs our worship. I've come to care for you, Kel, but I do have needs…" She left off on a blush, lowering her head until her chin dropped to her chest. "Occasionally I must have control. At least in this room."

She ripped his *shert* open, pressed her face to his chest and laved his nipple. "I must have a bit of control. At least once in a while." She rubbed herself against him as Wray fondled her from behind. "But tonight I sense your need and I bow to you. Make me yours." Straightening, she turned to Wray. "Mate with me. Both of you."

Kel needed no other invitation. His hands moved to her hair, pulling her to him for another soul-deep kiss. He needed this—needed her—in every way that she would have him. Releasing her hair, his hands trailed down her body, feeling her soft curves. He pushed the thin scrap of material from her breasts and feasted his eyes on her luscious curves. Bending down, he lowered his head to her breasts, suckling the tight rosy peaks.

He watched as Wray moved his hand lower, burying his fingers in her juicy cunt, wondering if he would ever have the patience to wait his turn at her tight vaginal hole.

"I don't want you to wait," Ana said, her breath coming in little pants. "I want you both at the same time." She blushed prettily and it was almost his undoing. "The others have told me of a way for us all to reach our pleasure. I wish to have you both this way. Please," she begged as her legs gave out and they carried her to the huge bed in the center of the large cabin.

After gently undressing her, they lay her on the bed to remove her thin sandals. They both massaged her calves and feet as they unlaced the long ties that bound them to her feet. His heart slammed erratically in his chest as she watched them undress with wide eyes.

Kel wanted to prolong it. He needed to stretch this agony out as long as possible. A part of him urged him to hurry but another part insisted he allow her to see every muscle of his body—every inch of his straining erection. His cock sprang free of the constraining cloth as he unbuttoned his *trews.*

Reaching up, she took hold of their bobbing shafts as they knelt beside her on the soft bed. Kel watched as her beautiful rosy-tipped breasts moved in time with her measured strokes through his half-closed eyes. It wasn't long before they both reached down to still her hands on their raging cocks.

She smiled coyly, gazing up at them with a lust-filled gaze.

"Suck it," he rasped, his voice barely more than a memory. His mind, like his voice, was gone. Taking with it any ability he'd ever had to make an intelligent decision. Every cell of his being was centered on this one woman as she slowly leaned forward to wrap her lips around his straining erection.

"As you wish, my lord," she whispered, just before her full, pink lips closed over the head of his eager cock.

Kel inhaled deeply, sucking enough air into his lungs to live for a week. He loved the scent of his mate's arousal. It was like an aphrodisiac, the strongest of drugs made to drive him wild with need.

She licked the length of his shaft. The stroke of her tongue sent pinpricks of ecstasy through his blood and he threw his head back. The sensation of her tongue sliding over the smooth flesh of his hardened organ nearly drove him over the edge. Gentle fingers cupped his balls and squeezed lightly, her nails softly scoring the underside of his sac. Lost in a forest of need, he buried his fingers in her hair and held her head as he pistoned his cock into her talented mouth.

The scent of her desire assaulted his senses and nearly drove him mad. The heady perfume of her body's musk had him licking his lips with the need to have her, to taste her. Finally gathering his wits, he looked down when he heard her long, guttural moan and grinned. It seemed his triad mate had the same idea. Kel watched with ever-growing need as Wray slid his tongue through her glistening folds, drawing mewls of ecstasy from their once reluctant lover.

Each moan, each cry of pleasure that Wray wrung from her luscious lips reverberated over his cock as she continued to take him deep into her throat. Still, he kept his hand fisted around the base of his cock, lest the great length choke her.

WRAY HAD WATCHED as long as he could before finally giving in to the need to taste his mate. Her flesh was sweet. Her body's fragrant perfume taunted him, begged him to lean down and stroke his tongue through her glistening folds. Her lover's cream seeped from her beautiful pussy as she continued to suck

Kel's cock. The sight of her full lips wrapped around Kel's organ had nearly been his undoing. It was all he could do to sit and watch for a time without jerking off and embarrassing himself on the sheets.

He settled himself low on the bed, maneuvering between her silky thighs. He almost came when she moaned deep in her throat as he tongued her erect clit. He grinned, knowing by Kel's guttural groan that her reaction had nearly sent him over the edge.

Wray watched as Kel, obviously too close to his climax to continue, pulled his cock from her mouth. If he hadn't been preoccupied with dining on Ana's precious cunt, he may have gone for a bit of that himself. Instead, he continued to eat away at her gushing pussy as Kel suckled her pert breasts while she came into his mouth.

Sitting up, he gave them both a practiced grin. "Top or bottom?" He asked, raising his brow. "This is your night, your choice, Kel. It is our gift to you."

"Bottom," Kel said, his voice no more than a guttural grunt. "I can't wait to feel her atop me, riding my cock, her breasts jutting toward me." He lay down on the bed and waited for her to lower herself over his large penis, his eyes glazed with need.

Wray couldn't blame him. He would love to feel her clasping vagina on his own cock. He watched as she slowly impaled herself on Kel's massive organ and leaned forward, pressing her breasts against the other male's chest. Wray looked down to the once forbidden hole as the little puckered ring winked up at him. He licked his lips. He would have her there. It was what she wanted. She reached back and wet the tiny ring with her own juices, waiting. They were both waiting.

He fell on them with a groan. He needed to feel the flesh of her tight ass sucking the cum from his cock. He longed to feel the pulse of her orgasm as she came with them both inside her. Damn if he didn't want to know what it felt like to have another man's cock stroking his through the thin barrier between her two holes.

He placed the head of his cock to her wetness, gathering the slick evidence of her desire; he coated the head of his rod before moving to her smaller bottom hole. Gritting his teeth, he pressed the head of his cock into the tight ring. Everything within him told him to ram his cock home, instead of easing the massive organ into her back entrance.

Still, he went slowly, enjoying every moment of his slow possession. His eyes squeezed closed, he wondered how he would ever last long enough to bring Ana to her pleasure.

She moaned beneath him and he stopped. He prayed to the Goddess that she wouldn't ask him to leave her. He wasn't sure he could.

"Should I stop?" he asked between clenched teeth.

"No. Goddess, Wray, don't stop now," she begged then wriggled backward seating his cock deep into her ass. "Yes," she keened into Kel's chest. She wriggled again, nearly unseating herself from Kel's eager shaft. Wray cupped her ass, holding her in place until his need to climax passed. Kel lay still beneath them, his eyes closed tight. If his shallow pants and clenched teeth were any indication, he was close to cumming, as well.

Wray gritted his teeth and tried to think on other things. He wanted—needed—to pleasure their lovely mate so she would allow this type of mating again. There was no doubt in his mind that triad mating could become addictive. Perhaps it was too late and he was already addicted.

"Stroke her clit, Kel. Make her scream for us."

No sooner had Kel reached between them, than she stiffened. Lifting herself away from him, she bared her breasts to his hungry mouth. A scream bubbled from her throat as Kel leaned up and latched on to the hardened nipple of her right breast.

Wray squeezed his eyes closed, his hands gripping her hips as he continued to drive his hard length into her forbidden channel.

ANA'S THROAT HURT from her continued screams as climax after climax overtook her. Kel's tongue circled her nipple, his teeth lightly abrading the turgid tip. Wray's hands caressed her back and bottom, squeezing and molding the soft white globes of her ass. The delicious fullness she'd felt at her first claiming was nothing compared to this. The pleasure returned tenfold with the two of them moving deep within her quivering body. Her heart slammed in her chest until she was certain she would die from the promise of such unbearable pleasure.

"Yes!" she screamed, fighting to make them move faster. Still, her two mates worked in a slow, agonizing rhythm that made her want to scream. They brought her to her pleasure again and again, yet she wanted more. She needed more. She needed them to lose themselves in her as much as they wanted her to do the same.

No sooner had the thought formed in her mind than Kel growled, his eyes changed, looking more like those of his animal side. His incisors lengthened and he spoke, his voice sounded strange. Deeper. Perhaps it was from his partial change.

"Will you bind with me?" He looked over her shoulder to Wray and nodded.

"Will you bind with us?" Wray added from behind her as they both stilled. They waited for her answer, their cocks still buried deep inside her.

"Don't stop," she begged. "I'll do anything. Please!"

Kel leaned up, wrapped his fingers around the back of her neck and pulled her down to gently press his lips to hers. "Shh... Ana, my love." He pushed the sweat soaked hair from her brow and gazed deep into her eyes. "It is not our intention to torment you. We wish only a blood bond with you."

She pulled away—what little bit that she could. "A—A blood bond?"

He nodded. "It would tie us three together. More so than the *Tigerian* ceremony already has. It would make us all *Tigerian, Lupin, and Carrillian.* Our life-forces would be bound together, extending your life considerably."

"Blood bond?" She asked, her voice nothing more than a terrified squeak. "Extend my life?" She asked, latching on to one good thing that she could see come from such a bonding. "By how long?"

"We would all remain as we are for another eighty years or so." Wray answered from behind her.

Ana's eyes widened and she licked her lips. She wriggled her hips in an attempt to keep them interested lest they should lose their lovely erections. *Eighty more year of this? By the Goddess, only a madwoman would refuse such an offer!*

"Yes," she said with a nod. "Will it—will it hurt?"

Kel gave her a curt nod. "For a bit. Then you will feel the ultimate pleasure as our blood blends and binds us together. Only then can we lose ourselves in your softness. A human's body is too frail for us to truly lose control."

How could she say no? Why would she want to? She leaned forward to kiss Kel, her lips trailing over the muscles of his chest. She gasped when Wray slowly pulled his cock from her ass then slid it back in—a reminder to her they awaited an answer. She almost snorted. As if it were likely that she'd forget.

"Yes." She leaned back and turned to press a sweet kiss to Wray's lips, lest he feel left out. "I want it all."

Again, Kel's teeth lengthened and he leaned forward to sink razor sharp incisors deep into the flesh of her breast. At the same time, Wray pierced the skin of her shoulder and she screamed from the mixture of pain and pleasure. She climaxed again as they held her immobile and drove their cocks deep inside her.

A different kind of pain shot through her as her body suddenly reacted to their saliva in her blood. Her gums ached, her incisors grew and she knew an unnatural need for their blood. She clasped her hand to her mouth. The last thing she wanted to do was hurt either of them.

It is not unnatural this time, little one, Wray whispered into her mind. *This time it is as natural as childbirth or breathing.*

Kel pulled her down to him, his fingers feathering through her hair, soothing her, even as they continued to move inside her. They were driving her wild with need. Never had she wanted anyone as much as she did these two males. She couldn't get enough.

"You must do this thing to bond with us," Kel said, petting her head, his large hands soothing her jangled nerves.

Wray massaged her body, his hands moving in soothing circles over her flesh. "Kel is right, little one. You must do this to bind our life-forces."

They both wrapped their arms around her, holding her close until she was filled with the need to sink her teeth into Kel's flesh. "Do it," he urged. Unable to deny the need any longer, she sank her new teeth into the heavy muscles of his chest.

Kel threw his head back and groaned, his erection growing impossibly larger. Large hands moved to her hips, alternately lifting and lowering her over him. He relentlessly pounded his hard cock into her as she raised her head and watched the marks slowly heal and fade from his flawless chest. She looked down at her breast with wonder. There were no marks marring the smooth, ivory flesh.

She took a moment to revel in the new sensations, the new emotions that accompanied her altered state as her two mates continued to thrust themselves deep inside her. Still, they didn't release the tight rein they held on their control.

Ana turned her head and looked at Wray through half closed eyes. She could barely keep them open, her pleasure was so great. He smiled and leaned closer as her teeth grew once again. Unable to reach his chest, she sank her teeth into his shoulder and his cock jerked inside her.

"Ana," he growled. "I hope you're ready. I can't—"

"We can no longer hold back," Kel completed Wray's sentence as they both began to drive into her with a force she never thought possible. The two males worked out a rhythm that nearly drove her insane. Each of them impaled her ruthlessly with their frenzied thrusts. Kel's hands tightened on her hips to the point of pain.

Wray's gentle kneading of her buttocks, as he drove inside her, only added to the endless stream of sensation and she screamed out another seemingly endless climax as they took her ever higher.

Her two mates took each other's wrists and completed the blood triad before they both growled through their own release. Their cocks pulsed inside her, shooting hot jets of cum deep inside her body. The pulsing of their cocks drove her over the edge once more and her body shuddered through her final climax. Seconds later, she collapsed onto Kel's chest, spent.

Three weeks later... Tigeria

ANA WOKE TO the call of a strange animal. *What strange and loud thing is that?* She grimaced and reached to pull her pillow over her head and realized she was not alone. One at her front, the other pressed to her back, the heat from her mates' bodies kept her warm from the morning chill. Closing her eyes, she inhaled, loving the scent of their combined musk.

The strange animal crowed again and her eyes flew open. *Damn that noisy creature! Can't a body get some sleep?*

Gingerly sitting up, so as not to wake her mates, she looked toward the window and made a face. Damn it was early. The gray light of the approaching dawn filtered through the sheer curtains. Climbing from between the two men, she got out of bed and padded to the window to greet the morning and curse that infernal beast whose noisy calls rattled her nerves.

Fire burned in the distance as the *Tigerian* sun moved higher, finally breeching the horizon as it filled the sky with a rosy glow. Gooseflesh rose on her arms as she watched the new day come to life.

She smiled as Wray's warm arms wrapped around her from behind and Kel stepped up beside her, his hands already straying to her hair. She leaned back and allowed her mates to comfort her.

"We leave for Wray's world today," Kel said, grasping her hand. "But we shall return here often."

Ana sighed. She certainly hoped so. Her newest and best friends could be found here as well as such glorious mornings. This is the kind of life she would wish for all her people and the *G'recians,* she thought. This was a peaceful world where they would lead peaceful lives filled with beauty, wonder and love. What more could they ask?

KIRI WOKE UP and glanced at her adopted son. Pushing back his sandy blonde hair, she pressed a loving kiss to his forehead. She knew she should have left him in his own bed, in his own room. He must learn to depend on her less as he grew older. Still, he needed her near him for a while yet. Even after these last few weeks, nightmares of the hideous *Hienials* still plagued him.

A strange light appeared in the far corner of the room and she quickly placed herself in front of him like a shield. Her mouth dropped open when a woman stepped from the center of the light. It was the Lady Goddess. Her body began to quake when she realized her visit could only mean one thing.

"You have been through a great ordeal, Kiri." She turned her gaze to Ryo and smiled. "It is good that you protect him, but there is no need. It shows much of your character that you can so dearly love the son of a beast."

Kiri fought the urge to cover the boy's body with her own. He wasn't a beast. Never that! Her heart stuttered in her breast. How could she protect him from a Goddess?

Ryo cowered behind her shaking. Sending waves of love and reassurance, she reached back to comfort him, her heart breaking. His fear and his trust in her nearly undid her. The poor boy knew so little of love—only what she herself had shown him. So many people had already attempted to end his young life. It didn't matter that he was small. It was his heart she strove to protect. His heart was larger than the planet he'd been born upon. The boy had an endless capacity to love.

The Goddess smiled at him and her expression gentled. "Your time will come, young Ryo. Soon you lead your people against a great enemy. There is goodness inside you unrivaled by any other. And a time will come when that goodness is needed. Have faith in yourself, in your abilities and in the people you hold dear." She laid a gentle hand on his hair. "Many blessings upon you." Ryo stilled, finally comforted and fell into an exhausted sleep.

The Goddess turned her gaze back to Kiri and smiled. "I charge you with his safety. You guard him like a young lioness, as is fitting. Your mates will be pleased that you will guard your children with such zeal." She leaned forward and whispered. "And they are coming, young protector. You are the next."

SEX ME OUT

Kiri Leran sat on her bed in shock. She dare not say or do anything. Poor Ryo had just fallen into an exhausted slumber and she didn't want to wake him. The poor dear needed his sleep. Yet she knew she would get no sleep this night, despite the comfort of her accommodations. Looking around the room, she realized the furnishings were expensive. At least they hadn't locked her in a barren cell. Still, they'd locked her in. What did they expect her to do, run—kill someone? No matter how luxurious her surroundings, a prison was still a prison.

She chewed her nails, wondering when the men would come to claim her. Her belly clenched and she also wondered if she'd be able to hold down her last meal. How would she know her two men? Was the *Lioni* male one of them? He'd already made his claim at the temple. She squeezed her eyes shut. She didn't know if she could stand it. How could she welcome two men in her bed after all she'd already suffered? How would she ever keep her sanity?

Ryo stirred behind her, whimpering. He tossed his head on the soft pillow and she turned to pull him into her arms. Kissing his forehead, she brushed the dirty blonde strands from his face and looked down into the visage of innocence. How could anyone not love such a face? What kind of animal must a person be to kill such a child, regardless of his parentage and the circumstances of his birth?

The child was nothing like his parentage would suggest. She worried about that sometimes. What was it that made the *Hienial* men so hideous, so evil? Was it the evil within them that twisted their hearts and souls and made them such ugly creatures? Ryo was the epitome of the perfect child. Kind, handsome, full of love, he was perfect in every way. How could someone so good turn to something so bad, so evil?

She inhaled deeply, loving his scent. He smelled of the soap and lotion she'd applied to his dry skin after his bath. She stayed on the bed next to him, holding him close and waited for the sun to rise. The new day would come and she would face her new life with courage. Nothing, no one could be as bad as three *Hienial* males. She would survive this and raise Ryo into the man who would lead his people from evil.

She hoped.

DRACE VANIER STARED at the door in front of him. Beyond the thin barrier was his mate. He knew he couldn't go to her yet. She certainly wouldn't welcome him after the abuse she'd suffered at the hands of the *Hienials*. He would need more patience than he'd ever needed before. The raging of his body wouldn't make it easy though. Just knowing she was aboard made him hard. Her scent nearly drove him wild and he feared he would lose control and try to force her like some untamed beast. He took a deep breath and held it. He would control his base urges, if for no other reason than to make his mate comfortable. His beast would just have to suffer, for the time being.

His first glimpse of her had nearly unmanned him. He'd known the minute he laid eyes on her that she was his. He ran his fingers through his hair, frustrated that he'd have to share her. He'd searched worlds for her, spent endless years yearning for a mate of his own. What was it about their galaxy that females were so few and scattered? What horrible thing did they do to deserve such hardship when it came to their women?

He paced away from the room, slammed his fist into the nearest bulkhead then sighed heavily. How would he ever convince the woman to accept him when he couldn't control his anger, his rage? Closing his eyes, he thought of his best friend and went to the nearest transport pad. Fury would know what to do. If not, he would give him the diversion he needed so badly. A few rounds of *Pal'alshok* would knock some sense into him and Fury was just the man to do it. He punched in the coordinates for the *Polaris* and sent himself to see his friend.

He shimmered into view on the pad on the other ship and nodded to the guards there. "Where is your master?"

"He is on the bridge, sir," the man said with a bow. "He knew you would come. He awaits you with *Carrillian* whiskey and game of *Nos'tak*."

"Just what I need to relax." It wasn't a physical game, but working his mind would have a similar effect. He left the transport chamber and strode toward the nearest *Trans-lift*. "Deck four."

The doors of the lift opened just outside the bridge and Fury stood waiting. "I knew you would come. I felt your uncertainty in waves. It is not an easy thing thinking that you must share your woman with another."

"How would you know?" Drace snapped. "You have no woman and when you do find her, you will most likely not have to share her with a stranger."

"Do you think it would be easier to share her with a friend?" Fury asked, his tone clearly stating he knew it wouldn't be easy regardless. "Still, a mate shared between two men is better than no mate at all. Is it not?" He grinned. "Besides, just think, the rest of your life would be filled with such escapades as we have been known to have with the *Banchal* females. They do love threesomes. Too bad they are born immune to our seed. I would have chosen one of them to mate long ago, if it weren't for that little fact."

Drace smiled wistfully at the memories Fury invoked. "If my triad mate were you, I don't think I would feel such revulsion to it."

"Hmm... You think you would not." Fury led him onto the bridge and they sat at the gaming table. "Do you still wish the diversion, or would you rather talk?" he asked, pouring two glasses of the expensive sapphire drink.

Leaning forward to accept the glass, Drace shrugged. "I don't think I could concentrate on the game now. I would surely be too easy a conquest for you."

"What is your excuse any other time, old friend?" Fury chuckled then downed his drink in one large gulp. "And don't tell me you let me win either."

"Back to the woman," Drace said, swirling the sapphire liquid in his glass. "I'm not sure I could share her, Fury."

Fury sat forward in his chair, his elbows on his knees and gave Drace an unreadable look. "Even with me?"

Drace snorted. "I think you are the only male that I *could* share her with."

"Then perhaps it is best that I am the third in your triad."

Stunned, Drace sat back in his seat and stared at Fury. "How can you know that when you haven't met her?"

"You know I have special...abilities. You've always known that we were linked the moment our blood blended in that brawl on *Truan Four.* The minute you saw her, I knew."

"Then why did you not say something sooner?"

Fury snorted. "And say what exactly? That I'm glad you found your mate and would you hurry up and introduce us so I can take her to mate as well?"

"I don't know. Perhaps waiting for me to come to you was the best thing you could have done." He couldn't believe the relief he felt knowing that Fury thought himself the third in his triad.

"How long has she been resting now?"

Drace glanced at his timekeeper. "About twelve hours. I think perhaps she's waited long enough. She knows I've made my claim. The waiting could be harder on her than the knowing."

Fury arched an ebony brow. "It could. She needs to know we don't intend to force ourselves on her, that we're willing to give her the time she needs to come to trust us. The last thing she will want is two males falling on her in a mating rut after all she's been through."

"You're right. And we should all be on the same ship. She needs to get to know us both."

They stood at the same time, pushing their chairs back an almost identical distance.

"We cannot allow this to come between us. We must both accept her and accept each other. I don't know about you, Drace, but I want this to work between us. I look forward to a lifetime of loving the same woman as we have done countless times throughout the years."

"Perhaps our earlier escapades were in preparation for this very thing." Drace turned toward the door. "Come, let us find our mate and introduce ourselves."

FURY INSTRUCTED HIS people to put away the gaming table and whiskey then followed Drace from the bridge. They entered the transport chamber and stepped up onto the pad. Turning, they looked at each other then grabbed each other's forearms in a warrior's embrace.

"I am honored to be your beta, old friend." Fury bowed his head in deference to Drace's superior rank. "I would have followed you in death. Now it is time to follow you in life."

Drace swallowed visibly and Fury knew he had not made a mistake. His brother could lead their people without him. Damek was the eldest and heir. With his stable of councilors, he didn't need Fury as beta. He turned toward the nearest crewmember. "Leave me here with Drace. Take the ship back to my brother and his council. Tell him…" He paused, not wanting to hurt his brother. "…Tell him that I have finally found my place and wish him well."

"Yes, sir," the crewman said with a salute. "As you will it."

They shimmered into being on board Drace's ship, the *Revenge,* and immediately strode toward the woman's cabin.

The distinct sound of battle reached them followed by a child's fearful cry.

"I won't let you take him!"

They rounded the last corner on a run. Fury grinned, amazed at his mate as he watched her brandish the legs of a chair at the crew members in front of her, their arms raised to deflect the woman's blows. Pride rushed through him when he saw that she was not easily intimidated. She fought for her cub with bravery, like any good lioness or mama bear.

One of the men turned and ran to Drace when he saw them. "We were only going to take the boy to the infirmary. He's so small, the doctor wanted to see him, to see if he has a growth deficiency."

"Ryo goes nowhere without me!" she snarled, brandishing her weapons at anyone brave enough to even come close to her.

Fury drew himself up, pushed past the men trying to enter the room and stood in front of her door, his arms crossed over his chest. "Leave them be. If she agrees, Drace and I will escort them to the infirmary."

The men turned to Drace, and at his nod, turned and walked away. They left Drace and Fury to handle the little spitfire who was their mate. Fury grinned and turned to face the open door. Bowing, he introduced himself. "Hello, mate. I am Fury."

"And I'm furious. We should make a lovely pair," she shot back, not missing a beat. "Now, if you don't mind, I'd appreciate it if you would close the door."

Drace followed him into the room, allowing the door to slide closed behind them.

"I meant with you both on the other side."

She gathered the boy into her arms then placed him behind her. She began to tremble as they both merely stood watching her. Tears began to stream down her face as she stood facing them, her back straight. The legs of the chair she'd broken rested on the bed beside her, ready for her to make a hurried grab at them. Fury was determined to see she would never think to do so.

"We are your mates. We thought to give you the opportunity to get to know us," Drace said as he stepped closer. "We do not wish to frighten you or bully you in any way."

"Ha! Is that why you sent your men here to me?" She clearly didn't believe him.

"We have no reason to lie to you, mate," Fury added, moving to stand beside Drace. They both stood and stared at her. Fury couldn't believe how lucky they were to have such a beautiful mate. She would complement them both. Her children would be as stunning as she, and with luck, as courageously ferocious.

Fiery red hair cascaded down her back in long curls. Green eyes flashed up at them, accentuating her high cheekbones and full red lips. Everything about her stirred his blood, making his gut tighten in reaction. There was both a delicacy and strength in her features. Even her nose was charming. Short and straight, it was a perfect fit for her delicate face. Her short stature did nothing to make her seem less formidable. Her fierce love of the boy and her willingness to die for him made her a force to be reckoned with.

Drace slowly approached them and knelt in front of the child. "I am Drace Vanier," he said holding out his hand. "I wish to be husband to your mother, would you allow that?"

Fury joined him on the floor, making himself as small as he could so as not to frighten the toddler. "And I am called Fury." He chuckled when the boy backed up. "It is my name, boy. Not my disposition. What is your name?" he asked, giving him the smile he usually reserved for his mother, younger brothers and nephew. "Are you going to tell me your name? It isn't fair, you know. You now know my name and I still know nothing of you."

The boy peeked out from behind his mother's legs. "I am called Ryo." He looked up at his mother, presumably for encouragement. "Mama says it means strong of heart."

"That is a good name for one such as you. A warrior must always temper strength with compassion."

"That's what Mama says." He nodded earnestly. Growing braver, he moved to his mother's side. His small hand still held onto her skirts. His bravery did not extend to completely leaving his mother. "Mama says she will not allow me to become like—" Tears filled his eyes and he started to tremble. "She says I will never be so bad."

"Of course you will not," Fury agreed with a curt nod before he turned his attention back to his mate. "I am called Fury."

She rolled her eyes. "As you said to the boy."

"I said it as a courtesy to you. I had hoped you would take the hint and offer your own name to me."

She snorted, showing her derision. "Why would I do such a thing when I know that names have power? It would be careless and stupid. Even Ryo knows enough to not give his full name."

"Be that as it may, I would still like to know what to call my mate." Fury watched as her eyes widened in fear before she dropped her gaze to the top of the boy's head. Her hands trembled within the small child's grasp.

"My name is Kiri," she whispered, her soft voice trembling.

Fury would have preferred to have her look him in the eye as she gave her name, but after all she'd suffered, he'd take whatever he could get.

"Thank you, sweetness, for gifting me with your name. It is almost as beautiful as you." Beside him, Drace shifted, obviously impatient to have her acknowledge him as well. He could actually feel Drace's urgency, his desire through the bond they'd long ago established between them.

"Now, I'm sure you want to do what is best for your son. What harm will it do if our medical personnel look at the young one? You can stay with him the entire time. No one," he said, with a quick glance at Drace, "especially the two of us, would ever wish harm upon you or yours. You are our mate, Ryo our son. We would defend you both with our lives if need be."

Fury watched with one eyebrow raised as Drace scooted closer to the boy, and ran his hand through the cub's already tousled hair, quickly skimming his fingers across the back of Kiri's hand. "Kiri, please allow us to escort you and Ryo to the infirmary. I would very much like to make sure you are both healthy and will live long lives with Fury and me. Is that so much to ask?"

Fury almost snickered but managed to control himself. Barely. He'd never thought to hear the mighty lion practically beg a female for anything. This is definitely one memory he'd keep tucked safe in his mind. One never knew when it might be useful for blackmail in the future.

After the longest minute of his life, his mate nodded warily. He couldn't blame her. She didn't know them, didn't know if they were honorable or not and after what she must have suffered at the hands of the enemy he couldn't imagine how terrified she must be to put her trust into a stranger. The courage and bravery she showed by doing so was truly awe-inspiring.

"I will do this. For Ryo." She gave them both a look that would have unmanned lesser men. "I do this for the boy. Not for you."

Drace stood and offered his hand to the young boy. Ryo looked at his hand with longing. His face showed the craving a boy felt to have a father, a man he could trust to look up to and emulate. He bit his lip, looked between the two of them with wide eyes before he offered his hands to each of them.

Kiri gasped and scowled at them both as if, by their mere presence, they took her son away. Crossing her arms over her chest, she strode to the door, waiting for each of them to take one of the boy's hands. Fury swallowed thickly, knowing what courage, what heart, it took for the young one to embrace them both into his life.

"I will follow behind you to witness all that transpires between you as you lead us to this infirmary."

They stopped in front of her and Drace reached out to chuck her under the chin. "There will be naught but our journey to the infirmary where we shall see to your health and...other needs."

"OTHER NEEDS?" KIRI felt a bit cornered. She glanced from the dark-skinned man named Fury, to Drace, the huge blonde *Lioni* male. Certain they meant she should see if she was capable of bearing their children, she trembled as she followed them. Part of her feared the outcome of her examination, another part dreaded it. She wanted to bear children again someday. She just wasn't sure she wanted it now, with these men.

"We thought you might need to talk about what happened."

"Talk about it? What good would that do?" She didn't want to remember it, let alone talk about it.

"We have found that it heals the mind to talk about that which has harmed you."

Her mouth dropped open. "And you have special healers for this type of thing?"

Drace nodded. "My father found such healers on a distant planet. He brought a few willing to leave their world with him to help our people—women who needed their minds repaired by such a healer. Women like you."

She looked down at her feet, blinking back the tears that threatened. How did they always seem to say the right thing? Whenever she thought the worst of them, they surprised her by doing something selfless. "I don't know how talking about it can help. But if you think I should talk to one of these healers, I will try."

Within minutes, they stopped in front of a solid *Illuma-glass* door. As soon as they entered the large room filled with strange looking equipment, she reached for Ryo. He took her hand and smiled up at her. His fingers curled around hers with familiar warmth. She blinked slowly when she realized that in her attempt to comfort him, he had reached out and done the same for her. They truly were a pair.

The healer approached them with a smile. Kneeling down in front of Ryo, she smoothed his hair back from his face, her hands checking his head. "How old is he?"

"He is nearly five summers."

"Five?" The healer frowned. "I didn't realize he was that old. He looks no more than three."

"He was born three moon cycles early." She looked back at the men who claimed to be her mates and swallowed. She hoped they didn't try to take him from her after her admission. "The woman who birthed him was dying. She made me promise to do everything I could to save him and keep him from the man who fathered him." Her heart clenched at the memory. Ryo was the only thing left to remind her of her lifelong friendship with Ryanza. "I cut him from her womb the moment she took her final breath."

The memories haunted her. She closed her eyes as if the action would keep the vision of the last time she'd seen her friend alive at bay. The sight of taking a knife to her friend's rounded belly as Ryo kicked frantically inside her. It as almost as if he'd known his mother was gone and he had been trying to kick his way from her womb.

"He...he was so small. So Tiny. Barely old enough to survive outside his mother's womb, still, he thrived when I took him. I fed him the milk from my own breast." Tears slid down her face as she continued her story, determined that they know all of it. "My own son had just been seized. He was only nine dawnings. They took him. When they found that he had been born without one of his fingers, they killed him." She gagged. "Then they ate him in front of me."

Kiri shook the memory off. It was in the past. A past she wished she could change. That was why she'd taken Ryo and run. That is why when any *Hienial* asked, the beasts were told he was a new child. Until he reached two he was safe. When he'd reached two summers, he looked old enough to take. But she knew. She knew deep in her stomach, where all of her premonitions came from, that they would kill him when they realized he wasn't growing as quickly as he should. That was when she ran.

"No sentient being should be so ghastly as to eat their own young." Her body began to tremble. "How can they be so disgusting?" She barely noticed when the one called Fury pulled her to her feet and wrapped his arms around her. Sometime during the retelling, the healer had taken Ryo across the room. How much had he heard? Goddess, she hoped he hadn't heard all of it. She'd been so careful to keep most of the horror of his parentage from him.

"It's all right, baby. I've got you now. No one will ever hurt you again." He smoothed his large hands over her back. She should have felt threatened, afraid, but she only felt...safe.

Kiri stood within his embrace, allowing Fury to hold her. She absorbed his warmth, feeling safe for the first time in years. She couldn't explain it, if she lived to be a hundred. She could feel his emotions. She felt his need to keep her safe, even from him. And that comforted her more than she'd ever thought possible.

She watched Drace as he stood with Ryo as the healer examined the boy. Drace glanced over at her and smiled. Kiri attempted to return his smile as she stood within Fury's tight embrace. When Drace turned to hear something the healer said, she closed her eyes and leaned into Fury's strength. Just for a moment. Then she would pull free and be strong again. Just this once, she needed to lean on someone.

"HE'S AWFULLY SMALL for his age," the healer whispered to Drace. "To save a child born three months early is a feat without specialized medical equipment." She smiled at the boy and gave him a few sweets. "There you go, sir. You were so brave, letting me test your blood. You and your mother will be happy to know you're very healthy. She will be so proud. Shall I tell her, or will you?"

Ryo inhaled deeply, his little chest puffing out. "I want to tell her. She's always so worried about me." He sighed and looked down at his feet. "I'm too small. She always says that."

The healer ruffled his hair. "You are small, but we have special food here that will make you grow quickly. I'll see that it is sent to you. Will you eat it?"

He nodded quickly, his face alight with the possibility that he would soon begin to grow. "Yes. Yes, I'll eat it. Please." He glanced back at Kiri. "I want to grow big and strong so that I can protect Mama."

Drace smiled and offered his hand. "Fury and I will protect your mother from now on, son. It is your job to grow strong to protect your own mate." He helped the boy hop down from the examining table and glanced back to the healer. "You may want to speak to his mother. You have much to talk about."

"Yes." She sighed. "I heard." The healer glanced back at Kiri. "I don't know how she survived. Seeing my child..." She shook her head. "Watching those animals do something like that would have driven me mad. She needs to talk to me alone. She will never say more in front of the boy. Tell her to join me in the other room." She indicated a small glass enclosure. "Where she can talk and still remain in sight of the child."

"I'm glad you have that small room. She never would have agreed to leave the boy out of her sight. I don't think he's been away from her once since he was born."

"It wouldn't surprise me." Glancing back to the boy, she lowered her voice to a whisper. "I can't tell you how I'd feel if some hideous creature killed my child then ate him in front of me."

Drace strode to the examining table, picked Ryo up and set him on his shoulder. "I know how I would feel and I think she feels the same, if her behavior earlier is any indication. Heal her mind, doctor. I can't bear to see the fear in her eyes."

Handing Ryo to Fury, Drace pulled Kiri into his arms. He needed to feel her in his embrace, just once. To feel the soft curves of his mate pressed against him was a luxury. No. It was a miracle. She was his miracle. He looked over her head to Fury. She was their miracle—their life. And her son was as their own.

"Your turn, *mi ama*. It is time you were healed, as well." He gestured toward the glass room. "We will stay here with your son." He smiled at her sharp look. "Yes. He is still your son. The boy is as much your child as if you'd given birth to him." He nodded his head toward Fury. "And though you don't believe we think of him as our own son, you soon will. But for now, you can watch us through the glass as you talk through your pain."

She pulled from his arms. A sharp pain stabbed him in the heart at her rejection and he raised his hand to the center of his chest. He rubbed the spot absently. She looked up at him through sorrow-filled eyes. Her lips trembled as she tried to smile.

"Someday I may look upon you with love. I truly hope this comes to pass if you are my mates." She shook her head slowly and cast her gaze downward. "But for now, I can only tell you I will try. For now, my heart breaks for my dead son, my departed friends and all of the women left on the surface—those who have no one to turn to." She placed her hand on his arm. "If you care for me as you say, find them. Find them all and help them as you would help me."

Drace nodded, swallowing thickly as her fingers squeezed tight, her nails biting into the thick muscles of his forearm. "It will be as you say. I will send a transmission to the other ships. They will help. Our healers will treat their many wounds—even the invisible ones."

Tears filled her eyes, trembling on her thick, red lashes, glittering like *moina* stones and her grip gentled. "Thank you, sir."

"Drace. My name is Drace. Please call me by my name."

"Thank you for your understanding...Drace."

He grinned at her. "There, that wasn't so hard, was it?"

She blushed prettily. His cock twitched at her nearness and he thought of his mother's friends, knowing only the memory of those old biddies would make it behave. He glanced over at Fury and almost scowled at the stupid grin on his friend's face. But he checked that too. He didn't want to frighten his apprehensive mate any more than she already was. She didn't need to witness his temper when she was not the object of his ire.

KIRI EYED THE medical doctor warily. Though the blonde woman looked friendly and appeared to truly want to heal not only her body, but also her mind, Kiri just didn't know what to think, what to do. She couldn't deny that getting the memories of her time with the *Hienials* out of her mind would be a blessed thing. How could just talking about what happened, reliving it again to another person, help her? It just didn't make sense.

"Kiri, there is nothing to fear from me. My name is Brandy Vanier. I'm Drace's adopted sister. I'd do nothing to harm my brother's mate, my new sister." When the doctor reached out and took her hand, a soothing balm of warmth spread throughout her body. Kiri shuddered as the heaviness that she'd lived with these past five years lightened, just a bit.

"How? How are you doing what you're doing?"

"It is my gift. A gift my family has encouraged me to use to help others. I'm an orphan really, brought as a child from a planet many, many light years away. When the Vanier Alpha found me homeless and starving, he took me in. His people have given me the world. Helping others is the least I can do."

"So, what do I need to do? Do I tell you all about the last five years I've lived as a repository for the *Hienial* seed?" Kiri's body shook so badly, she knew she was about to fall apart. She straightened her spine, intent on showing no weakness.

"Why don't you sit on the cot over there?" Brandy pointed toward a low cot covered with a homey looking quilt and several fluffy pillows, "While I lower the lights and light a few scented candles."

"What? Why? Don't I just tell you what happened and you'll allow me to leave?" Kiri twisted her hands together, her stomach churning. Regardless of how strange it may seem to lie on a couch, in the near dark, smelling flowers, if there was any chance it may help her, she'd do it.

"There is no reason *you* can't be comfortable when the telling is not. Is there, Kiri?"

Kiri shook her head, making her way to the low couch. The intricate design of the quilt drew her attention. It was almost as if the swirls and other designs moved as she touched it, drawing her fear and pain away from her. The feeling intensified as she lowered herself to lie down on the quilt.

"No, Kiri." The healer hurried to her side. "You must be beneath the quilt for it to truly help you." She helped Kiri to stand then pulled the covering aside to wait until Kiri lowered herself to the cot again.

The quilt covered Kiri with warmth and…love. She was surrounded by it. The sensation of being held in her mother's arms coiled around her, through her. Her heart warmed, her mind settled and her pain receded to a place where it could no longer touch her, hurt her—a place where she could pull it out, look at it and finally banish it from her heart.

The healer sat on a low stool near her, her hand resting on the quilt. "Do you think you can talk about it now?"

Kiri nodded and sifted through her memories. "Where should I start?"

Brandy smiled at her. "Start wherever you wish, sweetheart. But I think the beginning is always the best place."

"The beginning…" Kiri leaned back and shook her head. "No, that would take too long. I don't think any of us have the time for that." Besides, this made her uncomfortable. The pain was no longer debilitating, but she knew she couldn't spend the rest of her days beneath this lovely quilt. Sooner or later she had to return to Ryo and they both needed to learn to live again.

"Our government received a coded message from the *Carrillian* authorities or at least someone posing as their leader." She gripped the quilt tightly. Her fingers found a spot to trace and her pain receded a bit more. "The man begged for our help, saying they were under attack. Every man of warrior age, every boy nearing the *turun'ca* boarded ships and left to help them. We haven't heard from them since."

The healer tilted her head a frown marring her brow. "*Turun'ca?*"

"The coming of age."

"Oh. And what age would that be?"

Pain gripped Kiri's chest and the quilt warmed before the sensation faded. "They were all just approaching their fifteenth summer."

"Fifteen! All of your men and boys above the age of fifteen are gone?"

Tears slid down Kiri's face as she nodded. The quilt grew warm again, so warm she almost threw it off, but the pain she knew would wrack her if she did so, stopped her. "Every one of them. Only the old and infirmed were left." She attempted to look back, to remember without feeling the complete loss and rage she'd grown so used to over the last few years.

"After the males were gone, those animals came. They killed everyone not of breeding age. They took the sterile women away. I have no idea where. Several of them took a female. Three of them took me to my home and they— they raped me repeatedly until they got me with child. Only then, did they leave me alone. Then they waited for me to give birth and nurse my son so they could take him. I hid him when I realized they would consider him deformed. I knew what they would do. But—" she sobbed, the quilt glowing as it absorbed her sorrow. "But they found us."

Kiri threw the quilt off and stood. Grief and rage nearly consumed her as she paced the small area. She glanced out at Ryo, still held in Fury's arms and tried to bring her emotions back under control she had to do this. For Ryo.

Brandy stood and came to stand beside her. "I know the rest. You don't have to relive it again." She placed her hand on Kiri's shoulder and warmth and peace stole through her again. She reached up to finger a beautiful multi-stoned pendant, obviously distressed by the story.

Before Kiri could mention the pendant, alarm bells blared through the healer's office. Through the clear glass, she watched Drace and Fury stiffen. Even Ryo closed his eyes and cringed. Something serious must be going on.

Together she and Brandy ran into the main clinic, her to Ryo, Brandy straight to her brother's side.

She pulled Ryo into her arms. His little hands clutched at her shirt, then reached up and twisted in her hair.

"What is it, Drace? What's going on?" the healer asked.

Kiri listened intently, knowing that with so many of the enemy out there, both *Banart* and *Hienials*, danger was always near.

Drace grimaced while Fury paced. Neither would look Brandy in the eye. Finally, Drace answered, his voice gruff. "There is a damaged slave transport asking for assistance. There are wounded *Hienials,* as well as the women and children they've kept as slaves who require assistance."

Brandy's spine stiffened, and then she nodded. "I will do all I can, for all the injured."

Knowing it was her calling, and that she had no real choice but to volunteer the use of her gifts, Kiri turned toward the healer. "I have some small gift at giving ease to those in pain. If someone can care for Ryo, keep him safe, I will do all that I can to help you."

She was surprised when Fury walked up to her to lightly run his finger down her cheek. "If it pleases you, I will stay with Ryo."

Startled she nodded. "Thank you. It is important that he is protected by someone I can trust." She glanced down to the floor for a moment, searching her thoughts. "You say he is a son to you. I will take you at your word, but know this. He is the most important—the most precious—part of me. If anything happens to him, it is you who will suffer my wrath."

Drace moved toward her other side, placed his huge hand gently atop her shoulder. "I shall accompany you to the surface. They were so far out of the known galaxy, they have crash landed on an uncharted planet, so not only will there be danger from the *Hienials* themselves but we know nothing of what we'll find on the surface."

Kiri searched his gaze—for what she didn't really know. Maybe she wanted to believe that these men truly only meant to cherish her and her son. Nodding, she stepped away slightly, suddenly uneasy being so close to her mate—mates—she corrected to herself, glancing at Fury who even now gently held her son in his arms. She relaxed a bit as she watched him rub soothing circles on Ryo's back with his large hand. A man so gentle with children couldn't be all bad, could he? She bit her lip and looked away before he caught her staring.

DRACE STEPPED FROM the large personnel transport and looked up at the huge winged animals flying over their heads. What had Brandy called them? He glanced over at her as she stared up at them with awe.

"Look at them all," Brandy breathed, her eyes wide and glistening with unshed tears. She didn't show a bit of fear even though hundreds of the colorful but deadly looking beasts circled the landing site like carrion closing in for a fresh kill.

He raised his energy weapon when one flew lower, the claws from its feet barely missing their heads.

"No!" Brandy grabbed his arm, keeping him from killing one of the huge beasts. "Don't hurt them. They aren't here to harm us. They—" She glanced up them and smiled softly. "They aren't what they seem."

"Then what are they?" Drace asked, itching to shoot them from the sky. "It's obvious they've killed the *Hienials* and the people who once occupied the empty city we spotted on our way down."

"No, Drace. They have done nothing, but defend what is theirs. They didn't kill the occupants of the empty city. They *are* the occupants."

Drace whipped his attention back to her, searching her gaze before he returned his attention to the pale orange sky of this unknown world. "How do you know this, Brandy? I will allow neither you nor my mate to wander here if there is any chance that such creatures will do you harm. There is enough to worry about with you both working among the *Hienials*."

He heard her wistful sigh, but kept his attention on the creatures still circling overhead. "I can feel it, Drace." She reached out and gripped his arm.

"My planet's history has told of such creatures for many centuries. Long ago, they disappeared from my world. Most believe they are naught but a fairytale," she shrugged as she dropped his arm to step forward and gaze back up into the sky. "Or nightmare," she added, "depending on their beliefs. Perhaps they'd visited my world long ago, or originated there and came here when they weren't welcomed with open arms. For me though, Dragons have always fascinated me. To see this," she said waving her arms overhead as she turned in a slow circle, "to see this is every dream and fantasy come true for me."

"Are you sure it is safe then?"

"Yes," she nodded. "Very sure."

"Good, let us not tarry here then. Do what you need to do to make sure the survivors are well enough to transport and I'll gather my mate. They may be friendly now, but we know naught of them or their feelings toward trespassers. It is best to leave here quickly."

Drace watched as his little sister gave a rather wistful and reluctant nod before she rushed toward the rest of the medical team, her gaze darting from the rocky ground to the sky the whole way. Running his hand through his hair, Drace sighed. *Goddess, don't let coming here be a mistake*, he prayed. If anything happened to his mate or his sister, he would never forgive himself.

Turning away from his sister, Drace headed back toward his mate who he imagined was none too happy at being ordered to stay aboard ship until he could determine whether it was safe enough for her to help his sister. Of course, there were many possibilities in easing her anger. Perhaps, it would give him the perfect opportunity to get her used to his touch.

He was almost to the transport when the telltale tickling at the base of his spine warned of approaching danger. Dropping to a crouch, he quickly scanned the area, before spinning around to look behind him. There, coming up fast, a *Hienial*, raced toward him with a small battle sword in his hands, pure hate gleaming in his eyes. He had no time to strip and change into his lion form while wearing clothes would only hinder, not help him.

Before Drace could even reach for his weapon, one of the great beasts overhead swooped down and grabbed the *Hienial* with its clawed feet before again racing toward the sky at an incredible speed. Never had Drace seen such coloring on a creature outside his dreams. The dragon's armored scales ranged from the softest blues and silvery hues of a new moon to the dark blue of the sapphires his father had brought back from Brandy's planet so long ago. It essentially glowed. Its strange, changing iridescent colors glimmered as it flew away, carrying the enemy with it.

196

As the dragon beat his monstrous wings, and launched himself even higher in the sky, the *Hienial* thrashed, screaming his terror as they flew into the heavens. Drace watched, as the changing silvery blue dragon seemed to hover in mid-air. Another dragon, this one in shades of orange, gold and red, approached the first, and with his clawed forelegs extended, grabbed a hold of the *Hienial's* kicking feet.

He watched in horror, as the two dragons, separated, ripping the *Hienial* in half in mid-air. Drace shuddered, swallowed the bile rising in his throat. How could Brandy say they were safe after what he'd just witnessed? Still, he noticed that every one of his team remained on the ground unharmed, as did he. He couldn't discount the fact that the blue dragon had saved his life. The *Hienial* beast had been too close to him to draw his weapon. The beast surely would have killed him with his deadly sword if the dragon had not dragged the other creature to his doom.

He turned toward the transport, ready to tell his people to regroup. He was taking his mate and sister from this place before they were injured. He would not risk their safety.

"Stop!"

Where had the voice come from? It had seemed so close. It was almost as though he'd heard the voice in his head, the way he and Fury sometimes communicated. However, that was not Fury's voice. Drace heard the unmistakable sound of the beating of dragon's wings as he spun around in a crouch, ready to draw his weapon.

Two men stood before him. They were dressed strangely. The armor they wore looked like the scales of the dragons that had just ripped one of the *Hienial* in two. One dressed in varying shades of blues and silver, the other in varying shades of red and gold. He looked up toward the sky, searching for the two dragons that saved his life. It was impossible to tell if they were up there circling the sky with so many others flying overhead.

Both men were tall—taller even than he was. Their long black hair billowed behind them as they approached. Neither of them appeared to be armed. Drace studied them, assessing the danger as they approached. His head told him they were very dangerous creatures. His gut told him they had no intention of harming either him, or his people. Still, he watched them with caution. He would be a fool to do otherwise.

"Where are the dragons I heard swooping down upon me?" He looked around, still not quite believing they had been able to disappear so quickly. He heard them. He knew he did.

The two men looked at each other and grinned. "We *are* the dragons you're searching for. We apologize for giving you a fright earlier, but the man would have killed you and taken your women."

Drace nodded, still eyeing them warily. "Yes, they are good for that." Making a decision he wasn't quite sure was wise under the circumstances, he held out his hand in greeting. "I am Drace Vanier, leader of the *Lioni* people. When we discovered the distress call from the *Hienial* slave ship, we came here to provide medical treatment and retrieve the women and children used as slaves aboard this vessel."

The man dressed in blue stepped forward and took Drace's hand and arm in a warrior's embrace. "It is good to meet you. I am Damir D'rakionier, leader of the *Drakonians*. We have been searching the worlds over for a race with females. Ours are few. Our women no longer give birth to female children and our males long for mates."

"We have a theory about that." Drace continued, noticing their raised eyebrows. "It seems that an ancient race experimented with a virulent virus to commit genocide on what we believe to be the *Hienials*. We believe it attacked the genes in our bodies that determine the sex of a fetus." Drace nodded to the other *Drakonian* while he continued with his explanation, "It seems the virus worked all too well. It attacks the sex determining genes in every shifter race. The only people who seem immune to it are humans. Since they cannot shift, they do not possess the affected gene. Either that or they possess a natural immunity to the strain."

Damir glanced at Drace then nodded to his companion. "This is my best friend and second in command, Kaylen Di'nios." He looked past Drace to the transport. "You have your mate with you." It wasn't a question. "That is why you were so suspicious." He looked back toward Brandy who was already administering first aid to an injured woman. "You are lucky. She is beautiful. I don't blame you for being so careful with her safety."

Drace looked back over his shoulder and smiled. "She is beautiful. I forget to notice that sometimes." He smiled at the incredulous and almost angry looks of the *Draconian* males. "But Brandy is not my mate. She is my sister." He shrugged. "My adopted sister, but still not one I could ever look on with lust. To me she is still the young frightened girl my father saved from certain death on a faraway planet. One that he swears is teeming with fertile females."

Drace didn't miss the speculative looks the two men gave his sister. He wasn't sure he liked the idea of his little sister participating in the kinds of escapades he and Fury had when they were younger, but if these two men were ready to claim her as mates, he would not stand in their way.

He turned back to the transport just as Kiri rounded the corner and stood in the doorway, glaring at him, her hands on her hips.

"It's about time you returned for me." She raised one copper-colored brow. "Have you determined it is safe for me now or do I have to wait here in this sweltering transport twiddling my thumbs for another hour?"

"We feel for you, sir," Damir said with a grin. "Her tongue is nearly as sharp as a *Drakonian* female's."

She stepped from the ship to stand beside Drace. "What makes you think I'm his mate?" she asked stubbornly thrusting her chin in the air.

Kaylan chuckled and pointed at Drace who stood looking extremely uncomfortable. He looked as though torn between hugging and chastising her. "Because only the sharp words of a mate can put that look on a man's face."

Kiri's face turned a lovely shade of red at that comment and Drace laughed, joined by the two Draconian males. He decided he just might like these people.

KIRI'S FACE BURNED as she wished the ground would open up and swallow her. Why did men always stick together? Even when they knew nothing of each other they still sided with the males. She attempted to shrug off her embarrassment and moved closer to Drace. She wasn't sure why she felt more comfortable standing closer to him with these other males around, but she did. It wasn't as though she felt evil from them. On the contrary, she felt they were good. Very good. And they possessed a form of magic as well.

She'd watched with her heart in her throat, as the two dragons dove from the air above Drace. They headed straight for him. Just before their giant feet touched the ground, they both shifted forms in midair to land behind Drace fully clothed and armored.

When she stepped up beside him, Drace wrapped his arm around her waist and pulled her close. She kept her usual panic at bay by telling herself that Drace would never harm her, never force her to do something she didn't want to do and he would never allow these two males to touch her either.

Crossing her arms over her breasts, she put a hand to her throat and nodded at the other two. Her ire and courage suddenly deserted her and she smiled at them nervously.

Soothing warmth spread through her mind. She darted a glance to Drace who still looked upon the other two males with a degree of suspicion while he protected her with his body.

There is nothing to fear from us. We can even erase the horrible memories buried within your mind if you wish. We realize you belong to him…and another. We, meaning all of our males, will honor your choice.

Her sharply drawn breath caught Drace's sudden attention. "What is wrong, Kiri?"

She glanced at the two strangers and licked her lips. "They have magic. Did they tell you this, Drace?"

"We haven't had the opportunity to say much of anything, actually," one of the *Drakonians* answered.

"What do you mean?" Drace asked her, giving her his full attention. "Why do you think they control magic?"

"Because they shifted instantly in midair and clothed themselves before their feet even touched the ground. And…" She allowed her words to drift off, unsure whether she should say anything. What if Drace took their attempt to comfort her as a personal affront? He would never survive a battle with two such large and fierce warriors—especially if they shifted into their other forms. How much power, how much pure magic did it take to shift into a form with so much more physical mass than the forms they usually possessed?

"What else do you need to tell me, my love? You never need fear me in any way. Surely you know that."

Nodding, she swallowed thickly. She didn't fear Drace. She feared for him. "They can speak into my mind." Her gaze darted over the city, the buildings not so different from her own. Their method of transport so similar she could have been on any other planet. "Each of them just offered to remove my memories of the many *Hienial* violations I have suffered." If they did that though, she would lose so much more—her memories of her son, and his mother Ryanza. She would also forget the other women—friendships born and forged in fire. She may even lose the inner strength she'd earned in the process. Moving back, she allowed Drace to step in front of her. She couldn't allow them to remove her memories. Without them, she wouldn't be the same. She would be a stranger, even to herself.

The pained wailing of the wounded finally drew her attention and she looked out over the crash site. The ship lay on the ground, listing to one side. Large gouges were ripped from the side where it hit the side of a mountain in the distance. A long, mile-wide swath of destruction lay in its wake. Trees and buildings lay smashed and broken. A wide trench of ripped landscape littered with debris lay behind it.

Women and children huddled together, cowering away from the monstrous *Hienials* as the creatures tried, in vain, to maintain a least a bit of order. It was impossible. Hope shone in the eyes of the captives as the mighty dragons flew over their heads, attacking the evil *Hienials*. The older, more hideous of the creatures seemed to have a perverse taste for torture. They wielded whips against their captives, even the children, until the dragons swooped down from the sky and grabbed them in their great claws, carrying them to the skies and a horrific end.

The younger *Hienials* didn't seem to have acquired a taste for such abuse—yet. The young ones backed away from their older counterparts, alternately horrified and entertained by the violence that surrounded them. Kiri moved toward them, a whimper of understanding in her throat.

Drace protested, grabbing her arm when she attempted to approach a young male who fell to his knees clutching his middle as he laughed and cried at the same time. "He is *Hienial*. He is not worth your time."

Kiri turned, glaring at him. "Ryo is *Hienial*. Are you saying I should treat him with less kindness because of who his father was, how his father would have treated him if he'd been taken?" She shook his hand off with a scowl. "There is still good in him. If the *Hienials* have not destroyed all of the goodness in him, there is a chance to reach the human child still within." Reaching out, she placed her hands on the adolescent's head and closed her eyes.

Searching through the torture, the humiliation, the boy had been subjected to as a 'hideous' human, she poured warmth, love and human compassion into his soul. His aura became visible. Cloudy at first, it swirled with darkness, showing the evil the *Hienial* adults attempted to instill in him. Tears ran down her face as she saw his memories of them raping his mother continually in front him. She felt his shame, his feelings of utter despair that he was too weak and too frightened to stop those who attacked his mother until she'd gone completely mad.

She left the boy unconscious, healing from his painful exposure to those who would claim to be his kin. Moving on to the next, she did the same. One after another, she healed the *Hienial* adolescents, ridding them of the evil inherent in the adult *Hienials*, while Brandy healed the women and children they had kept as slaves. The powerful dragons still flew overhead, dipping and swirling, ferreting out the evil adult *Hienials* as they attempted to hide amongst the boys.

Kiri felt for the adults, exposed to evil for so long, they could remember no other way of life. She could find no goodness to cultivate in any of them. Every time she found one too far gone to heal and passed him up for another, a dragon would swoop down and end his life.

"They merely put them out of their misery, Kiri," Drace said, his hand moving in soft soothing circles over her back. "You should stop this now. You have already helped too many. They will still be here tomorrow. You must rest."

"No. I can't stop. I can't stop until I've healed as many as I can this day."

"How will you know when to stop, Kiri? When you fall to the ground exhausted?"

"If that is what the Lady Goddess has ordained, then yes, when I collapse. There is one out there, who must be saved. He is so close to being lost. When I find him, today's task will be through. Then and only then will I rest."

She moved through the people huddled around her, healing as she went. Her energy waned as she continued to touch every *Hienial* she saw, insisting on healing their emotional and mental turmoil.

After healing twenty-six of the hopeless creatures, she stumbled. Drace grabbed her by the arm and began to drag her back to the transport. It was then they heard the bloodcurdling scream that sent Kiri to her knees. She stood. Wrenched her arm from Drace's grasp and ran toward the horrible sound.

Several *Hienials* stood around one of their own, torturing him. "You will kill when we tell you to kill!" They hit him several times with a laser whip. "You will reproduce with the females of your choice. They have no say in the matter!" Again, they whipped him. He fell to his knees and nodded his head.

Kiri felt the goodness leaving him. The evil the others attempted to brainwash him with took over more and more of his consciousness. With every crack of the laser on his back, shoulders and legs, evil filled his mind. Their ideas began to take root and she screamed. "No!"

The incredibly loud sound of the dragon's screeches over her head, and the flapping of their wings beating the air as they descended on the adult *Hienials*, made her duck as they swooped in and pulled the three into the sky. She blocked out the sounds of the screams and ran to the one kneeling on the ground. What little good left inside him slowly seeped through the holes in his mind where the pain receded to blessed darkness. She reached for him.

Placing her hands on his cheeks, she lifted his head and stared into his eyes. "You will not lose yourself to the monsters. You are strong. Come back to us." She drew the pain from him, even as it filled her and she began to shudder from the weight of his burden. The welts of the laser whip grew faint as she returned the kindness back into his heart.

Kiri's back and legs began to burn as his welts became her own. She sobbed aloud as she took his incredible pain inside her and returned it with peace and love. Her grip on the boy's face tightened when Drace would have dragged her away. "No! Leave me! He is the one."

She stared into the boy's eyes. "I won't leave you, Keahi." She shook him. "Do you hear me? I feel the good in you. They haven't driven it out of you, yet. I feel our mother's goodness in you. What those animals did to her, to you, is an unspeakable thing." She hugged him, pressing his head to her shoulder. "She escaped them all those years ago and hid you here with us, with her people. Our mother knew your capacity to love would overrule their hatred, their evil. Her kindness lives within you." She placed her hand over his heart. "Here. It lives here. Come back to me, Keahi. Come back and love me. Love my son, Ryo. He also needs you. He will need your love and guidance in the years to come. He, too, is the product of those beasts. You must live. If you ever truly loved Ryanza, you will come back to me and love her son."

Keahi's eyes cleared as a part of him remembered his half sister. Slowly, he raised his hand and ran a finger down her cheek. "They told me they killed you. They told me they killed your son."

Tears streamed down Kiri's cheeks and she nodded. "They did kill Zahur. He wasn't whole and they killed him."

Keahi guessed the rest. "And they ate him in front of you. Don't try to spare me the details, Kiri. My hate for them helps. They tried to teach me to despise you, to loathe the others. The more they beat me, the more they convinced me their way was true. It changed me, making me want to kill you and those like you." He squeezed his eyes closed and tears streamed down his face.

Kiri dropped to her knees, still keeping her hands on him, still exchanging his pain for her kindness, her love. The evil she drew from him filled her, made her feel dirty. The oily sensation of pure hatred washed through her as she cleansed her brother of the taint of the *Hienial* deceit. They had almost convinced him that torturing those he'd once loved was a way to end their misery a way to cleanse their souls before death.

"I love you, Keahi. I need you in my life. Do not fight the goodness within you. Embrace it," she whispered, before she collapsed into Drace's arms.

STANDING WITH KIRI in his arms, Drace nodded to the two dragon leaders.

"Watch over him for me, will you? It seems he is to be my brother by bonding. I propose a friendship. I offer you the help of my people and my trust." He looked over his head at the still circling beasts above. "I can see you are strong, but I would still make a strong adversary or ally. I would prefer the latter."

He looked down at the boy, who only moments before had small boils covering his body. As the evil that had begun to distort the *youthling's* good looks left his body, the boils and markings of a *Hienial* left him as well. One would think that perhaps the boy would be handsome once again. If he was lucky.

"I must return to my ship and care for my mate. She has exhausted herself in her search for her brother." He looked to the other young males who were not quite *Hienial* and not quite human. "Kill those who are pure evil. Leave those who still have consciences to my mate. Once she has rested she will insist on bringing them back from the hell the *Hienials* introduced them to."

Damir stepped forward and nodded. Helping the boy to his feet, he and Kaylen flanked him. "We will watch over them but those she has not touched will remain in strong confinement. The others will be taken to guest rooms under guard until we can determine whether to trust them or until you take them from here."

"That is fair enough. I will send some of my men down to help if you wish." He shifted Kiri in his arms, brushing his lips over her pale cheek. "You will excuse me to care for my mate. She is in need of attention." He turned with a nod and strode back to the transport.

Stepping on a Transport pad, he nodded to the technician and they were instantly transported back to the *Revenge.*

After barking orders to his crew for food and medical supplies, he carried her to his chamber. He felt the need to wash the *Hienial* taint from her mind and body. When she sifted through her brother's mind, he felt the oily taint of evil. The unclean thoughts that made her feel dirty.

Since she was too weak to bath herself, he would bathe her. It would kill him to be so close to her, touching, even stroking her naked body, but he would do it. He felt her need to wash the *Hienial* taint from her body. She needed to be clean or she would slowly go mad.

He pushed the silky red locks back from her face and kissed her forehead. Her body may be exhausted, but her mind raced as he held her. Her heart sped up when he placed her on the bed. Leaving her for just a moment, he hurried to the bathing chamber to run the water into the large, deep tub. Her heart beat faster when he removed her clothing, picked her up and carried her into the bathroom.

Kicking off his boots, he stepped into the tub and sat on the wide ledge, still holding her in his lap. Her eyelids fluttered, she turned her head and licked her dry lips. "I—I thought..." the words were barely a whisper.

"I am your mate, Kiri. I will never force you to do anything you do not wish to do. Even now, you know you want this. You would rather be here, naked in my arms as I wash you, than to endure another moment of feeling the *Hienial* filth upon your flesh."

Drace began to wash her body. Starting at her scalp, he washed and rinsed her hair before moving lower. It nearly killed him to move the cloth over her full breasts, down over her flat stomach to delve into the secret recesses of her most private places.

He closed his eyes, trying not to imagine how it would be to caress her there, move his fingers over her hardened nipples, circle her clit with his tongue as he drank the nectar of her body from between her legs. Suppressing a groan, he stood with her still in his arms and exited the tub. Sitting her on the wide edge that surrounded the frosted *illuma-glass*, he dried her with a thick towel, even going so far as to gently comb the knots from her long hair.

She looked up at him as she moved to sit on her own. "I'm feeling a bit better now." She blushed. Her already pink skin from the warm bath grew even redder as she struggled to take the towel and cover herself. "I can dry myself now."

He held her hands for a moment and she looked up into his eyes. Her tongue trailed slowly over her lower lip and his cock jerked in his wet trews. He'd been a fool to get into that tub with her. He would have been a fool not to.

"You're still weak. Allow me to help you."

She shook her head. "I'm fine. Please, let me dry myself."

Releasing the towel, he stood and walked away from her. "I'll be just on the other side of the door if you need me, just call."

He'd no sooner closed the door, than she called him back into the room. "Drace, I—I"

He opened the door and found her standing in the room, her towel wrapped securely around her. He rushed back to her before her legs gave out again. "Yes?" He cupped her face and gazed into her eyes.

Her face reddened and she dropped her gaze to her feet. "What does it feel like to—to kiss someone?"

Drace swallowed thickly. He could smell her arousal and her fear. He couldn't believe that a woman as beautiful as his mate had never been kissed. He was speechless for a moment. As many times as those animals had forced her to their will, in her heart, Kiri was still a virgin.

Leaning down, he cupped her cheek and gently pressed his lips against hers.

DRACE'S TONGUE SLOWLY traced her bottom lip before delving into her mouth. She moaned, unable to hide her response from him. What was wrong with her? She'd only just escaped the *Hienials*. How could he make her want him so soon, after what she suffered at the hands of her enemy?

He pulled away to nip at her bottom lip, forcing her attention back to him. She opened her mouth wider, frantically tangling her tongue with his; desperate for more but unsure if she could go through with it. But, this— kissing Drace she could definitely handle. They were both breathing hard when he pulled back. He reached for one of her hands and drew it toward his erection, pressing it there as it throbbed. She whimpered. Could she? Could she make love to him? She just didn't know.

Drace met her gaze, he lowered his head ever so slowly then covered her lips with his, but this time he took a little bit more control, forcing her hand to stroke his cock through his still damp pants. Why wasn't she screaming at him to leave her alone? Why was she allowing this to continue?

As his tongue mated with hers, his big body shuddered. She could feel his pleasure, his happiness that she hadn't pulled away. Kiri groaned, desperate to feel more of their bodies touching, desperate for relief even knowing that he was so much bigger than she and that if he chose he could use his greater size to hurt her. If she were honest with herself, deep down she knew he'd never purposely harm her. It just wasn't part of his makeup. He didn't have the cruelty or the evil inside him that the *Banarts* and *Hienials* did. She knew he didn't.

He pulled away again, his face tight with need, his eyes dilated. "Make a decision, *mi ama*."

She cocked her head, licking the taste of him from her lips. He'd called her that before. "What does *mi ama* mean?"

It means 'my precious' or 'my beloved'. It is what my father called my mother and what I dreamed I'd one day call my mate. Will you mate with me, Kiri? Will you allow me to be a father to Ryo and any other children we may be blessed with?"

Kiri lowered her head again, stepped back and turned away from Drace. She could feel his whirling emotions but anger wasn't one of them. He truly believed they were mates and she could feel his determination to wait if that was her decision.

She shivered knowing that as soon as she made her choice she wouldn't be able to change her mind. Not only would it be cruel to Drace, but she knew her own body's urgent demands wouldn't allow her to back out. Her body might ache for Drace, her pussy weep with want, but her mind rebelled, warning her to run as fast as she could if she wanted to remain free.

Drace didn't give her a chance to run. He moved in, closer, closer until his body pressed against hers, his arms wrapping around her. She could feel his heart beating against her cheek and knew she couldn't deny him, deny the mating or the bond growing between them. His mouth dipped, covered hers in a kiss that burned away all thought of fleeing from her mind.

Kiri whimpered and rubbed against his front. She could feel his steely erection pulse against her belly and she trembled. He must have been as desperate as she for the feel of skin-on-skin as his trembling hands quickly opened her shirt and breast bindings.

As he continued to kiss her, his fingers drifted across her nipples, once, twice feathering across the hardened peaks before squeezing them in time to the dueling thrusts of his tongue. Panting, Drace pulled away and lowered his hands.

She glanced up, looked into his eyes. The feral hunger she saw there made her shiver. He stood so straight and tall, his hands fisted and clenched at his sides, leaving the next step completely up to her. Would she go to him, mate with him or would she walk away? He truly was leaving the decision up to her. So, what was she going to do?

Kiri licked her lips then nodded. "Yes, I—I will mate with you." She felt his hands on her hips tugging her closer. As he kissed her neck and nuzzled his way up to her ear, she closed her eyes, just wallowing in the delicious sensations wrought by his touch.

"Please, Kiri. Tell me what you want. What do you want me to do, *mi ama?*"

"I want you more than I have ever wanted any man. I want...I want you to make love to me like you mean it. Like it means something to you other than making a child with me, Drace."

Just like that, she was in his arms and he was standing her beside the bed.

With shaking fingers, he carefully loosened her bath sheet. As the towel hit the floor, his eyes lit up and he gave a rumbling purr. The pleased sound of her *Lioni* mate made her nipples tighten. She knew she blushed when he focused on her breasts heat burned her cheeks and she fought the urge to cover herself with her hands.

"*Mi ama*, you are so beautiful. A feast for a starving man. Fury will be so pleased when he sees you, when he too gets to make love to you. I can't wait to share you with him, but first you are mine. Mine to have, mine to hold, and mine to please." He dipped his head, rubbing his face over her breasts and neck. "Let me please you."

Without realizing how, Kiri found herself on her back on the huge bed that seemed big enough to sleep a small village. She watched, her eyes hooded as Drace stood above her and peeled his still wet grey uniform pants from his waist and legs. When he revealed the size of his cock, she gasped. He was huge, swollen. As thick as he was, how would he ever fit inside her without tearing her asunder? She licked her lips, as a new wave of indecision flooded her mind. She didn't see any way it could possibly fit. Immense disappointment washed over her where just a moment before fear reigned. Would she always fear this? Would it be the same with Fury? For the first time in years a male was kind to her, felt for her and worried about her needs above his own. She wanted—no—she needed to be everything they thought her to be. This was a chance at happiness she never dreamed to have while in the cruel clutches of the slavers.

Drace started to kiss her. They were slow nibbling kisses. His mouth and lips moved across her lips and jaw, traveling down her neck until he finally reached her trembling breasts. He brushed the sides of her breasts with his thumbs, watching her nipples tighten as his hand moved lower, trailing his fingers down to her hips. Finally, his lips made their way to the nipples he had seemed to overlook and she groaned with fiery need when he latched on to the tip with his teeth. The tip was hard, begging for his touch. He laved it into an even tighter bud then sucked it deeply into his mouth, while using his other hand to give the same attention to her other breast. When its twin also stood at rigid attention, he let go of the nipple he'd suckled to move to the other. Only when both of her nipples were red and swollen and hard as *talia* stones did he lift his head away from her chest to look into her eyes.

Kiri arched her back, moaning with need. She longed to bury her fingers in his hair and drag him back to her chest. Demand he give her turgid nipples more attention. A fire burned in her middle. It was a sensation she'd never experienced before now. It pleased her, making her want more. Need more from this man. How? How could something that had always been so painful, something she'd always feared before have her writhing in such desperate need now? By the Lady Goddess, this was unlike anything she'd ever imagined it could be. She'd felt Drace's pull on her nipples all the way to her pussy, her clit. Cream now dripped from her center to the bedding beneath her. She writhed on the bed unsure of what she wanted from him. Her mind whirled with need, with a desire she never thought possible. Her body writhed on the bedding beneath them like a wanton and she knew she would go mad if he didn't do something soon.

Kiri felt his hard cock pressed against her hip and knew his need was at least as great as her own. She realized with another moan that she was rubbing her pussy against his thigh. She smeared her body's juices along his leg. Like the great cat he was, Drace purred in reaction. "Yes, *mi ama.* Just like that. I love it when you rub yourself against me, marking me with your woman's cream." He swiftly rolled on top of her, lifted her legs over his arms and spread her even wider. Then, before the fear could return, before she could even think to protest, with one long, slow thrust, he buried his shaft deep inside her.

He slowly withdrew and returned, getting her used to the invasion of his large cock before he began to pound into her in long, sure strokes. It felt like her body flew into a million directions, fragmenting into thousands, millions, of prisms of light as the pleasure-pain of her first male given orgasm consumed her. She saw bright flashes of color as wave after wave of pleasure filled her just before the dizziness of her sexual exhaustion became overwhelming. She squeezed her eyes shut, no longer able to bear the exquisite sensations.

Above her, Drace groaned. Her name spilled from his lips. The love she heard in his voice, felt in his kiss as he pressed his lips against hers filled her with an elation she never thought possible. She could feel the pulse of his shaft as his seed bathed her womb and he collapsed over her, resting his weight on his elbows, careful not to crush her. Tears filled her eyes at his gentle loving and she blinked them away. She would not hurt him by making him think she had not enjoyed their lovemaking.

Fury stood in the doorway and watched, unable to feel anything but joy as Drace and Kiri finished their coupling. There was never any room for jealousy through the bond he held with his old friend. He loved him as a brother, perhaps even more so. He could only be happy that Drace had managed to bring Kiri to trust him enough to give her the pleasure she so deserved. He'd known through his bond with Drace what he would find when he entered the room. He couldn't have stayed away even if that was his desire. He needed to see his mate receive her first bit of sexual pleasure. Needed to know if it couldn't be him giving her such mind-numbing delight, at least his bond mate was the one given the honor.

When they'd returned to the ship, he had intended to come to them then. He'd thought to bring young Ryo to see his mother, but the warning that Kiri was in need of rest had changed his plans. Instead, he'd taken the boy to his room and told him his favorite bedtime story as a cub. He couldn't help the wash of pride that swept over him as the boy avidly listened to his story, his eyelids growing heavier by the minute until he drifted off into a much-needed slumber. The boy needed rest, security and kindness—and not necessarily in that order. Now, with the young one asleep, nothing would keep him from his mate.

He'd been curious, needing to see her, yet he'd kept his promise to her about their young son. Seeing to his needs before all else. Now he was free to wonder why she was in need of rest when she returned to the safety of the ship. What had she done on the surface of the planet below that had worn her out? Even though she lay flushed and panting from the sex sharing she'd just had with Drace, Fury could see the shadows of strain below her eyes. Through his bond with Drace, he could feel his concern for her even as he leaned down to kiss her forehead.

"Are you well, Kiri?"

She smiled. It was a sleepy, well-sated smile that made him want to drag her to him and hold her tight and safe against him as she basked in her afterglow. "Couldn't be better," she murmured, her voice slurring as she began to fall into an exhausted slumber.

Fury chuckled. She was so sexy in her sated sprawl. He doubted she even realized who was speaking to her. He'd have to change that.

Straightening from the doorway where he'd stopped to watch them, Fury strode toward the bed. Stopping near her head, he reached out, pulled a lock of her curly red hair into his hand. So soft to the touch, he thought—such a beautiful contrast to his dark skin. "All went well on the planet then?"

A frown marred her brow. She turned her head away, and Drace rolled off her to pull her into his arms. He could feel her sadness, Drace's concern. The smell of sex in the room, stirred him. His body raged, needing the comfort and solace of his mate's soft body. Even knowing her body lay naked beneath the sheet and that she was his for the taking, he curbed his desire. His mind controlled his body, not the other way around and, right now, his mate needed her rest. Besides, something wasn't right. He could sense it. "What happened, *mi amá?*"

"There were many, many *Hienials* in need of healing. It was tiring."

Drace shook his head. "It was more than tiring, Kiri. You practically drained yourself beyond return, by healing the *Hienial* youthlings."

"What?" Fury shouted, began to shake. "You did what?" Unable to stand looking at her hurt expression, Fury whirled around and stormed out of the room. He didn't want to upset her with his worry. Healing the *Hienials*? Why would she do such a thing? He ran his dark fingers through his ebony hair and paced away from the room at a near run. He'd come back later when he could talk to her without his fear for her tingeing his voice.

NERVOUSLY, KIRI KNOCKED on Fury's cabin door. It had taken nearly a quarter of a dial to talk Drace into telling her where Fury may have gone.

After a few seconds, the door slid open. Fury was seated on his bed, his head down and his shoulders slumped. She noted the chair across from the bed and quickly crossed the room and sat down. Desperate to set things right, she moistened her dry lips. He raised his head, quirked his eyebrows questioningly. "Why have you come to me, Kiri?"

She noted his set face, his clamped mouth and fixed eyes. He stayed still, almost as though he thought any movement would frighten her. Kiri longed to feather her fingers through his dark hair. She wanted nothing more than to smooth the deep frowns from his chocolate face. Drace had introduced her to that delicacy a few moments ago and she wondered, her face burning, if Fury's skin would taste so sweet. She bit her lip, twisted her hands in her lap, unsure just what to say. What if he didn't want her? Well, she wouldn't know if she didn't speak to him about it. She raised her gaze to his. "You left, Fury. Once you found out what I could do, you left as though I disgusted you."

The lines of concentration deepened along his brows and under his dark eyes. "Is that what you thought? That using your gifts to heal others—even the *Hienials*—disgusts me?" He sighed, flexed his shoulders then stepped forward taking her hand in his.

"I only heard how you grew weaker with every healing. You put yourself in danger for those beasts and I find that hard to handle, Kiri. I left only to calm myself. To know that you were in danger and I wasn't there if you needed me, well, it angered me. Even if Drace was with you, I wasn't." His tone was apologetic, his gaze sincere.

She sighed in relief. "Thank you. I'm..." she paused, trying to find the right words to ease his worry. "I will do my best not to overextend myself again. I don't want to cause you or Drace any more distress."

When he spoke again, his voice was tender almost a murmur. "Oh, love. Don't worry about us." He cupped her cheek and she couldn't help but tilt her head further into his hand. "You were meant to heal others. It is your gift. Just know that you will never be alone when you use it. It is our duty—our privilege—as your mates to protect you even from yourself."

She felt a warm glow flow through her at his words. His simple statement of intent eased something inside her. "So, you didn't leave Drace's room because you couldn't stand the sight of me?"

He removed his hand from her cheek to brush his hair back from his face. A devilish look came into his eyes and his mouth quirked up in amusement. "Are you asking me if I find you attractive?"

Her breath quickened. Her cheeks became warm beneath his intense gaze. His thumb caressed the hand he still held tenderly. She saw the heart-rending tenderness of his gaze and all thoughts fled her mind.

Already, she knew he would never force her to be with him intimately. She could feel his fierce determination that nothing ever be allowed to harm her. Every time his gaze met hers, her heart turned over in response.

His gaze dropped from her face to her shoulders, then finally to her breasts. Slowly and seductively, his gaze slid downward. She cleared her throat, pretending his slow perusal didn't affect her. "Well, I guess I better..."

"You better stay with me. I want to make love to you, Kiri. Will you allow it? Will you give yourself to me?"

Kiri hesitated only a moment then nodded. This was right, the right thing to do. She didn't fear him or what they would do together. Drace had already showed her how a mate loves his woman and now she wanted to make love to her other mate, to Fury.

"Strip me."

Kiri stood up, stepped forward. With shaking hands, she reached for the buttons on his uniform shirt. "Yes, Sir," she said as she slipped the first from its fastening.

Each button bared more of his dark skin to her gaze. Closing her eyes, she nuzzled his chest, seeking one of his nipples. She pulled it into her mouth and suckled gently.

Fury's hand closed around the nape of her neck, holding her head to his chest as his fingers gently massaged her scalp. She slid her hand inside his shirt, using the pads of her fingers and her fingernails to stroke the other nipple into a hardened point. Where she got up the nerve to be the aggressor, she didn't know. But, somehow, it felt right to take the lead. To prove to him that she wanted him with everything inside her no matter her traumatic past.

She trailed her lips lower, placing open-mouthed kisses along the length of his torso. Fury groaned and Kiri smiled against his chest. Unbuttoning the rest of his shirt, she slid the confining garment from his shoulders, letting it fall to the floor in a puddle. She slowly lowered herself to her knees, placed her palm against the solid ridge of his still covered cock. She could feel his need, smell his essence through his clothing and it excited her more than she ever thought possible.

Fury's fingers closed on her shoulders, gripped her lightly. "Wait." Restraint filled his voice. Kiri sat back on her heels. She looked up at him, confused. "Why? Don't you like what I'm doing?" Her hands trembled against his erection. "Doesn't it feel good?"

"Yes, my mate. It feels too good, though. If you keep touching me, I won't be able to make love to you like you deserve."

Kiri unlaced his tight *trews*. His cock surged thick and strong through the opening of his pants. Her pussy clenched. She leaned forward and pressed a kiss against the weeping head of his shaft. "Then tell me what to do, Fury. Tell me how to please you."

She watched with hooded eyes as Fury trembled beneath her touch. "Just finish stripping me, *mi ama.*" She watched as he swallowed thickly, his hands clenched at his sides. It was then she realized the power she held as a woman with her two men. They may be physically stronger than her, but she held the upper hand right now. The thought had her smiling to herself as she watched her mighty warrior tremble beneath her touch.

Quickly she went back to her task, stripping his pants and boots from him with a swift efficiency she hadn't known she was capable of.

"Now, take off your robe," he said, his voice husky with desire, when she'd removed the last of his clothes. Without hesitating, she untied the belt around her waist and shrugged out of her only covering, letting it join the pile of clothes already on the floor of Fury's cabin. She vowed to stand there silently, refusing to shield her body from her mate no matter how ridiculous she felt remaining so still and exposed before him. What must he think of her? He stood so silent, his gaze so intent she didn't know what he was thinking. She couldn't begin to guess what he thought, what he felt, about the way she so shamelessly stood before him.

Kiri locked gazes with Fury, silently waiting for him to tell her what to do next. He held out his hand to her, and she gently gripped it, threading their fingers together. Fury smiled. Dimples winked in his cheeks as he stepped backward, moving her slowly toward the bed.

When they finally reached it, he sat down on the edge, pulling her between his thighs. Picking her up with ease, Fury pulled her over him. "Straddle me, my love. Ride me. Take as much or as little of me as you'd like."

Kiri could feel the smile spreading across her face. With Drace, he'd been in charge, controlling their lovemaking, the positioning and the pace. The idea that Fury would allow her to take charge was a blessing she wasn't about to snub. Nodding, she oh-so slowly poised herself above his cock. She reached down and circled his girth with her fingers. He was so big, she was thankful he'd made the decision for her to take the lead.

When her fingers closed around the base of his shaft, she slipped the head inside her. Fury moaned. She could feel his pleasure through their newly formed bond. She lifted her hips just slightly then lowered herself again, taking more of his cock inside her.

Her breath hitched. Her heart stuttered. He filled her passage to overflowing, stretching her unbelievably tight. She savored the feel of him inside her, stretching her, caressing her in places she'd never known existed before today.

"That's it, *mi ama*. You can take me," Fury murmured.

She slowly slipped, centimeter by centimeter, down his cock. Goddess he was so wide, so thick and hard inside her. She shuddered, sending him even deeper inside her weeping channel. She couldn't think, couldn't breathe. The feel of his cock so deep inside her sent her thoughts tumbling into the ether. She lowered herself the last few inches, until his entire length was clasped inside her channel. She could feel him pushing against her womb and began to shudder. He leaned forward, took her face gently in his hands and placed his lips against hers. She sank into the kiss, explored his mouth, luxuriated in his warmth and caring.

He filled her so completely. Her hips began to move restlessly, needing him to thrust, to make love to her. She gripped his shoulders to brace herself as she eased his cock almost completely out of her then slid down again. They rocked together in a gentle rhythm. Kiri struggled to retain some measure of control.

Fury reached between her legs and flicked his fingers over her pleasure bud. She pulled her lips from his. Sitting back on her heels, she looked him in the eye, swallowed thickly. "Please, Fury. Make love to me. Show me how you feel about me."

He gently took her breasts in his hands and lightly pinched her nipples.

Kiri cried out. The pleasure pain pressure of her climax hit her without warning. She leaned forward, screamed against his throat as the ripples of her orgasm roared through her body.

Fury obeyed her plea, rolling Kiri beneath him. She had the presence of mind to lift her legs and press her heels into his buttocks before he plunged into her. Her channel clasped his cock, refusing to release him as he thrust into her pussy. Over and over again, he drove into her until finally his entire body stiffened. With a roar, he came, his hot seed bathing her womb with jet after jet of his come.

Neither said anything for long moments. Finally, Fury shifted, rolled them until she was draped over his chest. "Why don't we get cleaned up, then sit in the chair and talk for a bit. I'm sure Drace will be along before we know it."

Kiri nodded and together the pair made their way to his bathing chamber.

IT DIDN'T TAKE LONG for Drace to join them. He entered the room, pulled her right off Fury's lap and out of the chair. The sheet she'd wrapped around herself drifted to the carpet as he clasped her against his hard frame, his chest to her back with his arms wrapped around her waist.

Fury stared at the hard points of her nipples, licked his lips. She could see the raw hunger in his gaze, felt his need to mate with her through their ever-strengthening bond. She shivered beneath his heated stare. Behind her, she felt Drace's cock rise and press against her backside.

Her response to both males was so powerful. It was almost overwhelming. They'd already had sex, and yet she craved them, craved something more than just the one-on-one sex sharing they'd participated in.

Was it lust or something more, maybe the first stirrings of love? Was it even possible for her to love a man after all she'd been through? Heat surged up her body and her pleasure bud throbbed for attention, yet again. If anything, the passion between them burned brighter and hotter than before. How could her exhausted body respond to them so quickly? After all of the loving she'd already shared with these two men, it only took one look from them and she was ready to make love again. A week ago, she never could have imagined herself feeling this way for any man, let alone two.

With one hand, Drace clamped her to his body. His other hand lightly caressed the slight curve of her belly before sliding all the way down to her nether lips and thrusting a finger into her gate. Her pleasure bud ached with need, throbbing against his hand as it begged for his attention. He leaned forward, brushing the soft stubble of his face against her cheek and nipped her ear with his teeth. His finger slid into her slit, then entered her weeping channel.

"As our mate you will never suffer loneliness again, *mi ama*. That means 'my precious or my beloved.'" Fury reaffirmed the meaning of the phrase while he cupped her breasts as Drace finally rubbed her clit. Kiri gasped as the sensations bombarded her.

Drace rubbed her clit a little harder as his breath teased her ear. He gripped her by the waist and lifted her so that her arms could slip over Fury's shoulders. "You see, Kiri, together, the three of us will create the next powerful triad and the love we shall build between us will extend to our children."

She grasped Fury's shoulders as Drace lifted her towards him. Fury released her breasts and grasped her trembling thighs instead. The large male easily spread her open even wider as the head of his cock nudged her gate and slipped into the wet folds of her sex. His cock thrust hard into her body as Drace, using the hands at her waist pressed her completely down onto Fury's length. Fury cupped her backside and held her still, impaled on his cock. She wanted to move but he refused to allow her to.

Behind her, Drace whispered against her temple, "No one could love you as much as we will, Kiri." Drace trailed his fingers down her spine then between the spread cheeks of her ass. Goosebumps pebbled across her skin as he traced the opening of her anus. She gasped but Fury leaned down to seal her mouth closed with a kiss. For several minutes, Drace played with the rosebud of her rear before stepping away. He quickly returned, soothing her anus with a lubricant of some kind. He coated the entire area several times before pressing a finger deep inside her back entrance.

She shivered. Something dark and needy echoed through her as he continued to press his fingers, first one, and then another into her ass. She could feel him stroking Fury's cock through the thin barrier separating her ass from her vaginal channel. She moaned as Drace pulled his fingers free and applied more lubricant before sliding them back in. Fury lifted his mouth and stared at her while Drace continued to insert yet another finger. He worked them in and out, repeatedly, until they could slide inside her tight, rear channel easily.

"Both *Lioni* and *Beariti* females stretch their bottoms as both our species tend to enjoy anal sex from time to time. It will come in handy for you to get used to being stretched this way in anticipation of being shared. You will enjoy being filled completely." He must have sensed her doubt because he added, "We will see to it."

Drace removed his fingers and pressed the head of his cock against her prepared bottom, slowly entering her for the first time. The skin stretched, and a burning pain seared her bottom. Drace froze instantly, waited for her body to adjust to his invasion. She wanted to moan, to whimper with the pleasure pain.

Drace's cock started to ease out of her bottom before he thrust slowly back into her, this time giving her more of his length. He repeated the process, over and over, until he was fully seated within her. She needed to move, needed to feel them thrusting inside her together, or in tandem, it didn't matter so long as they moved.

"Please, I need…"

"What do you need?" asked Fury.

"Tell us," demanded Drace.

"I need more. I need you to move, both of you to move."

The hands on her bottom tightened as Fury started to ease his cock from her sheathe. Drace thrust forward at the same moment and his cock sank deeper into her body. As Drace pulled loose, Fury thrust smoothly into her channel once more. It made for an insane sort of torment. They continued to thrust opposite each other. One entered her while the other withdrew.

Finally, she could take no more of their teasing thrusts. She needed more. "Together," she demanded and they instantly obeyed. She felt them push into her at the same time and something inside her eased. Pleasure-pain speared through her as both cocks entered her simultaneously. Her fingers dug into Fury's shoulders as she held on for the ride.

"Tell me you will face the bonding ceremony with us."

"We want your vow that you'll mate with us in an official mating ceremony both on the *Lioni* home world and on *Bearote*, Fury's planet."

Both men stopped mid-thrust as they waited for her to answer.

In that instant, she realized she had nothing to fear from them. She knew to the depths of her soul they would do all they could to protect her, Ryo and any other children the Mother Goddess blessed them with. There could be but one answer to their question. "Yes, I will bond with you."

As soon as she answered, they entered her in one thrust, pressing deep inside her as they held her between them. Drace's chest vibrated behind her as he purred against her back. Fury hid his face against her neck as his cock pulsed, releasing his seed against her womb. Pleasure ripped through her. Her muscles convulsed as another climax overwhelmed her.

Fury began to lower her legs. Pain ripped through her overused muscles.

"Did we hurt you?" Drace asked, his voice laced with concern.

"I'm just sore from all the lovemaking." Drace sent his hands over her shoulders. A little groan escaped her lips as he gently massaged the aching muscles of her back, her thighs.

Resting her head against Fury's chest as they continued to massage her muscles, Kiri sighed. "So, when do we head to your home planets for our mating ceremonies?"

One week later, Tigeria, home-base planet of the Mother Goddess' Triads.

KIRI LOOKED AROUND the meadow where the ceremony would take place, nervous now that the time to join her mates as part of a bound triad was near. Naked, she stood in front of the ancient looking standing stones, her mates on either side of her. Knowing what came next, she took a few steps forward until she was close to enough to touch the nearest pillar of stone and turned to face her mates. "I await your desires, my mates."

Fury stroked his cock slowly, while Drace did the same. With a wave of his hand, a pallet covered with the softest *Carrillian* silk appeared between them. He moved behind Kiri, seated himself on the pallet.

"How did you do that?"

Fury snorted. "Just a bit of Transport magic. There is much you do not know of the *Beariti* yet, my precious. Come here, Kiri. Sit on my lap, facing Drace."

She nodded and did as she was told. There was no hesitance as she followed his directions.

With a firm grip, he lifted her bottom. She felt his cock nudge against her gate and widened her legs just a bit. He slowly worked his way inside of her, careful not to hurt her. She still was unused to the size of their cocks, much bigger than both humans and *Hienials* alike. When Fury had seated his shaft fully inside her channel, Drace nudged her lips with his cock. Slowly Fury stroked inside her, thrusting shallowly. "I will fuck your mouth, Kiri, while Fury fucks your channel."

Kiri nodded. Tonight was about uniting them in a true Triad and only her men knew the rules for the ceremony in their entirety. She trusted them to know what she should do.

Drace's hands gripped her hair, pulled her closer to his throbbing shaft. She took him into her mouth, taking as much of his length as she could without gagging.

Fury's fingers found her pleasure bud, her clit. His fingers strummed it each time she went down on Drace's cock. Several minutes passed and only when Drace began to come did Fury allow her to reach climax. As the salty fluid of Drace's seed hit the back of her throat, her entire body seized. The pleasure pain of her release washed over her.

When Drace was completely empty of his seed, he knelt down in front of her, wrapped his arms around her shoulders as Fury began to fuck her in earnest. Harder and harder, he thrust, hitting her womb with every stroke. His fingers dug into her hips, holding her body with an iron grip.

Fury groaned. His body trembled. His breathing grew harsher. Drace reached down and pinched her clit. Ecstasy shot through her. Her channel clasped Fury tighter, milked him of his seed. Fury and Drace leaned forward and placed their mouths to her shoulders. They both bit down, marking her as their mate.

They held her sandwiched between them as their teeth sank into her flesh. After they took her blood, Fury and Drace licked her wounds closed before tearing into their own wrists with sharp canines.

"Drink of our life force, *mi ama*. Drink and we shall all be as one. You shall be joined with us in life as well as in body." Drace held his bleeding wrist out to her.

Nodding, Kiri gently took Drace's wrist to her mouth, sipped his blood. Once she licked his wound as they done to hers, she reached for Fury. She took his lifeblood willingly, knowing there was no going back after this. Tomorrow she would return to Ryo and to the war with the *Banarts* and the *Hienials*, but she would spend tonight loving her mates.

BRANDY ATTENDED THE bonding celebration for her brother later that evening. She wasn't sure she wanted to go, but she didn't want to hurt Drace's feelings.

What was there to do there? Watch everyone else with their mates? Watch everyone else dance and have fun while she stood on the sidelines and watched?

She gazed at the newest triad, watching from her hiding spot in the corner of the room farthest from the reception line. Soon the party would be in full swing. The new triad had just arrived moments ago with the other mated triads following not far behind. She sighed wistfully when she saw the rosy glow of happiness on Kiri's face. It wasn't hard to see that they were all happy. Obviously, their bonding ceremony had gone well.

She couldn't help but wonder what it felt like to be made love to by two men at the same time. Hellfire, she didn't even know what it felt like to have one man make love to her. She grimaced, remembering the few times Drace and her other overprotective brothers chased away any male she'd shown interest in. And, if any had shown an interest in her, they were soon chased off sporting more than a few bruises.

She watched as the three newlyweds moved out onto the dance floor. Kiri looked happy, comfortable, sandwiched between the two men. Unbidden, she thought back to the dragon pair she'd seen last week. What had Drace said their names were, Damir and Kaylen? She could picture herself with them— even envision herself between the two males as they swayed to the slow music, pressing their hard bodies against her. Her pulse sped up. Her heart slammed against her ribs as her empty channel clenched.

"Would you care to dance with us, Mate?" The husky voice behind her sent goose bumps pebbling across her flesh. Cream spilled from between her thighs. Then, with a start, she realized what he'd said.

"Mate?" she squealed. She spun around only to see the men she'd just been fantasizing about standing silently behind her with very pleased grins on their handsome faces.

SEX ME ALL ABOUT

Brandy watched her brother's mating ceremony, desire curling in the pit of her stomach. How she yearned for someone to love her as Kiri loved him. She didn't begrudge him his match. Never that. Yet she couldn't help the twinge of envy that speared her heart as they sealed their promises with a kiss. So like that of her own world. It seemed forever since Drace's father had brought her here to live. Still, she hadn't forgotten the customs on Earth. A marriage ceremony was always followed with a kiss.

She sighed forlornly as she looked on. How would she ever manage to get through the celebration that would follow? The heir had found his mate. There would be a great party to mark the event—and as usual—she would be alone.

Alone… She diverted her thoughts to the two handsome dragons. Too bad they were unable to attend the ceremony. She would have liked to have gotten a better view of that particular eye candy. She'd never seen two more handsome men in her life. Both were tall, exceptionally so, with long dark hair. Her one and only glance at them before she'd been shoved back into the transport was brief, but she knew the one who wore blue, had eyes the color of sapphires and the one in red had the greenest eyes. That they'd both been staring at her made her toes curl, then she'd learned they wouldn't be attending the bonding and her spirits fell.

What she would give to have them show up here and sweep her away. To feel the way their rumbling voices made her skin prickle and the hair on her arms stand on end. Her clit throbbed at the mere thought of them and she wanted to scream her frustration that she would never see them again. Her brothers were very protective of her. Only her mate or mates would ever get close enough for her to touch.

She followed the crowd until one of her brothers found her and dragged her up to the royal coach. She nearly laughed at that. The royal coach was a hovercraft almost the size of a football field back home. It had to be large—at least big enough to carry the entire royal family and their guards. She boarded the large craft and strayed to the farthest end away from the happily mated Triads. It seemed that every new Triad blessed by the Lady Goddess was here.

Brandy looked out over the side at the swirling water beneath the craft and wished for someone, even one man to love her. Even though she knew her adopted family loved her, she still felt like an outsider. She was full human. She couldn't change into another set of clothes if she wanted, without her maids standing there ready to dress her.

Have you heard the saying 'be careful what you wish for', young Brandy? Today is your twenty-fifth birthday. Have you, like everyone else, forgotten this day is special for you as well?

Brandy shrugged at the voice in her head. She'd heard the voice since she'd been a child. Either she was deranged, or it was her mind's way of coping. She rather liked to think it was the latter.

You know who I am. I think you have always known. For one glorious year I walked the earth as a flesh and blood woman. I loved a man. A human man...who loved me. A child was born of that union. A female child. She was given a gift. An amulet to wear around her neck every day of her life—the amulet drew her power from her, her knowledge. Everything she'd ever known, her daughter and her daughter's daughter and down through the line—all they have ever known, is stored within the amulet. You are the next female in the line, granddaughter. It is you who will help fulfill the Triad legacy. With your help and the help of the others, the Banart plague will end and the Hienials will finally become what they were meant to be.

"Wishful thinking, Brandy." She blew the blonde bangs from her face and stared down into the crystal blue waters of the *Lioni River.*

As the craft slowed and the water cleared deep below, she spotted a bed of the most gorgeous colorful stones she'd ever seen. They were so beautiful she was tempted to dive in and pick up some of the overlooked treasure as the ship passed over them. Instead, she stood rooted to the spot staring over the rail and fingered her amulet, which had grown warm. It was a warm day so it was easy to ignore the heat of the amulet as she had so often in the past. Soon, the sun would set and the air would cool and they would all be more comfortable.

IT WAS FULLY dark by the time they reached their destination. The mated Triads all departed the vessel first, behind her father and mother as was customary. Still she lingered behind, not wanting to join the festivities. There was nothing for her there but loneliness constantly magnified by the joy of others. The last thing she wanted to do was bring her brother's spirits down with her melancholy. This was his night. His time for celebration had finally come and she refused to begrudge him his happiness.

She hadn't really wanted to be here, but she knew her presence would be missed and the last thing she wanted to do was hurt Drace's feelings. She had nothing to do here. Nothing but watch everyone else have a good time with their mates. Was she just supposed to stand and watch everyone else dance and have fun while she waited and observed from the sidelines, like some sort of wallflower?

She gazed at the newest Triad, staying hidden in the corner of the room farthest from the reception line. Soon the party would be in full swing and she would be able to slip out. Besides, who would miss her? The newest Triad—Drace, Kiri and Fury had just arrived moments ago with the other mated Triads following not far behind, though from the heated looks on some of the males' faces, they wouldn't be staying long.

She sighed wistfully when she saw the rosy glow of happiness on Kiri's face. It wasn't hard to see that they were happy. Obviously, their bonding ceremony had gone well. And she was happy for them. Truly she was.

Still, she couldn't help but wonder what it felt like to be made love to by two men at the same time. Hellfire, she didn't even know what it felt like to have one man make love to her. Drace and her other overprotective brothers chased away any male she'd ever shown any interest in. And, if any male approached her without their permission, they were quickly run off sporting more than a few bruises. She couldn't blame her brothers for wanting to protect her. She knew how few women there were. Still, she would have liked the opportunity to date. But, here on the *Lioni* home world dating was an unknown concept. Either you were mates, or you were not. There was no in-between.

Seemingly a glutton for punishment, she stayed and watched as the three newlyweds moved out onto the dance floor, happy smiles on their faces. Kiri looked delighted, comfortable even, sandwiched between the two men. She sure had come a long way from the frightened woman she'd been only a few short weeks ago.

Unbidden, Brandy thought back to the dragon pair she'd seen last week. What had Drace said their names were—Damir and Kaylen? What perfect specimens of manhood! She shuddered. Just thinking about them caused gooseflesh to rise on her skin. She could picture herself with them—even envision herself sandwiched between the two males as they swayed to the slow music, pressing their large, hard bodies against her. Her pulse sped up. Her heart slammed against her ribs as her empty channel clenched. She closed her eyes, trying to imagine the sound of their voices, the very timber and cadence as they spoke. Just the sound of their voices had brought her as close to an orgasm as she'd ever been in her life.

"Would you care to dance with us, Mate?" The familiar, husky voice behind her sent even more goose bumps pebbling across her flesh. Cream spilled from between her thighs at the thought.

Yes, that's what he would say. Damir, the one who wore blue had a voice that could bring a woman to her knees. Then she imagined the other, Kaylen repeating the phrase and she whimpered, wishing they were here. Wishing she was their mate and they had truly come to claim her. It wasn't until she felt a hand land on each of her shoulders that she realized that what she'd heard was no dream. The two dragons were here, standing just behind her.

Then, with a start, she realized what they had said. "Mate?" she squealed and spun around only to see the men she'd just been fantasizing about standing silently behind her with very pleased grins on their handsome faces.

"Yes, woman." Damir leaned close, inhaled deeply and closed his eyes as though savoring her scent. "You are our mate. Do not deny that you want us. I can smell the sweet scent of your desire on you, even if I couldn't read your mind."

Her face heated. *Oh, my god. They can read my mind?* Inadvertently, she replayed every time she'd thought about them in their presence. How she'd admired their physiques, their taut stomachs and their rounded asses, which she wanted nothing more than to grab onto and squeeze with all her might.

She lowered her head as her gaze drifted down to once again, admire the incredible size of Damir's package before she caught herself, her face heating to match the fires that warmed the great hall in the winter. *Stop thinking like this!* She strained to remember about the dead rats she'd been forced to sleep next to before Drace's father had found her and brought her to his home, anything to keep her mind from sex, especially sex with them.

Even then, she couldn't stop thinking about her attraction to these two men. Dragons. Whatever! Her nipples pebbled against the lacy camisole she wore beneath her top. She crossed her arms over her breasts, in an attempt to hide her reaction, though she knew it was impossible. They were the magical, mythical dragons of her dreams and they looked at her as though she were a decadent dessert they wanted to devour.

"Well, we're not mythical, but you've got the rest right."

Dropping her arms, she turned and glared at them. It just wasn't fair. She didn't know what they were thinking. They shouldn't know what she had on her mind, either. "Just stay out of my head. It's not right. You don't see me running around inside your head, traipsing through your private thoughts and telling everyone your private fantasies."

Kaylen glanced at Damir and smiled. "At least she's admitted that we're one of her private fantasies." He waggled his brows. "Would you like to make it a reality, mate?"

"Oh, my God. If my brothers could hear you, you'd be dead meat, right now," she hissed.

"No, my dear. That is why it appeared as though we missed the ceremony. We had business with your father." Damir smiled, took her hand and pressed a kiss to the back of her knuckles. "We had to ask his permission to court you."

"You did what?" She lowered her voice when several people glanced their way, frowning. "You can't just go and ask my father permission to court me when you haven't even asked me if I'm interested." She crossed her arms beneath her breasts then quickly lowered them when she realized it pushed her cleavage up, giving the two dragons a better view of her overly abundant curves.

"Of course we can. It is the way of your people." He shrugged. "It is the way of the *Lioni* people and you accepted your position as his daughter long ago. Will you change your mind and shame him now?"

Oh, they knew they had her between a rock and a hard place. She frowned. Besides, why was she even fighting this? Isn't this exactly what she wanted, or was she just pissed because the choice had suddenly been taken out of her hands? Not to mention that it was as embarrassing as hell to have the two objects of your secret lusty fantasies tell you that it was no secret. Besides, it's a big step between fantasizing about taking two mates and actually doing it.

"You may not think it right, but after we mate, you will have the same abilities. You shall become like us, a dragoness, just as if you were born to it," Kaylen said, his gaze intent. It almost felt that he could see into her soul, see her secret desires. And of course, he could. "Can you imagine it, little one? Can you imagine what it is like to soar above the clouds, at one with the air, the skies?"

"Perhaps, that has always been your destiny, hence your fascination with our species," added Damir as he pulled her closer to the dance floor.

"You're manipulating me, aren't you? I'm on the dance floor, right where you wanted me."

"Well," Kaylen added, whispering in her ear, "you're not exactly where we want you."

Damir chuckled then. "No. Where we really want you, is beneath us, between us, sharing your body, your heart, your very soul with us." His hands moved up her sides, gliding around her shoulders to pull her against him.

Kaylen stepped behind her, pressing himself against her back, the hardness of his shaft resting between the cheeks of her ass. "Where it belongs. Where we both belong."

Brandy shivered. Gooseflesh trailed along her skin where they both had touched her and where she wanted them to touch her. Delicious heat pooled in her center, moving lower to her womb as her woman's cream slid from her channel to wet her panties. This was a dream—it had to be. Everything in her life had been so fantastic, so surreal, since she'd come to live with the *Lioni* and for the first time since that day, she wondered if this was real or if she was back on Earth, shut away in some asylum. Given the choice, she would be here with them—mad or not.

Brandy let the two men lead her along the dance floor, pressing against her, knowing she was the final female in the famed Triads formed to fight the *Banarts* and *Hienials.* She knew the two men holding her must be her mates. She lusted for them.

Even from the beginning, when she'd first seen them shift from their dragon forms to stride to the group she stood with, she wanted to make love to them. She had watched the males, her tongue practically hanging from her mouth as they both strode confidently toward her group. Her mythical beloved dragons...

"And now we have come," Kaylen said, stepping away so Damir could turn her in their arms to face Kaylen. She looked up into his perfect face and knew she must have truly died and gone to heaven. That these two very handsome, powerful men would want her—even with her too tall, too curvy body that bordered on chunky.

She deliberately looked up, meeting his gaze. She knew her unusual eyes were her best feature. The iris, a striking deep shade of violet, rimmed with the thinnest ring of gray; her lids framed by thick blonde lashes. Her brothers had commented too many times on the uniqueness of her eyes for her to not realize they were, by far, her best asset. It was just too bad the rest of her body wasn't so special.

Damir pressed up against her rear, his hands moving over her thighs. "What is wrong with your body, *aliante?*" He once again ran his hands over her hips. Reaching around, he pressed one hand against her rounded belly. "You are perfect."

Kaylen's eyes narrowed. A red haze formed over the whites of his eyes. "Who here has told you that you are anything but perfect?" His right hand moved up to cup her cheek when she would have looked away. Tears slid from her eyes and he thumbed them away before leaning forward and lightly brushing her lips with his. "Do not look away in shame, *aliante.* You are perfect in every way." His free hand moved to join Damir's at her hips. "Your full hips tell us you are capable of bearing many children." His left hand traveled from her hip to her full breast. "Your ample breasts tell us you will feed our children well. Your height—yes you are tall for a woman—only tells us you will bear us tall sons and daughters, those who will grow even stronger than Damir and me one day." He leaned forward to kiss her tears away. "Never think you aren't ideal in every way."

Damir pressed more firmly against her rear. "Now I would like to know who it was that made you feel less than wonderful, mate. I shall correct their opinion immediately."

"It was no one on this world." She let them pull her from the dance floor, escorting her to an empty balcony, which faced the palace gardens. When they reached the stairs, she took the lead, taking them to the center fountain where the water sprayed in a rainbow of color. It was one of the places where she felt the most comfortable.

"You know I am not *Lioni.*" She trailed her hand through the warm water and waited for them to acknowledge her statement. At their nods, she continued around the fountain and let her memories take her back to her home world. "You would never believe the number of women on my home world. I think we are more numerous than men, though I can't be sure." She swiped at a tear she swore she'd never shed and called herself weak for it. "When my father found me," she turned and added, "the father you know, he found me with two things, other than the filthy clothes on my back."

She reached down inside her blouse to pull the pendant from between her breasts. "This pendant in a box that my parents made me promise to keep with me always and a magazine with a picture of my mother on the front. She was a model. The world considered her beautiful. She realized too late that her career drew rabid fans and religious fanatics to us and she sent me out alone to find my grandmother. My father went in another direction with a bunch of my dirty clothes wrapped up in a blanket to keep them from finding me. It wasn't until I got here I realized that it was our current enemies looking for me.

"Anyway, the *Lioni* men found me several weeks later, starving to death in a ditch with my box and magazine clutched in my hands. They have been nothing but kind to me. No one here has made me feel less than what I am, only that one magazine from my home-world where thin women are revered and those who don't fit that mold are considered less than perfect— sometimes even less than human."

She buried her face in her hands and sobbed. "I hear you say I am perfect the way I am and still, somewhere inside me, this insidious voice whispers, 'You are not. You never will be, and soon, even these two men will realize it and leave you'. How can I fight this thing when it is inside me?" She looked up at the two gorgeous men who had moved to kneel in front of her. "No matter how many times you tell me otherwise, how can I think I am beautiful when everything inside me tells me I am not? When I am nothing like my mother?"

She looked at them and almost laughed. "On my world, two men like you wouldn't even give me a second glance."

"Then they are fools," Kaylen said with a growl. "We have known all our lives a woman's heart is what matters the most, not her body. When a woman loves, and knows she is loved in return, this is the shape her body becomes," he said as his gaze roved over her curves. "This is just the right figure for childbearing. Your body is designed for loving as you deserve to be loved." He leaned forward and kissed her deeply. One hand cupped the back of her head while his other hand cupped her breast, kneading its fullness, his thumb rubbing over the tight peak.

She gasped when she felt the sensation of fingers delving into her wet slit when she could clearly see neither of them were touching her there. She threw her head back and groaned when the warm wetness of a mouth closed over her bare breast. Yet she was still clothed! Fire licked at her skin as the two men held her in their arms. Damir sat next to her then scooped her into his arms. He did his best to hold her on his lap at the edge of the fountain while Kaylen kissed her senseless.

The two men breached her mind, touching her in places they shouldn't have dared until they were truly mated. She knew what her father would think of such a thing, yet she was powerless to stop it. Somehow, they penetrated her clothing without removing it. Somehow, she felt the mouth of one at her breast and the mouth of the other breathing fire into her nether parts. The hot wet tongue stroked fire over her clit before entering her channel. She should stop this, stop them. As the king's daughter, she should know better, but she didn't want to stop.

Cold water closed over her head and the three of them surfaced sputtering. Her father and brothers stood before them with fierce scowls on their faces. One of them must have pushed her in.

"You asked my permission to court my daughter, dragons. I do not remember giving my permission to mate her in my own gardens in the dark of night like a couple of thieves." Her father glared at her. "You know our customs, daughter. With so few women in our midst, this type of behavior binds you to them—whether you truly choose them or not. I can only hope your body has made the right choice for your mind."

Brandy rose from the water, her face burning with mortification as the steam from the two aroused dragons rose about her.

Steam rises from you, as well, aliante. *It can only mean you were meant to be our mate. Your father only speeds up the process of our courtship and mating with his decree. Do not fear this. This is as it was meant to be.*

Her father and brothers turned away from her. "Go change into something less revealing. Your wet clothing shows your body to anyone who cares to look." Her father's hands were fisted at his sides, showing her how angry he was with her. He'd never been like this before—at least not in front of her. She climbed from the fountain as he said, "And make it something suitable for the binding! Your ceremony is tonight."

Tonight? Her surprised gaze darted from her father's back to her brothers'. She had nothing to wear. All her life she'd planned to wear a gown like the one her mother had modeled in the magazine. It was a wedding gown of pure white. Tears streamed from her eyes as she pictured the gown in the magazine—the one tie to her mother that she would now never have. She nodded and wiped the tears from her eyes. "Yes, Father." She could not regret what happened. What she knew would happen when she brought the two men to this fountain. Her only regret was the loss of the dress she would never have the time to make.

Warmth and tingling surrounded her. She closed her eyes, unsure of what new dragon magic she would be subjected to. Air blew her body and hair dry. Long fitting sleeves moved down her arms, her body was cinched into what felt like a corset as heavy material settled on her shoulders.

Finally, finding the courage to open her eyes, she gasped. Long white sleeves tapered down her arms, a low neckline studded with pearls showed her cleavage to perfection. She felt her back. A row of tiny buttons ran the length of her back from her hips to her neck. She turned to see a long train of silk and netting trailing her. It was *the* dress! *But how...?*

She looked to her dragons, now garbed in the finery of their houses. They each wore black suits, uniforms that resembled tuxedos. One with a red sash, the other blue, both wore their suits to perfection, their shoulders back as they proudly displayed their medals.

Brandy reached up to feel the veil on her head. They had forgotten nothing, right down to the pearl studded gloves and the shoes she'd wanted to match her mother's.

She looked at Kaylen and Damir and smiled. Suddenly she knew everything would be all right. These men cared for her already. She could feel it deep inside her where she'd made all of her life-changing decisions. When she chose to accompany the strange men who offered her a safe home—when she'd accompanied Drace on his mission, knowing she could be killed. Still she wasn't, she'd found her mates. Now, she would choose to live her life with them. They thought she was perfect. She smiled softly as a tear slipped from her eye. Who was she to tell them otherwise?

DAMIR LOOKED ON his mate and nearly fell to his knees. She was already beautiful. However, the dress they'd picked from her mind made her look like the Lady Goddess herself. She was a vision of perfection, her white dress glimmering with something she called pearls.

Next to him, he felt Kaylen's similar reaction. *Had I known how beautiful she truly was I would have been at her feet begging her for her hand instead of taking advantage of the privacy of the garden.*

I know what you mean, dear friend, Damir said, his vision blurring with unshed tears. He blinked them back rapidly. He could not show weakness now. If her family should deem them unworthy, they could still stop the ceremony. Still keep them from her. He couldn't have that. Not when they were so close to having their mate.

"We will have her now, if you don't mind." Kaylen said, causing her family members to turn.

They gasped but it was her father who was first to speak. "We knew you dragons possessed a certain...magic other than shifting. We had no idea what it was," he said, obviously amazed.

"You still have no idea, Sir. But as you will soon be family, perhaps we will share some of it with you." Damir said, stepping forward. "But, for now, your daughter wishes a human ceremony—or as human a ceremony as she can remember. As we have no particular ceremony other than the claiming, we ask your permission to give this to her."

"She is not *Lioni* by birth, only by adoption. If it is her wish to marry in the ways of her people I shall allow it. But it will happen now."

Brandy turned and kissed her father on the cheek. "Thank you, father. And though I wish to be married in this way, it is only because it is the only tie I have with my real mother. She once wore a dress like this, she told me she was married in a dress like this. I wish to honor her by doing the same." She took his hands and met his gaze. "Otherwise, I am *Lioni* in all things and this is why I follow your decree." She turned to take both Damir and Kaylen's hands.

She felt Damir delve into her thoughts, knew he needed to know that she wanted them. He needed her to want them, not just join with them because they'd compromised her with her people. Through the merging, she felt Kaylen's need to know the same.

At his mental probe, she smiled and opened her mind to them. She wanted this, wanted them more than anything else. She only hoped they would continue to see her as perfect. She allowed Damir to see her fear that in time, they would tire of her, think less of her because of her full figure. She heard his thoughts on her worries. What he saw of the so-called perfect figure from her home looked pale, sickly, and certainly not strong enough to give birth to dragons.

Her smile widened and she squeezed their hands.

"Do you Kaylen and you Damir take me to be your lawfully wedded mate?" They nodded. "We do."

"Do you promise to love, honor, and keep me?"

Again they nodded. "We do."

"Do you promise to cleave only unto me, 'til death do us part?"

"We do."

Understanding that her knowledge of the ceremony grew thin, Damir and Kaylen knelt at her feet and continued, knowing what she needed to hear.

"Do you, Brandy of the house of *Lioni*, take us as your mates?" When she nodded and made to answer Damir held up his hand, silently telling her to wait. "Do you promise to love honor and keep us in sickness and in health and cleave only unto us, as we will you, until death do us part?"

Tears ran from her eyes as he added that bit of the ceremony buried in her subconscious that she couldn't remember and she nodded. "I do."

He stood and whispered in her ear. "Now who pronounces us men and

231

wife?"

Brandy smiled. "That would be my father, since he's officiating here."

Damir turned toward Darvin, with raised brows, "Well?"

Her father chuckled and after placing a chaste kiss on her cheek, he joined the hands of the newly mated Triad. "I now pronounce you officially mated."

Before he could announce that they could now kiss their bride, a magnificent ball of white light began to form right behind him. The light grew brighter until a form began to take shape inside. When it became too difficult to see through the magnificent brilliance, it forced them to close their eyes.

Damir's gut tightened. He knew what was happening and his heart clenched. Was the Lady Goddess here to bless their union or to renounce it? He could only pray that She was there to bless it even knowing that it would mean She had a mission for him and his new mates. If She renounced their mating, it would kill something inside him, and destroy his belief in the Goddess, for he would never give Brandy up.

Damir, how could you think I'd ever do such a thing? Brandy's happiness and well-being comes before all things. For now, she is the last daughter of my line, and I chose you Damir and your bond brother Kaylen as her mates. Do you think my decision is faulty? That I should choose another pair for her?

Damir winced. *I beg your pardon, Lady Goddess. I meant no insult. I just couldn't bear losing her after just finding her. Brandy already holds my heart and the heart of Kaylen in her tiny hands.*

You may call me grandmother, my son. Brandy will call me grandmother and the same of Kaylen. You are my family, and for now, the last of my line. I should like my line to continue through my granddaughter. Are you two up to the challenge? She looked between them and raised her brow.

Of course, as I'm sure Kaylen will tell you. But first, I imagine you have a mission for us. We are your last Triad, aren't we? The last group of three needed to defeat our enemies?

Yes, my son. You are the final Triad. Through you, the Banarts *and* Hienials' *reign of terror will end.*

Damir finally opened his eyes as the brilliant white light faded. *What will you have us do?*

The Lady Goddess smiled. Her flaming red hair seemed to have a life of its own and her sparkling violet eyes could light up a room. Her curvaceous body was the epitome of a mature woman. She didn't look a day over forty, though she had to be thousands of years old. Other than the more mature face, and the difference in hair color, she could be Brandy's twin.

I will have you celebrate your mating night then meet me and the other Triads at the glen beneath the Tigerian *standing stones just as the sun crests the horizon, tomorrow.*

And then?

And then all will be made clear to you, to you all.

Knowing that she wouldn't say anything more, he didn't want to waste what time remained of the Lady Goddess's visit without saying what was in his heart. *Thank you for giving your last daughter of the line to us. We shall cherish her forever.*

I know you will. That is precisely why you have her. No one can love her as the two of you will. The Lady Goddess lifted her head and faced the growing crowd. The six Triads were in the garden, drawn by the Lady's presence.

"I bless this joining and all the Triad unions these past six moons. May the love you share include many children and may your children bring you love and joy. Let them follow the guidance you give them, for they too will be important in the future."

Before any could speak, the Lady Goddess slowly faded away.

Turning toward the newly arrived Triads, Damir grinned. "I guess you were all invited here by the Goddess unexpectedly." That was an understatement—since all the Triads were in varies degrees of undress.

Beside him, Kaylen chuckled obviously noticing that the *Tigerian* Triad wore nothing but their smiles. Appearing from around the corner, Brandy's mother, Marva, had a handful of ceremonial robes, which she carefully handed out, keeping her eyes averted the whole time.

Dax snarled, apparently not happy. "Yes, you could say that we were otherwise occupied and not expecting to be transferred anywhere without notice. We were working on giving our mate a child this night."

After donning her robe, Minna slapped Dax's arm and when Rage chuckled she slapped his too. "Show some respect and think beyond your cocks. There must be a reason we were brought here and she spoke of our children." She put a hand over her flat stomach. "Who knows? She may have gifted us with a babe already."

Jaynee, Laynee, Kiri, Ana and their respective mates headed toward Damir and the new additions to his family. The twelve men and women, followed quickly by the *Tigerian* Triad, moved toward Brandy and began hugging her one after another, before moving on to him and Kaylen. After the congratulations were given, Damir finally answered Minna's charge.

"You are right, Minna. We are the final of the Goddess' Triads. We are to meet at the *Tigerian* glen beneath the standing stones tomorrow just as the sun begins to rise above the horizon."

The men—Wray and Kel, Dax and Rage, Fury and Drace, Dare and Luc, and finally, Fane and Sayre—stood at attention. Dare—the *Savari* leader and apparently appointed spokesmen of the men—nodded before speaking. "Then we shall all be there at the appointed time. I've acquired a few new ships that should make the three day trip in just a matter of hours. You all are more than welcome to join me and my mates aboard the *Savari* fleet for the voyage."

Knowing that their own ship wouldn't be able to make the journey as quickly, Damir nodded. What other choice did they have? None. "We'd appreciate that very much if you're sure that you have room for three of us."

"Absolutely. In fact, all three ships have VIP quarters that are large enough for a Triad and any children they may have."

Damir glanced down as Brandy stirred in his arms. Her cheeks were flushed pink and he could smell the scent of her arousal now heavy in the air.

He looked over her head, met Kaylen's heated gaze, could see the banked fire in his eyes. When Kaylen's nostrils flared, Damir knew time was growing short. If they didn't get to a bed soon, they'd be making love to their mate in front of an audience.

Kaylen cleared his throat, ran his hand through Brandy's long blonde hair. "We would appreciate it if you could make the arrangements for our travel, then."

Damir chuckled, as he watched Brandy's skin turn yet a darker shade of pink. When Dare nodded and began speaking into a wrist communicator, he felt something inside him ease. Soon. Soon, they'd be able to make love to their mate. For so many long, lonely years, they prayed to the Lady Goddess for a mate and finally She'd granted their request. The wait to make her theirs in both body and spirit would take every bit of his legendary patience and he knew Kaylen felt the same.

"Everything has been arranged. Several shuttles are on their way to pick us up. By the time we reach the Royal *Lioni* landing pad, they should be there."

Damir lowered his head. "Thank you." With Brandy's hand held firmly in his, he and Kaylen quickly made their way to the pick-up point. As their destination grew closer, the passion and lust in his blood grew hotter. Only the knowledge that his mate wouldn't appreciate an audience for their first mating, gave Damir the strength to keep going. No sooner had the three of them reached the landing pad, than six shuttles began to descend from the sky. Thank the Goddess they wouldn't have to share transportation. He didn't think he or Kaylen would be able to keep their hands off their new mate, even for the short voyage to the Savari ships currently circling the *Lioni* home world.

AS THE THREE of them stepped onto the shuttle, Brandy's heart rate increased. Her hands shook. Her skin itched. Her empty channel ached, desperate for her mates to fill it. By the Goddess, how would she keep her hands to herself until they reached their quarters aboard the *Savari* ship assigned to them?

Her gaze drifted around the shuttle. It was larger than she anticipated. There were at least three separate sections. The front of the shuttle was closed off, the pilots accessible through a door secured with an electronic security pad. In the middle of the small ship were four spacious seats with an aisle down the middle that led to a door identical to the pilot's section. She had no clue what occupied the rear of the ship. Perhaps it was naught but a cargo area.

As soon as Damir led her into the main portion of the ship, she realized they would truly be alone for the short voyage, just the three of them. Her heart pounded against her chest. She needed her mates desperately, wanted them to make love to her.

Though she may still be a virgin, her thoughts were anything but naive. She wanted both of them to fill her, be it her ass, her pussy or her mouth. At this point, she was so desperate for them, she didn't care what portion of her body they filled, so long as it happened soon.

Damir led her to one of the spacious seats but instead of sitting her in one, he pulled her onto his lap facing him. Behind her, Kaylen moved in, pressing the full length of his body against her back. She could feel his arousal, feel it pulsing in need along her spine. Before she could even squeak in surprise, the three of them were completely naked, her dress and their tuxedos gone as though they'd never been.

"Wh—"

"It's dragon magic, *aliante*," Kaylen whispered into her ear before laying tiny kisses down her neck and along her collarbone. Soon he was trailing his tongue down her shoulder, along her spine then she couldn't think at all.

In front of her, Damir raised his hands, caressed the side of her face before slowly running his fingers down her chest. When he reached her lush breasts, he circled her nipples in whisper soft strokes until they grew hard and needy. She could feel his cock pressing against her belly but she was too nervous to glance at it.

Her body quivered, gently at first, before shudders shook her from head to toe. Never had she felt such burning desire, such desperate, yearning need. She arched her back, pressing her breasts against Damir's hands, her ass against Kaylen's rock-hard cock.

Kaylen rubbed his cock along the crease of her ass, teasing her with shallow thrusts as his hands slowly moved from her waist to her thighs. She shivered, knowing that he wanted to fuck her ass. Even knowing what he intended, knowing that she'd never taken a male in her body and that their joining would probably hurt, she couldn't deny Kaylen's need.

"Please, I—I need…"

"What do you need, *aliante*?" Damir asked. She tried to answer, but he chose that moment to lean forward and take her nipple into his mouth. He suckled it in long, strong pulls while one hand gripped her hip and the other worked her other nipple, pulling and tugging it in tandem with his suckling.

Kaylen wrapped her hair around his fist while he moved his other hand further up her thigh. Before she had time to think, to worry, his fingers slowly sank into her wet channel, first one, then two, until she felt stretched to the limit. She groaned, unprepared for his invasion.

She was lost in sensation. Damir continued to suckle her nipples, first one, then the other, until they were so sensitive she wanted to scream her desire, her need at the top of her lungs.

Behind her, Kaylen continued to stroke his fingers inside her body, shallow thrusts then deeper, as he prepared her for their mating. Nothing she read, nothing she imagined, could compare to what was happening to her. She moaned, unable to remain silent as her mates continued to assault her senses. And when Kaylen knelt behind her, lifting her ass off Damir's lap and tipping her forward, she almost screamed in frustration. Instead, she shrieked in pleasure as his tongue stroked her flesh, swirling over her clit as he knelt directly beneath her.

Her hips bucked. Her nails dug into Damir's chest as she clung to him. Her channel spasmed, ached with wanting, desperate now to be filled. Her thighs quivered. Her pulse pounded. Her hips lifted in the air, searching, searching now desperate for relief. As Kaylen continued to fuck her pussy with his agile tongue, Damir reached down between their bodies and gave a sharp pull to her clit just as he bit down on her breast. The dual stimulation set her off. Wave after wave of pure pleasure washed through her as Kaylen lapped up her woman's cream and Damir pet her still throbbing pussy. Completely sated, she lay boneless in Damir's arms.

Her channel was still pulsing when Kaylen stood behind her. Once again, he pressed his body against her back. His erection felt even larger than before, if that was possible. His voice, so masculine and sexy, whispered in her ear. "It is time, my mate. Time to meld our hearts and souls as well as our bodies."

Strong hands lifted her astride Damir as he lowered the back of his seat slightly. She swallowed convulsively as she got her first real look at his cock. By the Goddess, he was huge. Erect, it was almost as thick as her wrist and easily reached his bellybutton. How would he ever fit inside her?

REACHING DOWN, DAMIR positioned himself at their mate's cunt. Kaylen could tell that it took all he had not to ram himself inside her. The knowledge that she was still virgin was what kept them from taking her as ruthlessly as their inner dragons demanded.

As Kaylen held Brandy's hips, Damir slowly entered their mate. He could see the strain on Damir's face, hear his raspy breaths as he tried to be gentle. Kaylen knew the moment Damir reached Brandy's maidenhead. He could feel his friend's panic, his fear that he would hurt her.

The pain will only be momentary. You must breach her, my friend, if you want to complete the bond with her.

Damir gave a slight nod before thrusting up into their mate. Brandy gasped, bit her bottom lip. A lone tear tracked down her cheek. Kaylen's heart clenched, knowing the pain he brought her, hating that he was the cause, but it couldn't be avoided.

When he was fully seated inside her, Damir stopped, pressed his forehead to hers. Behind her, Kaylen continued to surround her with his body, his strength. He'd offer whatever comfort he could, no matter how his body raged at him to participate in the loving. Soon, he told himself. Soon, she'd be lost in pleasure and he could join them. Only when the three of them were connected physically, and they both spilled their seed in her, one in her womb, the other in her ass, would their bond be forged and her transformation to dragoness begun.

She groaned when Kaylen reached around her, cupping her breasts. Before long, that wasn't enough for either of them and he began pulling and tweaking her sensitive nipples. When she began to grind her hips against Damir, Kaylen used his fingers to trace the folds of her dripping pussy. He gathered the moisture there and dragged it to her nether hole. So lost in Damir's lovemaking, Brandy didn't even flinch when he used her cream to lubricate her back entrance. Slowly, he stretched her bottom, using first one finger then two, continually adding more moisture as he prepared his way into her. When she took three fingers comfortably and began to fuck herself on them, he knew she was ready for his cock.

"Are you ready to take me, mate?" he asked, knowing that whatever her decision, he would abide by it.

"Yes. Yes, oh God, yes!" she cried.

Taking her for her word, Kaylen bent his knees, lining his cock up with the pink rosebud of her anal opening. As gentle as he could, he began to press the head of his shaft against her ass.

He moved forward, inch by inch, until fully seated inside her ass. Then he stilled, waiting for her to become accustomed to his cock. He could feel Damir's cock rubbing against his own through the thin membrane separating him from her channel and he shivered in reaction. He wasn't attracted to Damir in *that* way but he had to admit, he enjoyed the feeling.

After a minute, she wriggled and pushed back as though begging him to fuck her. How could he refuse her? He began to move in slow even thrusts, opposite to those of her other mate.

The pleasure was so intense, he threw his head back and groaned as he increased his pace to match Damir's. Before long, their passion took over, the hunger surfaced and they began to pound her ruthlessly. Brandy gave a low keening cry as her clasping channel clamped down on their cocks.

She pulsed around them, locking their cocks into her body as she reached her climax. They continued to fuck her as they drove toward their own climax. Kaylen dug his fingers into her hips, forcing his cock into her tight ass, rougher and harder than before. He was so close—so close. She met each stroke with one of her own, pushing back and down as they drove into her, until in a blinding surge of heat and light, she milked them both of their seed.

BRANDY COLLAPSED ON top of Damir, her breath coming in short gasps. The two men pulled from her slowly and she shivered, whimpering at the loss.

"We didn't hurt you, did we?" they both asked at the same time.

She shook her head, a sleepy smile on her face. "It hurt for just a bit, then it was wonderful. I never knew it could be so..." she let her voice drift off and her face heated with embarrassment. She buried her head in Damir's shoulder, unable to look at either of them.

"There is no need to feel shame, *aliante*. We are mated now. It was our right and our privilege to breach you," Kaylen said, nipping her back. "Soon you shall see. It is also your right to have your way with our bodies. I can promise you, you will want to, and soon." He pulled away, standing to walk to the door in the back of the shuttle. "I hope this is a bathroom. Though it pleases us to see you covered with our seed, the mark of our mating, it can't be comfortable for you. I would like to wash our seed and the evidence of your maidenhead from your body before we clothe you again." She heard the sound of a door opening then Kaylen's chuckle. "Come see this, Damir, and bring our mate."

Brandy whimpered when Damir stood with her in his arms. With her arms and legs stretched around him, she could feel the evidence of his renewed desire, but wasn't sure she could take them again so soon. Muscles she never knew she had before ached. What she needed was a nice long soak to ease her aching body.

She gasped when Damir carried her into the room. She shook her head, amazed. It was a hedonist's paradise. A large bed and hot tub dominated the chamber. She would have been hard pressed to say which was bigger. She'd heard the *Savari* had large sexual appetites, but she never guessed that they would shuttle travel in such sensual decadence.

Kaylen walked over to the already full and steaming bath. "It seems our friends knew our desire was great and we would never make it to the ship before having our mate." Damir set her gently in the steaming tub. "It would have been nice of them to enlighten us to this chamber's existence."

"Perhaps." Damir shrugged. "But we know now. Let us comfort and heal our mate while we await our arrival aboard the *Savari* vessel."

They both joined her as she leaned back, enjoying the soothing jets buffeting her tired body. She needed this. A bath and a nap, then perhaps, she would be up to taking on her mates again when they reached their quarters aboard the ship. She wanted to love them as much and as long as she could before the conflict began. Who knew when they would have another chance to be alone or if they would even survive the coming war?

As the heated water began to soothe her sore muscles, she watched her mates through half-closed eyes. With their long black hair, heavily muscled chests, and wide shoulders, not to mention their magnificent cocks and asses, she had a hard time not salivating in their presence, especially now they were mated and she knew exactly what kind of pleasure they could give her.

Still, even after all their loving, it felt awkward being naked in front of them. Their bodies were perfect. They weren't short, or overweight. They didn't have to worry about what others thought of them.

"And neither do you, mate" growled Kaylen. "We find you exquisite just the way you are. Have we not told you that already?"

Next to him, Damir straightened, flexed his shoulders before skimming through the water to stop right in front of her. He caught her gaze in his before turning his head to look at Kaylen. "I guess we'll just have to make sure she knows just what we think of her, how beautiful we find her—even if it takes us all night for her to believe it."

Kaylen smiled, licked his lips. His green eyes flashed red. She pressed her back against the tub, suddenly anxious.

"Oh, I think that's a wonderful idea. By the time we lick every centimeter of her skin, holding off her orgasms, she'll have no choice but to agree with us. Only when she truly believes in herself, will we let her come."

Brandy swallowed, knowing they were serious in their intentions. How in the hell would she survive the night? She couldn't. She just wouldn't.

"You can. You will," Damir vowed just before his lips descended to hers. His kiss was slow, thoughtful. She couldn't help but respond, parting her lips as she raised herself to meet his kiss. His tongue traced the soft fullness of her lips, demanding entrance, demanding her surrender. His kiss sang through her veins, firing her blood with urgent need. Before long, he was taking her mouth with savage intensity, no longer trying to seduce her, instead conquering her.

She couldn't think, couldn't do anything but surrender to the passion Damir invoked. When Damir pulled her off the sunken seat inside the tub, she went willingly. When he demanded she wrap her legs around his waist, she did that too. So lost in Damir's kiss, Brandy lost all track of Kaylen. It wasn't until he pressed against her back, that she even remembered he was there. She jerked back from Damir, breaking their kiss, though he continued to hold her tight against his chest.

Tsk... tsk... tsk, aliante. I should punish you for forgetting about me, Kaylen whispered through her mind. She shivered in reaction. By the Goddess, just the thought of Kaylen punishing her made her clit twitch. Shouldn't she fear punishment, not actually get hot thinking about it?

Not when you know we would never harm you. In your heart, you know that only pleasure will come from whatever punishment we give you.

She swallowed, uncertain just what they planned for her and unsure what she'd do if they asked for more than she could give.

"Don't worry about such things, *aliante*," Damir murmured. He placed his hand on the back of her head, pulled her toward his chest so he could tuck her beneath his chin. It felt so right being held there, her ear against his chest where she could hear the steady beat of his heart. With his cock pressed against her belly, and one hand gripping her ass, her desire grew, but more than that she felt cherished in his arms, something she never thought to experience.

As she slowly relaxed against Damir, Kaylen's hands began to glide down her back. She could feel the soapsuds on his hands and she relaxed deeper into Damir's hold when she realized that Kaylen was washing her.

His hands ghosted over her skin, massaging her aching limbs and washing away the sweat from their previous loving. Not a single part of her body was missed, from the tips of her toes, to the hair on her head, Kaylen thoroughly washed her. Within minutes, she hung within Damir's arms, boneless. When the back of her body was clean, Damir turned her, so that she faced Kaylen. She continued to lie limp in his arms and Damir chuckled. "Wrap you legs around Kaylen's waist, *aliante*. I'll hold the rest of you while he washes your front. Then maybe we'll get to the rest of our plans for you."

Brandy nodded then slowly lifted her legs until they gripped Kaylen's waist. Kaylen's lips tipped up in the corners and she watched his eyes light before he dropped his gaze to her body. Her nipples were pebbled, courtesy of the cool air from the bathroom vents that wafted over them. With his heated gazed focus on her breasts, her nipples grew even harder, standing up as if begging for their attention. Behind her, Damir's rigid cock pressed against her lower back. She squirmed when Damir slid his cock back and forth between her pussy and her ass. No way could she stay still with that kind of stimulation.

Kaylen smiled as he watched her squirm. His gaze grew hooded as he poured more soap into his hands from the dispenser sitting on the side of the tub. As he lathered up, he winked at her. She gasped as his hands zeroed in on her breasts. His fingers massaged the scented soap into her nipples, before moving onto the rest of her chest, her tummy. When his hands drifted toward her pussy, she stiffened in their arms, too aroused from her bath to take even the slightest stimulation. She shook her head. "No. I can't. I can't take any more."

"You can, you will," Damir whispered into her ear, nipping the side of her neck with his sharp teeth before soothing the area with his tongue.

When Kaylen began to wash her between the legs, she breathed a sigh of relief as he only kept his hands there long enough to wash her thoroughly before he moved on to her thighs. Pulling her legs from around her waist, he knelt in the tub and washed first one leg then the next. When he stood again, he dropped a gentle kiss to her lips. "Time to rinse off, *aliante.*"

Her muscles had gone to mush, so she sat on the sunken seat until only her head was above water. Kaylen shook his head and Damir chuckled. "Turn around little one, and we'll rinse your hair then get you out of there before you become waterlogged."

"That's easier said than done. You've worn me out. I don't think I can move without assistance."

"Oh, poor baby. Not to worry, we'll take good care of you, mate," Damir promised. Within moments, they'd rinsed her from head to toe, using their fingers to work the knots from her hair. She'd never had anyone take care of her like this. She truly felt cherished, loved as they bathed her. Even though they weren't trying to seduce her, their gentle care was having that effect. She wanted to make love to them again, craved it.

When she was squeaky clean and ready to sleep—in the water, if need be—Damir picked her up in his arms and carried her from the tub. He held her still as Kaylen grabbed a large, soft towel from the warmer and began rubbing her skin. She closed her eyes, luxuriating in their care. After a while, even that stimulation became too much and she began to squirm. She needed release and she needed sleep, in that order.

She didn't even realize she'd been laid on the decadently large bed until she felt the mouths of her mates cover her nipples. Then, her eyes popped open with surprise just before she squeezed them closed again as they both began to lick and massage every inch of her body. Her breasts, her stomach, thighs, even her toes did not go ignored. They worked their way back up her body to her thighs. She spread her legs, her mind begging, screaming, for them to make her come. Just one flick of a tongue over her turgid clit and she would shriek the shuttle to the ground.

"Oh, no you don't, *aliante.* There is still your back," Kaylen said with a chuckle. "You didn't expect us to forget we promised to lick you all over your scrumptious body, did you?"

They had no trouble rolling her over onto her stomach. She lay boneless beneath them, literally unable to move. With her upper body propped on pillows, she could only groan when they each took an earlobe in their mouths and suckled gently. They were killing her slowly with their tongues.

Fire licked along her skin, as they moved down each tonguing a buttock. She squeaked with surprise when one of them spread her cheeks and tongued her anus. Not only did it set her afire even more, it felt soothing—as though their saliva was healing her where they had earlier stretched her virgin holes. She sighed her pleasure as the other put his tongue deep inside her channel. Her eyes widened. She never knew their tongues were *that* long before.

After they had licked every square inch of her body, and nearly driven her mad, she finally knew they meant what they said.

"I believe you. I am beautiful in your eyes and there is no other for either of you. Now will you *please* make me come?"

Damir looked at Kaylen, his eyebrow raised. "What do you think?"

"I think she needs to be fucked by two very horny dragons, and we're just the men to do it."

Finally! She was finally going to get to come. Just one flick of a finger, one lick of a tongue would set her off. Kaylen lay on the bed and drew her over him. His cock slid inside her so easily she was surprised. She shouldn't have been, the water had been slightly oily and all that licking had made her wet enough to take both of them easily. She groaned with pure delight when Damir slid himself into her ass—even that was lubricated. All that tongue action must have helped. She smiled into Kaylen's chest.

Three strokes and she was about to get her wish, she could feel her orgasm, just a few more seconds and she would explode like a dropped bottle of nitro. Before she could come—before any of them could—the shuttle began to slow and they felt the unmistakable sensation of a starship's deceleration gravity kick on. She looked around for her clothes. "My clothes, my dress!" Her face burned with mortification. "We can't be found like this. Fucking like horny children in daddy's car!" She tried to get up but Damir held her in place on his still rigid cock as her dress magically wrapped itself around her again and the two men were clothed as before.

Kaylen and Damir still had their cocks buried deep inside her, yet she was clothed. Well, except where their bodies met. They both shuddered and grunted as they pulled from her tight body.

Kaylen ran his hand through her wet hair then whispered into her ear, "By the Goddess, *aliante.* You are so soft, so welcoming. I can't wait to be inside you again so we can finish what we started. But protocol requires us to leave the shuttle as soon as the exit lights indicate. As soon as we enter the shuttle bay, we'll find our quarters."

"Which, with luck, won't take long at all." Damir ran his hand down her face. "It's my turn to fuck your tight ass while Kaylen takes your sweet pussy." He leaned forward. "And I can't wait."

The bump of the shuttle landing had them jumping from the bed and straightening the covers. Brandy needed to come so bad she nearly shook with it. Every nerve ending screamed for release. Everywhere her dress and undergarments touched, only made her need it more. She was so frustrated she could scream.

Damir exited the shuttle as soon as the door slid open. Turning, he helped her down then lifted her into his arms. A *Savari* officer stood ready to greet them. "Where are our quarters, please? Our mate isn't feeling well and we must see to her needs."

"Follow me. It isn't far."

They followed the *Savari* male to their quarters and Brandy marveled at the fact that their race didn't seem to have any short plain people. They were a lot like the dragons—all handsome enough to die for.

"I hear your thoughts, mate. I do not think I like you lusting after these men."

She grinned up at him and placed her hand on his cheek. "None of them hold a candle to you and Kaylen."

He frowned. "What is this hold a candle to? Why would they do such a thing?"

She saw the playful glint in his eyes and knew he was teasing her. "Stop teasing me," she whispered. "You and Kaylen have done quite enough of that on the way here." She gasped when he leaned forward and snaked his tongue into her ear, then sucked and nibbled on the lobe before straightening again.

The Savari male discreetly disappeared after showing them to the suite of rooms that Dare had boasted could hold many Triads and their children.

It didn't take long to find a room to their liking. It seemed to have been designed specifically for the two men. The blue, red and gold decorations took her breath away. Yet, it was the huge bed dominating the well-appointed room that she couldn't ignore. Her gaze kept drifting from that to the large tub in the corner. It seemed the *Savari* knew how to live, she thought with a smile. Damir deposited her in the center of the bed and gave her a heated look.

"I want to keep this dress, you two. So don't go and make it disappear again." She grabbed a fistful of the material hoping to keep them from using their magic on it. She gasped when it blinked out of existence for a moment then appeared across the room hanging over the back of a chair.

Realizing she was nude in front of her two men, she squealed and dove under the covers. Instinctively, she held the sheet to her chin, her face blazing with embarrassment.

Kaylen locked the door behind them and slowly approached the bed, dropping articles of clothing with each step. "Just think, Damir, we're finally alone with our mate. Now we can take our time proving just how beautiful she is."

"I know you think I'm beautiful," she said fearing they would torture her with their tongues again if she didn't accept that they thought her every bit as beautiful as her mother—if not more so. She stubbornly lifted her chin when they both raised a brow and looked from her to the sheet she held. "I know it. I really do. It's just..." her face burned. "It was instinct, or something. It's not like I take my clothes off for every male I meet, you know."

"As it should be," Damir said with a growl as he lowered his naked body to the bed.

Brandy couldn't help but stare. He was beautiful. They both were perfection personified. And they loved her. The realization surprised her. Not because they felt such emotion for her, but because she could actually feel how much they loved her. The depth of emotion she felt coming from the two men was almost more than she could comprehend—and it brought tears to her eyes.

She released the sheet she'd held so tightly to her chin, letting it pool around her waist where it caught on her hips. She raised her arms to her men, took a deep breath and said, "Make love to me, my mates." She rose to her knees, further proving she was no longer ashamed of her body as the sheet fell down to the mattress, exposing her blonde down-covered mound.

They both fell upon her, Damir kissing her deeply, his tongue exploring every secret recess of her mouth. Kaylen was at her breasts, suckling first the right then her left breast while his hand splayed over her belly. His fingers caressed her, constantly inching closer to her throbbing pussy.

Brandy gasped, her muscles clenching with anticipation as Kaylen's fingers gently delved into her wet slit.

Damir moved above her, carefully lowering her to her back. He lowered his mouth to the tips of her breasts. Her nipples pebbled to hard peaks as he licked and suckled each one.

Kaylen spread her legs and settled between them. He lifted her hips in his hands as though she weighed nothing and slowly lowered his head to her quivering flesh.

Finally! They were going to allow her to come. Finally!

Kaylen lapped at her pussy, seeming to savor her taste—every stroke of his tongue slowly driving her mad as she waited for relief. Her body tightened into one quivering muscle as she reached for her pleasure. Why didn't he just suck her clit into his mouth and give her the relief she so desperately needed?

She'd barely finished the thought when Damir pinched her right nipple between his fingers and bit down on her left. Still, the pleasure-pain didn't distract her from the fact that Kaylen circled her pulsing clit with his tongue, before at last sucking it into his mouth.

Brandy screamed her orgasm. As with each pull on her clit from Kaylen's mouth and the pleasure-pain of Damir at her nipples, she exploded into a million shards of light. *At last!*

DAMIR GAZED DOWN at his panting mate and smiled. "I think she fainted, old friend."

Kaylen chuckled. "I don't know about you, but I'm not through with her yet. Perhaps we should kiss her awake. Do you think she would like that?"

Brandy groaned and tried to roll over. "You two aren't getting out of fucking me again that easily." She smiled softly. "Where were we before we were so rudely interrupted by the shuttle landing?" she asked, her eyes still closed.

"I think," Kaylen said, rolling her on top of him, "we were right about here." He held her up by the hips and drove inside her. "You feel so good, *aliante.* I could stay like this forever.

Damir moved behind her and gently spread the globes of her ass. The small hole was already covered with her body's cream. Still, he reached around, between her and Kaylen and fingered her clit, gathering more of her cream to rub onto the head of his cock, mixing it with the drop of clear fluid that was already present.

He looked down at this hard cock. He needed to come so bad, his shaft had grown huge. He refused to be the rutting animal they both had been aboard the shuttle. That was instinct. This—this was more.

He concentrated on using his magic to make his hard-on smaller so it would fit in her tiny hole with less pain. Once inside, he could let go and allow it to grow again as he fucked her. Positioning himself at her rear gate, he pressed against the small bud gently. She squirmed as he began to make his entrance. Kaylen reached around her and swatted her ass, then rubbed it as though to take away the sting.

"Stay still, *aliante*. We don't wish to hurt you." He wrapped his arms around her and held her tightly.

Damir took his time. He was in no hurry to work his way inside her. He wanted this to be good for her. He stopped moving for a moment when his balls hit her flesh, or maybe it was Kaylen's dick. Right now he didn't give a damn. All he could think of was driving his cock into her ass. He wanted to feel her muscles clench around him, milking the seed from his balls.

Kaylen moved first. Slowly, he withdrew, then slammed back into her. She whimpered when Damir withdrew almost completely from her ass. "Don't worry, baby, I'm coming back," he said as he pushed his still growing cock back into her. It didn't take long to work out a good rhythm with Kaylen, nor to reach his full size again.

Brandy tried to help a few times, eager for something more and they each swatted her for it. It wasn't until the third time, that they realized it was the spanking she wanted.

KAYLEN WATCHED AS Brandy's eyes glazed over when Damir swatted her rear again. *She likes it!* He shared the news with Damir. He almost shouted with happiness at the realization. It was rare to find a submissive female amongst their kind and all the males were born dominant. The new knowledge brought out the *dom* in him as it obviously did in Damir. Brandy groaned and her muscles tightened.

One more swat and she would come screaming, taking them both with her. Kaylen caught Damir's hand when he would have spanked her yet again. He didn't want this to end so quickly. Not now. He loved the way her tight cunt squeezed his cock. It was amazing how her wet-velvet walls clamped down on him. Hell, he even liked the sensation of Damir's cock rubbing against his through the thin membrane as they both took turns ramming inside her.

Make it last. Make her beg for it.

Damir's furrowed brow smoothed as he grinned. *What a great idea!*

They kept their rhythm, neither moving fast or slow, just deep, as the jammed themselves into her tight holes. Neither of them spanked her when she wriggled again and again.

It didn't take long before she began to sob above him. Yet, she was still too stubborn to admit her needs.

"Please!" she begged, as they took turns ramming into her. "Please!"

"Please what, *aliante?*" He asked, waiting for her to tell them. Waiting for her to admit she needed the extra stimulation to come.

She shook her head and wriggled again, attempting to make one of them swat her again.

Kaylen held her still. "We will give you what you need, *aliante.* Just ask for it. Tell us what you want us to do."

"I can't!" She shook her head and sobbed into Kaylen's chest. "I can't!"

"Yes, you can," Kaylen whispered into her ear as he laved and sucked on the lobe. "We love you. We shall give you anything you desire, you merely have to ask us for it."

BRANDY'S BODY WAS wound so tight, she was sure she'd soon collapse. Every withdrawal, every return thrust brought her closer to the edge—but she couldn't come. She'd never known that pain, even the slightest pain given in the right spot, could bring so much pleasure. What was wrong with her?

"What's wrong with me?" she cried. "Why? Why can't I come unless—" She cut herself off before she said too much and gave away her horrible secret. Why had she never known about this thing before now? She was strange. A deviant.

"You can tell us anything," Damir said from behind her. His voice sounded strained, as though he was ready to come. She sobbed onto Kaylen's shoulder afraid. Scared of what they might think of her.

"I can't tell you. It's…it's—"

"Wrong?" Kaylen asked on a grunt. "Nothing is wrong with you, trust me. Trust us. Please, Brandy, I don't know how much longer we can hold on."

"I need you to spank me." The last two words came out on a whisper. Her face burned with mortification.

"Louder," Damir said, panting behind her. "Say it louder."

"Spank me," she whispered a bit louder.

"Louder!"

Oh, God. They really *were* going to make her admit to it or leave her wanting. The bastards. Finally, when she realized they had reached a point where they would lose control over their bodies, she didn't care anymore. She needed to come more than she needed to breathe.

"Spank me!"

Damir's hand came down on the cheek of her ass harder than ever before. "That is your reward for admitting your needs."

"Again, again," she sobbed. Tears streamed from her eyes as he spanked her two more times before she finally came. She screamed so loud, she knew they'd probably heard her on the bridge. As soon as her muscles clamped down on their cocks, both of the men groaned. They kept their cocks buried deep inside her, their hips jerking uncontrollably. Damir gave her one more swat and she came again as the hot, thick jets of their seed burst inside her.

She mourned the loss of their cocks as Damir pulled his thick length from her ass and Kaylen gently rolled her off him to lay sandwiched between them on the large bed. She barely noticed Kaylen covering her before she drifted into an exhausted sleep.

ONE BY ONE, the mated Triads met at the *Tigerian* sacred standing stones. Brandy looked around her, her body shaking with both fear and the early morning chill. The power of the stones hummed about her as they waited for everyone to arrive. The leaves in the tall trees rustled gently in the early morning breeze. Damir and Kaylen placed her between them and surrounded her with their warmth. She looked up to them and smiled.

"Why do you tremble so, *aliante?*" Damir asked as they both wrapped their arms around her. Her face heated when her brother and his Triad mates entered the circle. Drace grinned at her and she couldn't help but think he knew what had happened to her since they'd last seen each other. She brazened it out, her face red, as she fought the urge to bury her face in her mates' chests.

"I'm just a bit cold." It wasn't a lie. She *was* cold. It didn't matter that she was embarrassed—she was afraid. What would happen to them if the *Banarts* and *Hienials* should find them and make slaves of them? Their enemies would kill everyone here, except possibly her and her mates. Being dragons, the three of them *were* the strongest of the shifters.

The area around the standing stones warmed as the last Triad and their child Ryo arrived. Why the child needed to be here, Brandy still didn't understand. Still, who was she to question the Lady Goddess?

Brandy hadn't noticed before, but each Triad stood in front of a standing stone as the circle grew warm and the ground began to shake. The first of *Tigeria's* three suns began to rise, casting a pearlescent pink glow over the glen. She heard bird song in the distance and smelled the heavenly scent of wildflowers opening their petals to greet the sunrise. She closed her eyes as peace and joy bathed her soul, filling her with calm.

Within moments, the air around them began to stir. She snapped her eyes open, ready to face whatever would happen next. The hair on her arms stood at attention. Then, a bright light appeared in the center, near the altar of power, and after a flash of bright light, the Lady Goddess stood before it, a gilded box in her hands. Setting the box on the altar, she opened it, almost reverently. What could make a Goddess cherish something so?

The Lady Goddess looked to the first Triad. *Come to me, my children and receive your amulets of power.*

The three stepped forward, the looks of awe on their faces was unmistakable. An expression Brandy was sure they would all have before this day ended. As the goddess stopped in front of the first Triad, Brandy's stomach clenched, excitement and dread warring with each other.

Jaynee, my most powerful and faithful priestess. You wasted no time in sharing with your coven sisters when you found the Book of Shadows, *did you?* The Lady Goddess pulled a silver chain from the box. *I bestow this clear quartz amulet upon you, brought to you from a distant place. It shall amplify your energy, magic and your psychic awareness.* She slipped the chain over Jaynee's head then turned to the woman's mates. *For you two...* She paused, then pulled two more chains, these made of gold, from the box. On the ends were amulets made of smoky colored stones. *The smoky quartz will soften the enemy's power. The stones will absorb their negative energies, while the positive energy of the others will counteract the evil of your enemy.* The two men bent down and the Lady Goddess slipped the chains over their heads, the amulets resting perfectly against their chests. Once in place, a strange glow emanated from the Triad's three stones until they each seemed to reach out to each other, connecting the three together. A few moments passed before the light dissipated and left the first Triad with a visible aura surrounding them.

The Lady Goddess then turned to the next Triad and smiled. *Laynee, equal in so many ways to your sister, yet always fearing her shadow. Your power has the potential to save everyone in this circle. Come to me.* She reached out her hand, the three amulets already glimmering as they hung from her slender fingers. Laynee, Sayre and Fane stepped forward, hand in hand in hand. They held their heads high, kept their backs straight. Brandy could see how serious this Triad felt about what would soon happen. *To the three of you, I give the Black Onyx. It will help shield you and those around you with strength, while protecting you from negativity.* She faced the men. *You are her strength and courage. You must stay close. As you all must stay close to your mates,* the goddess said, looking at each of the Triads in turn.

The Triad moved forward, each one accepting their stones in turn. Like the Triad before them, a bright light came from each stone, tying the three together before it dissipated. The Lady Goddess turned to the third Triad who had already stepped forward, eager to receive their gifts to help them fight the enemy.

Minna, you may have the worst gift. With it, not only will you see your enemy, but you will see their atrocities. Those they perpetrate now, those they have planned for the future and those that have already come to pass. To you, I gift the Seer's Stone, the Beryl. It is the telling stone. With one with your power, it can be a horrible burden and for this, I apologize. Yet, with this stone you will at least know who and what is your enemy. No one will have the power to hide their true form from you.

The Goddess turned to Minna's mates, Dax and Rage. *To the mage twins I award the twin opals. Identical in every way, like their wearers, this stone will increase your psychic bond with Minna. What she knows, you will immediately know. You will also have the power to heal her as she weakens through the use of her gift. She must not succumb to unconsciousness or you will lose her.*

Brandy watched as Dax and Rage visibly shuddered, then spoke as one. "It will be as you say. No harm will come to our mate."

After nodding at the twins, she turned to Kel, Wray and Rachana. *Rachana, I do not envy your bravery and cunning. Your love for it has brought you such terrible disappointment and heartache.* Again, she pulled three chains, two of gold, one of silver, from the box. *Rachana, I gift you with the stone of healing, Unakite,* she said as Ana bowed her head, accepting the powerful gift. *Not only does it heal the body, but it heals one's soul, even your own if you wish. This stone will help you balance your ability to connect with me, and others of higher spirituality, in times of need. Your spirit will flourish, for this stone will release all that keeps your soul from becoming what it should.* She turned from Ana to face the woman's mates.

Kel, I gift you with the stone of the truest love, Topaz, for I know you truly love Ana and would die to protect her. If you concentrate hard enough, you may visualize your outcome, which will transfer to the universal conscious. It will give you the confidence to do what you know must be done and the personal power with which to do it. Kel nodded, his Adam's Apple bobbing in his throat as she slid the chain over his head.

Wray, I gift you with the Sapphire. It is a stone with many, many powers. Yet, it is also the universal symbol of peace and harmony. This stone will protect you against those who would seek to deceive you. It will protect you from the wrath of your horrendous enemies. Wray leaned forward to accept his stone. The Lady Goddess ran her hand down Wray's arm, then turned to Brandy's brother and his Triad mates.

Brandy became more nervous as she watched the exchange and the Lady Goddess came closer to her own Triad. She'd known the Goddess was a woman, was capable of love—but she'd never dreamed she could be her granddaughter no matter how far removed. She feared she would disappoint the only blood family she had left.

Kiri, your capacity to love astounds even me. That you could or would love the son of a creature capable of such cruelty says much about your character. I bestow Rose Quartz upon you. It is the stone known throughout the universe as that of gentle love. As you love your son, so shall you love the sons of your enemy and deliver them from their waking nightmare.

Drace and Fury, I bestow the Tiger's Eye upon you both. It will enhance your perception and strengthen your willpower in times of need, which in turn, will allow you to strengthen your mate when she begins to weaken. Plus, it will bring you much luck, she said with a wink.

She smiled and looked down at the boy beside them and gently pushed the hair from his eyes. Kneeling before the boy she said, *Ryo, you shall not engage the enemy. However, you will be invaluable in the coming months. With this, I bestow my own Blue Topaz upon you.* She slipped a silver chain over her head and it magically turned to gold in her hand. *Known as the stone of love, it shall bring you happiness all your days.*

Brandy stepped forward, sandwiched between her mates. The Lady Goddess smiled. Leaning down, she kissed Brandy on the forehead. *These words are for you alone, Granddaughter. Never, never think you could ever disappoint me. I love you as I loved the man who was your grandfather. You are so much more like him and your mother than you could know. Do you still carry your amulet?*

Brandy nodded and pulled her pendant from between her breasts. "Yes, Lady Goddess."

Then again, everyone heard the Lady Goddess's voice. *Your mates shall have stones to match—every stone of every power surrounding a moonstone. The moonstone is My stone. It draws its power from the moons, from me, as I am the silvery moons in the sky.* She touched the three stones and they began to glow as she infused them with her power. *Now you have the power of the Goddess. It is the only help I can give you. If you weaken, let your stones draw more of my strength from the moon. It is right and good. Otherwise, I can give*

*you no further assistance. For this, I am sorry. Three times three is a powerful
number. You have two times this. It shall be enough. It must be enough.*

Brandy reached out and the Goddess pulled her into a warm embrace.
Remember. I am always with you and I will always be your grandmother.

When the Goddess released her, the three amulets in her Triad joined
together, just as the others had, locking them together, mentally and
physically. If what the goddess said it true, they could each draw from the
other's power.

Before she could think more on that, all nineteen amulets began to glow.
The golden aura spread from one Triad to another until all six Triads and the
boy were enveloped as though a magical shield of protection encased them.
The Lady Goddess stood back, a wide smile on her face.

*Take tonight for yourselves. Tomorrow you must leave—the witches of
Carrillia need you.*

The next day… aboard the Savari *vessel* Freedom

WHEN DAMIR SAW the number of enemy ships that ambushed them, he wanted
nothing more than to pull Brandy into the safety of his arms and hold her
there, where no one would ever harm her. The thought that he must take her
into battle with him rattled his nerves and tested his sanity. Both he and Kaylen
had waited too many long years for her for them to lose her now.

The captain of the vessel, appraised of Damir's rank by Dare, deferred to
Damir while he waited for Dare himself to arrive on the bridge.

"What do you think, sir? We're surrounded," the Savari Captain asked.

"Have there been any attempts at communication?"

The man shook his head. "Even our attempts to converse with the other
ships in our fleet have been unsuccessful. I think they may be jamming our
communications array."

Damir paced the bridge while Kaylen kept Brandy close. Where the hell
was Dare, anyway? He didn't know shit about what the *Savari* vessels could do.
What the hell should they do?

"Raise your shields if you have them and pray until Dare gets here. I'm not
going to be the one responsible for the first shot." Damir swung around at the
hissing sound of the doors opening and turned to meet the amber-eyed gaze
of Dare Raden. By the state of undress the man was in, he was certain he too
had been interrupted in the act of mate-pleasuring by the enemy ships

surrounding them.

"Report," Dare said as he strode over toward a chair, buttoning his shirt as he sat. A translucent console appeared before him along with a three-dimensional depiction of the three *Savari* vessels surrounded by five *Banart* warships and two heavily armed *Hienial* slave transports.

"They appeared from nowhere, sir." The Captain stood, faced the *Savari* leader and fell to his knees. "Forgive me for not thinking to travel under cloak. With our numbers and firepower it never occurred to me that—"

"That the enemy would consider this a fortuitous time to gather more women to perpetuate their race?" Dare scowled at the man. "We always travel under cloak. Just because we have made so many new friends over the past months does not make us invincible. Nor does it make us less hated by our enemies." He shook his head and sighed. "Get off your knees, Braka, it does not become you."

Dare turned and motioned Damir closer. "We handed these out last night after you left. We figured there would be time enough for you and your mates to get yours before the first battle. It seems we were wrong." He handed three tiny chips to Damir. "Go to the medical bay and have them implanted. These are for telepathic communication. They are, so far, undetectable and because they are implanted in the soft tissue directly behind your ears, the nanite's artificial intelligence will connect to the correct areas of your brain to link you with the rest of us. When you wish to use it, think the words, 'Com On' and for privacy, merely think or say the words 'Com Off'. Go now, follow the blue lights in the corridor and it will lead you to medical. The procedure is painless and takes only a few moments. Hurry! A few moments may be all we have."

Damir led his mates from the bridge to the medical bay. He didn't like the idea of the technology of another species implanted in his brain. Many people wanted the dragon's secrets. He just hoped this wasn't another way for them to try to get it. Yet, there wasn't much of a choice, a radio could be lost—but the added benefit would be he could still communicate with others not of his kind with an implant if he shifted.

"Have you felt the burning yet?" he asked, taking Brandy by the hand.

"The—the burning?" She looked up at him, her eyes wide. "What burning?"

"Your fire. Your dragon's fire. When you truly become a dragon, your body changes, your organs change and you grow the organ needed to make the fire." Damir put his hand on her stomach. "You should feel it here."

"I—I don't feel any different. When should this changing start?"

"It should have started the moment we both came inside you." Damir began to worry that perhaps it wouldn't work on her because she was the granddaughter of the Goddess. He thought about the many times they'd been interrupted and shook his head, wondering if that could be the cause of the delay in her transformation from human to dragon. Perhaps they should hop into a bathroom for a quickie and attempt to hurry it along. Instead, he followed Dare's orders and followed the blue lights in the corridors to the medical lab and hoped he wasn't making the biggest mistake of his life.

KAYLEN FOLLOWED DAMIR into the lab, both concerned about the procedure and amazed at the *Savari* technology. Brandy didn't seem upset about anything but the fact that she hadn't started her transformation into a dragon yet and he figured if there was anything nefarious about the *Savari* plans she would have said something by now—felt something by now. After all, she is the granddaughter of the Lady Goddess.

"I'll go first," he said as a med tech indicated that one of them should sit in a strange looking seat. This way he could both protect his leader and his mate. If something should go wrong and the implant didn't integrate with his system, his mates wouldn't have to risk themselves.

He sat in the seat and waited for the technician to install the device, hoping that it wouldn't damage him—yet knowing if it did, at least Damir would care for Brandy if he passed on to the next existence.

A sense of feminine ire drifted through his mind. *You and Damir have little faith in the people you would call friends and allies, Kaylen. Have I made a mistake in gifting you with my only granddaughter?*

No, my Lady Goddess you have made no mistake. I merely wanted to be sure it would not interfere with our physiology.

I do not want to have to tell any of you to call me grandmother again. Be sure to use that title the next time we speak. Please tell them all is well and to have every female take care as she fights. Every one of them carries someone precious.

Kaylen swallowed thickly. *Brandy already carries Damir's child?*

She carries a child for each of you. Twin girls should make you both happy.

By the time he finished the conversation with the Lady...Grandmother, the technician was already tilting the seat up and calling for another to take his place.

Com on… It wasn't long before his mind was filled with the chatter of the others making plans.

Damir looked at him, giving him a wink and a smile before sitting in the chair himself. He let him know without words that even though *grandmother* had spoken into his mind, she must have allowed them all to hear the conversation.

We are tied together, somehow. I realized it last night while you, while we were…" Brandy flushed.

No wonder she'd finally given in and said she believed them about her luscious body. She'd heard their thoughts.

I didn't hear them all, Kaylen. Only toward the end, was I able to understand how you felt about me. I was nearly convinced before I linked with you. She wrapped her arms around his waist and laid her head against his chest. *A lifetime of feeling inadequate is hard to overcome, Kaylen.*

"I love it when you say my name." He pulled back and bent to capture her mouth with his lips. Only after he'd kissed her long and deep enough to have her swaying on her feet, did he raise his head to whisper against her lips. "It's your turn, *aliante.*"

He grinned when she licked his taste from her lips. Her face grew a lovely shade of pink. Taking a deep breath, he gave her a slight squeeze then let her go. "I love you, mate. You stole my heart the moment I saw you standing in front of your shuttle with your brother convincing him not to kill my people. I was so relieved not to have to kill him to obtain you. He seems like a nice guy."

"I'm sure he would say that's impossible."

"Perhaps, but never stand between his dragon and his mate. I would have hated to make your brother crispy. What's the point? We don't eat other shifters," he said with a laugh. "Now go get your device implanted. " He turned her around, gave her a gentle push toward the chair and swatted her rear as she left him.

"Hey!" she turned and glared at him, rubbing her right ass cheek. "That hurt."

"You two need to stop playing," Damir said helping her into the seat. "It doesn't hurt and it works. I can hear communications between several of the Triads. They're making plans while we're in here playing around."

"Sorry, Damir," they chorused. Brandy waited for the technician to implant the device behind her ear.

She frowned after a moment. "What happens if this doesn't work after I change?"

"It will work, your brain won't change. You'll only grow a few more organs." Kaylen squatted next to her and patted her hand. "And it won't hurt much either."

"It won't hurt much?" Her eyes widened. "What won't hurt much?" she hollered.

"Done," the tech said. "You can rejoin the others on the bridge now if you'd like."

IT WASN'T UNTIL they were on their way back to the bridge that the first blast of a plasma weapon hit the ship. It lurched slightly almost knocking Brandy to her knees. Both Damir and Kaylen grabbed her, sandwiching her between them. If they fell, all the damage would be to one of her males as they both wrapped themselves around her like human shields.

"I won't break, you know," she said on a gasp as Kaylen scooped her up just before he and Damir put on a blast of speed and headed for the bridge. "Com on…" Brandy said, hoping the nanite chip worked. She wanted to now what was going on.

"We're grossly out numbered. Even our superior firepower isn't going to help us against seven armed vessels. At least our shields are holding. They haven't been able to hit us with anything that will do more than shake us up a bit."

She tried to place the voice. It was either Dare or his brother, she was sure of that. She just wasn't sure which one, since their voices were so eerily similar even when spoken audibly.

"I have an idea. I think we need to concentrate on joining our forces. Our life forces. I think…for some reason, I'm sure that is the way to defeat them."

"Jaynee, this is a time for action, not meditation."

Brandy was sure it was Dare who spoke that time.

"I'm serious, Dare. If we let our crews do their jobs while we concentrate on becoming one, we can defeat them. It's what She wanted. It's why we are here wearing these amulets. I can't believe we weren't meant to work together. The Lady Goddess said three times three is a powerful number and we are two times that. She meant for us to work together."

It was then that Brandy understood. Concentrating on her words to travel over the COM system she agreed with Jaynee. "Jaynee's right. I know it. We must allow our auras to surround us, as we become one. That is the only way we can defeat this many ships. My grandmother intended for us to work together. That is why the amulets all bonded with each other. They will again, and when they do, it will destroy our enemy."

"Okay, we'll try this your way, but if it doesn't work, we may be consigning the whole galaxy to hell," Dare finally agreed.

When they finally reached the bridge, Dare, Luc and Jaynee were sitting cross-legged on the floor, holding hands with their eyes closed. Brandy sat between her two males and they mimicked the other Triad, trying to tap into the common consciousness of the Triads.

Brandy didn't know why, but she felt she must watch the view screen as she opened her mind to the power of the Triads. *It is good to be the granddaughter of the Goddess. Your mind can compartmentalize your thoughts. You will learn to do more and more as you progress. You have my powers within you, you merely need to learn to use them.*

As Brandy watched, the amulets of both Triads began to glow. Staring at the three-dimensional view screen, she watched wide-eyed as the enemy ships pummeled the three Savari vessels. It was only a matter of time before the shields gave way.

A strange white bubble formed around one of the Savari ships, expanding out to surround each vessel until they were all enshrouded in its protective shield. The enemy's weapons merely bounced off the shield, no longer even giving the ships the slightest quiver. Silvery lights, thin as a spider's web drew the three ships together, joining them into one huge triangular-shaped ship

It wasn't until the ships were bound tightly together that she saw the white light emanating from each point of their triangulated position. The joined ships spun in a slow circle. A wave of energy pulsed from behind their shield, destroying each *Banart* and *Hienial* ship as the *Savari* ships rotated in their direction. Brandy stared with awe as she watched the ships destroy every one of their enemies using their combined powers.

Within ten minutes of the battle's start, it ended. Brandy could see debris floating in space, huge chunks of the enemy ships, all that was left of their adversaries. She stood, walked over toward the view screen, watching as the body of a *Hienial* slaver drifted by her. One of its legs was missing and part of an arm, but he was still easily identifiable by his furry face and twisted, misshapen limbs.

She shivered, knowing deep in her gut this attack wouldn't be the only one they faced before reaching *Carrillian* airspace. She could feel the trouble coming as though someone was whispering it in her ear.

Brandy crossed her arms, rubbing them as she continued to stare out into space, though she wasn't looking at the debris in front of her, couldn't even see it as she tried to process the information somehow bombarding her subconscious.

Come on, she thought, and at once she could hear the others on the other two *Savari* ships. There was much she had to say, but there was no guarantee they would believe her.

Behind her, she heard the others moving around. Within seconds, Kaylen and Damir were on either side of her. They each reached for her hands. Needing the connection, she held on tight, threading her fingers through theirs. *There is another battle coming, this one much larger than the one we just faced. We must defeat or evade the combined Banart and Hienial fleets and make it to the main temple on* Carrillia *where the Priestesses are initiated into the Lady Goddess' service.*

Why? Jaynee asked, her voice heavy with concern.

Brandy shook her head. *That I do not know, only that we must make it there. All of us if we are to win this war.*

Next to her, Damir squeezed her hand. *Then make it we shall,* aliante.

Do you know how many ships are in the enemy fleets? Dare asked.

Brandy nodded, though only those on the bridge of *The Freedom* with her could see the movement. *Yes, there are nine Banart warships and six heavily armed Hienial Slave transports between here and our destination.*

Within her mind, the voices of the other Triads began to speak over what another, making it difficult to hear whatever the universe was trying to tell her.

Beside her, Kaylen stiffened. His voice, harsh and impatient, overpowered all the others. *Enough, you're just making it more difficult for Brandy to function.*

Her mind grew silent, not even the otherworldly voice that had warned her of the impending attack spoke to her. "Now what?" she asked aloud, knowing no other answers would be forthcoming from the universe.

Damir turned her, pulling her into his arms. "Now we prepare for another battle."

Brandy nodded against his chest. She only hoped that the voice that spoke of the enemy fleet didn't remain silent for long. Against such a force, they could use all the help they could get.

As the hours passed and the ships drew closer to *Carrillia*, the tension on the ship increased. Damir hated that his mate was upset. He didn't want her in this battle at all, but he understood that without her, the enemy would continue to plague their known universe, and that couldn't continue. Not when they had the power to prevent it. Knowing that still didn't stop him from worrying, however, that his mate felt responsible for all of them because of her relationship to the Lady Goddess.

This waiting had begun to get on everyone's nerves, not just his mate's. He wanted to shift into his Dragon form and raid the sky, destroying their enemy one by one. Perhaps, before all was said and done, he and Kaylen could do just that. He turned to watch his mate, now asleep on the divan in their quarters. Kaylen sat next to her, her head on his lap. Kaylen looked up, met Damir's gaze. He could see that his Triad mate's need for action was just as great, if not greater, than his own.

As Damir made his way toward the couple, the ship shuddered beneath his feet. It didn't take a moment to realize the second battle had started. Brandy sat up quickly, no trace of surprise on her face.

"So it has begun," she whispered. When Kaylen reached over to comfort her she gave him a weary smile then stood.

Damir couldn't protect her, couldn't lie to her. "Yes."

"Then I suggest we get on the bridge before they manage to do any damage to the Savari vessels. We all must arrive at the temple."

Damir nodded, reaching for her hand as she passed him. Kaylen was right behind them as they ran down the corridors. The ship continued to shimmy and shake as they made their way to the bridge, once knocking Brandy to her knees. Shit. They had to hurry. *Com on . . .*

What's the status of the enemy fleet? Have we taken any serious hits? Damir demanded.

From the bridge, Dare's voice was harried. *Not yet, but not from lack of trying. We need you three up here and we need you here now.*

We're thirty seconds away.

Thirty seconds later, they reached the bridge. Damir's gaze jumped to the viewport. Ships were everywhere. Green plasma bursts lit up the black sky. Brandy squeezed his hand then pulled him toward the other Triad who'd already taken their places on the floor.

Damir took his position across from Dare. Brandy sat to his right across from Jaynee, while Kaylen took his place to the right of Brandy and across from Luc. The two Triads joined hands, linking them together.

Once again, the amulets of both Triads began to glow. As one, they turned to stare out the view screen. As their ship moved into position with the other Savari vessels, Independence and Liberty, the white bubble coalesced around their ships. Prepared this time for the strange phenomena, Damir didn't react, simply joined his power with the others.

Again, the enemy's weapons were unable to penetrate their shield. It didn't matter that they were outnumbered five to one. The enemy continued to fall to the *Savari* weaponry. Several powerful plasma bursts hit their shield, but they didn't waver, keeping their focus.

Damir could feel the goddess's power channeling through his amulet. The stone grew warmer the longer the battle raged, nearly burning his skin. For hours he held his concentration, staying linked to his Triad mates and the other five Triads. Sweat poured off his body but he refused to break the connection to wipe it away. He would stand by them, no matter his discomfort.

Another blast hit their ship and he felt their shield begin to dissipate and waver. *No we must continue. We cannot give in to the fatigue. Look inside yourselves and find your power,* he demanded through the link.

A surge of power ripped through his body. The shield flared, once again growing strong. Beside him, Brandy's spine stiffened and she grimaced. He couldn't blame her. Channeling the power the way they were was not only exhausting but painful—it felt like your nerve endings were on fire.

Finally, the last *Hienial* ship floundered in space, spiraling out of control. They couldn't allow the ship to run, to find some planet to put down. With their last bit of energy, Damir and the others focused on the flailing ship. With seconds, the Hienial slaver exploded into thousands upon thousands of pieces, littering the sky above Carrillia with its debris. Seconds after the ship exploded, Brandy collapsed against him.

Damir stood on shaky legs, lifted Brandy into his arms then both he and Kaylen headed off the bridge, intent on getting Brandy to their quarters where she could rest until they reached Carrillia and the Lady Goddess's sacred temple there.

The next dawning, *Forest of Tranquility, Carrillia*

BRANDY SURVEYED HER surroundings. Tall trees blocked the light of the sun, lending the forest an eerie feel. She could feel the whisper of power in the air, as though they walked on sacred ground, sacred burial ground—and perhaps they did.

She could feel the power beneath her feet, in the very air she breathed. But something evil was suffocating it, tainting it. Brandy stopped where she was, holding her hand up for the others to halt. *Com on… There is evil near, both* Banart *and* Hienial. *Be prepared for anything and look beyond what can be seen with the eyes.*

As they grew closer to where the temple should be, Jaynee and Laynee, the *Carrillian* witches and their mates took over the lead. Brandy didn't mind, it gave her more time to find her center, find the power and strength inside her because she knew, before this day ended, she would need to call on all her power and the power of her bloodline.

Less than an hour later, the six Triads slowed when they reached the line of trees surrounding the temple. The sense of evil grew thicker. She could smell the *Hienials* on the air—there had to be dozens of the creatures surrounding them.

Before she could let the others know, her lungs, her chest began to burn. Her fingers and toes felt on fire. She turned to Damir and Kaylen, unsure what was happening to her.

"What is happening to me?" she whispered, not even trying to hide her fear.

Kaylen took her face in his hands while Damir grabbed her hands. "What do you feel?"

She shook her head, unable to really explain. "I burn. There is a fire raging inside me."

"You sure do pick your times, don't you?" Kaylen muttered.

"What? What the hell is happening to me? Is it my grandmother's power?"

"No," Damir said, squeezing her hand in comfort. "*Aliante*, it's your dragon awakening for the first time. The dragoness can sense the danger surrounding you and is awakening to protect you and our children."

Her stomach clenched. Burning pain ripped through her abdomen, up her chest and down her legs. She doubled over, unable to stand the onslaught of pain. Kiri stopped, turned and ran toward them as soon as Brandy collapsed. Brandy shook her head, waved at her to keep going. "Go, you must get into the temple, but be aware of your surroundings. We are encircled by the enemy."

When it looked like Kiri would ignore her command, Drace and Fury stepped forward, pulling their mate to a stop. "You mustn't disobey Brandy right now, no matter how your heart begs you to. Her mates will allow no harm to come to her," Drace assured her.

Fury ran his hair through Kiri's hair. "Drace is right. There must be a reason this is happening now, and who are we to go question what must be."

Through her pain, Brandy could see Kiri's indecision. "Save your strength, Kiri. It will be needed shortly. It is just my dragon emerging, warning me of impending danger."

Kiri slowly nodded then turned back toward the other Triads. All fifteen members of the other Triads looked out beyond the tree line, into the meadow where standing stones surrounded the temple, leaving Brandy in the care of her mates. Brandy clenched her knees then shoved off until she was standing once again. "What do I need to do to quench the fire?"

Damir and Kaylen exchanged glances. Finally, Damir spoke. "You must shift into your dragoness form, *aliante.* Only then will the burning pain ease."

"You have got to be kidding me."

Kaylen shook his head. "Unfortunately, we are not. If your dragoness is emerging, then there is a reason she has chosen this moment to do so. You are as much dragoness as you are the Lady Goddess's granddaughter."

Brandy threw back her head in agitation. Another wave of fire washed through her body. Finally, she nodded, unwilling to ignore any type of sign at this point. "Tell me what to do."

"Look inside yourself, deep inside yourself, and search for your dragoness. She'll be there sheltering your soul, protecting all that you are."

Nodding, Brandy closed her eyes, blotting out everything happening around her. She mustn't be distracted—not now! As though she was just waiting for Brandy's acknowledgement, Brandy sensed her dragoness, just as her mates said she would. She could practically see her dragon. Already, it was fiercely protective of her unborn children, surrounding her womb with the protective magic of dragon kind.

Embrace her, Brandy, Damir whispered through their mind-link. *Follow us. We shall shift with you, showing you the way.*

Give yourself over to your dragon. Just let yourself go, added Kaylen.

In her mind, Brandy grabbed onto her dragon, merging their minds together before reaching out toward the link provided by her mates. As though from a distance she watched her body contort, felt her body change, yet there was no pain, no fear of the unknown. Her dragoness protected her from it, yet allowed her to know what was happening to her, and around her.

She could hear a battle raging in the distance, knew that she must protect the others. Finally, the burning stopped and she opened her eyes, only to find a red dragon on one side of her, a blue on the other. Damir and Kaylen—her mates.

Ahh, you make a beautiful dragon, Kaylen whispered through her mind.

Yes she does, Kaylen. And, she shares both our colors.

Just then, Brandy heard a loud bellow, then a lion's roar. *We must help the others. If even one falls, all is lost.* As though she'd flown as a dragon all her life, Brandy's wings unfurled and began to flap in the air. She looked to the sky, aimed her thoughts at the treetops, and as easily as that she was airborne. Within seconds, her mates were flanking her as they dived toward the meadow where a battle raged. The meadow was overrun with Hienials, yet tigers, lions, bears and wolves were overpowering them.

Jaynee and Laynee stood back to back, their arms raised as they tried to weave spells. From the corner of her eye, Brandy noticed a priestess from the temple approaching them. Something wasn't right about the woman though. As she flew closer to the twins, she noticed the priestess clutching a dagger in her hand.

Enraged, Brandy and her mates dove toward the priestess, breathing fire over the woman. An eerie and inhuman shriek reached their ears. Before her eyes, the woman began to morph, taking on a dozen different shapes before falling to the ground, dead. It could only be a *Banart,* hiding among the priestesses at the temple. How many more were inside, waiting to attack them?

Jaynee and Laynee, looked up at her and her mates, both smiling their thanks before going back to weaving their spells. The battle was wearing down, but not yet over, so Brandy in her dragon form and her mates, dove for the *Hienials,* either scooping them up to drop them from the sky, or ripping their bodies to shreds right there in the meadow.

Inside the body of the dragoness, Brandy shuddered, still not comfortable with the level of violence and bloodshed around her. Born a healer, she never thought she'd take a life when she'd spent years saving them.

You do what you must, granddaughter. You have become what you were meant to be, so have faith in yourself and your mates.

As you say, grandmother. Brandy searched the glen, circled the standing stones to see if any more *Hienials* hid nearby. Seeing no more of the enemy, Brandy headed toward the center of the meadow, where the others had come together.

As soon as her clawed feet hit the ground, she felt her dragoness recede. Back in human form, and dressed as she had been before her dragon emerged, Brandy looked around the glen. Dozens of *Hienials* littered the ground. None of them had survived the encounter. She couldn't help but be relieved even though it went against her training.

She looked over toward Kiri, needing to ensure that she could handle seeing so many dead. It was too late for Kiri to try to save their souls and she worried that it would be too much for the kindhearted woman to handle, but she found her surrounded by her mates, Drace and Fury.

Brandy's tension eased, knowing that she'd be taken care of. Rachana, Kel and Wray stood in front of the temple doors, waiting for Jaynee and Laynee to ensure that it was safe to enter. Sayre, Fane, Dare and Luc surrounded their mates while the witches began to chant in front of the temple. Minna, Dax and Rage faced outward, continually searching their surroundings for hidden danger.

Jaynee and Laynee clasped hands then turned toward the waiting crowd. "We sense no traps. Though I'd still be wary once we enter," cautioned Jaynee. Dare and Luc stepped forward, each grabbing one of the long cylindrical door handles. Dax and Rage stepped in front of the women, while Fury, Drace, Sayre and Fane, and Wray and Kel circled the party, with Brandy and her mates guarding their backs.

As they approached the altar, Brandy's gaze wandered the room. The walls of the temple were made of some type of white marble. The floors, too. The altar was made of a shiny black material with rose-colored veins through it. Hanging above the altar was the largest crystal Brandy had ever seen.

The crystal seemed to call to her. Her amulet began to glow and grow warm against her skin. She looked to the others, and noticed theirs, too, began to shimmer with a golden brilliance. The crystal above the altar began to sing and glow. The louder the hum grew, the more their amulets reacted, throwing off heat and light.

As before, knowledge bombarded Brandy's mind. This time she didn't question what was happening to her. "Everyone, form a circle around the altar then join hands. I want you to channel everything you are, your love, your joy, your happiness, and your goodness through the amulets. Infuse your amulets with your soul."

Quickly, everyone moved into position. It didn't take long for the bond to form, linking them and their amulets together. The amulet against her chest began to vibrate and hum, matching the tune of the crystal hanging above them. Within seconds, a bright beam of golden light shot out of her amulet, striking the crystal. Soon, the other amulets did the same. Eighteen beams of golden light infused the crystal, making it shake and shudder. The crystal began to glow even brighter. The humming grew louder. The doors behind them shuddered. The marble walls quaked.

Brandy looked around, afraid that the temple would collapse around them. A noise above her head had her looking up. A small gap formed in the ceiling. It grew larger and larger as the walls continued to shake. "Look," she gasped. As all eyes focused on the opening in the ceiling of the temple, a beam of such brilliance shot through the top of the crystal and out through the opening.

She could feel a blast of power leave the temple, similar to what happened during the space-battles. This time, however, the amount of power let loose had to be a thousand times greater. For several long minutes, they continued to channel their power, their very souls through the amulets until suddenly their amulets stopped glowing and the crystal above grew silent.

Brandy, staggered by the events of the day, looked to the others. "What do you think we just did?"

When no one answered, she looked up at ceiling where all evidence of what just happened was gone. The point at the top of the temple had closed.

A BRIGHT LIGHT appeared in the center of the temple near the crystal that had amplified the power of the amulets. It didn't take long for the light to change into the form of the Lady Goddess.

Grandmother, she gently reminded Brandy.

Yes, ma'am. She smiled, holding her hand over her stomach, still shocked to realize she was a dragon and pregnant with twins. She almost felt like giggling. Something she hadn't done in years.

She glanced at the others around her and realized everyone looked different somehow. Happier. More content. Perhaps they felt the same lightness of heart she did now. The evil was gone from this place. It was no small feeling.

I knew I could count on you all. I knew that the goodness in you would outweigh any pettiness or suspicion. Heed my words. You are good people. You will raise wonderful children. You no longer need fear the Banarts, nor the Hienials. There are no Banarts and no full-blooded Hienials left.

She waved her hand and Ryo appeared next to Kiri and her mates. She glided over to the boy and knelt in front of him. *The evil ones are no more. The Banart are gone and the Hienials are dead. Yet, they left behind them a legacy. Halflings, such as yourself. They will need guidance and it is up to you* to find and lead them. *Those who are older can never lead for their hearts were once corrupted by evil and they died with their Banart masters. You are the oldest. You are now their king. Find them and make a life with them.*

"But...what if I turn bad, too?" Ryo asked, his eyes wide and filled with tears as if he feared the worst.

Dear, Ryo, it was not the Hienial who were evil. It was the Banarts. They exploited the Hienials when they came to them offering help to find women and to experiment on the males to help bring girl children into the world.

The Hienial were a peaceful people until the Banart came and turned them into the monsters you all knew. The Banart are no more. The power of the amulets brought their demise across the galaxy. Each temple magnified the power until it was finally sent to the other worlds and other temples across the galaxy. Every Banart and evil Hienial everywhere are gone. Nothing is left of them but the horrible memory of their existence and the halflings. You must find them. It is your destiny as it will be for all of the Children of the Triad.

Children of the Triad series
Available now in e-book at:
www.extasybooks.com
Coming soon in print.

ABOUT THE AUTHORS

Tianna Xander is the author of several paranormal, time-travel and science fiction romance novels. She loves reading everything from romance novels, murder mysteries and encyclopedias, to handbooks on solar energy. Tianna is the first to admit she spends far too much time surfing the internet and chatting with her online friends and critique groups.

Having written many novels and working on at least one more at any given time, Tianna still finds time for her family, friends and her many pets. She currently lives in Michigan with her husband, two children, three cats, two big dogs and one occasionally terrorized Netherland Dwarf bunny. Her life is anything but boring.

Visit Tianna's website at http://www.TiannaXander.com

Hi there. My name is Bonnie Rose Leigh and I've been writing since I was just a tyke. I live in a small town in Upstate, New York and spend most of my time on the computer either writing, or visiting with my friends. If I'm not busy on the computer, I spend my free time reading. It doesn't matter what genre the book is either, though I am partial to romance novels. If I'm not in my office, I can be found sprawled in a chair with a book clutched in my hand and a cup of cocoa sitting nearby.

To learn about all of my upcoming releases, please visit my website at: http://www.mybonnierose.net

2051207